"*And the world will burn before her.*"

~Prophecy of the Three Goddesses

Other Sapphic Pixie Tales From Cassandra Duffy:

The Last Best Tip

Astral Liaisons: Lesbians in Space!

Demons of Paradise

Demons of Paradise 2

An Undead Grift for Christmas

The Vampires of Vigil's Sorrow

The Gunfighter and The Gear-Head

The Steam-powered Sniper in the City of Broken Bridges

The Gunfighter's Gambit

Divine Touched

Cassandra Duffy

Day Moon Press

2012

Day Moon Press

ISBN-13: 978-1479321896
ISBN-10: 1479321893

©2012 Cassandra Duffy
2nd Print Edition
Cover Design by Katiie Kissglosse
Edited by Nichole Mauer

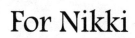

For Nikki

Chapter 1:

The Last Season for an Old Friend

The first storm of autumn darkened the sea to the northwest, rolling in like gray mountains across the sky, carrying with it the scent of the winter to come. The Last Road wound its way up through the granite, heading north along the coast, with the rocky shore to the west and the groves of stone berry trees to the east. Ahead, tall like a tooth of the Gods, stood the Screeching Peak, snow already dusting its jagged cap, stark white against the foreboding gray sky.

Harper walked slowly, careful to keep to the right of her warhorse, Aerial. The great gray mare, sixteen hands tall and stout like a brawny north man, was finally to be retired. Her coat was lined with scars equal to Harper's, although the final wound to end her career left only the tiniest mark, no bigger than an arrowhead. Aerial was only seventeen seasons with plenty of career left before her until she lost her left eye to a stone dart of all things at the end of summer. The armored head-crest she wore in combat would have blocked most projectiles much larger, but the stone dart found its lucky way through, given more force by attacking opposite a charge. Harper tried her best to heal the wound, dropping her attack when Aerial reared, yet even her magic couldn't spare her beloved horse's eye. Enough remained to stitch together a milky globe that Aerial could barely make out shapes with should Harper pass her hand in front of it. The rest of her company had already ridden ahead, giving Harper private time with Aerial for the last return to Griffon's Rock.

Tears rolled freely down her cheeks, pausing momentarily on the shelf of her high, refined cheekbones before tumbling free. Harper was part Sylvan-born on her mother's side, giving her slightly tapered tips to her ears, delicately triangular facial features, and an innate sense for magic. As she wore her honey colored hair long and typically free flowing, she passed easily for an exotically

Divine Touched

lovely human woman with the exception of her eyes. They were an otherworldly combination of green and blue such as a northern ocean after a violent storm when the world below the waves is churned to the surface and lit upon by rarified light breaking through the gray dome of storm clouds. Some said they shone with an inner light, although Harper was seldom near a reflective surface to verify.

Though Aerial had long since lost the need for a lead rope, Harper rested her hand on her equine friend's flank as they walked together. The ocean crashed against the granite shore down the boulder-strewn slope to their left and the autumnal winds blew through the golden leaves of the stone berry orchards to their right allowing them both to walk blind, guided north only by the sounds surrounding them.

Aerial sniffed at the air, flaring her nostrils to take in the scent of the approaching storm and rain striking saltwater to the north. Harper followed suit, breathing in deeply the blessing of the Sea Queen. Maraline, Goddess of the Open Sea, spoke to her followers like Harper through the ocean's song. Harper tried her best to see the approaching storm as a sign of a good resting season to come, a fine farewell to a friend's long service, before Aerial and Harper would finally part ways.

Griffon's Rock rose out of the base of the Screeching Peak like a shining jewel among worthless gravel. The city itself, the wintering home of Harper's company, was built from the ruins of the Dwarven City State that had inhabited the mountain a century before. The Dwarves had come to rely on the griffons that lived among the peak as their staple herd. Their end came when the dragons, who also fed upon the griffons, took umbrage with the Dwarves pillaging their food supply. The Dwarves were exterminated under the flame of the dragons and the dragons starved slowly after, consuming the last of the griffons without leaving generations enough to replenish the reduced numbers. The city of Griffon's Rock and the humans who inhabited it learned the lessons of foolish dragons and greedy Dwarves, focusing instead on the easily fostered crop of stone berries: the hearty, tree-grown nuts the griffons had once eaten. The shells of the stone berry were so hard only the griffon's beaks could crack them, or, as the people of Griffon's Rock learned, metal nut crackers in the precise shape of a griffon's beak. The nut within was often crushed, mixed with water, and turned into a gruel for marching troops or high quality mash for warhorses. The armies of the nation of Vaelandria marched on their stomachs as the old proverb went. And the stomachs of Vaelandrian horses and men alike were filled with stone berries grown by the people of Griffon's Rock. The secondary industry of Griffon's Rock was to offer winter housing for mercenary companies.

The treasure seeking season was coming to a close, although earlier than Harper might have liked. Harper's crew, the Dagger Falls Company had been beset by misfortune the entire season from spring's first thaw until they'd finally given up their endeavors a week ago. More fortunate companies would continue their work until the first snow, which wouldn't be for another two weeks, collecting coin and treasure for their benefactors before retiring to Griffon's Rock. The haul the Dagger Falls Company managed that season was embarrassingly paltry, and Harper didn't look forward to making their report.

They'd lost their Jack early in the season. Felix, a street urchin who had risen through the ranks of thieves guilds to turn adventurer and mercenary at the first opportunity, had served ably as the company's Jack for four seasons. Early in spring, when they were working as caravan guards to make their way into the east, a brigand ambush had struck the wagon train, felling Felix beneath a hale of arrows.

The company tried their best to replace the talented Jack with little success. Mettler, a grandiose figure with a flourishing rapier as his favored weapon and a bright orange sash tied around his head at all times, had hired on once they'd finished the caravan escort duty. The next job, and Mettler's only work with the company, was a reclaiming of a captive nobleman's daughter. Mettler was to scale the stone manor's wall, enter through an open window, and sneak through the mansion to open the gate for the rest of the company. The loud crash that followed from within, the shouting of guards, and then the frantic pounding on the interior of the keep's massive oak door told the company Mettler had failed miserably in his task. They'd gained entrance to the keep when the guards burst out the front door in great numbers to see if the foppish Jack was acting alone. The Dagger Falls Company battled well, slaying the guards through force of arms and dumb luck, and ultimately freed the nobleman's daughter in a distinctly ham-fisted fashion.

The second replacement Jack they'd hired on, and the one who managed to follow them the rest of the summer, was a Havvish woman—Havvish being the diminutive people having arisen from the union between a Gnome and a Brownie that supposedly took place two millennia ago—less kind origin stories for the relatively new race said they sprang from a swamp of particularly irritating water. Short to the tune of around four feet tall and delicately built, their work as Jacks was legendary and so the company felt themselves fortunate to find one available for employment. Unfortunately, so too are the Havvish people known for drinking, gambling, stealing anything not nailed down, and talking all waking hours and many slumbering hours as well. Brandinne was talented at her work, there was no doubt about that, fighting well with her crossbow and daggers, setting brilliant traps, and flicking locks from their mountings with little more than a look, but she drove them all to the edge of madness with her prattle and skunk-weed pipe smoking. Sven and Athol, the two brothers whose family was the company's benefactor, seriously considered stuffing Brandinne into a sack and drowning her on so many occasions that Harper actually started to fear for the Jack's life. Toward the end of the season, when they were camped at the edge of the Rusted Plains, Athol had stepped into a leg-turn trap, having somehow found his way toward Brandinne's side of the camp in the dark. The trap that cleverly combined sticks and ropes in such a way that would turn an ankle if stepped into, had served as a non-lethal warning. Athol claimed he was sleep walking. Brandinne superficially accepted this excuse, but the damage to the group's cohesion was done. Brandinne took her earnings and left them in the next town.

On the next job, Harper's trusted mount and warhorse of great import to the company's success, took the stone dart to the eye when they were to clear out a colony of goblins that had taken up residence in a town's only functional mill. The Dagger Falls Company took a vote, declared the season hexed beyond repair, and retired to Griffon's Rock to spend the winter months searching for a new Jack and better fortune for the spring thaw to come.

Harper finally strolled through the gates of the city's massive walls, once built by talented Dwarven masons. The cobblestone streets, brick buildings with thatched roofs, and hearty agrarian people all felt familiar and safe to Harper. The citizenry of Griffon's Rock were abuzz with preparations for the return of the mercenary companies. At least two dozen or more companies took their winter rest in Griffon's Rock, bringing with them wealth spent liberally on drink, entertainment, finery, and, if any was left over, supplies for the next season. The town greeted the companies with great hospitality, plied them with food, drink, and wanted wares, and then sent them on their way the following spring, picked clean of nearly every coin. Harper was different. As a Sword Maiden of the Sea Queen, she spent her winter months at the temple to Maraline, healing the sick, performing miracles in the name of her Goddess, and growing the flock of the faithful. Her wealth remained her own, saved in the temple's coffers, spared by her duty to her faith.

She walked the familiar narrow alleys along the outer wall to the livery where she would finally dip into her mountain of savings to provide comfort for an old friend who had served well. The livery master came out to greet her, dressed in the stained brown clothes of his work, his equally filthy hair pulled back into a long braid. He smelled strongly of the stables, of sweet hay, pungent horse manure, and leather tack.

"Greetings to you, Lady Harper," the stable master said, raising his hand in a three fingered salute meant to show fealty to an agent of the divine.

"Greetings, stable master," Harper replied. "I have need of new service."

"New or returned service, my lady?"

"Aerial has lost use of her left eye in the course of duty," Harper explained, gently turning her horse's head to show the stable master the truth of her words. "I wish her to rest in a retirement well-earned, paid for by the coin she helped acquire."

"Begging your apologies, lady, but we do not provide horse 'retirement' services here." The livery master fidgeted a bit, not wishing to look upon Harper when delivering the news. "Perhaps you should see to the butcher or one of the slaughterhouses for such a thing."

The implication struck Harper like a cold knife to the stomach, which she had experienced and hadn't enjoyed. "No, not in the sense of retire from this world," she said.

"Begging apology again, but what other retirement might a horse be offered?"

"To rest well, eat in peace, the occasional freedom to run across an open pasture, and then sleep in a dry stable." Harper held Aerial's head close to her own, breathing deeply of the warm, familiar smell of her beloved friend. "She has earned all of these things and more. Will you see to her comfort as a loyal servant of the Sea Queen?"

The livery master, still appearing baffled beyond understanding, nodded his agreement. "I do not understand your purpose in this, but if this horse is a servant of the Sea Queen, I will care for her as I would my own daughter." The livery master took the offered bridle, gave the horse a perplexed look, and led her into the stable.

Harper considered correcting the livery master before he departed, to tell him she meant *he* was a loyal servant of the Sea Queen as she had seen him come within the crystal-lined walls of the temple, but she thought better of it. Aerial could certainly be called a favored child of the Sea Queen and if that helped the livery master understand the request better, then Harper was glad to see it done.

The first rains of the coming storm struck her before she could even turn to take her leave. She tilted her head back to take in the blessed storm, bathing in the baptismal of her faith as she walked the streets toward the Thundering Dawn Inn. People gathered beneath awnings, at windows, and even dared to stand at the edge of the road to watch her pass, Sword Maiden of the Sea, drenched and happy. Harper knew this was as close to the divine as many would come. Few witnessed Gods and fewer still received the personal boon that was magic of the holy—Harper had done both.

She was but a child of single digit years, the daughter of a fisherman in Anilthine, when she beheld Maraline in all her glory. A blockade had shut the city's bay to the world over a trade dispute, keeping Harper's father on shore to fish from the docks with a pole like a common angler. She had joined him at the edge of the jetty, the manmade barrier of piled rocks to partially close off the bay to the wild waters of the ocean. On that fateful day, she went to see the hulking ships of a rival city bobbing along the lazy blue waves as she'd heard they were fantastically different. She was nearly out of her father's line of sight, although not entirely as this would raise his voice and she didn't want that, but she had wanted a closer look at the great warships. At the furthest edge of the jetty, where the sea spray washed over her whenever a wave crashed against the rocks, she finally saw the whole of the armada blocking in their fair city. A storm unlike anything she'd seen before or since, rose like a spear in the sky, slicing across the open ocean as no weather could. The men upon the blockade ships shouted, attempted to raise anchor and set sail, but it was all in vain. The storm slashed through their ranks with determined vengeance, shattering ships with lightning, colossal waves, and sail-tattering winds. Standing amidst the storm, gigantic like the statue of the Goddess within the city's square, was the Goddess Maraline incarnate. She walked along the ocean, smoothing the water as she went, creating a causeway in escort of a lone ship. She passed by the jetty, a few dozen yards only separating Harper from the Goddess of the Open Sea. She was magnificent, beautiful, glowing like the noonday sun set to bounce off the water. Harper felt her power in a way she'd never felt anything before. The touch of the moment lingered, found a resting place in her, and dwelled there like a flame. Her father ran to her, attempted to collect her from the end of the jetty, but he too was struck by the power of the Goddess and, like his daughter, could only hold his ground in awe of witnessing the divine. The ship the Goddess had personally escorted through the blockade held a high priestess with the power to raise the dead, or so the stories went. All Harper knew was that she must devote her life to this great and powerful lady of the ocean.

The ember of the divine planted in her from proximity to the Goddess had remained, growing slowly, the source of Harper's magic and anchoring her connection to the deity she served. The rain soaked her hair, made heavy her linen tunic, and seeped into her leather riding boots, but she didn't care. The rain also grew the ember of the divine within her and she felt closer to the Goddess because of it.

Divine Touched

Alarm rose out of the west. Someone was ringing the great iron bell above the western walls, calling aid to the docks and the lighthouse. Harper snapped out of her reverie. People rushed toward the sound of the clanging bell. Harper joined them in the charge, sprinting through the puddles collecting in the street. The lateness of the hour and the darkness of the storm clouds left little light to follow by. The storm prevented any torch from gaining purchase, leaving the help called by the bell to flow through the streets almost blindly.

When she broke free of the city, Harper got her first look at what raised the alarm. The great stone lighthouse on the edge of the jetty lay dark, likely losing its light under the ferocity of the storm. White-capped waves smashed upon the rocks, rolling out of the angry North Sea in gray mountains of water. Amid this turbulent hell of livid water, the remains of a ship was being battered against the rocks beneath the lighthouse. Cargo crates, barrels, debris, and people bobbed as black dots amid the choppy water of the bay, washed over from time to time when a colossal breaker roared over the jetty.

Great pyres of pitch laden logs began lighting around the bay, finally granting light enough to effect a rescue. Men with ropes and floats rushed to the docks and onto the jetty. They struggled hard to pull the sailors from the angry gray waters even as the spray and wind threatened to pluck the rescuers from the wooden planks of the docks and granite boulders of the jetty.

Harper rushed to their aid, making her way down the path toward the lighthouse. She slid her slender, two-handed sword from the scabbard across her back. The beautiful, holy weapon imbued with the power of the Goddess sprang to life when the rain struck it. This was no accidental squall of the coming season. The blade recognized the hand of the divine in the waters. What could the Goddess wish to destroy on that ship, Harper wondered. She braved the crashing waves at the end of the stone precipice the lighthouse was perched upon, raised the beautiful blade of the Goddess high above her, and bathed the entire bay in the soft blue glow of the guiding light of the Sea Queen.

Rescuers did their best to work by the light, hauling man after soggy man from the waves by the light until the storm finally battered the last of the ship into little more than kindling, and the entire hulk disappeared beneath the darkened waves.

Chapter 2.

A Not Unwelcome Prisoner

The storm abated almost immediately after the ship vanished beneath the turbulent sea, confirming Harper's initial belief that the storm was of divine origin. She slid her sword back into the leather scabbard across her back and wiped away a few wet strands of her hair that had blown across her face during her attempt to light the bay for the rescue efforts. She gazed out across the calming ocean, listening to the waves rolling along the coastline in increasingly regular intervals. Harper believed she had come to know the Goddess over the many years she'd spent in her service—someone aboard that ship had angered the Sea Queen. If the Goddess wished Harper's help in continued punishment of the offender, she would willingly act as the landlocked hand of her deity.

She made her way back through the crowds gathered to aid in recovery of the shipwreck. Faces gazed upon her in awe. The temple would be stuffed to the rafters the following day and perhaps for a few weeks after as the miracle storm and the lighted blade held by the Sword Maiden would spread increased belief in the Goddess of the Open Sea. The Goddess might find worthy among them and might not; it was not Harper's place to guess what use the divine might find in people. The Gods needed people rarely or not at all and seldom gave favor without very good reason. Indeed, it took a great deal of intelligence, devotion, and skill to catch the eye of a deity.

Harper's path carried her back toward the livery, hoping to see Aerial again before she slept. Her horse was a calming influence and one Harper desperately needed after seeing her Goddess smash a ship and no doubt drown many men in frightful retribution for a slight that Harper would not blaspheme to ask about.

The livery was quiet and dark, strange considering the hour was not so late as to put all work aside. Harper strode into the darkness of the stable out of the gathering dusk. She called upon the power of the Goddess within her to create a floating globe of light. It was referred to as the Mariner's Lantern, a use of divine magic common to followers of the Sea Queen. The faintly glowing light illuminated much of what one might expect from a livery: hay on the floor, horses anxious in their stalls, and various tack and care items. The halo of light finally illuminated the livery master she'd spoken with that afternoon, hogtied and gagged.

Harper drew her blade.

A shovel swung at her head from behind, sending a shadow through the light cast by the Mariner's Lantern, which gave Harper just enough time to duck the attack. She wheeled around with a defensive slash that cleaved the head from the shovel's wooden handle.

Her attacker, clad entirely in black leather armor and dripping wet, danced back out of the halo of light in a tactical retreat. Harped moved forward fully on guard with her sword held at the ready in front of her and the Mariner's Lantern following closely behind.

"I just need a horse," her attacker said in a stifled, hissing voice.

Harper glanced to her right. The only stall door opened was the one for Aerial. Her horse and longtime friend stood idly by, watching Harper calmly. Harper couldn't abide theft and she certainly wouldn't tolerate the theft of *her* horse.

"I suggest you begin walking to wherever a horse might carry you," Harper said. The stable was shaped in a T with the crossbeam intersection behind her. If she did have the thief cornered on the main corridor, she could force the fight back out the entrance to the street where she would have the advantage of more light and open ground.

"And risk a blister? I think not," the thief said in the same obscured voice.

Another shadow flickered through the light of the Mariner's Lantern telling Harper of another attack from behind. She wheeled around to find a horse blanket sent to swing along a rope from the exposed rafters. She returned her guard to the other side just in time to bat away a bucket hurled with surprising accuracy at her head. Before she could even get her sword around again, the thief was upon her, brandishing bailing hooks in each hand in expert strikes reminiscent of a tiger's clawing assault. Harped gave ground, dodging and yielding space as she couldn't effectively deflect the speed and fury of the attacks with her five foot blade, especially not in the confined corridor of the stables.

In the slightly more opened area of the crossed intersection, she stepped under a slashing hook, and made an arcing attack of her own at the momentarily exposed stomach of the thief. The thief's other hook caught the attack, turned the blade down into the dirt floor as Harper expected. She let the downward momentum carry them both lower and let go of the sword's handle when she felt the thief's weight bearing down on the blade. The maneuver set the thief off guard as Harper hoped, giving her the opportunity to bring a swift kick up into the thief's downward facing head.

The thief lost both bailing hooks in the process, but managed to remain standing. Harper lunged across the weapons they'd both dropped, planting her shoulder in the thief's stomach, knocking the black-clad attacker backward. The thief let out a decidedly feminine grunt at nearly having the wind knocked from her. Harper straightened up and willed the Mariner's Lantern forward. The light flashed across the thief momentarily with her cowl knocked back. Her attacker was indeed a woman and a strikingly beautiful one at that. She had the pale blue eyes and solid jaw of the Vaelindrian lowlands and the dark burnished bronze hair of the colonies in the deepest southern reaches. The woman's appearance clearly unbalanced Harper enough for a resumption of attacks. The thief threw what looked to be a wild punch, which Harper easily ducked, but followed it up with a handful of stone berry shell dust plucked from a nearby bucket. Harper staggered back, momentarily blinded by the powder used for drying wet tack, giving the thief the opening she needed.

Aerial was out of the stall with the black-clad woman riding bareback, heading for the stable entrance. Harper could barely see the horse and rider, yet she knew enough to know the thief would need to duck to avoid being struck by the doorway's arch. Harper let out a sharp whistle causing Aerial to leap as if to avoid a trap her rider had spotted but the horse hadn't. The rider, not expecting the sudden lunge, struck the beam with her head in a resounding thwack that plucked her from the back of the horse and deposited her on the stable floor.

Harper wiped the dust and tears from her eyes with the damp sleeve of her tunic, retrieved her dropped sword, and made her way across the stable to check on the condition of the felled thief. The light of the Mariner's Lantern illuminated her former attacker turned current patient. The woman was unconscious with a sizable knot on her forehead. Harper sheathed her sword as Aerial returned. They both looked down to the thief and then back to one another. Aerial let out a little whinny and nudged one of the thief's boots.

"Care for a fallen foe is your recommendation?" Harper asked of her horse.

Aerial mouthed the toe of one of the thief's boots, which Harper took to mean the horse hadn't taken the theft as personally as Harper had.

"Very well, mercy it is." Harper knelt beside the thief's wounded head. She touched her hand to the knot and called upon the glimmer of power within her granted by the Goddess. Mending, soothing magic flowed through her into the unconscious woman, easing the gruesome bump to a relatively unmarred state. Harper stopped short of pouring enough healing energy into the thief to bring her back to the waking world. She would have her bound and ready for questioning before that particular mercy was imparted. Thankfully, the thief had provided binding rope and left it conveniently tied around the livery master.

The livery master wasn't as happy in his rescue as Harper had hoped. Indeed, when Harper told him she didn't plan on letting him kill the thief, he'd told her he wouldn't participate in any nonsense of horse retirement then. She slung the bound and unconscious thief across Aerial's back and took her leave of the shouting and angry livery master who swore he'd have payment from the thief for the broken shovel.

The walk back across the city was blessedly quiet, with the clip-clopping of Aerial's hooves calming Harper in the familiarity of the sound. She was going to have a far harder time actually parting from her mount of nearly a decade than she thought. The thief on her horse's back should have been in the forefront of her mind as she still hadn't decided what she would even do with the woman. She tried to will herself to think about the conundrum, but couldn't come up with anything.

She walked Aerial and her thief cargo up to the great double doors of the Thundering Dawn Inn. The massive stone structure that dominated the end of a cul-de-sac near the orchard entrance on the eastern wall had spread since Harper had last seen it, enveloping several of the surrounding houses to add their rooms to its own. She hoped Sven and Athol's father had also expanded the stable facilities so she might board Aerial where she was staying.

Her musings were interrupted when the massive oak doors burst open to deposit a familiar figure face-down in the street. The man was of average height and musculature with brown hair cut nearly to the scalp on a square-ish head and an equally shortly tended beard. He was drunk and apparently in the middle of losing a bar fight. He looked up to Harper whose feet he had fallen at and smiled dimly to her.

"Are you planning on finding a room for your horse as well?" Sven asked, not bothering to pull himself from his prone state on the cobblestones.

Before she could answer, a much larger and wilder version of the man at her feet strode through the open doors, holding a limp man by the belt in one hand and a second, struggling man in a headlock with his other massive arm. Athol of the Stone Hammer boasted a wild mane of hair and an equally epic beard. Unlike his younger brother, he was built large and solid like the mountain they grew up in the shadow of, an advantage on full display. He tossed the unconscious man he held in his right hand to land beside Sven in the street, which freed up his fist to rain punches down on the head of the man he had in a headlock until he too was rendered limp. He dropped the second body on the other side of his fallen brother and then plucked Sven from the stones.

"Take heart, brother, we are victorious!" Athol bellowed.

He and Sven laughed drunkenly to each other.

Athol left Sven's side, dropping his brother to sit hard on the steps of the inn. He strode with purpose to Harper, more interested in the bound woman on Aerial's back. "Look, Sven, our swordswoman has been victorious as well," Athol said. "What have you found here, Sword Maiden?" Athol roughly grasped the thief's hair at the back of her head and lifted her face for inspection.

"Looks like a Jack to me," Sven said drunkenly from the steps. "Typically we hire those with contract and coin, Harper, but I suppose beating one into submission is a new plan worthy of consideration with how the last two hirelings faired."

"She's a horse thief, not necessarily a Jack," Harper said.

"She's dressed like a Jack." Athol let the thief's head drop. He plucked the woman from the back of the horse and slung her limp form over his shoulder. "Let's dunk her in water to revive and hear from the horse thief's mouth what skills she might have."

"But she no doubt is wanted by the law to attempt such a desperate stealing of a horse," Harper protested.

Sven stood on shaky legs to follow his brother into the inn. "What concern is that of ours?" he asked. "I am certain that blasted Havvish Jack we employed was irritating enough to be deemed illegal. To employ a Jack is to employ a checkered past."

Harper huffed her rebuttal to which Sven paid no attention. The brothers often acted unilaterally when sober and constantly when drunk, which was their obvious state from the ruddy complexion they both sported across cheek and nose. They were the sons of the company's benefactor and the presumptive leaders of the band because of this. Athol was a budding warrior of great skill with charisma flooding from every pore while Sven was reasonably quick of mind and educated—between the two of them they comprised a sound captain. Still, Harper would have liked to have seen their fourth get more time to speak for the company. Their Sorceress, Ezra, was wise beyond her already advanced years, intelligent to a fault, and well-studied in more topics than Harper could even imagine. She kept her own counsel though, followed begrudgingly most of the time, and spoke at length only when forced. Ezra and Felix, their original Jack, had gotten along well and she hadn't warmed to anyone since his death.

Harper walked around to the back of the inn to seek out the stable facilities, hoping the thief would awake and give the brothers an embarrassing lesson as she'd done with Harper in the stables. It'd serve their drunkenness right.

Divine Touched

Explaining the concept of retiring a horse to the stable master at the Thundering Dawn was no easier than at the livery. Finally, she'd made known to the man what she intended by explaining her horse was to be treated like a feckless old nobleman—fed, coddled sweetly, and encouraged to grow blissfully fat. The stable master exclaimed it was a waste of coin on a bizarre flight of fancy, but who was he to question how she spent her money.

Harper could hear the great hall of the inn long before she passed through the darkened corridors to it. The hall had once been an armory of some kind for the Dwarven city. Sven and Athol's great grandfather had converted it into an inn nearly a century ago. The massive vaulted ceilings of the rectangular room soared above the stone floor with colossal beams crisscrossing above like the ribs of a giant, granite beast. The bonfire in the lined pit at the center of the open floor heated the entire inn fairly effectively, losing some of its power in the distant wings. Several bars and kitchens branched off the main hall, occupied by contractors who brought in food and wine from other lands to compete within the open floor of the inn's great hall. Despite the earliness of the resting season, the hall was in fine spirits when Harper came upon it. Jovial music of a slapdash band filled the air and festive shadows cast by the bonfire danced along the tapestry-lined stone walls.

Harper stood aghast at the source of the merriment. The thief woman with the lovely eyes and swarthy skin twirled at the center of the festive atmosphere, drawing men and women from their seated task of drinking to join in the chaotic dance around the fire. Athol and Sven were sloshing grand tankards of frothy ale as they stumbled about, sweating in their heavy hide and fur clothes from the exertion of what looked like their version of dancing.

Harper was about to protest, to shout at their foolishness, but the wave of dancing crested upon her and she found herself dragged from the doorway she'd entered through by the very thief she'd rendered unconscious not an hour before. The woman held her close and twirled her into the dance without real recognition of who she'd grabbed. When she made to leave Harper's company to drag another person into the dancing parade, Harper held tight to her, pulling her back with a firm hand on her hip and another on her shoulder. Only then did the thief recognize her.

"I wondered where you'd gotten off to," the thief said boldly. Her eyes were sparkling with drink and fun; her skin was flushed from the heat and activity of dancing in leather armor.

Harper held her still, unsure of what she'd expected, but clearly displeased by the brazenness of the thief's response. "You act as if nothing has happened," Harper growled.

"What cause have you for anger?" the woman said with a smirk. "I did not steal your horse and I am still somewhat captured." To help this point, the woman reached a hand down to loop Harper's fingers through a belt cinched tightly around her hips.

Sven and Athol found their way through the dancing crowd to join Harper and the thief who were still awkwardly locked in something of a waltzing embrace.

"What drew you off course of questioning her?" Harper demanded of Athol.

"We did question her," Athol said.

"Mightily with much chest thumping and..." Sven said, trailing off a bit when he remembered his hand held a drink he didn't wish to neglect.

"...chest thumping and manly threats," Athol finished for his brother while he drank. "She answered well, but then asked us if we could drink and dance at the same time."

"We had to prove ourselves as she didn't take our answer at face value," Sven said, coming away from his tankard with foam clinging to his moustache and beard.

"I would ask the same of you," the thief said to Harper, "but we danced earlier tonight and you were in marvelous form."

"Ah, indeed," Athol exclaimed. "That must be how you came by the bruise on your forehead." He gestured to the purple welt marring the thief's otherwise stunning face where formerly a sizable knot had been.

"After a fashion," the thief said. "I had come out well ahead from the dance and was on the way to making my escape when her blasted horse bested me."

The woman was self deprecating in the most charming of ways and while Harper knew the comment could be taken as a slight against her swordsmanship, the admission that the thief had then been felled by a horse was cover enough for Harper to forgive the insult.

"To beat back the mighty Harper only to fall prey to her half-blind warhorse!" Athol guffawed with a spray of ale and spittle.

"Harper is your name then?" the thief turned back to her idle dance partner.

"We didn't manage introductions when you were throwing dust into my eyes," Harper said.

"Call it an even trade for the kick to the face," the thief said, turning her cheek to show Harper the lump raising there. "Had I not turned, you might have broken my nose."

Strangely, Harper felt a little bad about the bruise and was thankful she hadn't broken the thief's nose, which was cute upon closer inspection, button-ish even with a golden hoop piercing the left nostril.

"Warm blessings. You may call me Harper if you tell me your name," Harper said in the fashion of the lowland etiquette.

"Well spoken," the thief said with a surprised smile. "I am Calista of the Southern Reaches, Jack-of-all-Trades and, as you've seen, an inept horse thief." Calista spun Harper once and threw her into a dip. The adept dance maneuver left Harper dangling in Calista's arms, her heart thundering in her chest, looking up into a smiling face. They were about the same height and build, but Calista didn't seem to strain in the slightest to hold Harper's weight in the dipped position.

"I would tend to your wounds further," Harper stammered.

"And I would be glad to have you do so," Calista said, "but only after we finish our dance and share a drink." Calista spun Harper back up into her arms, the band kicked up, and they were once again twirling across the floor.

Harper's concerns about Calista's attempt to steal her horse resurfaced only once when she saw Ezra's disapproving scowl from amidst the crowd gathering to watch the great dancing ring flowing around the bonfire. When they circled back around to the place she'd seen Ezra, the Sorceress was gone.

Chapter 3:

Nearly in Agreement

It was deep into the night before the completely unexpected celebratory mood abated. The Dagger Falls Company retired to a private booth at the edge of the main hall where they sat on cushioned seats around a massive stone table lit by a cluster of candles in the center. The candles had melted into a single entity bearing half a dozen flames, becoming a stranger creature with each drip of wax.

Athol and Sven were well into their drink and eagerly consuming more while Harper and Ezra abstained. Calista remained somewhere in the middle, both in terms of drink and location. Harper saw her drink, but she didn't appear altered by it. Calista sat to Harper's right and Sven's left, the direct center of the company with two women to her right and two men to her left.

"The short of it, and we mentioned this already no doubt, is that we are without a Jack," Athol began, slurring and wavering in the saying of it.

"But we are also short of coin, as we've had two hirelings who didn't work out and a season shortened several weeks due to the lack of a Jack and Harper's horse taking an egregious injury," Sven finished for his brother.

"This leaves us in the regrettable position of needing to bring someone aboard, but not having the means to support said person through the resting season," Ezra said, breaking her silence for the first time that night. "We will have to hope a Jack is available to hire when the spring thaw comes or travel south until we find one. We should not burden you with telling of our troubles though."

Harper glared at the Sorceress out of the corner of her eye. The shrewd woman in her late fifties was all sharp edges, hard lines from a lifetime of furrowing her brow at tomes, and thus she put a stabbing point on her words as if the world offended her constantly. Her nose was over large, her face was a plain oval, and her black hair, gone almost entirely gray, was always unkempt and held up in a stern bun. Harper doubted she'd ever been joyous, young, or fair. She was powerful though and smarter than the lot of them combined, which gave her value far beyond simple looks or charisma could ever hope to balance.

A Sorceress or Sorcerer only had a decade or so of treasure seeking in them as it took a lifetime of study and dedication to hone magical prowess to the point of any use and then old age usually made rough travel and sleeping on hard ground too unappealing to continue. Ezra was nearing the end of her adventuring years and didn't seem happy at all about it. This always perplexed Harper as the Sorceress didn't seem to enjoy life on the road, despite her reluctance to leave it; Harper concluded years ago that Ezra must hate the repetitive life within arcane schools and libraries even more.

They'd adventured together for five years, and Harper knew well the gambit Ezra was playing at as she'd used it before to good effect. By making the job sound entirely unappealing, the Sorceress hoped to turn Calista away without a vote needing to be cast. It was clear where Sven and Athol stood on the matter of inviting Calista aboard, which would make Harper the deciding vote as a clear majority was required for major business to pass within the company.

"The treasure hunting season isn't over yet," Calista said. "There are two good weeks left. Coin could still be earned."

"Most of our tactics make use of a warhorse," Athol said. "The lack of a Jack has been a hindrance, but in truth, we're left without open ground combat maneuvers if we cannot rely upon Harper mounted with lance."

Harper was flattered to hear Athol say so—Aerial was so important to her she'd forgotten how important she was to the party as a whole. She didn't entirely agree with Athol's assessment though. In Harper's mind the entire company existed to move Ezra into position and then shield her while she rained magical fury upon their enemies.

"Perhaps I have heard whisper of work that doesn't require open ground combat," Calista said. Her nose wrinkled a little when she smiled, setting a glimmer off the golden hoop in her nose; Harper rather fancied that.

"Whispers are not work," Ezra chided.

"Indeed not, but what sort of Jack would I be if I was not able to turn rumor into so much more?" Calista settled back in the booth in the midst of the company so she might see them all at once and at the same time be seen by them all. "I find myself in need of coin and you find yourselves in need of a Jack and paying work. We would all be fools to pass up such an opportunity because of hurt feelings over a misunderstanding about a horse."

"Leave us a moment to discuss it," Sven said. "You need not go far though. Mine and my brother's debate skills have been sharpened by drink and as you've no doubt concluded, we are the brains of the operation."

"As you say." Calista shrugged and smiled. She slipped beneath the table, emerging on the open end of the circular booth to walk away toward one of the bars still open for business. Her tawny hair bounced playfully in the ponytail she'd pulled it into and her hips swayed with a feline grace—neither of which escaped Harper's notice, indeed captivating it so that Ezra finally drew her attention back to the table with a sharp elbow to the side.

"We both vote in the affirmative," Athol exclaimed with volume left unchecked by alcohol. "I've spent far too long carrying the burden of being the most beautiful within the company."

"What say you, Ezra?" Sven asked. "She provided an answer to your attempt at dissuading her. Surely even you see promise in her words."

"I would not have her for a serving girl in a tea house," Ezra said. "She is a mix of the last two failures we had for the position of Jack and she certainly favors the negative qualities of each far more than the positive." The Sorceress looked to Harper as if the matter would be shortly decided in her favor, and normally Harper would have agreed. Attempting to steal her horse should have been an immovable problem, but...

"She bested me in combat while I had my blade and when she was armed with what she could scrounge in a stable," Harper said to Ezra, knowing her audience for convincing was entirely to her left. "Had she picked any other horse than Aerial, we would not even have the opportunity to speak with her."

"Then our foul luck continues!" Ezra stormed from the booth, fists clenched at her sides, stomping her way to the exit that would lead to her room. The company remained silent until they were certain she had fully retired from the main hall for the evening.

Quiet at first, Sven spoke, "you favor more than her fighting prowess, do you not?"

Harper snapped her head to him and glared. "I am a Sword Maiden of the Sea. My power requires me to keep the title of maiden in spirit and deed."

"You dodge his question," Athol said with a guffaw. "See how she dodges? Behold Harper's shield of maidenhood once again raised to deflect the reality of her humanity." Athol stood on shaky legs to toast the proverbial shield of Harper's virginity. "Only the Sea Queen shall unfurl her sails!"

"She dodges with an irrelevant point," Sven said, pulling his brother to his seat again with a hand on his massive shoulder. "What is done between two maidens behind closed doors leaves them both maidens when they emerge—at least, as far as the pantheon is concerned."

"What mean you?" Harper asked, warmth touching her cheek at the mention of it.

"He means your maidenhood cannot be taken by other than cock, and yon Jack by the bar is not so handsomely equipped," Athol said. "Bed her to your heart's content if her favors turn toward you. Or, should you find yourself lacking in the courage to try, stand aside and let me take my go." Athol hefted his tankard of ale and drank deeply, careful not to spill a drop out either side with the massive churning up and down of his Adam's apple.

Harper didn't even truly believe Athol wanted Calista. His tastes ran wild like everything else about him. He fancied burly men and bountiful women; sometimes one at a time, often times both if he could persuade them. Calista simply wasn't the bawdy bar wench type or the bearded brute that Athol favored.

"Look now," Sven said, "her cheeks touch with anger. You have offended her heart's desire mightily and she may have to defend the Jack's no doubt already tarnished honor!"

"Then let it be settled with a leg wrestling contest," Athol said, punctuating the comment with a thunderous belch. "I am too drunk to swing a weapon and she is too sober to take the dishonorable victory of besting me in such a state."

"Consider yourself lucky this is true." Harper slipped from the booth, straightened her tunic, and gave the brothers a sideways glance as she departed. "I will deliver the good news to our new Jack and see if I might find out what she meant by rumors of work."

Sven and Athol made a lewd gesture of holding forked fingers in front of their mouths to wiggle their tongue between. Harper was well on her way across the room before she realized what the gesture meant. She glared back at them which only encouraged a drunken laughing fit waiting only on her understanding and disapproval of what they'd done. They were children, as all adventuring men were, finding great pleasure in lewd gestures or etching phallic drawings where other treasure seekers might find them. Nothing irritated Harper more than battling into a bastion where treasure was supposedly held only to find penis graffiti and dirty limericks left by another crew who beat them there.

Harper turned her attention back to Calista, who was lingering at the bar, leaned forward onto her elbows, back slightly curved, standing almost entirely on one leg held straight with the other idly toeing the floor. Try as she might, Harper couldn't keep her eyes from the Jack's figure in the leather armor. It clung in places, obscured with belts and bands in others, but always flattered, especially in the leg and rear end areas. Harper stepped to the bar beside Calista and affected her warmest smile.

"I hope that smile and the raucous laughter portend good news," Calista said.

"We would like to extend an offer," Harper said.

"And your spell-flinger? She is in agreement on this?"

Harper cocked her head to one side and grimaced. "Not as such, but she…doesn't care for much of anyone, so this is not unexpected."

"Antisocial lot those magic users." Calista lifted the drink delivered to her, some sort of brandy Harper would guess, and drank the entire contents of the tumbler in a single gulp. "It's not that they abstain from carnal pleasures for virtue of magic, you know? They've all got brains too full of other nonsense for them to even notice when or if they need something else filled."

Harper furrowed her brow and tried her best to smile as though she understood.

Calista caught on the effort and let out a little chuckle, not mocking necessarily, but almost earnestly touched by Harper's naivety. "Never mind that, lovely one," Calista said. "It was a joke only and bad joke at that. Besides, I don't even know if it is true in the case of your specific spell-flinger." Calista turned from the bar, leaning heavily on it still, but to one side as to devote more attention to Harper. "Tell me though, why does your company employ two magic wielders?"

"Oh, I am no Sorceress," Harper said. "I am a Sword Maiden."

"So she casts spells with bits of dead frogs, potions, and waving about of lengths of wood while you…"

"…think upon my faith and draw upon the Goddess's power."

Calista's lovely blue eyes went wide for a moment and an appreciative smile played across her burgundy lips. "You are divine touched?"

"Yes, since I was a child."

"The Sea Queen judging from the silver sextant pendant you wear around your neck."

"Yes," Harper replied. "Have you sought blessing from a deity? Perhaps the Lord of Mask and Coin?"

"I'm not so important or talented as to attract the eye of the Thief Lord," Calista said with a shrug. She pulled away from the bar and gave a half-hearted bow. "The only possible purpose I could think of for him to even look upon me would be that of self-satisfaction if he should turn his gaze upon me in more intimate times." She added a little stroking hand gesture to get her point across.

Harper laughed and blushed. "Would that intrusion offend you?"

"I do my best work without an audience." Calista gave a little smirk with an accompanying wink. "But enough talk of the masturbation habits of the Gods. I will put ear to ground for the rest of the evening and see what more I can make of the rumor."

"Should we secure lodging for you?" Harper asked after the Jack.

"I'll find somewhere on my own," she said back over her shoulder as she made to exit through the main entrance. "Sleep well, Sword Maiden."

24

Harper's eyes followed the Jack as she departed yet again. Without Ezra to stop her stare, she lingered long on the more artistic lines of Calista's figure. Despite not having had a drop to drink, she felt drunk in the presence of the Jack.

Chapter 4:

The Lay of the Land

Calista was glad to be free of the Thundering Dawn Inn. The night air was cool and fresh on her face in stark contrast to the stuffy heat of the inn's interior. She needed the lay of the land and she had problems that drinking and dancing couldn't solve.

She let down her ponytail and pulled the black cowl up from the back of her armor to conceal her face. She smiled to herself at the miracle of showing a little neck and bouncing hair for the Harper woman. There was little doubt in it: she had the Sword Maiden thoroughly enthralled. Good use could be made of a divine touched innocent with an intoxicating case of lust and puppy love.

She'd spun her words well that evening, mixing truth and lie into a beautiful blend that all but the Sorceress drank like honey-wine. It was true, she was without coin—indeed, she had nothing but the clothes on her back. She'd lied in claiming she knew of any rumors at all, let alone one as specific as a job that didn't require open field combat tactics. If they'd known she only arrived in the city that evening and hadn't done anything but try to steal a horse before they met her...they still might have offered her a job, Calista mused with no small portion of self-satisfaction. The brothers were completely charmed by her and the seed of Harper's infatuation was obvious. There was no small amount of dumb luck to the evening, which was a smart Jack's most prized possession. Better to have dumb luck than no luck at all.

Two problems remained to address: she needed to continue south and she would need to do so by land, which meant coin enough to make an effective trip of it. She'd erred in her panic when she'd tried to steal a horse without supplies enough to even get to the next town down the Last Road, which she knew from a brief glance at a map on the Thundering Dawn's wall was more than a three day ride away. Getting knocked from the horse prevented her from going through with a completely ill-conceived plan. Now that she had time to stop, think things through, and formulate a better plan, she knew she needed money, supplies, replacements for her weapons, and a horse with two functional eyes.

She doubted the Dagger Falls Company could help her get any of these things. They drank too much, struggled to keep Jacks alive, and their key strategy relied upon a woman who was bested by a thief armed with bailing hooks and a bucket of dust. What the company could provide her with was legitimate cover while she procured the supplies she needed. Even an obviously amateurish band such as theirs wouldn't steal in the same city they spent their resting season. She required their name only and time to work. With luck, she would have what she needed before the Sorceress figured out the game and expelled her from the company, which should correspond nicely with an influx of other mercenary companies arriving in the city. She would slip out amidst the excitement without being noticed, likely on a better selected stolen horse.

She strolled the streets, keeping to the darkened edges beneath the awnings and overhangs of the buildings. Clouds occasionally blew across the twin moons, giving her a chance to cover larger distances within the sleepy city without being seen. She needed to find the edge of respectability where a night life might draw predators to drunken townspeople. She need only follow the sound of merriment and the salty sea air to a district near the waterfront where sailors and longshoremen took their drink among wealthier merchants and even some slumming highborn.

Lanterns lit the night in the open square around the statue to the Sea Queen. A mere fifty feet up any road, the lanterns vanished. The edge of this protected land would be where she would find the prey she was after. She followed two men, full of drink and leaning heavily upon one another. They were dressed well enough to speak of a merchant's life perhaps. Calista followed, waiting for the predator she was seeking.

Her luck held, or perhaps it was desperation in the lateness of the hour. A man dressed as a ragged beggar that the two men overlooked, threw off his costume and set upon the duo with a truncheon. The heavy club dropped them both before they even knew they were under attack. Their groans and writhing as the mugger set about looting them said the victims hadn't been killed by the blows to their heads. Basic, to be sure, Calista thought, but not without skill enough to leave them breathing. Muggings that turned to murders tended to result with the mugger's neck on a block awaiting an axe.

She followed the mugger through a maze of dark, fetid alleyways that he clearly knew, but she did not. She'd nearly lost him on his way to his stash when the sound of his heavy breathing stopped her in her tracks, still concealed within the darkness of the intersection between two buildings. The mugger was on his hands and knees around the corner, drawing up a storm drain grate. A rope was tied to the under-handle and a large sack dangled from it. The mugger apparently only had the one stash as Calista expected. A smart thief would spread their take over several stashes and work a much larger territory in their thievery—she was glad he wasn't a smart thief.

She found a discarded shutter latching pole. It was clearly meant to close the top most shutters on buildings without opening windows, but was left to molder in the alley when it broke. Calista selected a chunk around her height and made her move from the dank little alleyway. She cinched the leather strap of her armor around her throat until the buckle dug into her voice box enough to alter her voice but not cut off breathing.

"That's a heavy sack," she said in her obscured voice that came out a little raspier and more masculine than her normal speaking voice. "I'd lighten it for you if you're smart enough to take the offer."

The mugger dropped the sack behind himself and drew a rusted old blade from beneath his tattered coat. Calista sighed—she wouldn't be getting new weapons that night—it was a lofty hope that such a slapdash thief would have a weapon of any value anyway. He stood a bit shorter than her and from the antsy footsteps he took from side to side she assumed he didn't have the faintest clue how to fight with a knife; he was not a match physically for her, but sadly, she was the only one who seemed to know that.

She shook her head. "Make this easy on yourself. Just give me the stash."

He lunged forward, a feint only to threaten her away as he was still well out of knife range. She spun one full revolution to gain momentum and stepped into the attack to put her full weight behind the strike. The staff swung down at his lunging weapon hand, making solid contact with the knife and fingers holding it. Fingers and blade broke, depositing the weapon on the cobblestones in two pieces, handle and blade, and the mugger on his knees, gripping his wounded digits.

An obvious defeat still wasn't obvious to the mugger. Immediately upon his recovery from the shock of a couple broken fingers, he made a lunge for the bag to escape with his stash. Calista reacted first, rushing past him to sweep his legs from beneath him with a strike from the staff. The mugger went airborne for a moment, landing hard on the backs of his shoulders with his swept legs still running in the air above him. She heard the air burst from his lungs and the strange groaning gasping sound of a man who had the wind knocked from him. She dropped the staff beside him, strolled casually to the sack, and collected it.

She walked several streets up, ducked into an alley and doubled back, heading the same way she'd come but one block over, whistling a jaunty tune, sack slung over her shoulder like a sailor on leave, right back into the lantern-lit district.

The mugger was from a guild or a gang of some kind, Calista concluded. An independent operator wouldn't have taken the risk of injury over such a light stash. The man had a quota to fill, and, judging from the last ditch run to keep his gains, was behind on filling it. It was sad that she'd had to break his fingers—he'd likely have to turn to begging in truth until they healed.

She found a low thatched roof opposite one of the interior city walls near enough to one of the lanterns for her work. She tossed the sack over the wall to land on the shed's roof and then scrambled up herself. Stepping lightly, she walked down the narrow stone wall's top and hopped into the shadowed portion of the shed's roof. She remained hidden with her stolen stash just on the edge of the shadow, able to briefly dip an item into the light for closer inspection should the need arise.

There were half a dozen coin purses within the mugger's stash. She emptied the pitiful sum of money within them into the coin compartment built into the girdle of her armor. Of the few bits and pieces of jewelry, two pendants and four cheap rings, only two were likely worth anything. Still, she tossed them all into one of the emptied coin purses. Without a known fence she could trust, all of the jewelry was fairly worthless. Still, she didn't like the idea of wasting a take, and so she slipped the purse down into the top of her boot, securing it within the loops meant to conceal a dagger's sheath.

The last item, and the one she was a little surprised the thief knew to take, was a crudely drawn map with an accompanying bundle of letters, all bound with a few bits of sturdy string. Dumb luck indeed, Calista mused. The map led to an ancient burned farm on the far edge of where the orchards met the forest in the east. One of the letters indicated the farm may have been built upon a dragon's lair, hence the burned-ness of it, but that something else must have taken up residence in the dragon's place at some point, preventing any serious attempts at looting. Apparently the man who was mugged, and to whom the letter was addressed, was a retired adventurer turned information broker who might know someone interested in purchasing the information.

Calista bound the map and letters together. She could sell it herself or give it over to her new company. It was impossible to know which take would be larger considering the alleged lair might turn out to be nothing more than the ruins of a farmhouse burned by a badly tended cooking fire. Obviously, if she sold it, and it did turn out be a worthless lead, the jilted party might coming looking for a refund, and there was little chance the money would be enough to actually fund her escape. Still, even if it did turn out to be a bust, or more than the Dagger Falls Company could handle, she could always sell it after the fact. At least, knowing the lead wasn't worthless could help her set the price, and if some creepy-crawly thing living in the old dragon's lair did happen to kill her company, excepting her, the retelling of such a story could certainly drive the price up. Walking away from a losing battle unscathed was a Jack skill she excelled at, as was storytelling.

Calista sat for a moment, tapping the tips of her index and middle finger against her lips as she thought. If there was a thieves guild operating in the city or a series of gangs, which was almost a certainty, picking off lone muggers would only get more difficult.

As a Jack-of-All-Trades, she did know a bit about burglary and pick-pocketing, but only enough to feed herself a short time, and no doubt the pickings would be slim if there were other thieves already out and about.

She was still in the middle of mulling over her options when she heard a couple of low voices growling to each other. She tossed the empty mugger's sack and the already looted coin purses down into the narrow gap between the shed and its parent building. She crept lightly to the crest of the roof and peeked her cowl-obscured head above to better eavesdrop.

Two men were having a bit of a chat in an alcove created for holding refuse bins, which they'd apparently hurled over the wall near the shed to clear space for themselves. They were obviously muggers in their own right, using the alcove as their rally point at the end of a night's work. Neither man held their stash, which meant they didn't trust each other fully, confirming what she'd already expected. They were both vying for position within a guild. Calista didn't like the lousy luck of that development.

"…rumors about something valuable being aboard," one of the men was saying.

"The *Enolla*? The one what sank before supper?" the other asked.

"There you go, thinking with your stomach. Yes, the one that sank before you stuffed your fat gob."

"How'd you catch wind of that?"

"Because I'm an excellent bloody thief."

"So you keep sayin' when your mouth ain't busy gobblin' your own knob about it."

"Your words wound me. Keep it up and I won't let you in on the score."

"You don't even know what was what from valuable on that ship. More than that, you don't know nothin' about swimmin'."

"Ah, but I don't need to know how to swim. I heard the valuable thing made it off the ship before it sank."

"Likely it'll have security then."

"Likely some, but how much security could it have with such an unscheduled stop and so few crew remaining to guard it? Likely they'll rely on a clever hiding spot to secure it. Which means it's likely to be easy pickings."

Divine Touched

"Yeah, yeah, that all sounds as proper likely as you say. You're figurin' to find out what it is, where they're stashin' it, and then get a few boys together for an ol' fashion smash-n-grab?"

"Those are the broad brushstrokes of the plan, yes. I'll be keeping the largest share as the most difficult work will be in finding out the what and where, but there should be plenty left over for the crew to make off well enough."

"You let me know when you get your part done and my mates and I will put brick and bat to the purpose."

Calista slid away from the conversation back down the other side of the shed's roof. She briefly considered following the smarter of the two back to his stash. He would be easy to spot as the thinner thief since she hadn't actually seen the men speaking. They were both smarter than the mugger she'd rolled earlier and the thinner one was smarter of the two who had spoken—she doubted she would be able to roll him with a broken shutter stick. Not that he would hurt her, but if he was worth a damn and smart enough about it, he would escape and tell the guild someone dangerous was in town, making her life unduly difficult.

Rumors were moving quickly already; she needed to move up her departure date. The question of what to do with the lead was settled—she would copy the map, hand it over to the Dagger Falls Company, and hope they were more competent than they seemed or at least good enough to give her a chance to escape should the lair raid go badly.

Calista was nearly asleep on her feet when she made it back to the Thundering Dawn. Her day had taken a substantial toll on her. An achy stiffness was making its way through her body. The bumps and bruises, which she hadn't let Harper fully heal, were now throbbing. More than anything, she was exhausted.

As much as she would have liked to have purchased a room of her own, the coin she'd stolen would clearly be asked about and she doubted there was enough to rent an opulent enough room for a ruse to be worth the effort. Instead, she wandered into the inn's stables where she found a familiar face.

Aerial whinnied when Calista slipped in through one of the unoccupied horse runs. She crept up close to the warhorse's stall and gave her a long, weary look in the graying light of the morning. Aerial strained her neck and blew a hot breath across Calista's face.

"Are you complimented that I thought you worth stealing even with your bad eye?" Calista asked of the horse. She leaned forward, resting her heavy head against the blaze along the horse's nose. It was a strange thing to even say aloud and she realized only after that she was instinctively charming the horse as though it were a part of the Dagger Falls Company. "Be glad you threw me or we both would have been doomed by it."

The horse nuzzled in closer to her with a strange gentleness from such a powerful animal. She pulled back and gazed into Aerial's remaining good eye. The horse stared back as if expressing curiosity or something else intelligent that Calista hadn't expected to find within a horse.

"Now you're trying to charm me," Calista told Aerial.

She shrugged off the strangeness of the exchange—delirium from lack of sleep and a few bonks to the head, she surmised. Calista scaled the beam nearest Aerial's stall, hoisting herself up into the hayloft. She didn't like sleeping in her armor if she wasn't on the road and she didn't like sleeping without something covering her. It didn't matter what her preferences were. Sleep found her almost immediately.

Chapter 5:

Bacon and Benefactors

Calista awoke only a few hours later to the sounds of the stables. Horses chewed noisily on grain and hay while the stable hands rattled buckets and tack, joking loudly with one another in their work. Calista pulled herself from her uncomfortable loose, hay bed, swearing she would pay for a room of any kind and think of a way to explain it later rather than spend another night in the hayloft.

She slid down the ladder into the midst of the bustling stable and stumbled groggily for the door toward the inn. She was young and not necessarily pampered, but she preferred ample amounts of sleep, ideally through the daylight hours. The stable hands paid her little or no attention as she made her way past them into the inn. Maybe she looked too grumpy to bother with questions.

She somehow found herself wandering through the servant's corridors until someone grasped her by the arm and guided her out into the main hall. The Dagger Falls Company was around their usual circular booth. They beckoned her over and she joined them.

"You look like you slept in the stables," Sven said when she was close enough to hear.

"I did sleep in the stables," Calista replied as she took the seat next to Harper.

"You should have told me." Harper fussed over Calista a little, plucking errant bits of hay from her hair until Ezra gave her a sharp glare.

"You are also still dressed in armor," Ezra said. "I assure you, the inn seldom sees full scale battles worthy of so much protection."

"I was going to go buy some clothes today," Calista said.

A serving girl came by the table with several platters on a rickety wooden cart. Calista's mood elevated immediately when the girl began setting out the metal trays, one of which contained a small mountain of smoked bacon. She plucked a piece from the tray before it was even fully settled onto the table and bit into it with great relish, letting out a contended hum as she chewed.

"By your leave, Mistress Jack," Athol said. "Let us eat."

"I could live entirely on bacon or things cooked within the grease of bacon, dying fat, happy, and with greasy fingers," Calista mused to herself, not really realizing she had an entire table listening to her devour the bacon and wax poetic about it.

"A woman of truly intelligent tastes," Athol exclaimed.

"Yes, I am seeing an entirely new side to her," Ezra snarked. "What random street urchin couldn't boast the same lofty goals in life?"

Harper slid a metal plate across the table in front of Calista, should she decide to partake of more than just the bacon one piece at a time. "I wouldn't have you concerning yourself with clothes yet," Harper said. "You can borrow some of mine as we look to be of similar height and dimension, but then we must go to the temple to heal your wounds and the wounds of those who survived the shipwreck."

Calista normally would have protested, not wanting to feel beholden and certainly not wishing to set foot within the temple of the Sea Queen, but all the bumps and bruises of the day before were compounded by a lousy night's sleep in an uncomfortable stable. She would risk all she had and more to simply feel clean and well.

"As you wish, Sword Maiden," Calista said, grasping more bacon for her plate.

"My brother and I should tend to our benefactors if our Sorceress of accounts is finished compiling the season's books," Sven said with a grim edge to his voice.

"I have, and it is as we feared," Ezra said. "Little in the way of profit, barely enough to support us through the resting season, and certainly not enough to keep a new hireling Jack." Her last comment came with pointed tone and a jagged look in Calista's direction.

"While you slept, spell-flinger, I turned rumor into evidence of riches and a map to locate it." Calista plucked the bundled letters and map from the back of her belt and tossed it onto the table. It slid between the platters toward the brothers until Sven's hand intercepted it.

He flicked the strings away, handing half the bundle of papers to Athol while he glanced through the rest. "It would seem she has indeed," Sven said.

"Jevvon's company has been seeking the exact location of this very cache for two or three season now," Athol said. "How did you come by this information?"

"A good Jack never tells and..." Calista began the mantra all treasure hunters should know.

"...a smart benefactor should never ask," Sven finished for her, "but we are not your benefactors."

"There other sayings we both know," Calista said, "like foolishly looking a gift horse in the teeth."

"She speaks true, brother," Athol said. He set a calming hand on Sven's shoulder. "We might move to provision and put off the discussion with the benefactor until we have seen what more might be made of the season."

Harper began to usher Calista from the table. Before Calista could be moved entirely, she plucked the final piece of bacon from the tray and smiled to the scowling Sorceress. "Thank you for the breakfast, compatriots," Calista said, taking a bite of the bacon. "Be ready to have your fortunes changed tomorrow."

Harper became more insistent in her guidance of Calista, taking her by the arm to lead her away before Ezra did something everyone would regret. Calista, for her part, allowed herself to be led, finishing the bacon before they were even to the stairs. She shifted the position of Harper's hand on her arm until their arms were linked. This brought a faint touch of blush to the tips of Harper's ears, which Calista caught out of the corner of her eye as they walked—slightly pointed ears; that was interesting.

"Ezra is a talented Sorceress," Harper tried to explain. "Please, give her a chance and I will encourage her to do the same for you. In truth, she genuinely seems to like Jacks. She adored Felix and was the only one of us who could stomach Brandinne in long sittings."

Calista laughed a little and leaned in firmly to Harper's side. "Not even you managed to keep a civil tongue with your last Jack?"

"I did, but it required great effort," Harper said.

"You are honey filtered through sugar, Sword Maiden," Calista said. Again, she glanced out of the corner of her eye to find this compliment touched not only Harper's ear tips with color but also the peaks of her cheeks.

Harper led Calista up several flights of stairs and down a hall wide enough for a dozen burly men to walk abreast. As her surroundings changed, Calista began to marvel at the opulence they were apparently walking toward. Much to her surprise, Harper produced a key and opened an ornately carved door along the expansive hallway. The room on the other side of the door surpassed what Calista might have considered royal accommodations in most inns. The bed was a massive circle carved from a single slab of a giant redwood tree. Two great stone fire places warmed the room, one nearest the door and another beside the bank of multi-paned windows on the other side. The room was clearly intended for high ranking officials within the Sea Queen's clergy as a maritime theme touched everything within the room. Carvings of fish, dolphins, whales, and other more exotic sea creatures decorated every flat area, ship lanterns dangled from the exposed rafters to light the room, and beautifully woven tapestries of the Sea Queen's triumphs lined every stone wall.

"You must be a little more than divine touched to be given a room like this," Calista said, wandering deeper into the palatial accommodations.

"The inn's owners are the benefactors of a dozen treasure hunting companies," Harper explained, "I am simply the most recognizable member of their mercenary stable." She closed the door behind her and began searching through her things for clothes that Calista might favor, which were strewn about the furnishings near one of the fireplaces. "The patriarch of the benefactor family and primary owner of this inn is Sven and Athol's father—a fact that comes with its own set of benefits and challenges."

Calista watched Harper search. She was guileless, apparently a little messy, and possibly far wealthier and more competent than Calista had given her credit for. Regardless of her error, which she was willing to attribute to overconfidence in her own abundant skills and a difficult day prior, she was bound and determined to find her way into similar accommodations, be it her own room or sharing Harper's. She walked closer to the faint light filtering in through the window and slowly began shedding her armor, certain to drop the right piece at the right time to get Harper to turn and look at her.

Her breastplate hit the floor with enough force to draw Harper's attention, viewing the backlit silhouette of Calista topless in the tight undershirt worn beneath leather armor. The form-fitting garment peeled away as well, and as Calista expected, Harper averted her gaze, although a few moments after what would be truly modest.

"You don't lack for confidence," Harper muttered, having settled on a dark blue tunic and tan, woolen breeches.

"I don't lack for talents either," Calista said with a grin. She shed the rest of her armor, standing naked with the exception of her undergarments, which really only amounted to a linen wrap to hold her breasts in place and matching shorts that covered only as much as was needed, both clinging to her like a second skin. She walked to Harper, touched her on the shoulder, and took the offered clothes. "My goodness, you're a demure thing."

Harper turned toward her at this, a surprising move in Calista's estimation. Her eyes were fiery and defiant. "I am not so demure as you think." As if to prove her point, Harper looked brazenly at Calista's form in the state of near-nudity. "You have lovely…breasts—full and of ample size for your height and weight."

Calista had to practically bite her tongue to keep from laughing. She wouldn't mean it as a mocking laugh, but she was certain it would be taken as such. She smiled, trying to smooth the edges to affect a flattered appearance; perhaps even hoping the rising color of amusement in her cheeks might be mistaken for blushing. "Thank you," she said. "You are equally blessed in that regard." Calista pulled on the tunic to find that it fit her body as loosely.

"I hope I was not too forward with my words," Harper said. "I am like that, though—careless…or even wanton at times with my compliments of lovely women."

Calista doubted that statement from front to back. Judging from the red rush of color running across Harper's face, neck, and upper chest, the Sword Maiden hadn't ever complimented anyone's breasts and seemed to be having a remarkably excited response to the first time.

"Oh, I like forward and wanton women." Calista smiled and winked to her with such practiced grace and speed she thought Harper might faint. She pulled on the breeches, cinching the waist using her own girdle from her armor with the secreted items still held in their built in compartments. She pulled on her own knee high boots as well and tucked the cuffs of the breeches into the tops. "How well do I transform into a respectable member of the company?"

"Well enough although your hair still speaks of a rough night in the stables," Harper said.

"Could you tend it for me as I appear to have forgotten mirror and comb?" Calista had seen a mirror on the other side of the room when she was undressing, but she didn't think Harper would mention it either.

"Indeed, I was about to suggest precisely that."

Calista took her hand and guided her to sit in one of the chairs before the fireplace. A whale bone comb with a scrimshawed scene of a sailing vessel on the handle sat on the table beside the chair she placed Harper in. Calista sat before the Sword Maiden, back turned to her, and awaited Harper's touch.

Harper took the comb to Calista's hair in timid, reverent strokes, plucking out errant pieces of hay when she found them. Calista, for her part, turned her head, tilting this way and that to give Harper greater access, and sighing in a way that bordered nearly on that of sexual pleasure.

"I love having my hair tended and stroked," Calista murmured, knowing the lowered sultry quality of her voice combining with her sighs would drive Harper's desires for her.

Harper responded with increased fervor as though Calista's hair indeed was an erogenous zone to be exploited. "You strike me as a woman who knows things," Harper said, as if to distract herself from the near moans escaping Calista's lips.

"Not the sort of things one might read in a book," Calista said.

"Other things though, worldly things?"

"I suppose, yes."

"Do you know how to bed a woman while maintaining her virginity?"

"You are indeed wanton with your questions!" Calista said playfully.

"I am?" Harper dropped the comb to the floor in a clatter so she might cover her mouth with both hands.

"I tease." Calista turned quickly to pull Harper's horrified hands away from her offending mouth. "Yes, in answer to your question—I do know how."

"I swear, I asked only to verify the truth of a comment Sven made last evening."

"Don't swear to that being the only reason just yet," Calista said. She stood and helped the flustered Harper from the chair. "Now, if you don't mind, Sword Maiden, I would see you to your duties at the temple."

"And I would see that bruise eased." Harper passed her hand across Calista's forehead with gentle fingertips.

Calista, in spite of herself, rather enjoyed the sensation.

Chapter 6:

Familiar Fractures

Harper and Calista walked the streets of Griffon's Rock, chatting lightly about the resting season to come and what might be done with the downtime. Only after they'd exhausted the small talk did a real conversation arise between them.

"You are from the low country then?" Harper asked.

"I am the daughter of a Duchess's former florist in a region known for flowers," Calista said cryptically.

"Your father was relieved of his duties?"

"In a sense. He died of the wasting fever when I was in the midst of my adolescence."

They walked on awhile longer in silence.

"You don't want to know where I come from?" Harper finally asked.

"You are a fisherman's daughter, from Anilthine by your accent," Calista said.

"How did…?"

"The divine touched of the Sea Queen are almost always fishermen's daughters," Calista said with a wry smile. "She has a weakness for people who were raised to revere the sea as both provider and killer."

"You know a lot about religion," Harper said.

"I know a little about everything," Calista corrected her. "It is the job of a Jack-of-All-Trades to know the lore of the land, have an ear for accents, and gather new knowledge whenever the opportunity should arise." She linked her arm through Harper's who seemed nervous at the gesture at first, only relaxing when Calista didn't appear to be going any farther in her advances.

The temple of the Goddess of the Open Sea was beauty embodied. The building rose like a lighthouse unto itself, constructed of ship timbers, sandstone, crystals, and dredged coral. The Sisters of the Sea, attendants to the temple and keepers of the written words of the Sea Queen, came out from the temple's entrance onto the cobblestone street to greet Harper. They were dressed in the blue silk robes lined with the spotted gray fur of seals. Their hair was all grown long and held in a rope braid that could only be managed by a specialized tool unique to the order.

"Greetings, Sword Maiden," the revered mother said with a respectful bow. She was an older, happier looking woman with a bit of plumpness to her and a long rope braid of silvery white hair. "The ranks of those seeking knowledge of the Sea Queen have swelled in light of your blessed beacon upon the bay."

"Then we should make good use of their curiosity and show them miracles worthy of the Goddess." Harper parted from Calista's side and walked into the temple with the revered mother instead.

Calista fell a few steps back, allowing the other sisters to place themselves in the procession ahead of her. Within the main chambers of the temple, the truth of the revered mother's words became apparent. Men, women, and children filled the sanctuary, a great vaulted room of chiseled sandstone with massive flying buttresses supporting the domed ceiling. Painted carvings in the walls depicted the various miracles of the Sea Queen along with the words she spoke to her prophets, recorded precisely as they were spoken. Harper separated herself from the revered mother, found her way back to Calista, and took her by the hand to lead her to the main dais of the temple. Calista allowed herself to be led, curious of what Harper had in mind. Once they were positioned atop the stairs leading up to an open giant clam shell, with the back half taller than Harper by half again, the Sword Maiden addressed the gathered throng.

"The Sea Queen offers miracles in exchange for your belief and sacrifices," Harper said, her voice took on a tone of authority as it boomed across the sanctuary. "Blind faith is not the way of the ocean, nor is it the way of its Goddess." Harper leaned in close to Calista's side to whisper to her, "kneel in front of me."

Calista smirked and did as she was told, positioning herself in front of Harper to kneel before her. She looked up the Sword Maiden's body and smiled at how lewd the angle could have been in a more intimate setting.

Harper blushed and tried to force a smile. "Facing the crowd," Harper whispered.

Calista dutifully turned until she was facing the gathered hopefuls with Harper at her back.

"Behold this woman's wounds, received in combat against one of the faithful," Harper continued her sermon. "Watch as they are healed by the power of the Sea Queen as a gift of forgiveness for her transgressions against the divine." Harper pressed her hands gently to the sides of Calista's face. Her hands were smooth, soft, and cool to the touch. A soothing sensation of tepid water began flowing over Calista's skin, carrying away the aches and bruises on her body. She felt the swelling of her bruises subside to be replaced with remarkable innervations. From the sounds of awe being muttered by the gathered people, Calista guessed the appearance of her wounds were diminishing as well.

The audience, as Calista saw it, responded to their performance with murmurs and excitement. Calista tilted her head back into Harper's hands and opened her eyes to look up at her healer. Harper smiled down to her. Calista stood slowly, held back her hair to show the bruise on her jaw and forehead were completely healed, and strode from the dais with a bounce in her step.

With the power of the Sea Queen proven, the gathered throng moved under the guidance of the sisters to form orderly lines to drink of their communion and bestow their offerings to receive the Goddess's blessing. Calista moved out of the way to find a vantage point where she could both see everything yet remain somewhat inconspicuous.

Perched on one of the ledges of the interior buttresses supporting the domed ceiling, Calista watched the procession of those seeking the Sea Queen's favor. Harper healed throughout the day, seemingly energized by the process. People drank from a large fountain of sea water set in the far wall. They would pay their tribute, usually in coin or goods, and then they received Harper's blessing or healing. The more Calista watched, the more she realized what was actually going on. The tribute or sacrifice was often paltry, unimportant, or useless. Several times the sister in charge of taking the tribute wouldn't even record the collection. In contrast to the lax policy of collecting alms, the sisters in charge of dispensing communion were rigid in their application of the sea water. Nobody made it past them without drinking and they often sent someone back for more if it was felt they drank too little. Many of the Gods had their favored forms of tribute, burning of crops, blood sacrifices, animal slaughter, sexual acts, or planting of trees—apparently, the Sea Queen wanted new followers to drink salt water.

Toward the end of the day, Calista began to doze off. The business of religion was boring after a poor night's sleep. She came to at the right time to see Harper healing a familiar man and his broken fingers. Calista smirked to herself. So the little mugger man wasn't as incompetent as she thought. He would be back to his unassuming beggar routine that very night if Harper had anything to do with it. Calista slipped from her perch on the little sandstone ledge and snuck around the outer edge of the dwindling crowd to keep her eyes on the mugger. If he was a fool, and she still suspected he was, he would head immediately for the thieves guild to report his hand was fit for that night's duty. If she followed him, she would know where their base of operation was and she might learn more about who else was operating in the city.

She was set at the door to follow the now healed mugger out, when a commotion stopped the entire temple in the middle of its business. Dockworkers and salvagers made their grand entrance, carrying a parcel of apparent importance. They showed a sister what they held beneath the cloth they carried, and she immediately bade them follower her to Harper. Calista was torn between seeing what they had and following the mugger.

They showed their package to Harper, who reached into the cloth and withdrew a dagger familiar to Calista. It was a gently curved blade with an index finger ring and shark skin handle capable of holding a grip even when slick with blood. It was an assassin's blade of exceptional make. Harper seemed to know precisely what kind of person it likely belonged to. Calista could wait no longer. The mugger was nearly out of the temple, and she would need to follow or let him go.

She turned her back on the mystery of the weapons and what might become of them, following the newly healed mugger into the dusk. A haze of smoke from wood stoves hung low over the city in the fading light of the day. She followed at a respectful distance from the thief she'd bested the night before, but she didn't see much reason. If he knew to check for a tail, which she suspected he didn't, he was far too excited about his newly healed hand to bother. Still, she obscured her movements as much as possible. If the man was part of a thieves guild, he might well be watched, and if he was watched and she was brazen, she might well be spotted.

He led her deeper and deeper into the city toward the wealthiest districts where the Dwarven homes set into the rock of the mountain were occupied by people of importance. The primary hall of the Dwarven keep, smashed in several areas as it was by dragon attacks, still housed the Duke of the city, his family, and what qualified as a court in the far-flung northern reaches. Calista had picked up enough information about the city in her day of listening at the temple to know this district of all places was the least likely for a mugger to seek out other disreputable sorts.

He vanished into a Dwarven statue garden on the edge of an estate in the darkest shade of the mountain, and then disappeared altogether. Calista waited for more than an ample span in the shadow of a coal cart parked beside the outer wall of a manor. Nobody else came or went as she hoped they would, and so she finally slipped from her hiding place to check the statue garden. It was as empty of muggers as she suspected it would be. While she made an elaborate show of inspecting the statues, she actually searched for the secret passage that must exist. There was barely enough light left to make her ruse of perusing the statues a believable one when she gave up the search. She was pretty adept at spotting flaws in masonry that might be used as hiding places and she hadn't seen anything out of the ordinary after several laps through the modest statue garden. It could only mean the passage was Dwarven, built when the city was, and went into the original construction of the garden. No other stone masons could manage to hide something so completely and anything added after would have left evidence of the alteration.

Whoever was in charge of the thieves guild was clever, connected, or...the realization hit Calista like a dead fish to the side of the head on the walk back. The thieves guild had a Dwarven member, or more likely one of the stout folk as its leader. The realization was an unwelcome one. Dwarves had an insatiable thirst for wealth, gold in particular, and if this Dwarf knew of the passage in the statue garden, there was no telling what other secrets within the city the thieves guild might be exploiting. Crossing Dwarves was a dangerous practice as they had an entire professional cast devoted to inventing and building torture devices. Increasingly, Calista's hopes rested on the Dagger Falls Company to gather the gold she needed.

To that end, Calista returned to the temple to wait outside for Harper. In short order, the Sword Maiden emerged, sadly, not with the bundle of assassin's tools. Calista's heart sunk at this. Luck might have been on her side if Harper had chosen to claim the daggers and other equipment. In truth, they weren't even supposed to be findable. The enchanted assassin's tools held a very specific curse to make them nearly impossible to find if ever lost. An unlucky owner of such items might walk past their own weapons a dozen times, lying in plain sight, if they didn't keep them close at hand or in the same location when not wearing them. Calista couldn't figure out how someone simply salvaged them from a wreck.

"I am sorry to leave you for so long," Harper said as she walked up to Calista. "Had I realized how tedious that all must have been for you, I would have sent you to aid Sven and Athol in the outfitting of our group."

"Think nothing of it," Calista said. She linked her arm with Harper's again on the walk home, cuddling closer this time, which seemed to please the Sword Maiden. "I was able to eavesdrop on a few interesting conversations to keep myself entertained."

"I don't know if you stepped out before the salvagers brought in their find, but that might have been of some interest to you." Harper seemed practically giddy to share information that Calista thought she might have to finesse from her.

"Oh? What did they find?"

"Within the wreck of the *Enolla,* they discovered a set of honest to goodness assassin's tools. There was a Dark Stalker on the ship, or, at least, there were the tools of one."

"I didn't think a Dark Stalker's tools could be found."

"The storm that sunk the *Enolla* was of divine origin," Harper explained. "The magic used to batter the ship against the rocks no doubt also washed away the magic on anything within the ship."

"Ah, that explains it," Calista said through clenched teeth. She willed her jaw to relax before asking the follow up question—the most important question. "What did you do with the assassin's tools?"

"One of the sisters will sail south with them to take them to the Thief Lord's temple in Ovid. Hopefully someone there will know who they belong to."

"A wise decision," Calista said. "Best to be rid of items like that." It was a lousy turn of already lousy luck. It would no doubt take a week of sailing to get down to Ovid, maybe a couple more weeks to determine who the blades belonged to, and then another week for the Thief Lord's Dark Stalkers to come seeking out the owner of the lost weapons...it all shifted her time frame up.

"I don't know about that," Harper said, breaking Calista's train of thought. "They're weapons of a faithful servant of the pantheon, no different than my sword in how they are used in service of their patron deity. I just think it is a shame the Dark Stalker didn't survive the shipwreck."

"Yes, I'm sure he would have made marvelous company for a Sword Maiden," Calista teased.

"I didn't mean it that way. Your company is more than satisfactory."

"More than satisfactory? You flatter me, Lady Harper."

Harper blushed and hugged tighter to Calista's arm. "I did not mean to offend. You are charming beyond reason, quick-witted, and...um...pleasing to look upon."

"Now you do flatter too much," Calista said.

"Speaking of weapons and to change the subject, I would see you armed before we depart for the rumored lair. What weapon do you favor?"

Calista brought them to a stop beneath a street lantern that had just been lit. Ahead of them, walking smoothly on stilts, was the lamplighter. The lamplighter carried a torch on a length of pole as long as himself, wore a metal helmet over his brainpan, and walked on lofty stilts muted with leather-bound feet on the bottoms. Calista had always supposed if her current work ever failed, she would make an extraordinary lamplighter—she was good on stilts and liked working at night.

"Look me over," Calista instructed Harper. "Tell me what weapons you think might suit me best. Take your time for there is a prize in guessing correctly."

Harper seemed amused and a little flustered by the strange contest, although she also seemed eager to succeed in it. Harper stepped back to take her in fully. She walked slowly around Calista who stood ready for inspection. Harper gently lifted one of Calista's hands for a closer look and then the other.

"Had I not seen you fight, I wouldn't suspect you were able," Harper deduced. "You bear no callous, no training scar, no limp, no prejudiced musculature…you've fought only with balanced weapons requiring of two hands or two single handed weapons of equal size. You must wear gloves even when training."

"You are correct thus far," Calista said.

"I would suppose a staff, although your work with the hooks felt practiced, and yet neither weapon would seem to match your aloof personality."

Aloof, Calista thought, is *that* what she's decided. "Then you've made up your mind?"

"I should guess a bow with silencing fur upon the string so you might strike from the safety of darkness," Harper said.

It was true enough, Calista supposed. She'd used such a bow before and she likely would again. While it wasn't her weapon of choice, the ruse worked best if Harper was called right regardless of her guess, and Calista could fight reasonably well with many weapons.

"A perfect guess," Calista said. "I do indeed favor a composite bow of yew and ash with a muted string."

Harper practically beamed at the validation of her guess. Try as she might to conceal her pride, it came shining through in the form of an unwavering smile and fidgety hands.

"What prize shall I receive for obtaining such a bow for you?" Harper asked.

"For the actual obtaining of the weapon? I shall have to consider this carefully," Calista said. "In guessing correctly, you have earned a prize already. What might your heart desire?"

"A kiss then," Harper said, her cheeks alighting with fresh blush.

"You ask much, but have earned much." The little imp within Calista, the one that always forced her into pushing limits, urged her to push Harper further. She liked seeing Harper react to her advances; indeed, she liked seeing the vibrancy of Harper's reactions to most things. She wore her emotions openly and it thrilled Calista to see someone behave so naked to the world. "If it pleases you, I'll even let you name where I place your prize."

Harper's reaction wasn't as initially satisfying as Calista hoped. She appeared more confused by the offer than titillated. "I do not understand…" was all she managed before she did indeed understand. Her reaction after was interesting to say the least. Calista could see, painted clearly on her face, as Harper's mind ran through a dozen possibilities she hadn't considered before. "My lips, of course, my lips."

Calista stepped closer to her, licked her own lips to put a wet sheen upon them, and leaned in to lay the softest, sweetest kiss she could manage on the still flustered Harper's mouth. The Sword Maiden let out the slightest murmur of delight when Calista's lips left hers. Still close enough for Harper to feel the breath behind Calista's words, she whispered to her, "find me the bow, and ask for more."

Chapter 7:

Eager Bedfellows

The Thundering Dawn Inn's main hall was predominantly quiet when Harper and Calista strolled in. The hour was not so late for merriment to subside, but Harper recognized the stocking taking place as more and more mercenary companies would be arriving shortly, leaving little chance to re-supply again in the coming months. Ezra sat at the usual booth, reading a book and writing down something on a handful of scrolls. Calista and Harper made their way over to the Sorceress.

"Good eve, spell-flinger," Calista said.

"Find your way to the stables," Ezra said without looking up. "We get an early start tomorrow in pursuing the lead you found."

"What flaw could anyone find in the manners of a magic-user?" Calista asked with a smirk. "Where are the brothers?"

"Getting a full night of rest, no doubt," Harper explained. "Neither enjoys an early start, nor do they rouse well after too much drink."

"Yes, the meeting with our patron did not go well," Ezra said, finally looking up from the spells she was poring over. "We are to make up the difference from promised projections with additional work or pay it out of our own pockets. What little luck there is to be had came in the form of Sven not yet selling off our surplus of supplies, so we are outfitted well for another week or so should more work find its way into our lap."

"Not to wash away the color of that good news with more bad, but we need the key to the armory and the company seal," Harper said sheepishly.

Ezra rolled her eyes and sighed dramatically. "Yes, of course, our Jack provides work but before it can even be completed she is in our pockets for weapons." Ezra removed a book from the stack to her right and flipped open the ledger. "Be reasonable in your selection and keep in mind, it is a borrowing only. We do not have the coin to fund a purchase."

"Understood," Harper said.

Harper and Ezra looked to Calista, who apparently hadn't been paying all that much attention to the Sorceress's grumblings.

"Oh, right, a borrowing," Calista said. "I promise not to carve my name into anything then." It would be a moot point if Harper hadn't sent away the salvaged assassin's tools—try as she might, Calista couldn't think of a way to convince Harper the weapons should be given to her.

"Find your respective bed and hayloft when you are done." Ezra handed over the key and company seal. "I still have preparation to make and would have silence to work in."

Harper took the offered items and guided Calista away, whispering under her breath when they were well clear of the Sorceress, "two things annoy her above all others: spending coin and preparation for the unknown."

"If that is so, a librarian's life would suit her far better than this one," Calista whispered back, bringing a giggle from Harper.

Harper guided Calista to the inn's armory where weapons would be stored through the resting season and surplus meant to equip the benefactor's companies would be held. The armory door looked more like an impenetrable vault where metal and magic guarded the weapons within. The key Harper used and the turning of the wheel required to unlock the door spoke of immense value beyond. Even recognizing all these indicators, Calista was unprepared for the scope of the armory. The cavernous room in the basement held weapons enough for a small army with empty room enough for two other small armies to store their gear.

"Pick as you like," Harper plucked the ledger from beside the door along with quill and candle.

Guided by the tiny light Harper held, they walked along the weapon racks containing blades and bows until Calista spotted what she wanted. It was a modified hunter's bow, meant for accuracy and stealth with reasonable power. Of middling size, the bow was not the compact type for firing from horseback or the colossal monstrosities carried by massed archers and wall patrols, but sat in the middle, meant to be carried by deer and elk hunters, or, as Calista understood it, assassins with skill in poisoning arrows. Harper's key unlocked the chain around the weapon rack, granting Calista access to the bow and an accompanying quiver of broad heads. Harper wrote down the lot number from the bow and quiver in the ledger, dripped wax from the candle beside it, and pressed the company's seal into the wax.

"Settled enough for the moment," Harper said. "Let us escape the dust and darkness."

They replaced the ledger, blew out the candle, and locked the great vault door behind them. Before they were to part ways, Harper grasped Calista by the back of her belt.

"I would feel better if you had other weapons as well," Harper said.

Calista glanced back to the locked door. "You might have mentioned that before…"

"Not borrowings. I have some spare items you can use not requiring of the armory or its ledger," Harper said. "Besides, your exact words not two hours ago were, 'find me the bow, and ask for more.' I have found you the bow, and now I would ask."

Calista stepped in closer to Harper, an intrigued smile painting her lips. "Ask as you desire then."

"Share my accommodations with me," Harper said.

"That sounds like more of a command."

"Please, would you share them with me?" Harper asked in hushed tones as Calista came close enough for whispers to pass easily between them.

"I am beholden, yet delighted to comply," Calista said.

They walked up the stairs to Harper's room both a little giddy and tired. Within the plush accommodations, locked away from the world, Calista waited to see what Harper's intentions truly were. She'd been invited by women to rooms before; however, in the past, the intent was clear. Harper began undressing herself, well away from Calista on the other side of the room without an obvious goal of seduction. The fireplace nearest the window acted as the only light on the far end of the room, illuminating Harper's form in the flickering rosy glow of the dwindling fire.

Calista crept closer, easily keeping silent on her approach. Harper's body was lovely. Though she and Calista were around the same height, Harper had far heartier musculature. She positively rippled with amazing muscles that could well have been carved from marble. What truly surprised Calista were the scars. Harper's milky white skin was marred in dozens of places by a myriad of scar types, although most were obvious blade slashes.

"You've seen combat," Calista said in hushed tones.

Harper turned her head, holding her removed shirt to her bare chest. "Fighting as a Sword Maiden can be a painful experience. We are not to trust our armor or sword. We are to trust our healing magic above our own strength of will. We are to pour wounds like water and let the Goddess close them."

"What does that mean?" Calista took a few steps nearer, finally putting her close enough to reach out and touch her fingertips to one of the longer scars along Harper's back. The chosen scar cut a jagged swath from the point of Harper's right shoulder, down along the blade, finally ending where the spine created a natural dip between. Her flesh was taut from the powerful muscles below and as smooth as spun glass.

Harper did not pull away from the touch, but also did not make mention of enjoying it. "We train for years without armor to learn never to balk at a strike. Even after we receive our plate, we fight one day a year without armor to remind ourselves that the armor is not where our strength lies."

"It seems like a hard reminder," Calista said.

Harper turned to her, giving her a strange quirk of the eyebrow. "Do you not have scars?"

"A few," Calista said, "but as you know, Jacks strive not to hold identifiable marks. We do work where it is best not to be recognized after."

"I find it hard to believe that you would be difficult to identify."

"I have talents to alter my appearance or armor to conceal it entirely depending on the needs of the work," Calista ran her fingers down another scar on the front of Harper's left shoulder, one she recognized. Judging from the cross-shaped puncture wounds next to one another, it would seem the Sword Maiden had been struck by a flanged mace. "I have other talents as well, not healing magic as you understand it, yet soothing nevertheless."

"Your touch alone is calming and exciting at once," Harper said. "Does that make sense?"

"In so many ways." Calista slowly walked her way around Harper. Her one-handed caress turned into two at Harper's back. Talented, strong fingers found weary muscles and sought to release them. Calista had massaged the wounded bodies of warrior lovers in the past and well knew the surface scars only hinted at the extent of the damage below that might cause constant pain. These places she sought out and pressed her soothing touch into them. Now, Harper voiced her approval with a weary sigh. "You grip tension like it is your last coin," Calista said.

"I did not know it until you sought to relieve it," Harper murmured.

"Indeed not, but let us move to the bed so I might make better work of it," Calista's partner was so supplicant under her touch that she suspected she could probably coax Harper from the room and into the street in her state of undress without much protest. She guided Harper to lie upon her stomach across the top of the bed. Before she joined her, Calista removed her boots and belt.

"Would you have killed me in the stables?" Harper asked as Calista began her work to relieve the tension within the powerful muscles of Harper's back and shoulders.

This was not unexpected. Often the soothing touch created honesty as though the tension was holding a person's tongue. "I did not when I had ample opportunity," Calista said. "You were blinded and I left you unmarked."

"Why?"

Calista reached up to sweep a few locks of hair from the side of Harper's face. "Because I thought you beautiful," she said, and found she truly meant it. To that point, she hadn't questioned the motives of her own actions over the past few days. The truth came to the surface on its own quite easily though. "This is no mean feat to make me say so either."

They continued on for a time. Calista's hands found the tension and injuries within Harper's body and sought to relieve them. "Don't you want to know why I didn't kill you?" Harper asked, finally breaking the silence that to that point had only been broken by the gentle crackling of the dwindling fires in the fireplaces.

"If you want to tell me."

"My horse likes you," Harper said.

"Through no mercy of your own then?" Calista asked, giving Harper's ribs a light tickle to make the girl squirm.

"I was on the fence, but she is a better judge of character than I am," Harper teased.

"I should be brushing her coat in gratitude rather than massaging your back it would seem," Calista said with a smirk.

Harper rolled onto her side, careful to cover her bare breasts with her arm. "I promised a gift and I should give it now in hopes of smoothing my comments," she said. "Check my bedroll near the far fireplace."

Calista slid from the bed to do as she was instructed. The bedroll was easy to find as the lone item of Harper's road gear that had not been unpacked and strewn about the room. She untied the straps binding the blanket and unrolled it to reveal a cavalry pick-hammer and a straight-blade dagger. They were quality weapons to be certain, definitely meant for work from the back of a horse, but Calista believed she could make good use of them, one to each hand, if the need should arise.

"This is an oddly sweet gesture," Calista said.

"I saw what you could do with baling hooks," Harper replied, adding a tiny, involuntary yawn to the end. "I would not have you unarmed should something make it past your arrows."

"Would you not defend me?" Calista asked.

"I would, although I suspect you would not need me to."

Calista smiled at this. "Thank you for both the weapons and the kind words."

"I ask only that you feed and stoke the fires before coming to bed," Harper said.

Calista did as she was asked, placing several fresh logs in both fireplaces from the wood hoppers beside each. The room lit up from the roaring blazes. In the new light, Calista found Harper fast asleep on top of the bed. Her arm had fallen away enough from her chest to expose one breast to the world.

"Tired little Sword Maiden," Calista whispered. "With really nice breasts and arms as it turns out." She undressed to her underclothes and slipped into bed. It didn't take much coaxing to get Harper to groggily join her under the covers.

Calista sat awake for awhile, simply watching Harper sleep. It startled her how easily and completely Harper trusted her. Calista couldn't decide if the naivety was endearing or saddening. She joined Harper in sleep with the question still unanswered in the forefront of her mind.

Chapter 8:

Odorous Lair

They awoke, dressed, and readied for departure far earlier than anyone wanted to. Discussion was raised of using Aerial as a packhorse to save on expenses. Harper flatly refused and found an ally in Calista who also staunchly opposed the idea. Ezra reluctantly threw her vote to their side to move things along. Sven and Athol grumbled about the votes moving along gender lines, but said no more once the matter was settled on renting a couple of mules that could carry far more than a warhorse.

Armed and armored, they set out on foot with their camp supplies strapped lightly to the backs of the mules. They walked out the eastern entrance to the wall, passing over the stone defensive bridge set above a small ravine. The company immediately entered the farm lands and orchards which were all dressed in beautiful autumnal glory.

Equipped for adventure, the band more closely resembled what Calista originally thought of them with the exception of Harper. Athol wore layered hide armor with spots of chain and carried a colossal steel hammer with spikes on one side of the head. Sven sported laminated armor of interlocking plates encased in leather while carrying a round buckler shield and a broadsword—his gear looked old, perhaps heirloom old. Ezra, like all arcane practitioners Calista had known, dressed as though she were a hair's breadth from homeless. Her robes were mended in a dozen places with mismatched patches over the larger holes and she carried only a gnarled walking stick that might serve no other function than ease of hiking. In contrast to the others, Harper appeared blessed by the Goddess in her plate suit. The gleaming, and obviously magically imbued, armor was not the only trappings of her faith as she wore a tabard coat of arms in the brilliant azure of the open ocean with the mariner's anchor and sextant crest upon her chest. Calista remembered back upon the first meeting of the

Divine Touched

company where they stated Harper and her horse were of key importance to much of their tactics—seeing them assembled, this comment made far more sense.

They broke free of the road to head in a northeastern direction, cutting across an orchard that was already plucked of rock berries during the harvest. They walked in silence the entire day, wary and on guard as though the orchard might not truly be safe. Calista appreciated this small measure of professionalism among the company; they might not be the best equipped bunch, but they at least seemed to know the basics of travel.

As the sun began setting at their back, they reached the original forest of rock berry trees that the orchards were culled from. The straight rows of well-tended trees gave way to haphazard gnarled trunks. The old growth forests outside the orchards were of little value in harvesting rock berries as the nuts grew sparsely and only near the tops of the difficult to scale trees. The leaves of the old growth were long gone, leaving only the tangled barren limbs above them as the day gave way to chilly dusk. Just before dark, they found the stream that was to indicate when they should turn north. They made camp on its banks with a roaring fire to drown out the babbling of the creek.

"Calista, your navigation was straight and true," Athol said with a mighty yawn. He settled his bulk down upon the nest of bear hides and discarded armor he created for his bed.

"Indeed," Sven agreed. "It's good to have a competent Jack again."

Harper beamed a little at Calista as she walked past her toward the creek to refill water skins drained during the day's walk. Calista lounged on the bedroll apparently left over from Felix, far enough away from the fire to be difficult to find while wearing her black, leather armor. She took the compliment in stride, instead following Harper's form with her eyes. The Sword Maiden looked lovely in the just the chain suit of her armor with the plates removed and stacked carefully. Harper's hips curved appealingly to either side of her tabard, showing her womanly form even in her armor.

"Do we set a watch schedule?" Calista asked, finally pulling her eyes from Harper's muscular backside to look in the general area of the rest of the company around the fire.

"We use a sentinel spell from our Sorceress," Sven explained.

As if on cue, Ezra jabbed the end of her walking stick into the fire, murmuring a quick incantation under her breath. A glowing red ball, around the size of an apple rose from the flames and proceeded to hover above the ground as if suspended upon a string.

"It keeps the fire going too somehow," Athol said.

"The magic is born out of the fire sphere of the..." Ezra began to explain.

"Gods damn it, you glorified school marm, I covered the explanation with 'somehow' already," Athol bellowed.

"...I walk into that one every time," Ezra grumbled.

Sven, Athol, and Harper laughed.

"I wouldn't mind hearing the explanation," Calista said.

All eyes were upon her. Athol and Sven exchanged a glance that carried an infinite amount of information in a form only the brothers could understand. Ezra retreated to her bedroll to bury her nose within a book, signaling the end of her participation in anything else that night. Calista looked to Harper who strode over with a peace-keeping purpose.

"Felix would always make a similar comment when Athol cut off one of Ezra's explanations," Harper whispered to her. "I think his willingness to learn is why she favored the Jack so much."

"Then I doubt she liked hearing it from me," Calista muttered.

"Give her a chance," Harper said with a smile that encouraged Calista to do precisely as she was asked.

"I couldn't help but notice your bedroll is well away from mine," Calista whispered to her.

"Yours is too far from the fire."

"I could keep you warm if you moved here."

"I could keep you safe if you moved there."

A twinkle of appreciation arose in Calista. Harper had gleaned why she obscured her sleeping place so far from the light. "Fair enough," Calista said, "I'll move to where you are."

In full view of the others, Calista gathered her handful of things and walked with Harper back near the fire to place her bedroll beside the Sword Maiden's. The brother's exchanged a glance that once again constituted communication only between them, but made no comment.

Divine Touched

As they all settled to sleep, Harper's hand made it across the finger's width of distance between her bedroll and Calista's. She sought out Calista's hand and gently held it as though it were all the contact she could ever want. Calista catalogued the gesture as yet another adorable habit of Harper's.

≈♥≈

Harper awoke first the following morning to a chill in the air and a low hanging autumn fog that restricted vision to a dozen yards or so. At some point in the night, she and Calista had moved almost entirely onto Harper's bedroll. The beautiful Jack stirred at Harper's side, apparently roused by the tiny change in Harper's breathing from asleep to awake.

They shared a smile before rising for the day. They roused the others, ate a quick breakfast of stone berry biscuits, apples, and jerky, and strapped on their armor.

Following the river north for several hours, Harper hoped the fog would burn away with the coming daylight, but apparently above the fog was an overcast sky, holding in the moisture and blocking out the sun. They smelled, rather than saw, the den through the fog long before they reached it.

"Ogre," Athol grumbled to give voice to the concerns at the forefront of everyone's minds.

The scent of the Ogre's lair, which could easily be smelled up to a quarter mile away depending on the wind and terrain, was akin to burning rotted vegetable garbage, the foulest body odor in the world, and a fetid musk capable of putting an army of skunks to shame. Breathing or fighting in an Ogre's stench was nearly impossible without magical protection. To add to the complications, Ogres were a diverse, if solitary race, with a dozen harmless mushroom farmers for every bloodthirsty marauder. While many mercenary companies would kill an Ogre for simply existing, Harper refused to allow the Dagger Falls Company to slay innocents regardless of how bad they smelled.

"Off to have your parlay, Sword Maiden," Sven said. "We'll wait here should you need us."

Calista glanced from the brothers and the Sorceress who appeared to be setting up a defensive position with the mules

60

protected in the rear. Meanwhile, Harper was tying her sword into its scabbard with a white cord to indicate she not only meant no harm, but would be physically unable to do any.

"Are you all mad?" Calista demanded.

"She refuses to let us kill Ogres without first learning their disposition," Ezra said.

"We agreed she would get to chat with them first if she went alone," Athol said.

"You would let her go alone because you don't agree with her stance on senseless slaughter?" Calista asked.

"They are not punishing me," Harper explained. "I want to go alone to prevent the Ogre from feeling threatened. I believe we may have killed Ogres in the past that simply reacted aggressively to our numbers."

"I'll go with you," Calista said. "I can remain unseen easily in this fog."

"Please don't." Harper placed her hand on Calista's shoulder to still her attempts at following. "I would not be able to lie if he asked if I was alone and we would be right back to the Ogre feeling threatened if he knew someone was watching him from the fog."

"Call out if you need help," Calista said sternly. "I can be at your aid in a flash."

"Let us hope it doesn't come to that," Harper said with a smile.

She walked off into the fog, passing almost immediately out of the visible range of her party. The fog thickened as she continued north along the creek bank. She willed an area of clean air around her, a blessing of the Goddess, to blow the stench away as she walked forward. Without the magical protection, she knew her eyes would be watering and her stomach churning by then. The dead grass on the bank slowly gave way to frosted over mud. It was likely the only warning she would get for her nearness to the den.

She'd parlayed with Ogres alone before, but never with such poor visibility. In the past, she was usually able to discern from a distance if the Ogre was peaceful enough to talk to or if it was a slayer of men. Most Ogre dens of the murderous types contained heads of various animals on pikes around the entrance. Since

Harper likely couldn't see such a warning until she was nearly upon the den, she hoped her luck would hold.

A low, crackling fire created a rosy dot in the fog ahead. Something big and lumbering was tromping through the creek ahead, banging around what she guessed to be a giant iron cooking pot from the hollow sound of it as it clanged against the rocks in the river. She let out an audible sigh of relief when she heard the Ogre humming a jaunty tune.

As she came even closer, she saw the full size of the Ogre faintly through the fog. He was enormous, even for an Ogre, well over ten feel tall, narrower at the shoulder than at the stomach, with long, powerful arms that reached down near his knees.

"Good morning there, friend," Harper called out to him.

The Ogre stood bolt upright, clutching the massive, black cauldron against his chest as though it were a precious child. He scanned the fog as she walked toward him, finally locating her by the clanking of her armor, and then fixating on her when she came into view.

"What want you, little knight?" the Ogre asked in his deeply rumbling voice. He had lower tusks with an impressive under bite that spoke of well-advanced years. His skin was mottled gray, his long, black, greasy hair held in a ponytail at the back of his head, and his brow had grown ridged and low across his eyes until they were nearly impossible to see.

Judging from his appearance, Harper guessed the Ogre was well over a century old. Ogres weren't like humans in that they never stopped growing—an Ogre would grow to the size of the food supply they could manage, making them voracious eaters. His ridged brow spoke of his true age and it likely offered protection to rival a steel helmet.

"To speak awhile if you would be willing," Harper replied.

"Bring you sword to talk?" the Ogre said in the disordered syntax typical of Ogres who spoke the common tongue of the coast.

"It is tied and will offer you no harm." Harper reached back over her should and gave the blade a harsh tug. The knot held the blade in the scabbard and to her back.

"Come then closer and we speak some." The Ogre dipped the massive pot into the river, gulping up the frigid water still trickling out of the mountains. He hauled the pot up from the bank and beckoned with one of his long arms for Harper to follow him toward his lair. He hadn't offered his name and hadn't asked hers; trivialization of names was a common Ogre trait, but it also said he was still wary of her.

The Ogre's den was actually fairly pleasant. A few rabbits, cleaned and skinned, hung over the fire to smoke. Baskets woven of stone berry branches held dozens of the hard-shelled nuts to either side of the sunken cave at the edge of an ancient foundation of a rock farmhouse. Harper was a little surprised to see the baskets, indeed many other vessels woven of the unyielding stone berry branches. It must have taken incredible strength and the patience of a mountain to bend the branches into usable shapes. This was a very strange Ogre indeed.

The Ogre plunked the water-filled cauldron down upon the stone hearth at the edge of the fire pit and set to loading in tubers and roots from one of the many baskets. "You have meal of the midday yet?" the Ogre asked. "It be hours will until ready still."

"Your offer is appreciated," Harper replied. "If our business should stretch so long, I would certainly join you." It was all a nicety as she knew better than to eat anything within an Ogre's stench.

"Business of what kind?"

"In digging your den, did you come across any items a dragon might have left behind or perhaps any evidence that a dragon had ever been here?" Harper asked.

"Dragon leave so much junk," the Ogre grumbled. "Dragons know not what valuable is. Little knight, tell me, of what good gold coins? Cannot coins eat. Cannot coins anything build. Coins catch light and hurl it in eyes. I ask little knight, of what good coins?"

"You don't want the treasure?" Harper asked.

"What use have I of tiny flimsy cups, silly trinkets of soft metal, and accursed coins?" the Ogre guffawed. "I hauled junk of dragon from the hole and hurl upon filth pile where belongs it."

"We would trade you for these things."

The Ogre roared with laughter, so much so that he nearly upended the cauldron he was filling with vegetables and tubers. "Should I trade you rubbish why? Trade you rubbish and become I rubbish trader. You take all want, but warn you I do, it unpleasant will be."

"With your permission then, I would bring up the rest of my group and our mules to begin collecting what we may find in the filth pile," Harper said with a trill of excitement tempered by the dread of having to dig through an Ogre's garbage heap for dragon treasure.

"Provide food for the pot if they want eat with me," the Ogre said. "If appetite they still have after."

"I shall return with my companions, of which we have a Jack who might share a story or two with you while we work," Harper offered. She was surprised to find she didn't want Calista soiling her hands in the vile task ahead—there was some level of perfection she wished to maintain in Calista that would no doubt be ruined in time, but didn't need to be spoiled so soon. If it was put to the group that Calista should spin tales for the Ogre to keep him happy, they might accept the Jack not doing any of the actual sifting of treasure from filth.

Chapter 9:

Staked Claims and Lines Drawn

Harper's happy return to the company was instantly ruined when she spotted Athol, Sven, and Ezra facing off with four human men and two dwarves; Calista was nowhere to be seen. As Harper neared, she recognized the leader of the other company. Jevvon was arguing vehemently with Sven about something. The two men were about the same height, armed similarly with sword and shield, but Jevvon was clearly a decade or more older than Sven as his long hair and beard were already touching with gray.

"Again, you claim the maps were acquired by a Jack that cannot be produced," Jevvon roared at Sven.

A much older man, far too old for the treasuring hunting trade, stood with Jevvon's crew. His head was wrapped in a bandage and he neither wore armor nor carried weapons. He stepped forward at this point to join in the railing against the outnumbered Dagger Falls Company. "I was bum rushed and felled by several stout men with truncheons," the older man said. "I bet it was these two...probably with friends. It is an affront to the information broker trade, which is vital to the treasure hunting profession. They must not be allowed to profit from such thievery."

Harper paid close attention to the two Dwarves upon her approach. They were dressed in the studded leather armor favored by Dwarven trackers and each carried two long knives common to their people. If she had to guess, they were hirelings brought on by Jevvon to track any company leaving out the east gate. If Jevvon was out money on the trackers, he'd be nearly impossible to dissuade with simple words.

"Wait there, Jevvon," Harped called as she stepped from the fog to join her company. "We might still settle this with words."

Jevvon's demeanor softened an iota upon Harper's arrival. "How might we do that, Sword Maiden?"

"Do you smell that? The treasure we both seek is currently in an Ogre's care." Harper stepped to the middle of her group, directly in front of Jevvon. She saw his eyes flicker to the peace-knot upon her blade, and she inwardly grimaced. He was too cunning and seasoned not to notice she was effectively unarmed. "I have spoken with the Ogre who is of the peaceful type. Allow us to retrieve the treasure without bloodshed as the Ogre has stated he would permit, and we will share with you a percentage of the spoils depending upon what we find."

Jevvon folded his arms over his chest and looked down his nose at Harper. "Or we could simply combine forces, slay the Ogre, and take whatever we all can carry."

"You cannot fight the Ogre without me to cleanse the air and I won't help you kill an innocent," Harper said.

Jevvon nodded in the direction of the two Dwarves and shook his head. "Those two can kill the Ogre just fine without your help, especially if he is as peaceful as you say. I only offered to join forces as a kindness."

"I will not let you harm the Ogre who has raised no weapon against anyone," Harper growled.

"Just kill her and let's get on with this," the information broker piped in.

Before any real decision could be made upon either side of the standoff, the sound of quick violence echoed out of the fog—a wet smacking followed by a muffled grunt and a gurgling, choking sound. Calista strode from the fog with a loaded crossbow in one hand and Harper's bloody dagger in the other. She tossed aside the crossbow, knelt to slide the dagger back into the sheath on her boot, and slipped her bow from her back.

"Your Jack is dead," Calista announced, "and I've about had it with you throwing idles threats around." She plucked half-a-dozen arrows from her quiver and stuck them in the ground before her for easier access.

Athol let out a mighty battle roar mixed with a healthy dose of glee. He slipped his massive hammer with the sixty pound head on a six foot shaft off his back and swung it in a deadly arc in front of him, the spiked head aimed first. Sven and Harper ducked beneath the attack while Ezra took several steps back to avoid the follow through. The hammer swing passed harmlessly over the two

Dwarves. Jevvon raised his shield to deflect the crushing blow from caving his unprotected head. Athol's hammer skipped off the convex face of the shield, altering its angle just enough to catch the next man in the row across the top of his bronze helmet, which normally would have spared him were it not for the spikes biting into the metal enough to gain purchase. The warrior's head snapped to the side with a sickening pop as the force of the swing snapped his neck.

Harper struggled to untie the cord on her sword's handle with the blade still strapped to her back. The first Dwarf to draw steel came directly for her, but stopped short when two arrows sprouted from the side of his neck. Calista had them flanked and the second Dwarf appeared to understand this better than his dying brethren.

The other Dwarf tracker fell in behind the older, unarmed man before Calista could get an accurate shot off at him. Her next two arrows struck home in the information broker's stomach. He pitched forward from the wounds and the Dwarf took flight. Calista snatched the last two arrows from the ground and gave chase before the Dwarf could reach the relative safety of the fog.

"If you run, you'll only die tired!" Calista called after him.

She fired on the run, missing with the first arrow, but hitting with the second, low in the Dwarf's back. His hand reached around to grasp at the arrow jutting from just above his metal girdle. Calista tossed aside the bow, drew the cavalry hammer and dagger, one to each hand, and easily walked at a brisk pace to catch up with her staggering quarry. She batted away the defensive knife the Dwarf clumsily brought up to protect his face when she caught up to him. She carried through the strike and slashed the already bloody dagger through the Dwarf's beard, severing the windpipe below. The Dwarf expired at her feet in a gurgling heap. Harper lost track of Calista in the fog after she saw the Dwarf fall.

Jevvon and his lone remaining companion didn't appear to think their chances had been significantly diminished by the loss of the majority of their party. Jevvon lunged into the fray with shield and sword at the ready. He knocked Sven off his guard and pressed the advantage. It was all Sven could do to keep his limbs intact as Jevvon came after him with expert strikes from sword and shield.

Harper finally managed to free her sword from its scabbard just in time to deflect an incoming attack from Jevvon's remaining warrior. The man was larger than her, nearly as large as Athol, wielding a full body shield and a swirling flail with a wickedly spiked head. She did a quick shoulder roll to escape his next swing of the flail. The length of chain binding the spiked head to the handle gave the warrior remarkable range and he brought the head back to twirling so quickly and easily, Harper wondered if she could even get inside the man's guard.

She looked to Athol for help, but found the mighty barbarian had leapt to his brother's aid already. Even with Athol's help, Sven was still giving ground under Jevvon's attacks. Athol's hammer couldn't swing fast enough to catch Jevvon and every time he tried, Jevvon forced Sven toward the follow through of the swing to unbalance them both.

The flail head came for Harper again and she had to give ground until she was entirely too far out of range to make even a wild attack with her sword. The warrior was bedecked in banded metal armor with a thick, steel helmet. Even if she managed to get inside the deadly radius of the twirling flail, she would have her work cut out for her in getting through the shield and armor.

As Harper planned her next assault, she heard Ezra's voice join the battle, chanting quickly to weave magic to her will. The flail-wielding warrior heard her as well and broke off his attack on Harper to turn his attention to the unprotected Sorceress. Ezra finished the spell before he could complete the full turn of his guard. A salvo of quick-moving, burning rocks struck the man in the side and bounced off his shield and helmet. He seemed perturbed by the magical attack, but not particularly wounded by it. The warrior made a remarkably quick charge on Ezra, barreling down on her with armor clanking and flail head whirring through the air. Harper sprinted to make up the ground to aid the Sorceress, but she knew she wasn't going to make it in time—he'd driven her too far out of position and he had a head start of several steps.

A black flash of leather armor and a shock of burnished hair struck the warrior's side at below waist level. The cavalry pick Harper had given Calista was buried in the flail-wielding warrior's left knee, jutting out the other side with a trickle of blood. The warrior's charge came to a stumbling stop well short of Ezra. He listed to his left to lean heavily on the full-body shield he carried. This gave Ezra all the opening she needed. A second spell came to her lips before the warrior could get his flail's head swinging again. A flash of light and clap of thunder emanated from the Sorceress's hands. The warrior's body went rigid as arcs of electricity jumped from the plates of his metal armor, eventually seeking out the ground. The scent of burning human flesh filled the air. The flail-wielding warrior crumbled forward, cooked alive within his own armor.

Harper turned her attention to the fight between Jevvon and the brothers. Sven and Athol were both wounded in a dozen places, losing energy against Jevvon who didn't appear to be so much as scratched and showed no sign of flagging. Jevvon was using the river well to reduce the effectiveness of their number advantage and he looked ready to cull Sven from the duo to remove the advantage entirely.

"Jevvon!" Harper shouted, "bring your fight to me!"

In response, Jevvon knocked Sven into the river with a harsh shield bash, and cut Athol's leg nearly to the bone with a slash from his sword. Ezra ran to the scene of the carnage even as Jevvon was walking away. She fell to her stomach to grasp at Sven's flailing hand when the river threatened to drown him in his armor.

Harper and Jevvon met in the space between. Her blade clashed against his shield with a clap of thunder as the Goddess's power flowed through her. His blade made it easily through her guard, but did little damage against her plate armor. The electrical shocks coming off her sword as she only pecked at the surface of his guard began to take their toll even as the tiny cuts and bruises managed by him against her armor wore on her strength. Try as she might, she couldn't administer anything but a glancing blow with her huge sword and try as he might, he couldn't get close enough to swing from the hip to force his sword through her armor.

They were both breathing hard, both bleeding, and the space between them lengthened between attacks as each tried to rally enough to finish the other off. After another clash of steel against steel in which neither managed to land a blow, both retreated to take a knee. Harper looked across the expanse of the dozen or so pace opening they'd created between them to see if Jevvon might be willing to surrender. She found his eyes as weary as hers with a growing respect within the stern gray orbs. He had the look of a man ready to compromise.

In the moment after, the light went out of his eyes as a dagger was drawn across his throat. Calista stood behind Jevvon's collapsing form even as it sprayed blood from the neck the entire fall to the ground. She held Harper's dagger in her hand and wore a satisfied smile upon her full lips.

"I gave you as much of a chance as I could stand before intervening," Calista said.

"He might have surrendered," Harper exclaimed.

"And he might not have," Calista said. "We cannot deal in possibilities. Find your feet and accept victory. Athol and Ezra have plucked Sven from the river, but the brothers will need your healing if they are to walk anywhere." Calista stepped over Jevvon's fallen form and helped Harper to stand to her full height.

"Of seven, you killed five," Harper said in an awed whisper when the realization struck her.

"The old information broker was an accident," Calista said.

Before Calista could help Harper limp to the rest of the company, Harper stopped her. "What are you?" Harper demanded of her.

"A Jack-of-All-Trades and a master of none—I do my best work after the setting sun," Calista recited the old rhyme.

"I would argue you are a master of at least one trade," Harper corrected her.

"Give me two chances and I'll prove you right twice," Calista said, "but for the time being, you should conserve your words for your Goddess to cobble back together our broken group while I see what spoils might be stripped from the bodies of the fallen."

Calista made her way to the information broker she'd claimed to accidentally shoot. The man was still alive, groaning weakly as one of her arrows had likely punctured his diaphragm. She knelt beside him, making a show of searching his clothes.

"Who provided the Dwarves?" Calista asked of the wounded man.

"Please…" the old man gurgled. The frothy blood spilling from his mouth with the words mixed into the scraggly gray beard, slicking it to his gaunt neck. If Calista didn't get answers from him quickly, she wasn't likely to get them at all.

"Answer my question or I'll salvage my arrows before you expire," Calista hissed. To get her point across, she grasped one of the shafts jutting from the man's stomach to let him feel what pain the tiniest shift in the arrow could cause. "Who provided the Dwarves?"

"Randolph made me bring them to Jevvon, but Jevvon didn't trust them," the information broker groaned.

"Nor would I." Calista slid her dagger between the man's ribs and pushed until she felt the blade puncture the bottom chambers of his heart. He died a second after. Of course Jevvon didn't trust them—he knew they were from the thieves guild. She hadn't been sure, not really, until the second one tried to run. The Jack she'd killed in the forest was likely Jevvon's man, but the Dwarves were clearly after their own agenda, which may or may not include an ambush on the return to the city.

Calista glanced back to the rest of the company to find Harper and Ezra well into the process of patching the brother's back together. She didn't have much time before they would come looking at the bodies.

She searched the Dwarf corpses first. The stocky little men had quick draw sheaths for their knives and blackened belts that would fit her. She salvaged both sets and strapped all four along her hips, two to each side on staggered levels. She checked and adjusted the weapons until she could draw both sets easily. The furthest Dwarf, the one who tried to run, possessed the mark she assumed they both carried although his was more obvious as she'd cut away most of his beard when she slashed open his throat. Above the laceration mark that ended his life, she found a branded scar of a downward facing horseshoe with horns. She didn't recognize the guild crest, but she assumed if she showed it to the rest of the company one of them would know.

The fog was finally clearing and with it came a redoubling of the stench from the Ogre's lair. Calista found what coins she could on the corpses and headed back to the group. She'd gained weapons of her own, knowledge of the thieves guild marking, and a name of possible value—Randolph.

"I lost my sword and shield in the river," Sven grumbled when Harper turned her healing magic to him.

"You can take Jevvon's," Harper told him. "I think his equipment is better anyway."

"We thought she ran away," Ezra muttered under her breath. "As soon as the men came upon us, she vanished, likely without them even seeing she stood with us."

"If she hadn't, we might all have died," Sven said.

"Don't doubt the owner of the crossbow that she killed had his sights set on you, Sorceress," Athol said through gritted teeth. The wound on his leg was deep, more than deep enough to sever a few necessary tendons while missing any blood vessels likely to kill him.

"If that is true, then she saved you twice in one encounter." Harper glanced over her shoulder to Ezra even as her hands glowed with the healing magic to smooth the wounds over Sven's sword arm and shoulder.

"You would have reached me in time for the man with the flail," Ezra scoffed.

"I appreciate the compliment to my speed over open ground, but we both know my lack of swiftness is the reason I do most of my fighting from horseback." Harper turned her attention to Athol's leg when Sven's sword arm seemed reasonably mended.

"If that's true, then why could she reach me in time?" Ezra said. "I don't mean to look a gift horse in the teeth…"

"Yes you do," Sven interrupted. "It's one of your favorite things to do."

"…but how is it that she could kill so many so effortlessly?" Ezra finished. "Of all of us, she faced no open attack and suffered no wounds, yet she felled five of their numbers."

"I'm going to give her part of your triumph over the flail man," Harper said. "We'll call it five and a half." She focused much longer on Athol's severely wounded leg, warmth and light poured from beneath her hands as though she held a small lantern to his skin.

Athol and Sven laughed.

"Fine, do so, it only strengthens my point—she's not a simple Jack," Ezra said, folding her arms over her chest.

"No, I am quite the clever Jack as it turns out," Calista said, having easily snuck up on the chatting group. "Their horses are tied up down stream of here. There are two traveling horses among their number, likely the mounts favored by the Dwarves, if our spell-flinger would like to take one."

"What of the bodies?" Sven asked.

"Yes, aside from the knives you've already claimed, what gear might we add to our own?" Athol asked. Harper helped the massive barbarian to his feet, which was a struggle for them both.

"Items well worth using to upgrade your own gear and whatever else deemed unusable will make an easy sale on the open market," Calista said. "Judging from the way this dust up settled, I would say they expected trouble and came eager to meet it with steel."

"All too true," Harper said, "and we're glad you were equal to the task, aren't we?"

"We may have underestimated Jevvon," Sven said, quietly adding, "and overestimated my ability to swim in armor."

"Aye, it was a worthy battle where the mighty Athol struck the first blow, felling a man with a single swing of his hammer!" Athol bellowed, clapping his brother on the shoulder.

"Second blow, actually," Ezra corrected him. "The Jack she killed in the forest would be the first."

"Our mathematician is correct," Sven said, "a point Harper has made several times to us already. Really, Calista, you should hear how she gushes over you—it's appalling."

Harper tried to hide her blushing with a quickly turned head, but out of the corner of her eye should could tell Calista had seen and wore a satisfied smirk as evidence.

"We'll have to inform the scribe of the mercenary ledger of what transpired today," Ezra said. "It'll mean a lot of paperwork to catalogue those we rightfully killed in the course of a legitimate job."

Divine Touched

"That's what we have you for," Harper said with a wry grin, glad for the change of subject.

"Not to add to your work, spell-flinger," Calista said, "but only four of these men were mercenaries. The Dwarves bear the mark of a thieves guild and the old man without armor that I mistook for a Sorcerer was apparently a freelance information broker."

"Let's get a look at the mark," Sven said, his tone suddenly grim. "We may have really stepped in something filthy."

"Speaking of filthy," Harper said. "About our Ogre friend's treasure…"

Chapter 10:

Unhealthy Apples

Gratitude for the collective turning of the tide of battle accomplished by Calista in several individual fights helped in the vote to allow the Jack to sit out the dirty work of sorting the Ogre's filth pile. Calista, who claimed to know a few songs and stories the Ogre might like, gladly and with remarkable civility, kept their host company at the front of the hut while the rest of the company toiled in the back.

"Why anyone would keep their filth in a pile is beyond me," Sven muttered on their approach of the vileness barely enclosed in a bulging pen woven from sticks.

More than just the usual filth an Ogre might produce from bodily function, the pile also contained kitchen leavings and random dead things the Ogre dragged home. If any of them had been farmers, specifically root vegetable farmers, they would have immediately identified a marvelous concoction of composted and manure. The quartet was exceedingly glad the magic zone created by Harper prevented anyone from smelling what they were about to be elbow deep in.

Athol took the duty of scooping the filth from the colossal bin to hand to Harper who walked it to the stream where Sven and Ezra washed it and catalogued the pieces to the best of their ability. It was agreed they wouldn't stop until three of the four were so disgusted and tired of their duties that they couldn't carry on. It became a source of pride among the longtime friends—who could withstand their putrid task the longest. They stripped off their clothing and armor to don just the bare minimum of attire that they could stand to part with as there would be no salvaging any cloth that came in contact with anything from the Ogre's filth pile.

Calista perched herself on the widest fencepost she could find and watched the Ogre in his work of creating stew from a harvest of every edible thing he could get his Ogre paws on. She was a bit hungry herself and so plucked an apple from one of the packs they'd brought with them and slipped one of her new knives from her belt to cut slices off the fruit.

Calista strained her neck a bit to see around the hut. Harper was walking another sack full of disgusting items down to the stream. Her strapping arms were flexed in an appealing way that showed off some lovely definition and the round muscles of her shoulders were visible through the gaps in the tattered tunic she wore. If Calista didn't intellectually know Harper probably smelled terrible from the work she was doing, she would have considered it an entirely appealing scene.

"You not help others with sort of pile?" the Ogre asked her, drawing her attention away from watching Harper's backside when she bent over to set the sack down between Sven and Ezra.

"Where I come from, the Jacks entertain the Ogres and the others sort the filth piles," Calista explained.

The Ogre smirked with his broken yellow teeth and immense lower tusks. He shook his head and his smirk broke into a full smile. "You know not much of Ogres, little Jack."

"Why do you say that?" Calista said, cutting off a slice of the apple to pop into her mouth.

"I tell when finish apple you do, or let you find out maybe yourself."

"Fair enough," Calista said. "I've never conversed with an Ogre. I honestly had no idea Ogres were so well-spoken and clever."

"Ogres like people of kind any," the Ogre said, piling a basket full of what looked like skinned skunks into the bubbling stew cauldron. "Some speak, some fight, some smart, some smash— some good of the cook like me."

"A philosopher, a chef, and a hermit," Calista said, slipping another apple slice into her mouth before she'd fully chewed the first. "I've known humans like you, although obviously not with the strength of appetite you have. There's something about solitude that makes a man want to consider the mysteries of the world and make stew."

"You have food add to stew?" the Ogre asked cryptically.

"Just the apple, I suppose," Calista said.

"Throw in."

Calista shrugged and tossed the apple into the pot. It disappeared into the murky brown sludge with a little splash. She wiped her knife blade off on her leg and slipped it back into its sheath. She watched patiently while the Ogre crumbled several handfuls of homegrown herbs into the pot and gazed deeply into the bubbling stew.

"You know what I now do?" the Ogre asked.

Calista shook her head.

"Future told from stew if wants me to you do." The Ogre looked up from his cooking to lock eyes on Calista and, for the first time, she had the distinct impression of how inhuman their host really was. Aside from his size, jutting lower jaw, greasy hair, rubbery skin, and pronounced tusks, his eyes were ancient in ways even the oldest humans never could be. The Ogre was aged enough to have seen the world in ways most species simply couldn't.

"I'm supposed to be entertaining you, but if you'd like to tell my future, I'm game," Calista said, trying to affect a breezy tone to replace the casual ease that was shaken straight out of her by the abrupt shift in the conversation.

"Ask question, honest only question or stew get angry," the Ogre said.

Without even thinking about what she might say, which was unlike her on every level, Calista blurted out, "Will Harper and I end up together?" She could kick herself for the candid response to a request she normally would have lied about regardless of how angry it might make the stew—there was some magic at work about the Ogre and she wasn't as resistant to it as she thought she should be.

The Ogre stirred the stew slowly with a length of oak that was worn so smooth it looked like polished bone. His slow, deliberate motions were broken up by the inclusion of strange, jerky patterns traced through the thick concoction in the pot. As Calista watched, she suddenly regretted throwing the apple in as requested; it was clearly a component for an actual spell and not just some eccentricity by a hermetic Ogre who fancied himself a fortuneteller. The Ogre finished his stirring work, tore the oak rod from the mixture, and stared hard into the hole left behind where the wood exited the incredibly thick slurry. It filled in slowly and the Ogre nodded his understanding of what he'd seen in the depths of the stew.

"Lie to her you do," the Ogre said. "The you she love not a real you. When she see the you that real, burn the world around you."

"What's that supposed to mean?" Calista asked, a little annoyed that her fortune would be so accurate at the outset, yet so vague when things got important.

"Stew say no more," the Ogre said.

Calista narrowed her eyes at the Ogre soothsayer and cocked her head to one side to study him with an intensified interest. "You're divine touched," she said as a statement of fact. "Some Ogre God or other speaks to you and grants you favor."

The Ogre shrugged as though such a thing were beneath consideration or note. "Questions many better to ask by you in opinion mine."

Calista shrugged off the peculiar interaction and went to check on the progress of the rest of her cohort. Sven and Ezra didn't look remotely interested in clean, spry company as they were both filthy from their task of washing treasure in the river and they both were constantly stretching their backs as though they weren't used to toiling so long while hunched over. One look at Athol told Calista she shouldn't bother him. She'd heard him making a joke early on about the glorious work of adventuring being little better than sewer-sweeping—after a few hours of digging through an Ogre's filth pile, when he said the words, he wasn't joking anymore. Calista guessed from the look of him that he was the only member of their group actually coming in contact with truly vile things and the fact that he had a long beard meant he was having quite a bit of unwanted contact with it. Calista settled on Harper, who appeared the only person interested in talking to her and the only one not entirely bedraggled by the task. Harper smiled to her upon approach and Calista fell into step along side her as she walked another load of treasure down toward Sven and Ezra at the riverbank.

"How is our Ogre host?" Harper asked.

"I think he might be divine touched," Calista said.

"I thought there was something special about him. Probably the King of Stews or some such lesser god."

"There's a King of Stews?"

Harper shrugged and shook her head. "I have no idea, but if there were a God for stew makers and eaters, could you imagine a better acolyte than an Ogre? They're all stomach and have no concept of what is and isn't putrid."

Calista smiled. "Was that a joke from the chaste Sword Maiden?"

"I'm full of surprises," Harper said with a wink.

Before they could fully make it down across the field to the riverbank, a bout of extreme stomach cramps overtook Calista. She fancied herself fairly stoic in the face of pain, but the cramps doubled her over despite her best efforts to remain upright.

Harper stopped and turned back with her sack of filth-smeared treasure still slung over her shoulder. "Uh oh, you didn't eat the stew, did you?"

"No, I only ate part of an apple we brought with us," Calista said through gritted teeth.

"Just because you can't smell the stench doesn't mean it's not there," Harper explained. "That apple was likely covered with the stuff the second you took it from your bag. Let me get this load down to the river and I'll see to your tummy ache."

Calista fell over into the grass to hold her aching stomach in the fetal position. She glanced up to Harper a couple dozen yards away. The Sword Maiden was handing off the treasure to Sven and Ezra who seemed to think it was grandly funny that their new Jack made the mistake of eating anything in an Ogre stench zone. They waved to her and pantomimed shoving her fingers down her throat to make herself throw up. Calista felt a little hazed by the whole ordeal and she didn't much care for it, even if it was her own fault.

Harper took her time in returning, washing her hands and forearms thoroughly before coming back. She didn't seem nearly as amused by the whole thing as Sven and Ezra did, but she also didn't appear overly concerned with Calista's possible death, which carried a touch of hope. Calista felt like she was dying, but if Harper wasn't concerned about an imminent demise, she probably wasn't in danger of one.

Harper knelt behind Calista and gently slid her hands down over her cramping stomach, guiding away Calista's own hands in the process. Calista looked up to her and tried to smile although she was sure it came out more as a grimace.

"This will hardly put you at even with the rest of the company," Harper said.

"Is that another joke?" Calista asked painfully.

"It wasn't intended as one," Harper said. "Nobody here is foolish enough to think you didn't save us all back there. Sven may admit to it, and Athol will probably make a joke about it at some point if he gets drunk enough, but you'll never hear Ezra acknowledge what you did for her. Know that I know and take comfort in that."

Calista tried to laugh, but the slowly easing pain prevented her from truly finishing the chuckle. "Oddly enough, I think you're the only one who would have survived without my help."

Harper blushed. "Then I thank you for saving me from acquiring a new set of scars."

"Consider us even if you can ease this poisoning even to half strength."

"I can do better than that." Harper's hands began faintly glowing against the outer shell of Calista's armor and the pain not only eased, but eventually evaporated into nothingness.

The rush of numbing hormones meant to ameliorate the agony suddenly had the wall of pain pulled out from in front of them. They rushed over Calista unchecked, causing her to feel better than she ought to and even made her a little giddy. She gave Harper an appreciative smile and slipped her hands over Harper's to hold them in place despite the job being done. "I bet you could make me feel all kinds of good," Calista said, a flinty, seductive edge coming to her voice out of genuine desire.

At this, Harper looked as though she might want to take a quick dip in the river to cool the flush of heated red running across her skin. "I wouldn't know…do you really…?" her stammering response was cut short by a colossal holler of rage from up by the Ogre's hut.

"Harper! Another load up here," Athol shouted. His voice was angry thunder, leaving little question of his quickly fraying nerves.

"I should go get that," Harper said, pulling her hands away from Calista's stomach. "You should lie here a moment to recover."

Harper scampered off, leaving Calista to wonder why she'd been so forward without a goal in mind. Her seduction of Harper wasn't supposed to work backward on her—she was supposed to remain in control of the situation, turn it to her advantage, and…she couldn't even finish the thought with the intrusion of the impressive list of pleasures she imagined sharing with the demure Sword Maiden, who, as it turned out, was kind of funny.

Calista snorted at the last part of the thought. She never considered whether or not she even enjoyed a sense of humor on a woman. Certainly she liked when people laughed at her jokes, but to have someone make jokes she considered funny…she thought she might get used to such a thing. She snapped herself from the thought with the violent realization that she couldn't seduce Harper, not for real, not for keeps—she had to skip town and she would have to do it soon.

She pulled herself from the grassy field that was her brief convalescence bed and ran back up around to the front of the hut before Harper could pass her with another load of treasure. It was the battle, she told herself, or perhaps the healing magic that clouded her thinking so much—a little time spent chatting with the Ogre and thinking over her potentially catastrophic situation would help clear her mind. They would make enough money from the Ogre treasure for her to escape in a day or two; there really wasn't a functional reason to seduce Harper anymore.

She glanced up to the sky and the gathering dark gray thunderheads rolling in out of the north. A cold storm was coming down from the mountains, not from the sea, but from the top of the world.

Chapter 11:

The Stench of Success

They camped on the edge of the orchards, more than far enough away from the Ogre's lair that they shouldn't have still smelled it. Unfortunately, even with extensive magical cleansing and hard scrubbing, the stench followed them, clinging to their hard-won gains.

Sitting around the campfire, Harper was constantly smelling her hair and Athol would follow suit shortly after in smelling his beard. Even though they seemed to satisfy themselves the smell wasn't coming from them, they had to check again each time a little breeze brought the odor into the campsite from the pile of gleaming treasure they left well away from the campfire.

The clinging Ogre stench would decrease the value of the treasure immeasurably. Calista was the first to realize this, but she didn't want to voice what was already no doubt on everyone's minds. No noble woman would want to pay full price for a necklace or pin she couldn't wear in public because it still smelled like a combination of Ogre excrement and rotting table scraps. They could have sold some of the items retrieved from the other mercenary band they'd tangled with if Calista didn't need the knives she'd looted and Sven didn't need replacements for the weapons and armor he'd damaged or lost. The rest of the weapons and armor they scavenged from the men would be sold into the Thundering Dawn's armory, which wouldn't amount to much as the flail man's armor wasn't salvageable after being electrically fused together. Even with a friendly fence, which Calista doubted they knew of since the demise of their old Jack, the treasure wasn't going cover much ground.

Ezra looked up from some of the scribbling she was doing and cleared her throat, snapping Calista from her musings. "I've catalogued what we have and totaled some conservative estimates of what our take might end up being," Ezra said. "We will make little profit on the salvaged weapons, armor, and the horses as we are bound by contract to sell them back to our patron's stockpile. To purchase back the use of the sword and shield Sven took to replace his own, the four knives Calista claimed, and the rental of the two mules we ended up not needing, we're likely to manage a dozen silver pieces or so. As for the Ogre treasure…"

"Why do I suspect that grand pile of riches we acquired may as well be tin and flint?" Athol grumbled.

"We can try to fence it, which would likely fetch the aforementioned tin and flint prices, or we can have it disassembled, melted down to ingots and spare gems, to resell that way by jewelers and money changers," Ezra said.

Calista flinched at the second suggestion. Part of a treasure's value was the craftsmanship that went into its creation. Many of the pendants, rings, goblets, and other items they'd found were aesthetically beautiful and likely formed by hands of long dead artists. Reducing them to their raw materials, which may get rid of the stench, would also cost them money and reduce the total value of the haul significantly. If she knew a fence, one perhaps that could move items over seas or across borders, they might manage better prices. With the market being Griffon's Rock and whatever traveling merchants were currently inside the walls, she couldn't think of a way to convince anyone to pay even a fraction of market value.

"Will melting it down get rid of the smell?" Sven asked. "If so, we might try that with Athol's beard."

Ezra scrunched her mouth to one side and made something of a thinking face, ignoring Sven's joke; Calista suspected she would be a terrible gambler with such obvious tells. "Probably," Ezra finally said. "I think the smell is in the metal and not the gems, so at the very least, the gems will hold value better if they're freed from their respective pieces."

"What will the total coin be if we go that route?" Calista asked.

"After expenses and our patron's cut…somewhere in the area of eighty gold coins," Ezra said.

The news hurt. Calista could see it on the brother's faces as well that she wasn't the only one smarting from the low number. Still, Calista surmised it would be enough to get her outfitted for the road, or perhaps even rent a spot on one of the last caravans heading south. It would hardly be the lap of luxury, but it would buy her an escape in tolerable accommodations and a timely fashion.

"Let's take what we can get then," Calista said. "After all, we didn't have to pay a broker fee for the information, nor did we have to fight the Ogre who laid claim to the lair."

"We had to kill Jevvon and his crew," Ezra said.

"What is this *we* nonsense?" Athol asked. "The Jack you constantly insult did most of the killing and I took most of the injuries. In fact, I say Calista and I take a larger share each, or perhaps just me since I lost the most blood and will lose valuable beard hair to the sheers to fully rid myself of the stench. A gold piece for every inch of beard I lose should suffice."

"How are we to know the stench in your beard is from the Ogre?" Ezra asked. "You vomit into it so often when you're drunk, the odor might be from you."

"Can we consider the vote of paying for beard hair in gold?" Sven asked. "Opposed?" Everyone but Athol raised their hands. "Four to one, beard hair for gold fails to pass."

"You're all jealous you cannot grow such a fine beard," Athol grumbled.

"Spoiled beards aside, for a couple days of work without a lot of travel, the numbers are good," Sven said.

"Ignoring the fact that the treasure, were it untainted, would be worth ten times that, of course," Athol grumbled.

"Ignoring that fact, yes, dear brother," Sven said.

"It's a hard fact to ignore," Athol countered.

"Drink until you manage," Sven said.

This seemed like a proper course to Athol who hefted a heavy wineskin to his mouth to begin the process immediately.

"We'll call that four votes in the affirmative and one of abstaining then," Ezra said, glancing meaningfully to the sullen Harper.

Calista hadn't noticed Harper's silence until Ezra pointed it out. The Sword Maiden wasn't sitting apart from them or particularly distracted by anything, but she certainly didn't seem to be in the mood to discuss the treasure's value. She couldn't be sure of why Harper was upset, but since she would be leaving soon anyway, Calista didn't think it could hurt anything to give the Sword Maiden a smile.

"Care to help me check the horse's hobblings for the night?" Calista asked of Harper as she gained her feet. She offered a hand to help Harper up, which was taken with shy gratitude. Leaving the warm circle of firelight, Calista did not release Harper's hand.

"What might be the matter, lovely maiden?" Calista asked in a hushed tone when they were nearer to the horses than the company collected around the campfire.

"I thought you might think me tainted and vile like the treasure," Harper said quietly. "You seemed eager to be away earlier when I returned to the task of hauling the fouled gold."

"Perish the thought," Calista said. "I returned to my duties entertaining the Ogre so you wouldn't think me slothful. It would take a good deal more than a little labor in the muck to spoil your purity in my eyes."

"You always know precisely the thing to say," Harper said.

"The gift of a talented tongue," Calista replied.

Calista waited patiently while Harper saw to checking the first horse's hobble rope. When she rose though, Calista pounced, pressing her body flush against Harper's, urging her back to the trunk of the nearest tree. Calista's hands made their way inside Harper's heavy cloak to grasp at her hips, pulling her closer to engage in a knee-weakening kiss. To Calista's surprise, Harper appeared to be awaiting just such an instigation. She threw her arms around Calista's shoulders and returned the kiss with equal verve. They were of similar height, enfolding easily into each other's embrace, practically sharing Harper's cloak to hold in the building heat between them that eclipsed the fast encroaching cold of night and the gathering storm.

Calista broke the kiss, pressing her cheek against Harper's as she pushed in closer to whisper to her. "Concern for retaining your maidenhood should not prevent you from touching me as I've long since lost mine," Calista whispered to her. To encourage the point, Calista's hand came up to Harper's full breasts, cupping one of them with a gentle, but meaningful squeeze. "Do you not wish to touch me?"

"I waited only for a clear invitation," Harper gasped.

"Consider the invitation extended and open in perpetuity," Calista cooed into Harper's ear. "I am keen to be explored by you."

Harper's fingers were awkward, yet eager to find their way. Calista rather enjoyed the inexperienced pawing Harper was giving her as though she wanted to touch everything of Calista, but could not precisely focus on anything for too terribly long since something else always seemed to call her hands elsewhere. Calista placed a hand against the tree behind Harper for support as she allowed the awkward groping to proceed. Harper's hands focused first on her chest, although apparently not focused enough to make it through her top to the breasts beneath. Just as Calista was about to instruct her in how to get beneath the cloth tunic, Harper was already on to other areas of interest, grasping at Calista's hips and then reticently around to grip Calista's firm ass.

"You've combined the wrong elements in your efforts to please," Calista chided softly. Before the words could harm Harper's no doubt delicate enthusiasm, Calista continued, adding her own hand to Harper's body to demonstrate. "You can combine verve and focus to create pleasure." Calista gripped Harper's breast, rubbing her thumb in strong circles across the nipple she could feel rising to attention through the material. "This sort of intensity must remain focused to one area for some time though. Can you feel what I mean?"

Harper nodded shyly, a euphoric smile spreading across her lovely lips. She lifted her hand to Calista's breast to emulate the lesson, seemingly thrilled when she managed to draw a pleased smile from Calista in return.

"Or, should you desire to enthrall with soft, sensual caresses, you may spread them over a great many areas, although always moving with the fluid motions of water over skin," Calista instructed, following through with corresponding caresses to demonstrate. Her fingers deftly made their way inside Harper's tunic to find the warm, smooth skin beneath. She caressed in teasing, soft passes over Harper's ribs, down along the outer edge of her stomach and then tauntingly low across her hip bones, moving toward center to barely graze the softest hair just at the top of Harper's mound. "This creates delicious anticipation by making your lover wonder where your hands might wander next."

"Which do you prefer?" Harper asked.

"First one and then the other," Calista replied. "Your hands aren't the only implements you have for these tasks either." Calista leaned in closer until her lips were barely brushing against Harper's as she spoke the rest. "Your mouth can excel at both techniques as well. Think on that, my dear."

As Calista pulled away and headed back toward camp, she glanced over her shoulder through the curtain of her hair and spotted the desired smile on Harper's lips. The night was going to be cold, far colder than the night before, and the sharing of a bedroll with the attractive Sword Maiden sounded entirely enticing. Calista's mood was soaring with the knowledge she would soon be on her way south to safety, but in the interim couple of days, she would enjoy everything Harper had to offer with no greater goal than pleasure in mind.

Calista wasn't the only one to sleep well. After a cozy night spent in Harper's eager embrace, they were both rested and a little sickening to the rest of the company with how outwardly intimate they were after their night's rest. Ezra and Sven apparently slept fitfully in the cold while Athol drank himself into a stupor and was well on his way to picking up where he left off the night before on the ride back to Griffon's Rock. He was nearly falling from the saddle by the time they rode in through the eastern gates.

The company parted ways, although Harper left Calista's side reluctantly. Ezra was off to the smelter and money changer to see to the task of melting down the Ogre-stench infested treasure while Harper was to check in the bow Calista no longer needed and report to their patron as Athol was beyond even conversational slurring. Sven took on the unpleasant task of tending to his drunken brother who was of a mind to get even drunker if someone could be convinced to order for him. Calista took her leave of Harper with a brief kiss on the cheek, promising to return to the inn before evening.

She set out on foot after their mules were returned and procured horses sold. The city was alive with activity as other mercenary bands were making their arrivals. Calista walked through the packed streets filled with hawkers and family members who came out to greet the adventurers arriving heavy laden with coin and tales of adventure.

She passed around a corner into a narrow causeway between the guard barracks and the outer wall in hopes of finding a less congested route to the caravans off the edge of the bazaar. She stopped, almost out of habit, at hearing a clear voice filtering down from one of the arrow slits on the side of the building.

"...a Dark Stalker," the man said, and suddenly Calista was all ears.

"I seen the bodies dredged from the bay," another man said. "You go down and poke out which one is in the Brotherhood of Assassins. I'm tellin' you, dead sailors and a few immigrants is all they fished out of the drink from that shipwreck."

"Maybe the Dark Stalker was among them," the first man said. "If you were an assassin, wouldn't you want to blend in? A smart Dark Stalker can probably look like whoever they want."

"There you two go, telling stories," a third man said with a booming voice of authority.

"No, it's true, Captain," the first man protested. "My cousin is an affirmed sister at the Temple of the Sea Queen. She told me someone brought Dark Stalker weapons into the temple."

A long pause followed and Calista wondered if they were whispering out of earshot. Her fears were allayed when the Captain resumed speaking, clearly having mulled things over in the meantime.

"If that's true, and we'll have to confirm it before we act, we'll need to investigate," the Captain said.

Calista was about to move on at the mention of this. Confirming a rumor, never mind launching an investigation, was a laughably difficult activity for most city guards. The little chuckle she felt at the assertion caught in her throat like a dry hunk of half-chewed bread when the Captain continued.

"Didn't the livery master claim a shadowy figure tried to steal a horse a few days back?" the Captain asked.

"Tied him up like a present the thief did," the second man said. "He said the Sword Maiden gave the thief a thrashin' and took them into custody."

"Them? Did he say 'them' or are you simply too dockside born to apply a proper pronoun to the thief?" the Captain asked of the second man.

"He said 'them', Captain," the first man affirmed. "He said he didn't get a good look at the thief until after he was tied up and slung over the back of the Sword Maiden's horse, and then he wasn't so sure the thief was a him."

"It would seem that to confirm the rumor and begin the investigation you two need to speak to the Sword Maiden," the Captain said.

Calista left quickly, suddenly eager to find passage out of the city on the soonest departing caravan she could locate. She arrived in the bazaar to find it was doing a brisk business in just about everything. She squirmed through the crowd to the outer edge where she hoped to find a wagon heavy laden or being loaded, but the only full merchant's wagon she could find was in the process of unloading. She began asking around only to find the soonest departure was still a week away and she would need to come back and speak with the caravan driver closer to the date of travel.

She returned to the inn with a gloomy cloud both figuratively and literally over her as the evening's sky was darkening with the thunderheads off the ocean, bringing in cold rain and biting winds. If her luck continued its disastrous streak, she bet she would arrive back at the inn to find Ezra had already recorded into the guild ledger the slaying of the other mercenary band. Shortly after, Jevvon's group would be announced dead in a lawful altercation and then the thieves guild would begin asking around about the two Dwarves they'd sent along with Jevvon's company. Shortly after *that*, Calista would have people asking unwanted questions about her. She wondered idly if the thieves guild or guards were capable enough to find her before the week was up. She doubted either was, judging from the conversation between the guards and the thieves she'd dealt with to that point. She might escape town by the skin of her teeth, but she was certain she would manage to do just that. Still, she decided to keep a low profile in the meantime. A week spent in the inn drinking, eating bacon, and sleeping in Harper's bed sounded like a fine way to spend seven days lying low.

Divine Touched

She arrived back at the inn feeling significantly better. The momentary panic of the eavesdropping and irritant of having to wait a week for a caravan were behind her. The inn was lively and welcoming. Her company, minus Athol who was likely sleeping off his day of drinking, was at their usual table and they all looked pleased to see her, even Ezra after a fashion.

She slid into the seat next to Harper and gave her a lingering kiss on the neck. No need to back off the seduction now. She had a week to heat things up and create some fond memories for the long road south. Harper responded with a meaningful squeeze of Calista's thigh beneath the table, which was an entirely welcome surprise.

"I've been thinking about what you said all day," Harper whispered to Calista cryptically.

Calista gave her a puzzled look and a cocked eyebrow. Harper pulled her close to elaborate.

"About using my mouth the way you showed me to use my fingers," Harper whispered her explanation. "I've been so excited thinking about it ever since you planted the seed."

Calista smiled and cuddled closer to Harper's side. Teaching the virginal Sword Maiden the sensual arts would not only be an accomplishment worth cherishing, but a delightful task that could stretch over the full seven days if she meted out her lessons carefully.

"You're all set for the resting season, by the way," Ezra said, snapping Calista's attention away from the two or three finger widths of milky white cleavage showing at the top of Harper's tunic.

"What?" Calista asked.

"Your room and board for the next five months," Ezra said, "it's all under the company's account with your portion of the treasure securing your meals, room, and other expenditures."

"The gold is...?" Calista stammered knowing the answer to a question she couldn't stand to even finish giving voice to. The gold was spent already, her share, the share that would have bought her passage from the city, was already sunken back into the company's account ledger at the inn to provide for her the entire winter.

"...taking care of expenses," Ezra finished for her. "Don't worry, before the spring thaw I'm sure you'll have enough left over to finish outfitting for next year. You don't seem to have extravagant taste in food or alcohol."

Calista could simply scream in Ezra's face if she didn't think it would cause an enormous scene with no appreciable effect. Of course she wasn't going to see any of the money. The money wasn't even money yet. The smelter and money changer likely gave Ezra a promissory note, which was given to the patron, who put it toward the company's expenses. Profit sharing wouldn't happen until the expenses were covered, and, since Calista hadn't put anything toward the company's season, the entirety of her share would be soaked up. She'd never joined a mercenary band before, and now she knew why—it was royally difficult to screw over an ancient system designed to not allow people like her to screw it over.

"Are you okay?" Harper asked, jolting Calista from her fuming.

"Fine, I could just use a drink," Calista said through teeth that wouldn't unclench.

"You've got the tab for it now." Ezra lifted her own goblet of wine in mock toast and smiled a knowing half smile to Calista.

Chapter 12:

A Bad Day to Be Interrogated

The news of an expense account, as innocuous as the news seemed to Harper, appeared to suck all the desire out of Calista. Harper's awkward attempts at flirting went unnoticed, the drink Calista ordered went untouched, and eventually the Jack retired to her room in something of a funk. Harper noted glumly that she specifically retired to her *own* room.

The following morning, after a fitful night of sleep made lousy by sexual frustration and embarrassment spawned out of her rejection, Harper stopped outside the door to Calista's room. She considered and reconsidered knocking a dozen times over. Ultimately, she left the door unmolested and headed out for the day without so much as a sideways glance through the main hall on her way out of the inn.

What had she even been thinking? She was an inexperienced virgin with a body covered in scars. Of course the Jack lost interest in her after such a short time. Calista was beautiful, charming, exotic, well-traveled, astoundingly capable in battle, and romantically experienced—she could have anyone she wanted. Harper believed herself entirely foolish to even hope Calista was actually interested in her.

She made her way to the Temple of the Sea Queen with the intention of redoubling her devotion to the original mistress who showed only slightly more interest in her. There would be healing to do, potential faithful to preach to, and tithing to oversee. She made it no farther than the front door before two city guards, dressed in the gray and gold cloak of the Griffon's Rock banner, barred her entrance to the temple.

"What business does the guard have at the Temple of the Sea Queen?" Harper asked as they formed something of a wall between her and the door.

"We've got questions," the shorter, fatter man said in an accent reminiscent of the dock district. "Questions only for the Sword Maiden, and that's you."

"What my friend means is that we would like to ask you a few questions if you have the time, Sword Maiden," the taller man with a moustache-less bronze beard said. If Harper had to guess, the first guard was a commoner who lucked into a position as a guard while the second was probably a bastard of a minor nobleman who wasn't fortunate enough to be born before his older siblings devoured most of his father's influence and favors.

"Of course, although if you have no intention of tithing to the Sea Queen, we will have to hold our parlay outside the sanctuary." Harper guided the two guards to the side of the temple where a small stone platform overlooked the western approach to the city and the open sea beyond. She glanced around to see if anyone was meditating or praying among the stone altars to the great sea creatures that were the Sea Queen's favored children. When she was satisfied nobody was secreted away between the statues of leviathans, krakens, sharks, and mermaids, she motioned for the guards to speak their questions.

"We heard tell of assassin weapons being brung in here the other day," the shorter guard said. "Special assassin weapons, mind you. You seen anythin' like that?"

"Yes, a salvager brought in Dark Stalker equipment. It will be returned to the Thief Lord's temple in Ovid as soon as the sailing weather permits," Harper replied.

The taller guard nodded and seemed to consider the first matter settled. "As is your right to decide," the guard said. "We would also like to ask you about the thievery you prevented at the livery."

This made Harper cringe inwardly a little. She was fully within her authority to take possession of the Dark Stalker salvage and do with it as she saw fit. The city guard had little or no say over divine touched items. But a thief, a common horse thief as they saw things, was well beyond what Harper was allowed to pass judgment on.

"The thief only tried to steal my horse and I considered the bump on their head punishment enough for the failed attempt," Harper said. The shorter, fatter guard from the docks seemed reasonably satiated by the answer, but the taller man with the bronze beard had a flicker of cunning recognition in his eye.

"That's an interesting choice of words," the taller guard said. "Why say 'their head' rather than his or her head? You must have discovered the thief's gender in tying them up."

Harper sighed. She had no head for subterfuge and could not willfully lie without breaking the code of conduct demanded by the Sea Queen. "The *attempted* thief was a woman, but, seeing as she did not succeed in stealing anything, I do not think she is a matter for the city guard."

"Get a load of...not a matter for the guard? We'll be the ones decidin' what is and isn't a matter for the guard!" the shorter man griped. "We've got Dark Stalkers and horse thieves on the loose and you're playin' pronoun games with us." Harper guessed by the man's stilted pronunciation of the word 'pronoun' it was a recent addition to his vocabulary.

The shorter guard looked to be puffing up for another round of shouting when the taller guard placed a calming hand on his shoulder. "Never mind all of that," the taller guard said. "Your story matches up with the livery master's well enough. If you wish the thief arrested at a future date, we will be happy to accommodate her in the city stocks." The taller guard attempted to guide his compatriot away, stopping short at the exit of the sheltered alcove on the side of the temple. "Your company, the Dagger Falls, lost its Jack this last season—Felix was his name, I believe."

"We did," Harper said, not remotely liking the new line of questioning.

"That's a shame," the taller guard said. "I enjoyed going to the Thundering Dawn to watch the knife juggling displays he would put on during those long, winter nights."

The guards departed with not another word spoken, leaving Harper to wonder what they were really after. All their inquiries seemed incomplete to her. They'd only wanted to know if the Dark Stalker weapons existed, didn't seem interested in the horse thief's name, and didn't want to know anything beyond whether or not Felix was alive. Harper turned to head back out of the statue garden to consider the strange questions. Her heart leapt into her chest and she nearly jumped from her skin when she found her path blocked by a Havvish woman who seemingly appeared out of thin air.

"By the Goddess, Brandinne..." Harper stammered.

"The 'Goddess Brandinne' is it? I rather like that," Brandinne said.

"That's not what I..."

"I know what you meant and I know what I meant to hear," Brandinne said. "I hear a lot of things as it turns out. Strange things like a bunch of seemingly unfinished questions from an oddly matched guard pairing. Did it strike you as anomalous that they would match those two together? I imagine they were childhood friends of some sort. Do you have any childhood friends? Havvish don't keep in touch as much as we ought to, but I certainly know a few people like the short squat fellow who you would think couldn't possibly be as stupid as they appear only to prove they are time and time again..."

"Yes, I mean, no," Harper said, hoping to stem the astounding flow of words out of the Havvish woman's mouth by making a ham-fisted attempt at answering the slew of questions hurled at her.

Brandinne gave Harper a smirking little sideways glance. She tucked a few strands of her short, curly, black hair over her large, round ears with a distinct point at the top. "I liked you, Harper, still like you if we're being honest with one another, which was probably the only reason I stayed with your group as long as I did—did you ever piece that together?" Brandinne asked.

"Not really," Harper answered quickly before the Havvish woman could manage to squeeze any other questions in after the first one.

"You're sweet, incredibly sweet, and a little oblivious to certain things," Brandinne said. "I had thought to get you drunk to see what you might say, but you never showed any interest in spirits. I also thought to intrigue you with sparkling conversation, but you seemed to listen more than speak, which left me to wonder if you even liked the fine art of parlance. Then there were the two dopey brothers and the scowling mage, constantly telling me I talk too much, demanding I put something back that I don't even remember how I got it, and you can see why I had to take my leave when the big, hairy one thought to shove me in a sack for who knows what purpose."

"Yes, I suppose I can see your point," Harper said. Already the speed and verbal alacrity of the Havvish Jack was overwhelming Harper's ability to keep up.

"I knew you would!" Brandinne said. "You've got a head full of reason on your shoulders with some of the prettiest blond hair I've ever seen. We don't have much blond hair in the Havvish circles. I knew a redhead once. She was the backside of whatever farm animal you find most repellent though, if you catch my meaning. Thus you see my dilemma. It's difficult to fancy a fair-haired girl of my own kind when the only one I can find is a goat's behind! Which really does bring me back to the original reason I even joined your little company of drunks, ruffians, and frowners. Do you want to know what it was?"

"What? Um…yes, I wouldn't mind hearing that," Harper said, not entirely sure what she'd just agreed to.

"When I saw you, I thought, 'there's a tall bit of lovely I wouldn't mind climbing all over'," Brandinne said. "I thought that desire would fade away with a little pilfering, drinking, gambling, and causing of general mischief, but my luck didn't hold, even though my kind is renowned for our remarkable luck. Humans might call it divine touched how much the Brownie gods watch out for us, but that's your silly phrase for what we would call simply existing as charming creatures worthy of a deity's benevolent attention. I really can see what the Sea Queen sees in you though that she doesn't see in other humans. Snorting, clomping, incompetent lot, humans, but you're not really fully human, are you? You've got Sylvan blood of some sort in you, I can practically smell it on you. If I'm being honest, I did actually smell it on you, when you were sleeping, I crept over one night and took a long smell of your beautiful blond hair, which is how I know you've got Sylvan in you."

"You smelled my hair?" Harper asked.

"Of course, didn't I just get done saying I fancied you?" Brandinne asked, seemingly a little hurt or insulted by something Harper clearly missed.

"You did?" Harper asked, although from the enormous smile on Brandinne's face, which showed off the legendarily large mouths the Havvish people have, the little Jack took Harper's question as a statement of affirmation, further displaying Brandinne's previous statement that she heard what she wanted to.

"Good! You don't have to reply with anything right now. It'd be too tragic for me to know whether you fancy me in return just yet. I might hurl myself off this ledge out of joy or sorrow depending on your words, but the result would be the same, no? Splattered Havvish all over the streets below—nobody would even know why I did it. I guess I could say for sure if it was out of overwhelming joy or life-destroying agony of rejection right before I did it, but that would only burden you for the rest of your life with the knowledge that your words, good or ill, caused my death. I wouldn't do that to you."

"Um…thank you?"

"What I will do, is tell you what I think is really going on here, connect some seemingly unconnected dots, since I have a bit more ink and parchment on the situation than you do, if you catch my drift, and I'm sure you do."

Harper didn't, but she also didn't have enough of a gap in the conversation to say so before Brandinne was off again.

"I was skulking about a bit before you arrived, waiting for you if you're curious, and I overheard those two guards having a conversation," Brandinne said. "The tall, good-looking one with the beard, he seemed to put things together in ways the shorter, fatter one wasn't able. There were only supposed to be two questions. I knew that since they'd decided before you arrived that they would split them evenly. The third question, about Felix, was an impromptu query by the taller, smarter guard. He put things together from your answers."

"Put what together?" Harper asked.

"Come on, I know I don't have to do all the work for you on this," Brandinne said, waiting as long as she could for Harper to puzzle things out, which was less than a Havvish heartbeat before she continued. "The guards think the horse thief was likely the Dark Stalker belonging to those tools the salvager brought you, and the taller, smarter guard seems to think your new Jack is one in the same. If I followed them, and I was going to if I could have resisted talking alone with you, I'm willing to bet they went straight from here to the mercenary guild registry to find out what her name is. What do I win if I'm right?"

Harper was still a little behind in the conversation when the last question hit home. "What do you want to win?" Harper asked automatically.

"A kiss!"

"Sure," Harper said. A moment after her mind caught up to exactly what Brandinne intended. "Wait!"

But the little Jack was off, no doubt in search of proof that the two guards were indeed about to discover Calista's name from the mercenary guild registry. After Brandinne stopped talking, Harper's mind cleared a little, enough to think through everything she'd just been bombarded with. Calista was a Dark Stalker, which really made a lot more sense than any other explanation she could come up with. The guards were looking for Calista for some likely justified reason. And Brandinne was romantically interested in Harper. The rejected, hurt part of Harper's ego and heart, bruised by Calista's suddenly cold behavior felt a little vindicated in knowing the Havvish woman had been carrying some bizarrely small torch for her all these months. She walked around the side of the temple to watch Brandinne leave. She'd never really considered whether or not she liked Brandinne or thought of her as attractive. The Havvish Jack was incredibly slender, as was most of her kind, with almost entirely rounded features common to Gnomes. Harper had to admit she was a snappy dresser in purple silk attire, cordoned off at certain places on her frame by gold hoops slid up her limbs. Yes, Harper decided Brandinne was definitely pretty after a fashion. She couldn't help but half laugh and half snort at the thought of how easy it would be for Brandinne to baffle her into so many compromising positions though. If Calista's intimate words were a fine wine and a warm fire in their intoxicating effect, Brandinne's were akin to being spun in circles too many times and then hit in the face with a bucket of frigid water.

Still, Harper couldn't think of a reason she wouldn't reward Brandinne with a kiss as a matter of honor, and since seemingly nobody else wanted a kiss from her.

The other two reveals provided by Brandinne struck Harper in the moment after the whimsical mental image of leaning down to kiss the Havvish woman who was more than a foot and a half shorter than her. If Calista was the Dark Stalker, she might have use of her gear.

Harper raced into the temple to find the sister charged with returning the assassin's tools to Ovid in hopes of changing the order. She couldn't entirely vacate the command. The Thief Lord's temple would need to be notified as a matter of courtesy, but Harper could prevent the messenger from taking Calista's weapons with her. Besides, if she was to confront the smooth-talking Jack, she would need more evidence of her status as a Dark Stalker than the confusing words of Brandinne and a few disjointed questions from two oddly matched city guards.

Chapter 13:

A Bad Deal after Interrogation

Calista woke up late in a feckless, uninterested mood. There were too many pressures bearing down on her and too little time to do much about any of it. Despite the massive amount of paperwork involved, Ezra had indeed filed the listing of Jevvon's company dying at the hands of the Dagger Falls Company in a legal altercation over a treasure trove that rightly belonged to the Dagger Falls. While Calista was at the guild register's office, conveniently located on the other side of the street from the Thundering Dawn Inn, she spotted a few interested parties requesting similar information including a trio of Dwarves and then a few minutes later two city guards.

Suddenly, she was back to the desperate plan of stealing a horse and hoping for the best on the road with limited supplies and only a handful of coins. She instinctively went around the back of the massive Thundering Dawn Inn to the stables and lunging arena used to exercise the horses. She wasn't being cautious enough to truly case the place for potential horse theft later that night. Instead, she walked straight into the stables, brazen as she pleased, and sought out Aerial.

The great gray mare seemed happy to see her once Calista passed in front of her good eye. Aerial poked her head over the stall door and Calista gathered up under her chin to hug her neck. Aerial, knowing the gesture well, rested her head along Calista's back and gently mouthed the end of her hair. Calista laughed a little and pulled away.

"Who teaches their warhorse to hug?" Calista asked of the horse, but she already knew the answer. Someone as sweet as honey filtered through sugar, that's who.

"You'd think someone who was already caught trying to steal a half-blind horse wouldn't go right back for the same maimed mare," a man's voice resounded through the stables, snapping Calista's attention away from Aerial.

"Likely she's got a mind to skedaddle out of town," a vaguely familiar voice added.

Calista ventured around the corner, livid with herself for leaving her knives and armor in her room. She was dressed only in some of the plain clothes Harper gave her—wool britches, leather boots, a loose auburn tunic cinched tight around her waist with a wide, braided leather belt, and a heavy black cloak. If she were to get into a fight with anyone, she would be at a distinct disadvantage of being unarmed and entirely encumbered by clothing meant more for warmth than ease of movement. She poked her head into an open and empty stall where she heard the voices coming from to find the two city guards from the guild registry, lounging about on some stacked bails of hay in the stall turned storage.

"There she is," the tall guard with the bronze beard said. "She's prettier than you'd expect for an inept horse thief."

The shorter, fatter guard with him snorted. "You always were drawn to a pointlessly pretty face. Give me a wide hipped, big-titted barmaid any day of the week and twice again on my day off."

"You don't care if her face is fair or foul?" the taller guard asked.

"Why would I give a rip about that? Bent over a barrel she don't even need to have a face for what I'd be plannin'," the short, fat guard replied.

Initially, Calista took the superficial recognition of the two guards as likely the same two she'd overheard when she was eavesdropping beneath the barrack arrow slit, but the more she heard of their easy banter, the vulgarity peppered in by the fat one, and she knew she'd heard their voices before—they were also the same two thieves she'd listened in on after robbing the mugger her first night in the city. This was hardly surprising as many city guards tended to play both sides of the fence. It was a lot easier to rob people when you knew precisely where patrols would be. The only question that remained was whether or not they were part of the thieves guild.

"We're being rude, more specifically, *you're* being rude," the guard with the bronze colored beard said. "Here we have a lovely guest to talk to and we're talking to each other about bar wenches over barrels. Forgive us, Miss Calista."

"I must have left me manners in the gutter where I was born," the fat guard said, braying with laughter at his own joke.

"You know my name, or at least the name in the mercenary guild ledger," Calista said, "but what do I call you two?"

"That's true. When we checked the ship's manifest, which somehow washed up on shore as though it were meant to be found, there wasn't a single listing of a female passenger named Calista. In fact, there were only five female passengers on the ship, and all their bodies were accounted for after the wreck," the tall guard said. "You can call me Guard Ulrich, and my portly companion here is Guard Turbald."

"Why you got to be referrin' to me as a companion? Makes me sound like your dog or somethin'," Guard Turbald sniped.

Guard Ulrich ignored his companion and pressed on. "I find myself wondering if maybe you were traveling as cargo since the *Enolla* was a known smuggling vessel."

Calista knew better than to deny any of it. She wasn't dealing with a couple idiots, perhaps one idiot, but certainly not two. Trying to banter her way into convincing them she wasn't who they clearly thought she was would be a waste of time.

"Are you after me to give you swimming lessons or do you need an extra pair of hands for your smash and grab?" Calista asked, hoping to rattle them a little with information about them that they wouldn't expect her to have.

"I'd be proper impressed," Guard Ulrich said, "if I didn't already know you were a Dark Stalker. You could vanish before my very eyes right now, and I'd have to assume it was just another trick of the Assassin Brotherhood I wasn't aware of. Besides, why would I need to go looking for the hidden valuables from the ship when they're standing right in front of me?"

Calista hated when she found a competent guard—she hated even more when she found a corrupt and competent guard. Clearly the Guard Turbald was little more than violent muscle to sway people when Guard Ulrich's words couldn't convince someone on their own. She didn't want to underestimate the fatter guard as well in thinking she could easily best him in a physical fight, especially not when she was unarmed.

"Can we skip to the part where you tell me what you want?" Calista asked.

"I happen to have composed a list of people, a mental list at the moment mind you, but no less indelibly written," Guard Ulrich said. "This list has a number of people on it who aren't as accident prone as I might like. People fall off buildings, eat poisoned fish, and accidentally stab themselves all the time, yet the individuals on this list seem fairly adept at avoiding all these common missteps."

"And why would I help you change their fortunes to misfortunes?" Calista asked.

"There are two excellent reasons." Guard Ulrich stood, dusted the hay from his uniform, and then helped Guard Turbald to his feet. "I find myself in possession of information the Captain of the Guard asked for personally. This information could be made to seem as connected as it really is, or it could be made to seem entirely coincidental. A ship sinking, Dark Stalker weapons from the salvage showing up at the Temple of the Sea Queen, a failed horse theft by an un-apprehended thief, and a new Jack appearing in the mercenary guild registry could all be happenstance. Some of it could even turn out to be wild rumor if the investigating guard so reported. Suddenly these Dark Stalker weapons were simply antiques of no importance or value, the horse theft could easily be attributable to any number of known horse thieves, and the new Jack could turn out to be a dear old friend of a reputable noble house who happened to be staying in Griffon's Rock for several months before signing up with the Dagger Falls Company. It's really all in how a guard might report these things."

"Blackmail then, is it?" Calista said.

"Only a fool would hope to blackmail a Dark Stalker," Guard Ulrich said. "That sounds like an excellent way to get oneself assassinated. I offer the obfuscation of said information as a gesture of goodwill. I'll pay you for your work, of course. You need money to leave the city since your career as a horse thief was as inept as it was short. I can provide the money you need, in small amounts at a time, so you'll have the full sum when you finish the list."

"And when I'm done?"

"We'll part amicably having helped one another greatly." Guard Ulrich brushed past Calista on his way to the stable exit with Guard Turbald quick at his heels. He held his hand out from beneath the awning into the open air to feel a handful of snowflakes. "The first snow is falling. Soon, it'll be thick enough to choke the Last Road. I don't think a lone woman on a stolen horse could make it far enough south before she froze to death. We'll come back tonight for a drink and you can tell us if you agree with that assessment."

Calista spent the rest of the day tending to Aerial. She brushed her coat, cleaned her hooves, and meticulously washed her mane and tail. The uncomplicated work reminded her of simpler times when her life was equal parts training and labor. By the time she finished, the sun was setting and the snow was falling in earnest.

She made her way back inside the inn, tired but in fine spirits. She expected the Dagger Falls Company to be in the main hall along with the two guards, but she found the typical booth reserved for the company empty and she didn't see anyone among the smattering of patrons dressed in a guard uniform. It took her a moment, squinting through the gloom of the great hall to spot the tall man with the bronze beard and his squat companion sitting at a small table, conspicuously far away from anyone else enjoying a drink or dinner. They were in plain clothes and doing their best to look innocuous. To the untrained eye, they were doing a fantastic job, but Calista spotted Turbald's dagger handle poking at the side of his shirt whenever he leaned forward, and Ulrich looked to be drinking, but the level of wine in his glass chalice didn't seem to be going down even after several pantomimed sips.

She approached them brazenly, threw off her cloak and deposited herself in a free chair. The two men jumped, not having heard her approach, but quickly regained themselves as though they were more interested in avoiding the flourishing cloak.

"If you're going to pretend to drink so you can look the place over, you shouldn't order wine in a clear glass," Calista told Ulrich, "and your dagger is showing through your shirt like you're trying to smuggle a baby unicorn somewhere," she added, turning her attention to Turbald.

"Maybe I bring out that dagger and see if…" Turbald began.

"We appreciate the pointers," Ulrich interrupted his partner before he could get to the no doubt vulgar conclusion of his sentence. "After all, we wouldn't be asking for your help if we could tend to the list in question ourselves."

"Speaking of, let's see a proper list, not of the mental type, so I can get a clearer image of what you're expecting," Calista asked.

Ulrich seemed to consider her request for a moment as though he weren't sure such a list even existed. After a short pause, long enough to irritate Calista, he produced a small scroll from the folds of his cloak and passed it to her unceremoniously as though it were little more than a bill for wagon wheel repair. Calista was glad to see he possessed enough sense to make seem innocuous the highly important list to any prying eyes around them.

Calista snatched the scroll from his hand, crumpling it a bit in the process, and let out a huff. Unceremonious was one thing, but making it appear the recipient wanted nothing to do with the paper to throw a casual observer off the scent was another. To add to the ruse, Calista unrolled the scroll roughly, tearing it a little.

"These aren't the numbers we talked about," Calista said, a little loudly.

Turbald seemed confused by the entire exchange and looked to Ulrich a few times to see if he caught wise. Ulrich indeed did appear to understand what Calista was doing. He nodded to Turbald to let him know things were as they should be, and shrugged plaintively to Calista.

"I wish I could do better," he said, "but times have been tough all around."

In truth, the list was far longer than Calista anticipated. There were a dozen names, more than three times what she could reasonably be expected to kill in a week…except, they didn't know she planned to travel on the last caravan at the end of the week. The list was long, the prices fixed at an amount that would indicate sea travel. The port traffic was slow that time of year and the port authority was cracking down on stowaways after the *Enolla* sunk with more bodies on it than were listed on the passenger manifest. Ulrich thought she was planning on booking passage aboard a ship in three weeks, which would be the only way out of town by that point.

Divine Touched

Without looking up, Calista rechecked the list to find a few interesting names in the bunch. There were people she didn't have a moral dilemma about killing and several of them might even hold a significant amount of coin on their persons at their looming times of death. If she crosschecked the most morally corrupt offenders on the list with the wealthiest, she would certainly have the most dangerous targets, but she would also have money enough to book her passage on the caravan independent of what Ulrich was planning on paying her. Unwittingly, Ulrich handed her something far more valuable than the coins he promised her.

"I spent a little time outside the mercenary guild's registry this morning," Calista said. "I spotted the both of you, but before you got there, I spied a trio of Dwarves. They were grumpy looking fellows with shaved heads and braided brown beards."

"What says we know those types?" Turbald asked, narrowing his eyes shrewdly, perhaps too shrewdly.

"Dwarves make for marvelous drinking companions and possibly even good business associates, but can be lousy friends," Ulrich said. "I wouldn't expect this trio to buy you a drink or offer to lend you money, yet I don't think their inquiry will come to much since they are business associates of someone you're in business with."

And there it is, Calista thought with an inward smile. Not only were Ulrich and Turbald part of the thieves guild, they were willing to hold off other members of the guild while Calista finished her work. She wondered how cross the Dwarves would be with the both of them when Calista vanished a week later with the job less than a third done and no chance of revenge forthcoming. Try as she might, she couldn't be made to care what became of the guard duo.

"Then it would seem I must make the best of a bad situation." Calista stood quickly, snatched up her cloak, and stormed away.

She softened her approach to the Dagger Falls Company booth in seeing a figure sitting at it. The hall was large enough and their show boring enough that she doubted anyone really noticed what she and the two guards were talking about. She hurled her cloak into the curved booth and took her seat across the table from Ezra.

"Quiet night in here, eh, spell-flinger?" Calista asked. "Should we expect the brothers and the Sword Maiden eventually?"

"The brothers will likely be along shortly. The inn will begin filling up soon and they usually like being present when it does. Pick of the bawdy litter, so to speak," Ezra said without ever looking up from the open book before her.

Calista asked, "and Harper?"

"I passed Harper on the way down here. I believe she was on her way up to one of the sitting rooms with Brandinne," Ezra said, finally looking up with a wicked grin to revel in Calista's reaction.

"Who by the moons is Brandinne?" Calista asked.

"I'm sure we told you about her," Ezra said coyly. "She was the Havvish Jack we had before you. Apparently she was interested in catching up with Harper…alone."

Calista practically hurled herself from the booth, abandoning her cloak and nearly upsetting Ezra's goblet of wine when her knee banged on the underside of the table. "Which sitting room? This blasted inn has a dozen on my floor alone."

"Now why would I know a thing like that?" Ezra said.

Calista ran for the stairs. She was a mess, dressed for comfort rather than seduction, and she smelled like she'd been working in the stables all day, which, of course, she had. She debated with herself as she scaled the stairs over whether or not she had time to clean up and change clothes before searching for Harper. The fact of the matter was, she had no idea how long it would take to find the right sitting room in the labyrinthine inn and she certainly didn't have enough of a wardrobe to change into something more fitting to seduction as she was already wearing most of the clothes she had.

As she crested the stairs to the second floor, she considered turning right to her room or left to begin her search. She couldn't even truthfully say why she cared so much to be present when Brandinne and Harper were catching up. Would Harper's tastes in women even stretch to Havvish? Wasn't the consensus among the company that they disliked Brandinne's personality? Calista turned right to head to her room to at least get slightly more presentable. No, it wasn't true that the whole company found her irritating. The brothers did, she could remember them clearly railing against her, but Ezra never participated and Harper's response to the brothers' insults of Brandinne was to politely defend her.

Calista could kick herself for her reticence in letting Harper dangle so loosely for so long when she…Calista stopped in her vigorous scrubbing of her face, a little surprised to find herself not only in her room, but well on her way to undressing and cleaning herself up. She was going to leave in a week. Her armor was there waiting, she had four new knives to deal death with, and she now had a task to set everything to. And that task was not seduction. If she was being smart, truly smart, she would put on her armor, grab her weapons, and start looking for ways to whittle down her list.

Still, she didn't want to spend the week sleeping alone, and she didn't like the idea of losing a lovely, chaste, sweet thing like Harper to a rambling Havvish woman no doubt bonkers on skunk weed half the time.

She returned her attention to cleaning her skin of the day's work, and decided less would certainly be more when it came to her clothing for that evening.

Chapter 14:

A Difficult Night to Think Straight

Harper's heart wasn't in the act of taking tributes or healing wounds. She knew it was heresy to continue without her full attention on the task of channeling the Goddess's power into the potential faithful. She left the temple with a bundle containing the Dark Stalker equipment and more than a few curious eyes following her out the exit. She knew she wasn't behaving normally, but she didn't know how to stop.

As much as she would like to limit the amount of time she spent thinking about Calista, she found more and more hours of the day were occupied with the exotic southerner. Despite the sudden shock of Calista running as cold as the falling snow, Harper couldn't help but think fondly of the Jack and her flirtatious advances. She still thought of using her mouth as Calista instructed her, to cut slow teasing trails across her tanned skin with it, and then focus with verve when she reached something...

Her train of thought was broken near the inn when a pebble bounced off the back of her head. She glanced around to see who might have thrown it, but found nothing. When she turned forward again to resume what remained of the walk back to the inn, she found Brandinne standing directly in her path with a nearly ear-to-ear grin on her pert little features.

"You owe me a kiss and then some," Brandinne said.

They walked into the Thundering Dawn together, warming almost immediately in the cheery main hall where a great fire was aglow in the center pit. Harper glanced down to the Havvish woman at her side. The smile hadn't left her face and a few snowflakes were clinging to her short, black hair, catching the firelight in an alluring way. She hadn't noticed before how pretty Brandinne was when she smiled, or perhaps she didn't have many reasons to smile when they were adventuring together with how much Sven and Athol harassed her. Harper felt a pang of guilt run through her at this realization; she should have done more to cull the brother's abuse or better still, cut it off entirely.

"So, when are you going to tell me what's in the bundle?" Brandinne asked. "Or should I guess? Can I guess? Can we make it a game? Can more kisses be offered as prizes? Perhaps even…"

"Weapons," Harper said to cut off the quickening stream of questions that was heading toward a deluge. She immediately regretted it when she saw Brandinne's face fall. She was being a flirt, in her Havvish sort of way, and Harper stopped her rather than encouraging what should be wanted behavior. "I'm sorry. I didn't mean to spoil the game."

"That's okay," Brandinne said. "I'm sure I'll think of another one in a few minutes. Hey, it's Ezra!"

Harper glanced up from the remarkably resilient Jack at her side to find the Sorceress was indeed walking down the stairs into the main hall even as Harper and Brandinne were about to head up. A strange expression, equal parts unhappily surprised and suddenly intrigued, flashed over Ezra's face at being recognized by Brandinne.

"Hello there, Brandinne," Ezra said, affecting a notable facsimile of a smile. "It's so good to see you again. I wasn't happy with the way you parted from our group, but I can see our Sword Maiden has smoothed over some of those unfriendly edges already."

"She has and has made promises to smooth them further should they need further smoothing," Brandinne said. "We were going to go catch up some, talk a few things out, pay off some debts accrued earlier today, and possibly smoke some skunk weed in a quiet little corner somewhere."

"You were going to smoke skunk weed?" Ezra asked of Harper with a curious eyebrow raised.

"No, I was going to watch her smoke it and count the smoke rings," Harper said.

"More for me," Brandinne said. "You know the old Havvish proverb: the only thing better than more is even more. Now, I know what you're thinking, it can't be all that old since Havvish people aren't all that old, but really it's a matter of perspective in cultural matters since dragons probably have proverbs that are twenty millennia old while…"

"I won't keep you two then," Ezra said. "I'm glad you found your way north and back into Harper's company though, Brandinne."

As Brandinne and Harper departed from Ezra, leaving the Sorceress to take up position in the company's traditional booth, Harper couldn't help but feel that Ezra was up to something. She shrugged off the suspicions as likely unimportant. She trusted Ezra and didn't want to discourage her friendly demeanor toward Brandinne by questioning it. Harper tried to jump back into the conversation with the Havvish woman, who was chatting along happily at her side as they ascended the stairs, but she could see Brandinne was well past the genesis of the topic and picking up steam.

Harper made the decision not on a whim, although it had a wicked barb aimed at Calista in her motivation. She held back a pace or two as they crested the stairs onto the second floor. The hallway was dimly lit and cool compared to the main hall, and if nothing else the plan would warm things up. When she was still standing a step below the landing, she grasped Brandinne by the wrist and turned her back to face her. The Jack seemed surprised, but pleasantly so. Harper intended on asking her about whether or not she wished to collect the kiss, but Brandinne didn't need any such prodding as she practically threw herself into Harper's embrace and kissed her with girlish glee.

Brandinne was so petite and light against her, although her arms, which she threw over Harper's shoulders, were remarkably strong in holding their embrace. Kissing Brandinne was an entirely different experience than kissing Calista. Brandinne's mouth was animated in ways a human's mouth simply wasn't and her effervescent personality apparently extended beyond her conversation skills as her tongue was akin to a darting, playful little squirrel against Harper's.

Harper expected a quiet, reflective moment after the incredibly intense and highly enjoyable kiss, but Brandinne was energized if anything. Brandinne smiled brightly, showing off both rows of her teeth farther back than was humanly possible—she nuzzled into Harper's hair and let out a musical little giggle that was very Brownie like.

"That can't count as the kiss," Brandinne said. "You owed me the kiss, and we kissed, but that doesn't mean that was the kiss. I stole that kiss, you see. If someone steals something from someone who owes a debt, the debt isn't really paid since payment implies willing gifting of the..."

"No, that's okay, I'm happy to still owe you another," Harper said.

Brandinne blushed, an honest to goodness blush that colored her fair cheeks, setting off the faintest dappling of freckles that weren't easily visible otherwise. "Okay then, let's find someplace quiet," Brandinne said.

They found an out of the way little library with a bay window overlooking the square in front of the Thundering Dawn Inn. The fire in the tiny fireplace was barely holding onto embers, leaving a chill in the book-strewn room that clearly once belonged to a proper home the inn expanded to encompass. Harper stood at the window watching the snow fall silently outside while Brandinne saw to restoring the fire to a cheerful glow.

The revived fire did a fine job of warming the room and providing flickering light to see one another by. To add to the low light, Brandinne plucked a brand from the fire and set about lighting the handful of candles on a small, central table. Getting a better view of the room in the low light, Harper's suspicions were largely confirmed. There was little doubt the library was once a private study with ancient tomes in ceiling to floor shelves covering every wall. The books looked so old and so neglected though that Harper suspected they would fall apart in her hand should she try to pluck one from the shelves. At some point, likely after the inn took over the library, someone removed all the furniture from the room, save the little table, replacing what were no doubt thread-worn chairs and sofas with mismatched throw pillows and rugs.

Brandinne sat on one of the largest of the pillows near the fireplace and set about her lengthy process of getting comfortable. Harper remembered this from their brief time adventuring together. The little Jack went through a whole ritual in situating herself whenever she planned on staying in one spot for long—it seemed to involve equal parts stretching and trying every possible position to find the most comfortable. In the warm glow of the fire and candles, Harper watched Brandinne with growing curiosity. She was distinctly not human. Her facial features were human-like, but exaggerated. Her eyes were large, and a deep shade of purple. Her mouth was larger, wider, with shockingly animated lips. Harper also suspected she had close to twice as many teeth as a human since her mouth seemed to occupy far more real estate in her skull. All of these oddities came together to form an exotically pretty face. Harper wondered if she was considered beautiful among her own kind.

"The guards went straight from the temple to the mercenary guild registry, by the way." Brandinne settled sort of on her side, propped up by an elbow, with her legs crossed. She slipped a long, slender-necked bone smoking pipe from her satchel and set about packing the delicate little bowl at the end with pungent smelling plant flotsam she pinched from a leather pouch she kept around her neck like a pendant.

Harper wondered how Brandinne could possibly have come to the conclusion that the bizarre position she was in was the most comfortable. She shrugged off the oddity and found a comfortable place for herself opposite the Havvish woman on the pillow across the fireplace from Brandinne's. Harper watched the Jack's delicate, adept fingers as they filled the pipe with practiced motions. Brandinne's fingers were long, and all but the thumb and pinky were exactly the same length. Harper hadn't noticed this before either. Brandinne's hands were really quite incredible to behold as though every movement her fingers made were in a dance to music.

"You're kind of fascinating, you know?" Harper said.

"I'm quite fond of telling people that," Brandinne agreed, "regardless of whether or not they think so." She slipped the stem of the pipe between her lips, brought the little fiery brand from the fire to just above the bowl, and took a long, deep inhale of the skunky smelling plant. She held her breath for a time before exhaling the thick, green smoke out her slender little nose. "Are you sure you don't want some?"

Harper shook her head. Surprisingly, the calming effect of the weed was already slowing down how fast words were exiting from Brandinne's mouth. With a few more puffs, Harper guessed she would almost be down to normal human conversational levels.

"Are you considered attractive by Havvish standards?" Harper asked, realizing only after she'd said the words that she was probably being thunderously rude.

Brandinne giggled and rolled a little onto her side in a maneuver reminiscent of a cat in a sunny spot. She took another deep inhalation of her skunk weed before answering. "That's a fun question." Brandinne's words were given visible form by the green smoke exiting her lungs as she spoke. "A unified sense of Havvish beauty doesn't exist. We're a half-breed species so we are largely attracted to mixtures of all kinds, which is probably why I find you so eye tickling. I'll tell you though, we can see differences in each other that other races can't. My hair has highlights in it that are considered interesting by other Havvish, but you probably can't even spot them."

Harper stared hard at Brandinne's hair in the low light, but she simply couldn't see any color variations. She hoped it was a trick of the firelight rather than a lack of attention to detail or visual prowess."

"Don't worry about looking for them," Brandinne said. "They're there, and they're nothing all that special. But that makes a little sense, doesn't it? Most humans look about the same to me. When a human says this person is handsome or that person is ugly, I have to take their word for it. You're different though—you're a swan among ducks."

Harper felt the blush rising in her cheeks and a smile tugging at the corners of her mouth. "Thank you," she murmured. "For what it's worth, I think you're very pretty too."

"Tell me something, lady swan." Brandinne rolled onto her stomach to stare intently at Harper. Her eyes caught the firelight in an odd way, reflecting every flickering detail as though in a perfectly polished mirror. "Why aren't you in charge of the Dagger Falls Company?"

A shiver ran up Harper's back at such intense scrutiny from such inhuman eyes. She didn't know if it was a product of the skunk weed or the quiet surroundings, but Brandinne's attention was somehow far more intense even as her speech was slowing.

"Athol is the greatest warrior among us, and…"

"He is? According to whom?" Brandinne asked.

"We've sparred before, and without my magic, he's bested me every time."

"And that would be the key, wouldn't it? *Without* your magic, he bests you, but what about *with* it?"

"He's never wanted me to use it when we spar," Harper said.

"Gee, I wonder why," Brandinne said with a very feline, toothy smile. "I'll tell you what I remember of your company. You and your warhorse, leading the charge with lance gleaming, while everyone filled in the wake left behind you. I didn't mind; being behind you affords a lovely view, especially from my height, and I'm at my best when my enemies have their focus elsewhere. He may be bigger, stronger, and hairier than you, but whether or not Athol is the greatest warrior in your group remains to be seen."

Harper blushed again, growing increasingly sensitive to Brandinne's flattery in an intoxicating way. "It's all a question of second best at this point anyway," Harper said. "Our new Jack is a destructive force of nature."

"Ah, yes, *her*. I find it odd that you would sign on a Jack so quickly after she tried to steal your beloved horse."

"Calista is charming in a way that makes people forget things." Harper didn't know how else to explain it. Calista's words possessed a strange ability to find sensitive areas in people's minds, hers especially, and coax agreement from them in just the right way.

Brandinne took another long pull from her pipe, holding it and Harper's attention in the silence that followed. She exhaled slowly and quirked a delicate eyebrow. "You don't find that peculiar?"

Harper's answer, which she wasn't entirely sure of anyway, never found room to be heard as the topic of conversation poked her head into the study at that precise moment. Harper jumped at Calista's entrance, although Brandinne seemed unfazed by it, almost as if she expected Calista to enter at any moment.

Calista wasn't dressed appropriately for the sudden influx of cold over the past few days. She was shivering a bit, clad only in a tabard meant to go over other clothing, showing off the entirety of the outside of her legs and threatening to spill her ample breasts should she lean forward too far. Harper leapt to her feet and raced to Calista who still seemed a little unsure about fully entering the room.

"What in the world are you doing walking around in just a tabard?" Harper asked. She grasped Calista by the arms and began rubbing her palms up and down them to try to warm her.

"I was looking for you," Calista murmured.

"I would have thought you were looking for pants," Brandinne said.

"Come, warm yourself by the fire." Harper wrapped an arm around Calista and guided her to the fireplace and the pillow opposite Brandinne's.

"Care for some skunk weed?" Brandinne asked once Calista was settled and Harper was back on her feet, searching the little room for something to wrap around her.

Calista narrowed her eyes at the offered pipe. "Isn't that the same stuff that wiped out the Gnomes? Something about it eventually making them all sterile?"

"Only when it came to procreating with their own kind," Brandinne corrected her, returning the pipe to her mouth to take another long inhale from it. "Besides, the type of sex I have doesn't result in babies regardless of how much or how little I smoke."

"Brandinne!" Harper peeped, momentarily losing her focus in her futile search for a blanket.

"What?" Brandinne asked with the best feigned innocence Harper had ever seen. "I'm sure she knows exactly what I'm talking about."

"I just..." Harper trailed off, her mind hijacked by something else. "I don't think there's a blanket in here."

"You've got your cloak," Calista said demurely.

"Oh, I suppose I do." Harper began to remove her cloak, but Calista's hand placed on her leg stopped her.

"We can share," Calista said. "I don't want you to be cold."

Harper awkwardly sat next to Calista on the pillow, glancing furtively to Brandinne to see if she would object. When the Havvish woman rolled her eyes and shrugged, Harper felt she'd been given permission of a kind, and sat fully, offering Calista part of the warm, wool cloak. Calista took the presented cloak and a little more, snuggling against Harper's side and letting out a tiny hum of pleasure.

"That's probably my cue to turn in," Brandinne said, exhaling another stream of green smoke as she spoke. "If you want to find me, for anything, I'm staying in the lighthouse room." Brandinne stood, tapped out the embers of her pipe against the heel of her palm and kicked the little ball of ashes into the fireplace before it could fall to the floor.

"That was my room the first two seasons I adventured with the Dagger Falls Company," Harper exclaimed. The lighthouse room wasn't actually a lighthouse, but a circular parapet that was decorated with lighthouse bric-a-brac to give it a maritime feel.

"Was it?" Brandinne asked with a knowing grin. "You'll have to come up sometime and participate in a little nostalgia with me then." Brandinne walked delicately past them toward the door, turning before her exit. "Don't forget about what you still owe me," she said cryptically before vanishing into the darkened hallway.

The room filled with the sound of the crackling fire and little else for sometime after Brandinne's exit. When Harper was certain Brandinne hadn't stuck around to listen outside the door, she spoke, softly still in case she was wrong. "You and I have to have a conversation," Harper said, barely above a whisper.

"Certainly, but first I have to apologize for last night," Calista said, attempting to snuggle further against Harper's side without much response from her companion. "My mind went elsewhere, caused by nothing you'd done, and I should have simply said as much and excused myself to sort my own thoughts rather than sort them in front of you, giving you the impression I was ignoring you."

Harper was glad to hear the words, and accepted Calista's apology into her heart before she even knew what was happening. She had to shake off the warm, fuzzy feelings that immediately came flooding back at Calista's kind words. She reached over to beneath the table, where she'd hidden away the bundle she'd carried since earlier that day. She placed it in front of Calista on the pillow.

"Open it," Harper said.

Calista reluctantly slipped from Harper's side to untie the leather strip holding the cloth to a tightly held packet of something. As she pushed aside the wrapping, she immediately identified the items as hers, but showed no outward sign of recognition.

"What are…?" Calista began.

"Consider very carefully before you lie to me," Harper cut her off.

"They're mine," Calista whispered. She lifted the tightly packed little bundle of items. Her tools fit perfectly together into something of a cluster when she wanted to hide them. There were her daggers, one curved and one straight bladed. They were weapons of remarkable cruelty imbued with mystical poison and serration on one side to tear flesh and cause bleeding. There were also her lock picks capable of opening magically sealed locks. And finally, there was her miniature harpoon and chain. It looked like a tiny, wickedly barbed grappling hook attached to a weighted shaft no longer than her index finger, with a coiled chain attached to a reel that affixed to her belt. She wondered if Harper knew what it was used for.

"You're the Dark Stalker from the ship," Harper said. "Why was the Sea Queen trying to kill you?"

"I couldn't factually say," Calista said. "Until you told me so, I didn't even know for certain that the storm was of divine origin."

"Well, have them back, I suppose," Harper said.

Calista collected up her weapons and looked to Harper who was staring at the window and the snow falling outside. "Do you want me to leave you alone?" Calista asked.

"For now," Harper replied. "I need to think."

Calista slid from beneath Harper's cloak and made for the door and the chilly hallway beyond. Before she could close the door behind her, Harper stopped her with a comment.

"Brandinne seems to think the guards are after you."

"I think they are too," Calista replied.

Calista practically ran back down the hall once she was clear of the room, partially because she was cold and partially because she wanted to get her weapons concealed again before someone else could identify her by them. The wards on them that prevented them from being found would return with time and extended contact with her. If she spent the night with them in the bed next to her, they likely wouldn't be identifiable by the morning, and by the end of the week, they might once again be nearly invisible to anyone who wasn't divine touched.

She stopped at her door, checked the strand of her hair she'd plucked and tied around the foot of the door, leading over to the frame. It was broken. She slipped one of her daggers from its sheath and secured the rest of the bundle to her back by the leather strap. She opened the door softly, and crept in low with her blade at the ready for ambush.

"No need for that," Brandinne said from somewhere in the darkness of the room. "I'm not here to attack you." She wasn't audibly locatable as she was using a Havvish trick of throwing her voice. Their strangely large and animated mouths weren't simply for an interesting appearance, as Calista well knew. Being able to throw ones voice, to bounce it off hard objects, was a Brownie trait used to mess with outsiders in their forests—many Havvish were able to learn it as well.

Calista shut the door behind her and returned the dagger to its sheath. "Do you at least mind if I stoke the fire a little to get some warmth in here?"

"I do, actually, but feel free to bundle up. I'm a little disgusted by your slutty and desperate ensemble," Brandinne said, throwing her voice to seem as though it was coming from the corner behind Calista...or perhaps it really was.

Calista shrugged. The barbed comment was truthful enough. She'd felt desperate after hearing Brandinne and Harper were catching up alone, and she'd put on something overly suggestive to compensate. She actually felt a little better having someone else accurately identify what she'd done. She grabbed a blanket from the bed and wrapped it around herself.

"So, what do you want?" Calista asked. "I'm tired and not in the mood for guessing games."

"That's a shame," Brandinne said. "I like games, but you're right, we don't have that kind of relationship. In plain language, I want what you want."

"Harper?"

Brandinne giggled, which had a strangely sinister edge to it when she bounced the sound off three or four different places in the room to make it sound like there was a whole host of her hidden within the shadows, mocking a thoroughly surrounded Calista. Intellectually, Calista knew of the Brownie trick to do this to obscure their numbers, but she'd never actually experienced it. Firsthand, in a dark room, it was a little unsettling.

"In part, although you want to leave, and I want you gone," Brandinne explained. "I overheard your conversation in the stables, and before you get too nervous, no, I wasn't following you, I was following them. I'm offering to help you since our interests align so nicely in this one regard."

"How do you propose to do that?" Calista asked.

"You have a name on your list, again, don't worry, I didn't steal a look from the copy after it came to your possession, but I did watch when Ulrich wrote it out," Brandinne said. "Stevis Grayson—he's in shipping, or, more specifically, trafficking of sex slaves. If you were to kill him at the right time, you could steal enough money to escape the city in whatever fashion you saw fit."

The name hadn't stuck out to Calista when she first perused the list as Ulrich had only described him as an importer and exporter of rare goods. With the new information about what Stevis really did, Calista wondered why Ulrich would want him dead. The two primary reasons Calista could think of didn't fit Ulrich very well. He didn't seem like the type to try to take over Stevis's racket of kidnapping women and children to sell into prostitution overseas. It was possible that Stevis was paying one of Ulrich's rivals within the thieves guild for protection, but if that were the case, it would make more sense for the rival's name to be on the list so Ulrich could take over the protection work for an increased fee.

Apparently Brandinne accurately assessed what Calista was doing with the silence in the conversation. "Don't bother trying to wrap your head around why," Brandinne said. "The fat, stupid guard made fun of Ulrich when he wrote the name on the list. Apparently it's revenge for enslaving and selling off a girl Ulrich fancied."

Calista snorted. The entire job sounded downright appealing with more particulars added to it. She could avenge something worth avenging, shut down a despicable trade in the city, and get paid handsomely for her time.

"Very well, say we kill him together, take the money I need, and I get out of here the first chance I get…what do we do in regards to Harper in the meantime?"

"Certainly my intentions are more worthy than yours," Brandinne said. This barbed comment made good contact on Calista—leaving her with a harsh sting for how she was behaving. "I'll not pretend like I can convince you to do the honorable thing—honor among thieves being what it is. Let's just call it game on: you try your best to get what you want from her in the time allotted and I'll try my best to get what I want and we'll let Harper decide what she wants from either of us."

"Don't you think you have an unfair advantage in that scenario?" Calista asked. "You've known her a lot longer than I have."

Brandinne laughed again, bouncing it off several more surfaces until it sounded as though the darkness must be teeming with Havvish women. "I don't have your Dark Stalker trick of persuasion," Brandinne said. "Oh, don't look so shocked. I know full well you're a…what's the colorful phrase you Dark Stalkers use among yourselves to describe one of your members who has been divine touched by the Thief Lord?"

"Mistress of Masks," Calista muttered. Brandinne shouldn't have known such things even existed, let alone the term for it.

"Yes! Mistress or Master of Masks. Isn't it funny that you have this remarkably rare thing in common with Harper and yet you can't share it with her?" Brandinne snorted and for the first time, Calista thought she might truly know that the little Havvish Jack was near the fireplace. "Perhaps the Sea Queen is more selective in who she chooses for her divine touched. Take a look at Harper and take a look at yourself. Clearly the Thief Lord's standards are lacking."

"There's another way this could be settled," Calista growled.

"As much as I like solving problems with violence, it's second only to drinking contests in my estimation, I know better than to try in this case," Brandinne said, "and you'll know better since there's a good many people in this city you don't want finding out what you really are, not the least of which is Harper. Maybe you kill me, but maybe I have a contingency plan that would deliver your name and true nature to a select few regardless of whether or not I'm breathing."

"Fine, we'll see your plan through as you laid it out," Calista said.

"I'll be in touch, and remember: game on."

Calista couldn't be sure if Brandinne was truly gone from the room. She made immediately for the fireplace to stoke it back to life from the coals it slumbered in. The stack of wood she'd placed next to the hearth was gone and it took her a good deal of time to find it in the darkness. Of course Brandinne didn't want her stoking the fire. The chimney was her planned escape route all along. Calista found the wood tucked beneath the sitting chair nearest the small window of her room. She threw a few of the little logs angrily onto the fire and poked at the whole mess with the iron rod provided until the fire perked back up.

Game on indeed, Calista fumed to herself. Perhaps her intentions weren't entirely honorable before, but perhaps they could be made so. Harper needn't stay in Griffon's Rock. Maybe when Calista left, she would take Harper with her. She was too good for her current company anyway, and far too good to end up with a skunk weed smoking blabbermouth. She wouldn't kill Brandinne out of professional courtesy—she was clearly a worthy Jack and respect might well have blossomed into friendship between them if they weren't after the same woman.

First things first though, she needed to find out more about this Stevis Grayson.

Chapter 15:

A Challenge or Two

Calista awoke late, as she always did when given the chance. She was a late to bed late to rise type, which was fairly standard of Jacks, although she was also a fervent believer in sleeping as much as possible when a soft bed, cozy room, and warm blankets were available. Coming to the day took awhile for her and she only reluctantly left the comfort of the bedding to step into the relatively cold room as her fire had died down during the night. She dressed for the day, forgoing her weapons for the moment, wanting to seem a little unassuming since so many eyes within the city would be on her.

Within the main hall, she found a strange division among the Dagger Falls Company. Half of them were having a grand time over a late breakfast and the other half didn't seem to be enjoying themselves at all. The main hall was far more populated by adventuring crews than previously and would likely hold even more before the week was done. Even still, finding Sven and Athol, grumpy and separated from the massive stone table that was their company's right, was an easy matter as they were the only people in the entire hall not having a good time.

Calista slipped between serving girls and boys making their way around the hall to the brothers who had set up shop at a small table a span away from the booth. Their eyes were still glued to their usual seats though and the women occupying them.

"You two have the look of being angry at the morning," Calista said, snapping their attention away from the booth.

"The accursed Havvish woman has stolen our breakfast," Athol grumbled.

"I shall find a guard to serve justice for this purloined meal immediately," Calista said with a smirk. "Except, you seem to have found another breakfast. You didn't steal it, did you?" Calista glanced to the plates of untouched food sitting in front of the brothers.

"Fine, she stole our…something, comfort, I guess," Sven said.

"Aren't you usually the articulate one?" Calista asked.

"Are you going to help or are you just here to mock our exile?" Athol said.

Calista rolled her eyes and leaned back against the leading edge of the table to inspect the situation. Brandinne, Harper, and Ezra were occupying the Dagger Falls Company booth, talking, laughing, and apparently having a grand time playing some sort of word game.

"It's amazing to me how she manages to still hold the majority of the conversation while consuming most of the food," Calista mused. Indeed, Brandinne was talking as much as Harper and Ezra put together, yet tomatoes, ham, eggs, potatoes, and bread were all vanishing into her mouth between speaking.

"That is remarkable now that you mention it," Sven said. He and his brother cocked their heads to one side in unison to give the Havvish woman's habits a new consideration.

"Were you banished for being spoil sports or were you unable to keep up with the word game they're playing?" Calista asked.

"Neither," Athol said, although Calista could tell by the twitch above his eye that he was lying, at least in part. "We simply do not enjoy her personality."

"What would you have me do?" Calista asked.

"Take your place as our company's Jack and run her off," Sven said.

"Money," Calista said.

"What?" the brothers said in unison.

"How much money will you give me for this task? Her presence doesn't bother me in the slightest," Calista lied. "So, you'll have to pay me to champion you in this."

"A silver coin," Athol said shrewdly.

"Excellent, a silver from each of you." Calista turned on her heels before either of the brothers could object and sauntered her way over to the booth where merriment was indeed focused on the Havvish Jack.

"Good morning, Calista," Harper said.

"Good morning to you, Sword Maiden," Calista replied.

"I was told you fancy bacon," Brandinne said to Calista. "Sadly we've consumed all we have. If you don't mind waiting, we could ask for more, or you could just go steal it."

"Cute, but not why I'm here," Calista said, folding her arms over her chest.

"Then why *are* you here?" Ezra asked.

"Challenge." Calista affixed her gaze on Brandinne.

"Accepted," Brandinne said. "Field of battle?"

"Riddles before the public," Calista replied.

"Terms?" Brandinne asked.

"Any riddle asked by anyone and first to falter fails," Calista said.

"A brutal gauntlet indeed," Brandinne said with a twinkle in her purple eyes. "Are the stakes high enough to warrant it though?"

"An evening, with Harper if she is amenable, *alone*," Calista said. "Perhaps dinner, a bit of gaming, a stroll, sparkling conversation, and whatever else might tickle her fancy."

"Stakes worth any danger," Brandinne said. "Are you willing to provide such a prize, Harper?"

"If you both feel an evening with me is worth possible public embarrassment of your craft, who am I to tell you otherwise?" Harper said.

Athol, who had somehow snuck into hearing range, pounded his massive fist upon a nearby table, rattling every plate and piece of cutlery with the vibrations. He added a roar to echo through the room, "Challenge!" His mighty proclamation brought a grand cheer from the other mercenaries within the room who liked nothing more than a challenge between their members to pass the long, winter months, displaying for bragging rights and gambling purposes, which company had the most adept adventurers. Duels, archery competitions, knife throwing, singing, riddles, and magical mastery challenges were quite common during the resting season as hardened treasure hunters needed to keep their skills sharp by showing off for their peers, and more provincially to stave off boredom.

The men and women of the mercenary guild, a few dozen in all, jumped to under Sven's direction to create a space proper to a challenge. Two Jacks dueling with riddles, open to audience participation, was a treat indeed so early in the resting season. Two tables were shoved to the forefront. Calista and Brandinne were born to them by the hands of the audience and placed upon them in full view of the gathered adventurers.

"First to falter fails!" Sven yelled to the audience who echoed the terms.

"Stakes?!" someone from the gathered throng yelled.

"A quiet evening alone with the Sword Maiden Harper," Athol answered.

A hushed and excited wave of murmurs washed through the gathered mercenaries and a few even asked if they might join in the competition as well.

"Shall we allow age or beauty to start us off?" Sven asked.

"Start with age," Calista replied, raising her voice to be heard throughout the great hall. "I will gain her years, by and by, but she may as well have something to balance my beauty that she will only get farther and farther from."

The audience laughed and made taunting "ooooh" noises to the jibe.

"You'll find your reflection good company after you lose," Brandinne said. "Regardless, I accept." She made a grand show of thinking of what riddle she might pose, drawing the entire room to silence to await her words. "It may hold the knowledge of the world, or nothing at all. Always standing, but what lies therein always rests. Can hold a burden eternally, but can only ever be unburdened by another. Of what do I speak?"

"Am I to be impressed with your knowledge of ancient riddles?" Calista asked. "A bookcase, of course." Calista didn't wait to have her answer verified, as she could see on Brandinne's face she'd hit the answer easily. "There was a green house. Inside the green house there was a white house. Inside the white house there was a red house. Inside the red house there were a lot of babies."

"What Havvish wouldn't know the answer to this one?" Brandinne asked. "Food riddles are foolish in a competition against a people renowned for our stomachs. You speak of watermelon."

They thrust and parried at one another with riddles, although neither faltered. The audience, Jacks from other companies usually, injected an occasional riddle when an opportunity arose, and these too were answered by Brandinne and Calista. Wagers began trading hands as the competition stretched on through the first hour. Groups of adventurers took private counsel with one another to think up new riddles to baffle one or the other in order to win side bets, but even these concoctions failed to stump.

"He gouged out the eye. It is not the fate of a dead man. He cut the throat: a dead man," Calista said.

"A governor or government with the power to pass judgment," Brandinne replied. "The tower is high, as high as any tower, yet casts no shade. Of what do I speak?"

"A midday sun beam," Calista said. "What has four hands but none to lend?"

"A man carrying a clock," Brandinne replied. "Like a fish in a pond or like troops before a King. Of what do I speak?"

"Uselessness—the fish within a pond is not for eating and troops before a king are not fighting wars," Calista replied. In truth, Calista was getting bored, and even though she'd taken Sven aside to place a bet on herself with the coins owed to her by the brothers, she wasn't so sure she was going to win anymore. It wasn't that Brandinne knew more or superior riddles than her—she just knew she was likelier to slip up because of her boredom while Brandinne didn't seem to get tired of the game at all. The only riddle she kept in reserve for such an occasion was considered bad form in most competitions of wit, but Calista could tell their audience was interested in seeing a resolution as well and might not mind the riddle form of a swift kick to the groin if it ended the game and settled their side wagers. "How far can a wolf run into a forest?"

The room silenced and for once, Brandinne was struck speechless. "Philosphoical questions aren't riddles simply because they are puzzling," Brandinne protested.

"It is a riddle, but if you think it too philosophical, I will let you ask three questions so you might reassure yourself of its validity," Calista said.

"What forest do you speak of?" Brandinne asked without hesitation.

"Any forest," Calista replied, satisfying the universality of the riddle.

"Why does the wolf run?"

"The usual reason for running: to get from one spot to another," Calista said, drawing a laugh from her audience. The answer satisfied the need of the riddle to contain all necessary information to solve it within the asking.

"Is the wolf metaphor or literal?"

"Literal."

"If it is literal then the riddle cannot be answered without knowing what forest is spoken of," Brandinne protested.

"So, you have no answer?"

"It cannot be answered!"

"Halfway," Calista said, "because, after halfway through, the wolf is no longer running *into* the forest, it is running *out*."

"That's a stupid riddle," Brandinne huffed.

"Yes, well, you didn't know the answer, so what does that say about you?" Calista hopped off her table to a combination of cheers and jeers as the audience of a few dozen adventurers was split fairly evenly on who they bet on. Calista ignored both the comments about it being poor form and adulations about her cleverness alike, seeking out only Harper in the crowd. Surprisingly the Sword Maiden came to meet her halfway.

"You did all that just to have dinner with me?" Harper asked.

"I did all that to have dinner with you *alone* and I would have done more," Calista said.

"Then I suppose I must honor the deal," Harper said.

"Do not make it sound so unappealing," Calista teased. "I promise to have entertaining anecdotes and compliments aplenty to keep you from falling asleep during this chore."

"I didn't mean it like that," Harper said.

"After yesterday, would you rather I have lost?"

"I would rather you stop being so ridiculous about this and collect some of your prize now." Harper grasped Calista by the front of her tunic and pulled her in for a kiss. Calista was so taken aback in such a delighted way by the passion and force of the kiss that she forgot they had an audience until the entirety of the hall, excepting Ezra and Brandinne, burst into applause at the culmination of the victory.

As their lips parted, Calista was treated to Harper's full blush, having surprised even herself with such a bold gesture. "I will endeavor to find accommodations worthy of such a momentous night," Calista said, already counting the money she'd just won from the side bet as spent on her night with Harper. It was money she hadn't planned on having anyway, likely wouldn't need ultimately, and would be well spent on seduction if she truly planned to convince the Sword Maiden to leave with her.

"Then I will endeavor to dress and look the part when the time comes," Harper said cryptically, setting a little fire in Calista's imagination that she knew would only grow until her curiosity was satisfied that night.

Harper collected her cloak and Ezra, walking toward the door with many eyes following her departure. Calista glanced to Brandinne, who was still standing stunned on her table, and found the Havvish woman more intrigued than angry at the defeat.

She felt the bag of coins pressed into her hand before she spotted Sven at her side. She clenched her fingers around her winnings, mentally counting them through the cloth pouch.

"The odds were against you," Sven said, "so your take was good."

"Ten silver coins from the two you owed me," Calista mused, still watching Harper's exit from the inn, only turning her attention to the brothers when the door swung closed in a flurry of snow. "Five to one odds though?"

"She's Havvish and notoriously crafty," Athol interjected. "Besides, you looked unfocused and bored most of the time. Those who bet on you thought it was a tactic and those who bet against you won't likely underestimate you again."

"Perhaps you could challenge her in the future..." Sven began.

"...but to something more lethal and accidentally..." Athol continued, trailing off meaningfully at the end.

Calista glared at the brothers. "What grave injustice did she do to you two that you would want her dead?"

"She annoyed us," Sven explained, to which Athol nodded.

"That's it?" Calista asked.

"It was a severe annoyance spread over a goodly amount of time," Athol said. "Besides, we've killed men for less."

Calista didn't doubt that. She knew Harper to be the heart and soul of the group. She was their conscience and moral compass, but she wasn't an original member of the company. Ezra, Athol, and Sven adventured for a few years before her and she likely didn't have the sway she did with them until only the last few of their five together. Calista was hardly in a position to lecture them though. She was going to kill a few men for the gold of it all. Still, she saw far more value in Brandinne than she saw in the brothers combined. Adventuring men were violent, impulsive children for the most part, which was likely why she had long since lost her ability to even pretend like she was interested in men beyond meat shields to distract while she placed a dagger in someone's back.

"I wouldn't harm her and I wouldn't see her harmed by others," Calista said. "She's a worthy rival and were we not adversaries in seeking out Harper's affections, we might well be friends."

She took her leave from the stunned brothers and made her way up toward her room to gather her things for a little jaunt through town. It was to be enough of a walk to warrant arming herself although probably not armoring. She needed to find a restaurant worthy of an important night and she needed to get a better look at the city in daylight with an eye to assassin work.

Brandinne was outside the door to her room when she arrived. "I found your strand of hair at the bottom of the doorframe," the Havvish woman said, pulling herself from the casual leaned position she held against the wall. "That's a clever way to know your room was intruded upon or if someone might be waiting for you inside, and one an intruder couldn't really replicate unless they had the exact same hair color."

"I'm glad you approve," Calista said. She brushed past the Havvish woman and opened the door, unsurprised to find it was already unlocked.

Brandinne followed her into the room. "That was also quite the game-ending riddle," she said. "I'll have to use that in the future."

"That's how I learned it," Calista said.

"It's still stupid though."

"You still couldn't answer it." Calista grabbed her weapons from beneath the bed and set about finding hiding places for them among her clothes. The daggers and lock picks found homes easily, but she struggled to get the chain reel and mini-harpoon hidden beneath her sleeve.

"Let's talk about Stevis Grayson then," Brandinne said, shutting the door behind her. "I have two possible ways to enter his company. One you won't like, but the coin will be better, and the other is more dangerous, the coin is lessened, and I'll have to do the actual killing, which will require a cut of the spoils."

"Let's hear both for a laugh," Calista said.

"You could easily pretend to be a courtesan seeking transport and hope he attempts to kidnap you," Brandinne said. "You might well manage it within his office, which would then be open to looting."

"You mean use my womanly wiles to seduce my way into his graces to then kill and rob him?" Calista said. "Aside from that being wholly beneath a Dark Stalker's skills, it's also no doubt something people have tried on him already."

"I didn't think you'd like that one," Brandinne said. "The other option is to lure him to the docks where his ship is awaiting clearance to depart before winter ice closes the bay, and slay him among his body guards."

"How do you know where his ship is and how would we even lure him there?" Calista asked.

"His is the ship I came in on," Brandinne said. "He didn't know I came in on it, but it was the ride I made use of. He keeps a secluded section of one of the docks for his vessels alone for obvious reasons. It's quiet, devoid of witnesses, and a lovely place to dump a body that likely won't be found until spring if it is found at all."

"You still haven't mentioned how we would lure him there."

"With fire, of course."

Chapter 16:

An Exhilarating Evening

It took Calista most of the day to find what she was looking for among the narrow alleyways and quaint lanes of Griffon's Rock, but eventually her nose led her to what she sought. Spices in the air, the scent of roasting goat, and the exotic perfume of incense drew her to the tiny building off the main bazaar on the edge of the dock district and the marketplace—southerners from the lowlands creating a little taste of home.

She paused outside the restaurant to breathe in the scents of her past. A wooden sign above the door identified the establishment as Ghaf'nashi, which translated to a purple flower typically dried and smoked from a water pipe by old men, but also meant the act of smoking in such a way. Adept practitioners of Ghaf'nashi smoking could breathe irregular shaped smoke rings of vibrant colors through the light of oil lamps.

She pulled the rope handle on the door and pressed in. The restaurant and smoking den bombarded her with the thick air reminiscent of the city she grew up in. The small front room was hot and held a low haze of smoke around the rafters. Four crescent tables, half the height of normal tables, were set with low stools for sitting, each containing a water pipe in the center. Wax incense holders lined the shelves along the walls and bouquets of dried tulips dangled above every window and doorway.

Two older women, dressed in the wrapped purple cloth of the servant class in the south emerged from a draped off area at the back of the front room. Their jaws were stout and square and their hair dark brown, nearly black with streaks of gray. Calista guessed them to be from the southeastern baronies of the lowlands where the palm trees grew. They bowed to her and touched their foreheads. Calista responded in kind.

"Warm blessings upon you," the taller of the two women said.

"Warm blessings," Calista replied. She guessed the women to be related from the similar swoop of their noses and high foreheads, but their ages were difficult to discern, as was common among women of her homeland. One could be forty and the other seventy and they might both look fifty-five. She might very well be dealing with sisters or a mother and daughter.

"Travelers from the homeland are uncommon this far north," the other woman said.

"Indeed," Calista replied. "Imagine my surprise and delight at finding an actual tea house at the end of the Last Road." The southern most edge of the Vaelandrian nation, before the great salt flats began, was known for open grasslands spotted with beautiful flowers, heavily spiced foods, strong teas, and potent poisons. They exported salt mined from the flats, flowers plucked from the endless rolling hills and fields, and assassins. As warm as the two women were toward Calista, she knew there was an inherent mistrust of other lowlanders. They were smiling, but likely held daggers behind their backs.

"Perhaps you might enjoy a pot of tea then?" the taller woman asked.

"This evening," Calista replied. "I have a special someone whom I would like to share a bit of our culture with. Could something of a Dahlia's Feast be prepared on such short notice?" Calista removed the pouch of coins given to her by the brothers, letting the jingle of the bag sway their answer. "A single meal with four courses?"

"She must be a remarkable find to try to bring such festivity, even in part, for just her," the shorter woman said. "We held annual Dahlia Feasts for the first few years after moving here, but the northerners didn't seem terribly interested in our customs."

"I am certain to have a willing participant and would adore such a lovely reminder of home," Calista said.

The women glanced to each other and smiled. "Then we will begin at the setting sun, as is customary." The taller one snatched the coin purse from Calista's hand and they scurried back behind the draping.

Calista was so far removed from her own people she'd almost forgotten how abrupt they could be. Unlearning the grabby, demanding ways of the lowlands was difficult. What charmed in the south tended to exasperate everywhere else. The proprietors of Ghaf'nashi probably struggled still to find customers if they accepted payment in the lowland way as they had with Calista.

Harper was in for an interesting evening and Calista wasn't as sure as when she'd started her errand that it would be an entirely enjoyable one. She truly hoped a seasoned traveler like the Sword Maiden would have an open mind about such things.

Calista wished she'd held a few coins in reserve to buy new clothing even though Harper didn't seem all that concerned with sumptuary norms. She selected the mixture of clothing that matched the desired black and red of the Dahlia Feast host city. She found her way to Harper's room only to hear the sounds of struggles within. She thought to knock, but decided against it, bursting through the unlocked door with her hand on the hilt of her dagger.

Harper was within, and struggling mightily, but her adversary appeared to be a dress, or more precisely the dress's sleeves. The dress looked new, although not specifically tailored to Harper. It likely cost quite a bit and probably could have been altered to match her physique with more time. It was a typical maiden's gown of flowing blue and gray satin, belted low on her hips and cinched tight around her waist and chest with a corseted bodice to create voluminous cleavage. The main body of the dress appeared to fit reasonably well, perhaps a little tightly through the hips and squeezed Harper's already impressive chest up into a ridiculous collection of womanly bounty that looked like it would be exceedingly uncomfortable after a short time. The sleeves, however, which were meant to be tied on after the fact over the top of lace wrappings weren't nearly up to the task of encompassing Harper's powerful arms. A lifetime of swinging a massive sword and wearing heavy armor bolstered the Sword Maiden's arms and shoulders into downright brawny shape, which was ideal to their work, but far too big to fit within a maiden's sleeves.

Calista stifled her giggle at Harper's entanglement with the gown's sleeves. "You are meant to have help in putting those on," Calista said.

"I did until Ezra declared it a wasted venture and left me to my own devices," Harper said.

She was breathing heavily from the exertion, exacerbated by the constriction of her bodice. Her already cupped breasts were heaving up and down with every breath, catching Calista's eyes and they might have entirely held her focus if it weren't for Harper's arms and shoulders. The strain and struggle of pulling at sleeves and unintentional flexing brought her musculature into stark relief. Calista released her hold on her dagger to come to Harper's aid, and perhaps to touch the Sword Maiden's eye-catching limbs.

She gently plucked the sleeve from Harper's hand and rather than help her tie it into place, tossed it aside and began unwinding the lace wrappings which weren't nearly sufficient to cover the expanse of Harper's arms. In the course of her work, Calista ran her fingers along the definition of Harper's muscles, finding them as pleasing to touch as look upon.

"I would be of the opinion that such sleeves are intended for women with uninteresting arms," Calista said. "Your limbs stand in full glory without such adornment and so you have no need to wear them."

"You don't think me mannish for such hardened muscles?" Harper asked shyly.

Calista shook her head and smiled, tracing away the last remnants of the sleeves no doubt intended for a woman with arms a third the size of Harper's. She walked slowly behind the Sword Maiden, took her long, flowing blond hair between her fingers and began braiding it, interweaving one of the lace wrappings meant for beneath a sleeve. "If you were any more womanly in such a dress, I believe your breasts would spill out of their own accord," Calista said. "Men and women both have arms—how could they be inherently attractive for one gender but not the other? You have the arms of a woman who swings a massive sword. They would seem out of place on a nobleman. Thus gender has little to do with it."

"I have seen women admire Athol's arms," Harper said, "but have never heard compliments on mine."

"Athol's arms are large, but hold little else of value," Calista said. "Hairy, brutish, unkempt things appeal to base desires of base women." Calista finished the long, thick braid of Harper's hair and tied it off with the end of the lace binding; she'd hoped to have enough left over from the braiding to create a bow, but Harper's hair was far longer than she'd anticipated. She placed her hands on the warm, soft skin of Harper's shoulders, thrilling at the sensation of the strong muscles beneath. "I would compliment yours in saying they are beautifully shaped as though you were carved from the finest marble by a master sculptor who knew every muscle and sinew intimately and would only display them in their perfect form and balance. This dress was meant to be worn by you, but the sleeves would be an abomination to cover such flawlessness."

"You speak poetically about something I've never heard praised," Harper said, blushing in such a way that it showed through on the back of her neck, the tips of her pointed ears, and the sharp angle of her cheek bones.

"I could write epic poetry about your arms and shoulders," Calista said, "although I would prefer to write sensual sonnets about them. Come, we must make our way to the appointed evening before I change my mind and decide I would much rather cut the dress from you and compose a thousand odes to your nude form."

Harper accepted her cloak around her shoulders as Calista raised it for her. They strolled arm-in-arm from the inn, avoiding the main hall in favor of a side exit for fear of being spotted by many fellow adventurers who would no doubt have questions or comments that could only slow them down.

The sun setting in the west broke through the clouds that covered the city if only for a moment, casting golden light across the snow collected in the streets. Beams of warm light across the cold landscape lengthened shadows between buildings, illuminating the path of the duo as they made their way to the southwest corner of the city. Above them, the storm raged over the Screeching Peek amidst black clouds and snowy rocks. The break in the weather over the city though was a lovely reprieve for the moment.

"You seemed cross with me for a time," Calista said.

"It is hard to remain so under such compliments and acts of kindness," Harper replied, cuddling closer to Calista's side. "I am frightened by how much I care for you and how little I truly know of you."

"This evening should help, after a fashion," Calista said cryptically.

The tea house was as Calista hoped, dressed in lanterns on the outside, obvious in their approach that something special awaited them inside. Harper appeared to get caught up a little in the excitement, drawing Calista along faster toward the exotic destination. Calista pulled the rope, hoping for a bell, and wasn't disappointed as she opened the door for Harper and heard the ringing of three distinct chimes. It was a good omen that such detail was seen to.

"What is all this?" Harper asked as she stepped into the dimly lit tea shop, breathing in the wonder of the southern reaches that included enticing scents of spiced cooking and the smoke of incense.

"In the lowlands, there is a traveling celebration of the Wandering Goddess Lyndria, patron deity of the gypsies. Every year the celebration moves to a new city, calling women from all over to travel and partake in the Dahlia Feast," Calista explained. "Over the centuries, the main attraction of the celebration was in the Ceremony of Wandering Love."

"You get ahead of yourself." One of the women from before emerged from the back room where the drapes were pulled aside to reveal a door. She was still dressed in the wrapped robes of the lowlands, but her dark hair was held down flat around her head by three bronze diadems. "There is much to the feast to get to before we can speak of the Wandering Love."

"She is right," Calista said, guiding Harper toward one of the crescent tables that were now arranged in a ring with different color lamps glowing in the middle of each. Their first stop was the table with the lamp that burned with a faint blue color. Calista aided Harper in lowering herself to sit upon one of the half stools, which would have been difficult alone in the dress. "We must first lament the coldness of stagnation that presupposes a grand excursion."

Harper beamed to Calista, leaning in briefly to kiss her upon cheek. "This is like where you're from?"

"It is something I wanted to share with you," Calista said.

The starting course was chilled liquor with berries in the bottom. Harper abstained as part of her vows to her deity. When the proprietress left the room to fetch the next course, Calista drank both tapered glasses quickly.

"What is our hostess's name?" Harper whispered to Calista.

"I don't know," Calista replied, a shiver running over her from the potent, clear liquor. "It's considered rude to ask unless offered. There are people all over the lowlands who know favored proprietors for years without ever learning their names."

A bell was rung and they traveled on to the next table lit by a green lamp. Calista rather enjoyed the act of helping Harper from the stool and then lowering her to the next one as it afforded her ample opportunity to touch Harper's alluring arms and wrap her own arm around Harper's slender waist. At the second station, they were served the first course of food, which consisted of river crustaceans cooked in a fiery red curry and covered in a baked oat crust on the tops of the open shells.

"It represents the fire within necessary to experience change through travel," Calista explained.

Harper took a daring bite and was rewarded with watering eyes and flushed skin. She drank greedily of the potent mint tea provided in tiny jars meant to represent how tea is consumed while on the road. The tea seemed to help some, and to Calista's surprise, Harper was determined to try the crustacean curry cakes again once she'd rallied a little to.

"Who is Dahlia?" Harper asked as she fanned her face with her hands as if there were a literal fire to dispel.

"Dahlia was the mortal consort of the Wandering Goddess," Calista explained. "Eventually, she aged and died, as mortals are expected to do, and the Goddess Lyndria came to the world in disguised human form to travel the roads Dahlia loved in search of the same pleasures her former lover once found there. The foods we eat, the drinks we partake of, the songs we sing, the stories we tell, and the rituals we participate in are the same favored by Dahlia and later experienced by the Goddess who loved her."

"That is so beautiful and so sad," Harper said.

"Such is love," Calista said. "We are meant to cherish both sides of a connection—the joy and sadness."

They moved on to the next station with the lamp of faintest yellow light. In helping Harper to her feet and aiding her to sit, Calista found her eyes inexorably drawn to Harper's chest where the warmth of the room and the spice of the last dish drew a lovely beading of sweat between her breasts illuminated by the light of the lamp in an entirely enticing way. Harper caught her gaze lingering and blushed at the obvious admiration. When both host women were back out of the room to fetch the next course, Harper leaned in close to Calista to whisper silken words to her.

"Your eyes linger on my skin where your mouth might want to travel?" Harper asked.

Calista glanced down to Harper's hand on her thigh to find it shaking a little. She was so eager in her exploration yet so nervous in her advances. Calista adored the virginal inexperience and admired how artful Harper was becoming in her flirtations.

"I wait only for an invitation," Calista whispered in response.

"Consider it extended," Harper replied.

Calista leaned in closer, determined to taste the beaded sweat between Harper's heaving breasts, only to be cut short by the ringing of another bell, signaling the return of the serving women. She changed her angle to kiss Harper on the neck. The woman cleared her throat regardless and Calista returned fully to her own stool.

"The song of first love found in the journey of life must be sung," the woman said, setting a platter of steaming vegetables and hunks of goat meat between them. She poured from a terracotta pitcher a thick wine sauce over the dish. As the burgundy sauce sank between the hunks of food, it began steaming and boiling, cooked by the heat held within the platter, vegetables, and meat. "Would you like to sing the song yourself, or shall I fetch my cousin?"

"I'd love to hear you sing it," Harper said, "if you're willing and able."

"Certainly, although our hostess and her cousin may well have better singing voices," Calista said.

"No, we don't," the hostess said.

Calista straightened her back, cleared her throat, and began singing in a hushed tone, subtle in the dim interior of the little tea house.

Divine Touched

Under spring's cheery glow
I came to the river for a daily drink
Little did I know
I would end up thirsting for life.

Kiss me by the moonlight
Ask only my name
Love me in the morning
And I'll promise the same

By the balmy summer moon
We shared love's full embrace
By the light of the rising sun
We parted ways too soon.

Kiss me in the sunlight
Ask only for my hand
Love me in the daytime
And I promise to understand

Amid the fallen leaves of autumn
You gave me a ring
Without leave to say yes
I made you sing

Kiss me in the gathering night
Ask only for love
I'll love you in the evening
When the stars light above

"There's no verse about winter?" Harper asked as Calista fell silent.

"The romance of the Wandering Goddess and her beloved Dahlia ended too soon," the hostess said. "By an immortal's estimation, no love with a mortal could have time to fully mature into winter."

"That's the more depressing interpretation of the song," Calista said.

"You have a lovely singing voice," Harper said.

"She's a little better than my cousin, I guess." The hostess set the pitcher of wine beside the platter and handed Harper and Calista cloth napkins before taking her leave.

"No forks or knives?" Harper asked.

"We're meant to eat with our hands since young love is messy yet satisfying."

They plucked sauce soaked hunks of food from the mound with their fingers, eating slowly at first, and then finding their appetites as was intended when they realized neither of them could keep dainty manners while eating the dish. They were giggling, wiping each other's mouths with the napkins, and were well-fed by the time they were to move on to the final station with the red glowing lantern.

Harper leaned heavily on Calista when she was helped up, whispering hotly against Calista's neck, "I think there was wine in that sauce."

"There was, but I thought most of the spirits would cook out," Calista replied. "Is it against your vows to eat wine or simply to drink it?"

"Drink it, I suppose," Harper said. "It feels a little picky to say eating wine sauce on food is okay even though the wording of the vow quite clearly specifies drinking."

"I think if the Sea Queen meant to include eating of alcohol based sauces in the vow, she would have stipulated so." Calista helped Harper sit upon the stool at the final table, lingering a little behind her to trace her fingers along the tops of Harper's taut shoulders.

"The Dahlia Feast is a remarkable way to spend an evening," Harper said as Calista at last sat beside her.

"It typically takes four days and nights," Calista explained. "Each station consumes a full day and night, but since I only won a single evening with you and we're the only revelers, it made more sense to condense it to a single meal."

"What is the purpose of this final table?"

"The Ceremony of Wandering Love," Calista said. "As the Goddess Lyndria was no longer able to stand her loneliness, she sought out a new love after Dahlia's death. She knew her lover would not want her to suffer an eternity alone and so it was that Lyndria came to bless new couplings that took place on the final day of the feast."

"This means divorces and new marriages can arise in a single day." The hostess returned with two baked sweet rolls in a basket woven of reeds. "I changed lovers in my life three times during the Ceremony of Wandering Love."

Calista pointed to her own empty head. "That's why she wears three diadems."

"We do not frown upon polygamy in the same way the northern nations of Vaelandria do," the hostess said. "So the Ceremony of Wandering Love is also a way to add new spouses to households. My sister married two wives and a husband during Dahlia Feasts."

"What is the symbolism of the sweet rolls, aside from dessert?" Harper asked.

Calista scooped the closest roll to herself and pinched the flaky pastry between her fingers to tear it. Half an old silver coin dropped onto the table. Calista popped part of the little roll into her mouth and snatched the coin piece up on the first bounce with her free hand. She tucked the bite of sweetbread into her cheek and held out the half of the coin for Harper to inspect. "The other half is in your roll," she said. "Were there many revelers, the rolls would hold several such split totems meant to introduce new people to pairings fated by the Wandering Goddess."

Harper reached into the basket, plucked out her own roll, and tore it open to reveal the other half of the coin. "Since we're the only two here, does that mean our pairing is fated?"

"The Wandering Goddess does not make mistakes in this ritual," the hostess said sternly.

Harper and Calista finished their desert, thanked the cousins who hosted them, and stumbled out into the chilly darkness of the night, giddy with excitement and warm from good food and wine.

Calista for once leaned heavily on Harper, having drunk both shares of the ceremonial spirits to prevent insult from being done to the hostesses. It felt good to feel Harper's strong arms holding her for stability.

"You didn't seem to agree with the hostess's interpretation of the song," Harper said. "Why do you think the song doesn't have a winter verse?"

"The song is specifically about Lyndria and Dahlia, not simply relationships between deities and humans," Calista explained. "They could not get married as the song says, but not because one was immortal and the other mortal; Dahlia was already married to a jealous man who would not give permission for further marriage. Southerners are polygamous, but require equal acceptance by all participants, and Dahlia's husband did not think he could compete with a Goddess for his wife's affections. This didn't stop their ongoing relationship though and when Dahlia died after decades together, Lyndria lifted her to the stars so she might walk beneath the gaze of her lover in human form. There is no winter verse because Lyndria began her travels to heal her heart by then. The winter verse would start the song for her next love."

"Is there such a song?"

"Not that I know of," Calista said. "This all happened a thousand years ago, so I don't think one is forthcoming. That's a long time to find a new love, even for an immortal. I doubt she found anyone to rival Dahlia."

As they neared the inn, Calista could feel Harper's breathing and heartbeat quickening. An added benefit to the blood vessels in Harper's arms being so close to the surface was also being able to feel her pulse through the arm wrapped around her waist.

"I want to invite you to my room," Harper said, "to help me remove my dress."

"I would be honored to aid you in this," Calista said.

"And to take full advantage of me once I am naked before you," Harper said quickly.

"Yes, that part was implied in the first bit."

Chapter 17:

Unmarred Maidenhood

Harper eagerly pulled Calista up to her room. No one ever bothered to seduce her before and Calista did such a fine job of it that Harper was aching to find out what came next. Before she could even get to the door, Calista pushed her back against the wall, pressed her body full against Harper's, and kissed her in such a way that left Harper breathless and wanting.

Within the privacy of Harper's room, barely lit by the flickering flames of the dying fires in the fireplaces, Calista seemed to slow things down to an agonizing pace. Harper envisioned the aforementioned cutting of the dress from her in hasty fashion, but Calista appeared to have other plans, namely teasing Harper around the dress while she took an ample amount of time in unlacing the cords holding the garment in place.

Calista's mouth lit across the cleavage created by Harper's dress. Her lips were so soft, her tongue so warm, and her breath so enticing that Harper barely noticed Calista's hands wrapped around to her back, slowly unlacing the cross-cross pattern along the back of the dress holding the corseted bodice in place. After a lengthy caress of every inch of her mountainous cleavage by Calista's daring tongue, Harper was left panting and hungry for something she didn't even have a word for. When Calista finally pulled away Harper's loosened dress, she couldn't be rid of the uncomfortable garment fast enough.

In Harper's estimation, it was her turn, and though she was essentially fumbling blindly with how to do things in a seductive manner, she knew the basics of how to remove clothing and she needed Calista's clothing off! She drew Calista's face up from her breasts to kiss her. Holding her partner's attention with a kiss was easy; however, undressing Calista while her own focus was fragmented by the steamy kiss wasn't. Eventually, Calista caught onto what Harper's stumbling fingers were after and aided her in removing belt, breeches, and finally boots.

"By the Gods, you have remarkable breasts," Calista murmured, breaking the kiss. "I wouldn't have thought it possible to maintain such a chest when muscle clearly dominates everything else about you."

Harper giggled, still trying to work away Calista's tunic and the warm tabard she'd draped over it. "It is in my family's blood. Every female relative on my mother's side has the same ample chest regardless of height or weight. If anything, the training that carved away fat from everywhere else has tamed the familial trait of ever increasing bust size." Harper finally pulled away Calista's top, hurling it aside unceremoniously. Her lips found their way to Calista's exposed neck, just below her jaw line.

"The women in your family must have horrendous back problems as they get older," Calista whispered, losing steam in the conversation at feeling Harper's mouth.

"It is practically an epidemic, although I haven't felt any as I am accustomed to carrying such weight and more." Harper took a half step back from Calista to give her an admiring look as well. "You don't seem to want for womanly curves yourself, you know."

"You flatter me." Calista smiled, coyly cocked her hip to affect a demure posture that accentuated the curve of her hips and the swell of her chest even in her small clothes. She was a seductress of such practiced grace that she had the uncanny ability to make Harper feel strong in one moment and girlishly vulnerable in the next.

In an attempt to turn the charming tide back on Calista, Harper raised her arms to begin plucking her hair from the braid, having long since noticed how enamored Calista was with her musculature and long hair. Not to be out done, Calista closed the gap again, and ran her hands down the powerful lines of Harper's body, and kissed her way into a kneeling position before the Sword Maiden. Calista paid extra attention to the defined lines of Harper's abdominal muscles with a talented tongue. Harper's hair fell free of the braid, cascading in blond waves around her shoulders, and Calista treated herself to the view of the event with upturned eyes and her mouth flush against the flat circle of Harper's bellybutton.

Harper lost her train of thought, and certainly any thoughts of seduction in feeling Calista's hot breath continuing south along her skin. She ran her hands through Calista's beautiful, darkened bronze hair, only pulling her eyes open from focusing on the pleasant sensations when she felt Calista's hands tugging down the waistband of her under shorts. She knew she should have felt vulnerable in such a nude state before Calista, but all she really felt was an overwhelming urge to have them off and have Calista touch her.

Calista's taunting licks and kisses came to a stop though after she'd pulled Harper's underclothing down over her powerfully muscular thighs. She helped an entirely nude Harper step from the discarded pool of clothing. She guided Harper to the bed, laying her back out across the warm blankets and mountain of pillows. Harper eagerly allowed herself to be led, gazing deeply into the dark sapphires of Calista's eyes.

Calista straddled her waist rising tall and beautiful in the flickering fire light as she began peeling away the cloth bindings that held her own breasts. While Harper's eyes drank in the beautiful show of slow undress, her hands endeavored to learn the lines of Calista's hips, legs, and ass. She followed the instruction in the woods, letting her hands make smooth, taunting paths over Calista's smooth skin and supple curves. In response, Calista rolled her hips, writhing down onto Harper, and letting out a pleased gasp with a lewd smile splayed across her lips.

Calista slid from her straddled position with fluid grace, urging Harper up farther onto the pillows to sit up even as she made her way down between the Sword Maiden's powerful legs. Harper watched with electric anticipation as Calista's head made its way up her thigh to the point between. She vaguely knew the thick knot at the top of the woman's line was meant for pleasure although she didn't know how much pleasure until she felt Calista's mouth encircle it.

Calista's hand made its way up Harper's stomach, caressing at the ridges of her abdominal muscles even as Harper strained to arch her back; her other hand wrapped insistently around Harper's muscular thigh, intent on keeping her mouth flush to the work. Harper had never known such pleasure, such excitement, or such unbridled desire before. Everything felt new and wonderful and the source of it was Calista's mouth. It was building toward something within her. She arched her body this direction, rolled her hips another, seeking out ways to speed the swelling sensation in her. Calista kept up with her movements well, pressing on with tongue and suckling lips until Harper heard herself screaming wordless cries of pleasure as the rolling wave of satisfaction crested and crashed up on her shore in a way she could only describe as transcendent. As she came down from the tingling, tumultuous peak that Calista brought her to, she felt awash in emotions, most of which focused on a feeling of utter adoration for Calista and desire to be nearer to her.

Seemingly reading her mind, Calista came up to her side, kissing and caressing at Harper's body, and in doing so creating all new writhing until they were fully entangled. Harper's breathing refused to calm even as she wrapped her arms and legs in and around Calista's. She was sweating, trembling, and biting her tongue to keep the word 'love' from tumbling out.

"I have never felt such pleasure before," Harper murmured, her lips tickling across Calista's forehead.

"It is a magical little spot on the body that can bring enormous joy with the right stimulation by mouth or finger," Calista replied. "In time, you will know its power well."

"May I touch you?" Harper asked.

"It would be rude not to," Calista whispered.

Still entwined, Harper's hand made its way off Calista's hip, eagerly pressing away the underclothes in her way. Calista aided in this some with her free hand and angling of her hips until Harper was able to push them the rest of the way down Calista's leg with her toes so Calista might kick them off entirely. She knew it would've been easier to simply leave Calista's embrace, but she still felt too emotionally fragile and connected to want any reduction in the skin on skin contact.

She slid her hand up between Calista's legs, feeling the warmth built there and the smooth skin with soft hair at the very crux. Calista responded with pleased coos of delight as Harper's fingers explored her body. She was exceedingly hot, wet, and slippery to the touch. Harper sought again and again the matching nub on Calista, but it was elusive and hidden. In her consternation, Harper drew her gaze from admiring the beautiful expressions on

Calista's face to glance down to her work between Calista's legs and the corresponding parts on her own body. Hers was obvious, as she'd always known it to be, thick and round like the tip of her index finger while Calista's was too well hidden to even see.

Calista, catching on Harper's concern, reached down to guide her fingers to the correct spot.

Harper felt the hard nub, but the confusion remained. "Is it meant to be small like this?" Harper asked.

"You are blessed in part with Sylvan blood, yes?" Calista asked.

"Some on my mother's side," Harper said, not understanding why such a question would matter.

"Sylvan blood is a blessing indeed in certain areas," Calista explained. "Among them, some endowments are more prominent on men than women, but no less remarkable in both cases. Women who don't know this are typically in for a shock when sleeping with Sylvan men. As for me, it was a hope resulting in a pleasant surprise. Everything works the same, responds to the same caresses, but mine is simply a little smaller and more difficult to find."

"You are more delicate," Harper said.

"In many ways as it turns out," Calista said, "but it is a difference between us that I rather enjoy."

"You do not think it strange then?"

Calista smiled in a way that practically made her eyes sparkle. "I think it is wonderful!"

"How do I caress you in such a pleasing way as you showed me?" Harper asked, feeling enormously relieved that their differences were a source of delight rather than dismay.

"Soft and slow at first, with a single finger to warn my body of what you intend," Calista whispered against Harper's lips.

Harper followed the instruction, immeasurably satisfied to hear corresponding sighs of pleasure passing from Calista's mouth after such gentle caresses from a single finger. She pressed on, sensing an increase of desire in her partner.

"When you have me to such a state where I am eager clay in your hands awaiting more of your touch, you may add more pressure and another finger to rub," Calista said breathlessly. "In time, you will know these things simply by watching my body react to your touch and listening to the sounds I make."

Harper greatly liked the sound of that. She wanted to know Calista's body and enjoyment in so many ways—she needed to be a source of ecstasy for Calista. She rubbed with the requested second finger as well, adding a little speed, paying close attention to what appeared to increase Calista's breathing until she could see the building within her. It was awe-inspiring to see from the outside what she'd just experienced. Calista was drawing closer to the same crashing pleasure Harper was recently introduced to and Harper was in control of guiding her toward it. She rubbed eagerly, wishing to catch the backside of the wave to drive Calista forward, guided by the cues Calista said would become obvious.

Calista squeezed her thighs around Harper's hand, bit her lower lip in a delicious way, and stifled a high-pitched squeal of glee that Harper hoped meant she felt one of the pleasure waves as well. Calista reached her hand down to grasp Harper's wrist, putting an end to the rubbing for the moment.

"You are a quick study of providing female pleasure," Calista whispered before kissing Harper fiercely.

"I had a superb teacher," Harper replied when the kiss broke.

Hours later, after some fairly blissful sleep, Harper awoke in the cold room. A strange question of faith weighed on her conscience. She slipped from the bed and Calista's warm embrace under the guise of reviving the dwindling fires. She wrapped herself in the nearest cloak to the bed, which turned out to be Calista's. Huddled deep within the heavy wool, she crept across the chilly floor to one fireplace and then the other, revitalizing them with fresh logs and a few pokes of the iron rod to spark the coals.

She waited a moment near the window to watch the world outside. The light from the fires illuminated enough of the room and the space beyond to show a few heavy snowflakes fluttering down beyond the glass.

The Dahlia Feast, specifically the final station, weighed on her mind. If the Goddess Lyndria indeed blessed pairings in such a way, she was fated to be with Calista by a Goddess that was not her own. It was difficult to tell though. Some deities, her own included, cared little for humanity or anything mortals did. The Sea Queen Maraline favored her aquatic mortal followers of whales, sharks, and other more exotic ocean creatures, than she did anything that dwelled on land. But Lyndria might be one of the meddlers who enjoyed fiddling with mortal's lives. It certainly sounded likely from the stories and songs told during the Dahlia Feast, but Harper didn't know anything about Lyndria.

Calista was a Dark Stalker, which added another layer of questions. Certainly Dark Stalkers weren't necessarily divine touched as most were more akin to the affirmed sisters at the temples to the Sea Queen—devout followers and servants without any tangible recognition of their deeds by their patron deity. Still, Harper couldn't imagine anyone more deserving of recognition by the Thief Lord than Calista, although she knew her mind was a little clouded by newly formed attachments that no doubted biased her opinion.

It wasn't inconceivable that Lyndria would push two followers of two other deities together in one of her rituals without a clear reason. It did seem the pantheon enjoyed tweaking each other's noses in such ways. Harper never presumed to know the motivation of a God or Goddess though. Lyndria could very well be playing a prank on the Sea Queen or Thief Lord in repayment of a slight that was thousands of years old, taking place in lands Harper never heard of. It was all unknowable.

She couldn't ask Maraline either. In truth, she doubted the Sea Queen would care to answer. Harper wasn't meant to pester her Goddess with trivialities; she was meant to serve. There was a connection of some kind between the Thief Lord and Sea Queen, all the old scriptures of both faiths said as much, although nobody could precisely explain it. Certainly their followers overlapped as many sailors were smugglers or pirates and knew to offer alms to the Thief Lord to ensure their illicit activities would succeed. Likewise, many assassins used the ocean to dispose of bodies and would tithe earnings in hopes Maraline wouldn't wash their murdered victims up on damning beaches with evidence intact. Beyond this, the two immortals seemed to know one another, although the nature of the relationship didn't have a corresponding mortal equivalent.

Harper's vows to maintain a virtuous chalice for the Sea Queen's power may run into trouble with help from Calista. The activities of a Dark Stalker involved lying, cheating, stealing, murdering, and were often celebrated with alcohol. The lone issue dodged of Calista being ill-equipped to harm Harper's virginity seemed a little paltry in comparison to how many other parts of the vows might be in danger if their relationship continued as Harper truly hoped it would.

Harper glanced back to Calista's sleeping form. She'd curled up without Harper to help warm the bed. Even coiled into a ball, barely visible in the light of the crackling fires, she set Harper's heart aflutter. Harper desperately wanted to say the words, to tell Calista she loved her. Saying so too soon could be disastrous though and she couldn't even risk saying it to Calista when she was asleep since there were more than a few tales of Dark Stalkers sleeping with one eye and one ear open to the world.

Calista made her feel beautiful and desirable in a world that often saw her only as forbidden fruit or unfathomably sacred. In either case, few people showed interest in her romantically as the former wouldn't risk angering the Sea Queen for a cheap thrill and the latter wouldn't blaspheme to think themselves worthy of touching a Goddess's chosen in such a way. Until Calista's advances, Harper wasn't even sure she favored women. She knew men lit no fire within her heart or between her legs, but women were often confusing and the ones who did show even a flicker of interest in her weren't the types she wished would. Calista was different though. Harper's heart swelled at the thought of her, she ached for her touch, and Harper's eyes couldn't keep from roaming liberally over Calista's body. Were her desires for Calista simply carnal, she might have more control over herself, but she was so intrigued by her too.

Harper slipped from the cloak and back between the heavy blankets. Calista gathered her up as soon as she was within arm's reach.

"You're chilly," Calista muttered drowsily. "Let me warm you."

Harper melted under Calista's touch. She relaxed and felt safe with Calista wrapped around her and indeed, she warmed quickly from the tender caresses. She was glad she hadn't whispered of her love since Calista did seem to be a light sleeper. Although she wanted to say something to her, something of lasting value to express a fraction of what she felt.

"I like when you put your mouth between my legs," Harper said, immediately regretting the choice of all the things she might have said.

Calista paused in the gentle stroking of her hands up and down Harper's back and then she burst into a light laughter. "Then we are well-matched since I like putting my mouth between your legs."

"I meant to say something better," Harper said, glad of the darkness to cover the warm blush she could feel positively painting her cheeks.

"That was honest and complimentary, so it will suffice for words shared in the dark," Calista replied.

Harper fell easily back to sleep.

Chapter 18:

Fire and Ice

Calista and Harper hid away from the world for two days, calling food to them through the servant bell cord reserved only for the most opulent rooms. They made excellent use of the stone bathtub only afforded to the nicest accommodations. Two days passed in a blur of sexual exploration, physical intimacy, and quiet conversations before Harper finally declared they needed to return to the world of the living, if only for the change of scenery. Reluctantly, Calista agreed to let their vacation from reality end. The opportunity to speak with Harper about running away with her arose several times over the two days, but Calista could never find the nerve to say anything. Still, as they walked from the room that was their oasis, she felt confident she'd outdistanced Brandinne enough to remove the threat entirely.

Arm-in-arm, they made their way to the main hall. The evening was already maturing and the great room was abuzz with food, alcohol, and merriment. The last few stragglers of the mercenary bands meant to take their rest at the Thundering Dawn arrived that afternoon, and everyone seemed to think that was ample reason to splash stacks of coins for the purpose of celebration.

Calista half-expected to see Brandinne at the Dagger Falls Company booth, but only the brothers and Ezra occupied the benches around the stone table. Athol and Sven were in the midst of a drinking game of their own creation that didn't appear to have very well defined rules. Great mugs of frothy brew awaited consumption in front of both brothers while the Sorceress appeared to favor a goblet of wine. Ezra was adjudicating the whimsical game, but the clarity of her memory for the regulations apparently wasn't appreciated by the brothers.

"Confound it all, you prudish librarian's assistant, don't quote me to me," Athol bellowed, spraying a great deal of beer foam from his moustache in the process. His head was swaying so liberally it was difficult to tell if he meant the statement for his brother or Ezra.

Ezra and Sven exchanged a look and began laughing.

"Who would quote you to anyone?" Sven asked.

"Who would be interested in anything you had to say aside from you?" Ezra added.

"Ah ha! Two questions in a row starting with the same letter." Athol smacked his fist against the table in celebration. "You both owe me a drink equal to the number of birds I can name."

Ezra and Sven lifted their drinks to begin, awaiting Athol's list of birds to determine how much they would consume.

"Bats!" Athol announced.

Ezra and Sven put their drinks down.

"Bats aren't birds," Harper corrected him.

"Now you owe us all a drink for knowing what bats aren't! In this game you can only know what something is, not what something isn't." Sven said. "Since you cannot imbibe, might I suggest your glowing friend there take the drinks in your stead? I'm sure after two days alone of whatever it is you two were doing, one of you must owe the other favors equal to that."

"Before we join, are the rules to this game written anywhere?" Calista asked.

"Ezra started to, but Athol made a rule that for any Sorceress scribblings to be valid they must be penned in such a way that he could understand them while drunk," Sven said.

"Which put a worthy end to anymore of that," Athol said before filling his mouth with another swallow of beer. "I'm barely literate when sober."

In the communal laugh shared after, Ezra pressed a rolled note into Calista's hand. She subtly opened it and read it quickly. There was no doubt from the bizarre, loopy handwriting that it was from Brandinne. Harper caught the change in Calista before she was able to secret the note away, such was the growing connection between them.

"Is something wrong?" Harper asked, her eyes following the note.

"Brandinne asked for another Jack's help on something that I should see to," Calista said. "I'm sure she is cross with how long

I've been unavailable—patience and manners aren't things Havvish are known for, after all."

"I would be happy to help," Harper said with a bright smile.

"And I would be glad to have your help if you wouldn't be such a grand distraction for me," Calista replied. "My mind wanders to delightful places in your company and I lose my focus all too easy."

"Very well, I will remain here until you return and do my best to oversee this preposterous game." Harper collected Calista's face in her hands and kissed her. Calista felt Harper's hips pressed against her in what was becoming an increasingly familiar way. The Sword Maiden always seemed to angle her lower body in closer during a kiss. The habit was added to the growing list of things Calista thought were adorable about Harper.

She wandered toward the stairs to return to her room for weapons and armor, chancing a glance back before vanishing into the hallway only to find Harper staring longingly after her. Catching the Sword Maiden watching her in such an unabashed way sent a happy tremble through Calista's stomach, and she blew a kiss to Harper that set the Sword Maiden's face aflame with blush and a happy smile.

Focus, even out of Harper's company, was difficult to come by. Back in her own room, Calista's attempts at putting on her armor hit several snags as she couldn't keep herself from thinking of Harper and what she would prefer to be doing. There was no doubt in her mind, she needed Harper to leave with her so they might go off on their own adventures, or simply find a private room somewhere in the warmer south where they could wear one another out.

With her armor finally donned, her weapons equipped, and her cowl covering her face, Calista shook the more distracting elements of her infatuation and brought herself to consider the task at hand. Brandinne's note described where to find the docks, explained only one ship would need to be set ablaze, and gave a vague description of how to find the assassination target. Calista didn't much care for letting another plan her jobs, but Brandinne's course was simplicity itself and Calista couldn't think of what she would do much differently.

Divine Touched

Calista slipped from the window in her room and slid down the snowy, slanted roof to the ledge below before dropping into the shadowy alleyway. Sneaking through deep snow was difficult for a lot of reasons. Her armor was black, which helped at night, but not in an entirely white landscape. If she kept to areas without traffic, her tracks would be obvious though, and so she had to split the difference of avoiding people and seeking them out. She began to wonder if Brandinne took such considerations with her own travel within the city.

Getting to the private dock took longer than Calista expected with the added difficulty of the snow. She'd learned long ago how to keep her activities clandestine in such weather, although she'd always allotted enough time, knowing it slowed her. The dock itself was tucked away on a difficult to spot lobe of the bay, well away from the glow of the lighthouse. Calista guessed a ship would likely need a guide boat to even find its way in. She rounded a small, abandoned boathouse amid a grove of fir trees heavily laden with snow. The docking area was just far enough out of town to provide privacy without being so far away as to arouse suspicions.

The twin waxing moons broke free of the partially cloudy night enough to illuminate the bay. The ship in question was anchored a fair bit from the dock as ice was threatening from the edges of the shallower water. One of the mooring ropes bowed down enough under the weight of snow and ice to provide Calista with an easy entrance if she could reach the end held within the icepack and climb it above the open water.

She made no effort to conceal her path to the icy shore as she didn't plan on taking the same route back. She tested the ice of the bay with one foot first and found it reasonably thick nearest the shore. About ten feet out from land, she began to wonder if her plan was a reasonable one. The ice beneath her feet was groaning and she became acutely aware that she was exposed and moving very slowly. Blessedly, the clouds solidified enough to cover the moons, dropping the bay into darkness. She doubted even the keenest eye could spot her among the ice anymore, although she also couldn't see if the ice was cracking either. She heard again and again what she thought might be breaking ice beneath her increasingly cold feet, but the layer never perceptibly moved.

Finally, when she was completely certain her next careful step would plunge right through, she reached out to grasp the heavy rope. She held with both hands to dangle from it and slung her legs up to begin crawling along it toward the ship.

About halfway up the rope, it occurred to her that it would have made far more sense for Brandinne to be the one to set the ship fire. Calista probably weighed forty or fifty pounds more than the little Havvish woman and the ice might not have even noticed Brandinne. A sinking thought followed on the first's heels: it was a trap and a clever one that would require a long walk back from a burning ship across already weakened ice, and that didn't even take into account if there were slaves already on the ship. Calista wouldn't willingly burn innocent people alive just to create a distraction to kill a single target.

Calista continued on regardless, curious to see what she might swipe from the ship. She wasn't sure she was going to set the requested fire anymore, but there might still be a few things worth stealing. She swung herself up to stand on the mounting of the frozen rope, peering over the edge of the railing to see where a guard might be. Not surprisingly, the deck looked clear. Getting a rowboat to and from the ship would require a good deal of doing through the slushy bay, making intruders unlikely. She glanced down to the frigid black water below and back to the encroaching sheet of ice she'd crossed. Whatever the crew was going to do with the ship, they would need to do it soon or risk having it crushed by the winter ice pack.

She slipped silently over the railing and made her way forward along the foredeck. It was a large, square-rigged cargo carrack that sat high in the water. Any drop off the edge would be a dozen foot fall into freezing waters with little hope of rescue. Still, she considered that a good option for eliminating a witness if someone should spot her; distracting the crew with the futility of trying to rescue one of their mates might be a good way to make an escape.

She waited at the narrow stairs leading down from the foredeck to the main deck. The cargo ports were open, which seemed odd. If the ship was a slaving vessel, the cargo couldn't be moved onto the ship too early as the cold might kill them and certainly would if some thoughtless person left the covers open in such a way.

Calista lowered herself over the front railing onto the main deck, dropping the last few feet to avoid leaving footsteps in the snow gathered along the stairs. She kept to the shadows, following the thickest, darkest path provided by the mast. As she came upon the first ajar port of two, she listened carefully. There wasn't any of the thrashing or bemoaning of fate she attributed to slave trafficking. In fact, the cargo hold was dead silent. She craned her neck to look in and found the hold largely full of casks, none big enough to hold a person. If she had to guess, they were cooking oil created by pressing stone berry nuts. She checked the other port and found the same cargo.

That would be the trap then: a ship full of highly flammable oil without a slave in sight. Calista thought she should seriously reconsider whether or not to kill Brandinne. This thought was cut short by two unrelated, but equally terrifying things. The first, and the most noticeable, was the sound of a crackling fire and flickering lights along the side of the ship she'd just come from. The second was the groaning of the hull in such a way that spoke of a far more imminent danger. Certainly wooden ships creaked and groaned, even in harbor, that much Calista knew, but the ship she stood on seemed reasonably new, and the sudden influx of noise might have seemed out of place for it even in a gale.

She walked to the side she suspected was on fire only to find the black water she'd just climbed above was no longer there. Ice had filled in the long gap of open water and was threatening to crush the ship like a dried leaf. And, as she noted secondarily, the ship was in fact on fire, seemingly started from the far end of the mooring rope she'd just climbed up.

She ran for the other side of the ship, hoping ice enclosed that side as well. She was no longer concerned with remaining silent and unseen as any noise she made was more than covered by the sounds of the hull buckling and anyone who cared to look for trouble would likely see the fire long before they saw her. A couple confused men emerged from the forecastle looking alarmed without a clear direction for their fear. Calista sprinted past them toward the opposite side's railing.

"You're going to want to abandon ship now," Calista said to them as she ran past.

She caught her harpoon on the outer edge of the railing and jumped off, giving slack on the chain slowly to make as soft a landing as possible. The ice not only covered the outside of the hull, but appeared to encase the entire bay without a drop of open water between her and the opposite shore. She made a reasonably soft landing on the thick ice. Even with her full weight coming down at a bit of a fall, the ice didn't so much as creak in protest. The ship the ice was pressing against, however, was making all sorts of horrible noises.

Calista pulled the slack out of the chain on her harpoon and gave it a swift yank to disengage the mechanism for the barbs. The apparatus came down to her, drawn in by the recoil on its spool. She snatched the metal harpoon head out of the air before it could strike her in the stomach, and took off running for the opposite shore. The men she'd passed were at the railing, shouting something after her, but not heeding her advice to abandon ship.

The fire finally broke through to the hull and the ship went up like a shattered lamp. An instant after, the ice finished cracking the hull open like an egg, spilling the burning oil across the bay. Despite the thickness of the ice, the burning oil did its work and cracks began shooting along beside Calista, racing ahead faster than she was running. She turned the corner, knowing she couldn't make it to the opposite shore in time, leapt over a crevice that opened in the newly iced over bay, and ran for the nearest land she could see, which was almost exactly where she'd walked onto the ice in the first place. Leaving the same way she came might make her easier to catch, but being caught sounded a lot more appealing than being burned to a crisp and dumped into the frigid bay.

The cracks in the ice easily caught up to her again, crisscrossed in front of her, and the bay opened up. She leapt across the first gap, finding a chunk of ice ahead that she hoped was large enough to support her weight. She almost lost her balance when the piece of ice shifted under her landing. The force of her jump carried her forward, the leading edge of the ice dunked under the water, and she used the momentum to launch herself toward the next piece. This piece was much smaller, and in no way able to hold her. It threatened to buckle beneath her immediately, forcing her to hurl herself off one leg blindly toward whatever might catch her. To her immense relief, the ice she fell sideways onto was the thick, unbroken section nearest the shore with no unfrozen water beneath. The impact hurt, but a bruised hip and shoulder was far better than falling into the water. She glanced back to watch the burning ship descend into the jagged teeth of the icy bay.

She scrambled up the shore into the grove of snowy trees, eager to be off any sort of ice and out of the flickering light of the oil fires that were still clinging to some of the larger chunks of ice around where the ship had gone down. The fire was no doubt Brandinne's doing, but the ice was divinely sent. None but the Sea Queen herself could freeze a bay so quickly, which begged the question of who was trying harder to kill her. If the ice hadn't crushed the ship, Brandinne's plan to kill her likely would have succeeded. The fire had shot straight up the rope Calista climbed to board the ship, leaving little doubt the Havvish woman followed her across the ice to set it and block off her only escape route. So, in a strange way, the Goddess intervened with the ice, giving Calista somewhere to jump down to rather than a cold, watery bay. Or, Maraline was trying to kill her as well and the two attempts on her life offset each other since one was of fire and the other ice. There was also the possibility that the Sea Queen froze the bay for an entirely unrelated reason, perhaps even just to be unexpectedly wrathful—a common motivation for the pantheon, and it was just the luck of the Jack that it coincided with Calista's need for an escape route.

Calista snuck along the edge of the bay, looking for the entrance to the dock. Men gathered to watch the ship sink and the strange suddenness of the bay freezing over. But the men holding torches and standing about on the shore weren't all that interested in the bay. As Calista crept closer, she could see they were gathered around something in a ring, setting several men with their backs to the epic scene of a burning boat sinking in the middle of instantly iced over water.

Someone small, at the edge of the group, tossed a torch almost directly at her and shouted in a shrill voice from the other side of the crowd, "There's the assassin!"

The same shrill voice called from a different part of the gathered group of men, "She killed good old Mr. Grayson!"

"I sure did, and you'll never catch me!" Calista heard the Havvish voice shout from a few feet behind her, clearly bouncing off the tree she was hiding beneath.

"Quick, get her before she gets away!" the same voice shouted from the same area the torch was thrown from.

The men rushed from their gathered position to give chase. Calista slashed upward into the branches above her with one of her daggers. The cut wasn't enough to cleave the branch from the tree, but more than enough to send the mass of snow piled on the limb cascading down on her pursuers as they neared, dousing their torches. The snow in the tree was a bit of a house of cards. When the lower branches dumped their load of snow, a small avalanche followed as the rest of the limbs higher up followed suit until a few hundred pounds of snow held on the boughs of the sixty foot tree unburdened themselves after several days of accumulation. Rather than scurry out the other side of the tree, she dove into the falling snow and rolled forward into the downpour from the upper branches and entangled herself into the other bodies trapped in the tiny avalanche.

The second wave of men circled around the back edge of the tree, seeking out her path. They found the one she'd used to sneak up to the tree, and, not knowing any better, followed it back toward the boathouse. The third wave of dockworkers began digging out the handful of people caught in the wash of snow. Calista cried for help with her voice restriction strap changing her cry to that of a hoarse young man. She held out her hands when the rescuers reached for her. Two large dockworkers plucked her from the pile, dusted her off, and resumed their search for the remaining people.

"You okay, lad?" an older man asked, unable to get much of a look at her in the dimness created when so many torches were doused by the snow.

"Fine, sir," Calista said hoarsely. "That'll teach me to try to be a hero."

"You're a good lad for trying," he replied, but she was already vanishing into the gathered people.

She fell farther and farther back as the crowd turned their attention to search after an assassin already within their midst until the mob left her behind entirely with the other stragglers. She turned off into an alley as they passed around a corner.

On the long, cold walk back toward the Thundering Dawn, Calista decided killing would be too easy for Brandinne. She would need to concoct something truly wicked to teach the little Havvish Jack a lesson. Then, she would probably kill her.

Chapter 19.

Getting Back

Calista was freezing cold and fuming mad by the time she walked back into the main hall of the Thundering Dawn Inn. She would have loved to run upstairs with Harper to warm herself in a hot bath, but first she had to balance the scales a little. She slunk into the shadows to the side of the door and waited for Harper to leave the company's booth, likely in need of a break from the drunken rowdiness of the brothers. Once Harper was gone, Calista made her way over to the table. Sven and Athol stared at her for a time without recognition while Ezra was out cold, face down on an open book.

"Has Brandinne come back yet?" Calista asked.

"We definitely would have missed her," Sven slurred.

"Not tonight you wouldn't," Calista said. "She's going to be in a gloating, celebratory mood. When she does get here, I need you to keep her busy."

"We're too drunk for a task," Athol said.

"That's perfect," Calista said. "Challenge her to a drinking contest."

"We're already drunk," Sven said.

"You don't have to win; you just have to keep her occupied." Calista slipped away, barely avoiding Harper's return from the bar where she was refilling the warmed milk and honey concoction she favored.

Within the darkened confines of the labyrinthine inn at night, Calista was little more than a shadow. Sneaking calmed her nerves some and the warm interior dispelled some of the chill from her hands and feet. By the time she found her way up to the lighthouse room, she was practically giddy with the prospect of dusting off her burglary skills.

She traced her finger along the doorframe, easily locating the strand of black hair tied between the gap. If Brandinne didn't have such a big mouth to mention liking the trick, Calista might not have looked for it. She slipped the strand off its mooring on one end, flicked the lock open with a couple prods from her Dark Stalker lock picks, and gently opened the door a tiny crack. She slid the straight blade dagger of the dual set out of her boot. Running the slender blade gently along the gap, she stopped when she felt resistance. Not stopping at just locating the tripwire along the bottom of the door, she continued her inspection, finding another trigger at the top as well. She flicked the blade of her knife to trigger the top trap, hearing a thump strike the other side of the door. Next, she positioned herself to the side of the door and gave it a hard shove with one hand, quickly retracting the hand to safety. The only sound to let her know the second trap sprung was dripping liquid on the plank floor. Calista glanced inside the room with the fully opened door. The scent was subtle and sour. It was far too dark to see the liquid, but Calista guessed from the smell and use in a trap that it was likely an acid of some kind.

"Paranoid little thing," Calista muttered to herself.

She stepped over the puddle of acid into the room and gently closed the door behind her. A thick crossbow bolt was jutting from the interior face of the door, explaining the thumping noise of the first trap.

Calista stood in the center of the room and turned slowly to scan the entirety of the darkened, circular parapet. There was a sense to breaking and entering. Unpracticed, unthinking thieves simply rifled through everything, broke a lot in the process, and grabbed whatever they thought most valuable as it surfaced. A smart thief, one who didn't wish to be easily caught, deduced where the best items were hidden, took enough not to be readily noticed, and replaced everything so the owner might not know for several days that they'd even been robbed. Her gaze fell on the wooden lighthouse carving sitting atop a stack of little rocks—very carefully stacked rocks from the look of it.

Calista set aside the lighthouse and plucked the top layer of rocks free to reveal a bag. She freed the heavy sack of coins from the carefully placed pyramid of stones. When stealing a stash of money, an old thief master once told her, always change the container it is held in—coins become property of whoever possesses them, but the container will always belong to whom it is

164

stolen from. Calista snatched one of Brandinne's shirts from a neatly folded pile on one of the benches, laid it out on the bed, and dumped the coins onto it. Amid the coins, were a handful of tiny spiked balls that Calista would bet her life contained poison. Calista flicked away the poisoned caltrops with the tip of her dagger, leaving only the coins. If it were a warmer climate, she likely would have placed a snake or nest of scorpions into the bag for Brandinne to find, but, seeing as she was in the frozen north, she settled on the more poetic snow swiped from the sill outside one of the many tiny windows. She replaced the snow-filled bag, stacked the rocks around it, and set the lighthouse on top.

Calista reloaded the crossbow for the trap, collected her makeshift bag of coins from the bed, and slipped out the door, taking extra care to replace both the trap triggers and the hair across the frame. With any luck, Brandinne would find everything as she expected it, and step right across the threshold into the acid from her own sprung trap. When she found the snow in place of her money, she would know precisely who robbed her, but would only have quickly melting proof of the deed.

Pleased with her progress thus far, Calista decided it was worth it to create a stash so Brandinne couldn't counter with a similar trick. Certainly Calista's departure was only a couple days away, but there was no need to take any chances with escape so close at hand. She snuck down the back stairs and into the stables. She found Aerial's stall more by sense memory and feel than anything else. The powerful mare greeted her with a whinny upon approach. Calista instinctively shushed the horse, and, to her surprise, Aerial replied with a softer whinny.

Calista slipped into the stall, pausing briefly to caress Aerial along the neck. She knelt below the grating affixed to the side of the stall intended to hold hay and began digging. A foot down into the hard, dusty ground was all she could manage before she started hitting frozen soil. She placed the makeshift bag of coins in the hole and covered it. If she had to guess, she'd stolen between forty and fifty gold depending on how many of the coins were bronze or silver, which she couldn't see in the low light.

She gave Aerial a hug around the neck. The horse again settled its chin along Calista's back as if to return the embrace. "Guard our stash until it's time to go," Calista whispered to the horse. "The three of us will be on our way to a warmer winter in the south before you know it."

Back around the front of the inn, with every intention of re-entering as though she hadn't arrived yet, Calista was stopped by two familiarly shaped men in guard uniforms walking toward the front door. She gathered up a handful of snow and hurled the hard-packed ball, striking Turbald directly on the side of his dented helmet.

"Draw steel, I'm under attack!" Turbald shouted, drawing his own sword to fend off any other incoming snowballs.

Ulrich sighed and waited until Calista emerged from the shadows. "Could you have killed him?" Ulrich asked.

"I could have killed both of you, but why would I want to do that?" Calista said. "We're friendly enough, aren't we?"

"Just so." Ulrich encouraged Turbald to sheath his sword with a couple hard nudges of his elbow. "We were called down to a wealthy merchant's private dock this evening to investigate the murder of a kind, old exporter of cooking oil. Of all the heinous people in this city, we were a little shocked to learn someone would kill him first."

"I couldn't imagine what issues a person might have with an oil merchant, but as a Jack is prone to hearing tall tales from drunken louts in the wee hours of the night, I feel honor bound to say I know who is claiming responsibility even if I can't speak to their motivation," Calista said.

"And who might'n that be?" Turbald asked.

"A Havvish woman with black hair and exuberant personality was bragging up the coming downfall of some sort of thieves guild. I believe her exact words were, 'I'll snip the horns from the horseshoe since those dunces can't even defend the merchants paying protection.'" Calista saw the comment regarding the thief brand landed with both guards and members of the thieves guild in good standing. "It would seem a foolhardy thing to brag about if she didn't intend to supplant such an organization with one of her own."

Ulrich nodded his understanding. "This is grave news indeed." He slipped a small coin purse from his belt and tossed it to Calista. "There is payment of five gold coins for the valuable information. If you'd actually seen who killed dear Mr. Grayson, you might have made the full sum, but it would seem nobody will have easy work before them after tonight."

"Would that I made it down to the docks before such calamity befell so many." Calista snatched the thrown bag out of the air. What did she care if they shorted her on the assassination contract? She hadn't actually killed the man and even at the promised rate of ten gold coins, it was an insultingly low figure. Besides, she'd just stolen what she'd needed from the actual assassin.

"Speaking of which…" Ulrich turned on his heels as though he never intended to actually leave. "You may want to take a look at the bay at some point."

"It's froze over from land to horizon, it is," Turbald finished for his partner.

"It would seem, without ships to come in or ships to go out, we'll all be stuck with what we have at hand for the rest of the winter," Ulrich said. "Were I you, I would make myself comfortable with my current situation."

Calista strained to tamp down the smile tugging at the corners of her mouth, managing to strangle the smug expression into something of a grimace. "Is that what you would do?"

"Indeed, were I you. Have a good evening." Ulrich bowed curtly to her and walked off with a grinning Turbald at his side.

Calista waited until they were well gone before she ventured to the end of the lane leading up to the Thundering Dawn. Down the hill, through the haze of wood smoke, she saw the full bay, glimmering in the scant light of the twin moons, frozen for as far as the eye could see. If she wasn't sure before that the Goddess Maraline had a hand in the ice, she was certain now. She shrugged it off and ventured back up to the inn. Her plan never required the bay, and now that she had enough money from robbing Brandinne, all she really needed was Harper's agreement to leave with her.

The main hall of the inn was dying down quickly with the growing lateness of the hour. The Dagger Falls Company booth held three occupants, only one of which was awake and aware. Sven and Athol were face down on the stone surface, snoring loudly, hands still wrapped around massive tankards of unfinished ale. Brandinne was sitting between them, bouncing stone berry nuts off their heads into the drinks. Whenever she successfully got one of the nuts into the tankard, she took a drink of her own massive mug.

"Hey, partner," Brandinne said. "It's good to see you made it back after all."

"You couldn't have thought that would actually work." Calista folded her arms over her chest and raised an eyebrow at the little Havvish woman.

"It'd be pretty dumb to say 'yes' now," Brandinne said. "Regardless of what I did or didn't think, you're alive, you weren't apprehended, the target is dead, everyone got to see a ship full of burning oil sinking on a snowy night…I mean, we're all richer for the experience, right?"

Calista leaned forward, placing her hands on the edge of the table to stare Brandinne directly in the eyes. Her voice dropped an octave and took on a cruel edge. "You can't beat me at anything— riddles, betrayal, seduction, choose whatever you like and know that I'm better than you. In truth, I could kill you whenever I want, but you're not worth the time or effort it'd take to bury you in a tiny grave. Now, if you'll excuse me, I have a buxom, blond Sword Maiden and a comfy bed waiting to warm me up after a long night of making you look like a fool." Calista strolled away casually showing her back to Brandinne in a blatant display of disrespect between Jacks.

"This isn't over!" Brandinne's shrill voice shouted after her.

"Nope, but soon you'll wish it was," Calista replied.

Harper waited long after Brandinne returned from the errand that Calista was meant to be helping on. She waited even after Ezra drunkenly passed out, slept it partially off face down on the table, awoke, and stumbled up to bed. She waited through most of the drinking contest that arose between Sven, Athol, and Brandinne after the Havvish woman strolled in all grins and bluster. Finally, when her exhaustion won out over her worry, she could wait no longer and decided to head to bed. Brandinne said it was probably for the best as Calista might not come back to the inn that night, although she would say no more about the task they were supposedly working on together. It struck Harper as exceedingly odd that Brandinne remained silent on a topic.

Even within the comfortable confines of her room, Harper couldn't find sleep. She was yawning excessively and physically weary, but every time she laid her head down, thoughts of all the horrible things that might have happened to Calista flooded into her mind, rousing her to stand and pace. She was up and wandering her room for the fifth time in what she guessed was an hour when she decided it was time to get dressed to go look. A soft knock came at the door a moment after.

Calista opened the door gently and poked her head in. All the worry and energy drained from Harper in a sudden rush that nearly knocked her from her feet. She rushed to the door to pull Calista in and hold her close. Calista, for her part, returned the embrace although she didn't seem to share in Harper's relieved concern.

"I was worried about you," Harper whispered into Calista's hair.

"It was a lengthy errand, but nothing dangerous," Calista said.

"But Brandinne said…"

"That's just the thing about Brandinne—the more she talks the more apparent it becomes that she doesn't know anything," Calista said.

The comment struck on a strange part of Harper's still overworked mind. Brandinne made it all too clear that she thought Harper was worthy of leading her own group and was likely the most powerful warrior within the Dagger Falls Company. If Calista's assessment of Brandinne was accurate, then none of that could be true. It frustrated Harper that her mind would come to such a conclusion out of what was meant as a platitude from Calista.

"Are you okay?" Calista asked, drawing back to look Harper in the eyes.

"Yes, my mind is wandering from so much worry." Harper wondered if Calista shared Brandinne's assessment of her or if she simply saw her as an attractive, yet ultimately frivolous swordswoman in fancy armor. Calista was so dangerous, so fast, and so gifted with weapons that Harper couldn't imagine how she could ever match up. In the one, brief altercation between them,

Calista fought her armed only with what could be scrounged in a stable, and easily could have killed her once she was blinded.

"I am chilled from my long night and could use a good deal of warming up," Calista said. "If you're equal to the task of restoring feeling to my frozen parts, I would greatly appreciate it."

Calista's words cut through the muddled mess in Harper's head, striking directly on the part of her very soul that desired Calista's comfort and pleasure. Her hands were set to the work of disrobing Calista before she even knew what they were doing. The skin she found beneath the leather armor was indeed cold, and Harper's heart jumped with renewed worry.

"Perhaps it would be warmer in bed," Calista said.

Harper concurred. The bed was well stocked with thick blankets, seal furs, and puffy pillows. It also sat somewhat between the two fireplaces, making it one of the coziest spots in the room. She guided the increasingly nude Calista toward the bed while removing the final trappings of the freezing leather armor.

"The bed would be warmer with two," Calista said as she slipped beneath the covers.

This also made sense to Harper. The shared body heat between them always made the bed far more comfortable than when Harper slept alone. She slipped into the bed beside Calista and pulled her close so she might impart some warmth.

"It'll probably work better if your skin is pressed directly against mine." Calista's hands began gently tugging at Harper's night clothing.

The intent finally dawned on Harper when Calista had her nearly undressed as well. She aided in removing the nightgown and warm stockings, and pressed the entirety of her body flush against Calista's once they were equally nude.

"Your skin is warm, but I believe your mouth might be even warmer," Calista whispered against Harper's neck.

The words sent an excited tremble through Harper's stomach. Wishing to have the same effect on Calista, she whispered back, "Guide me to the parts you would like warmed by my mouth and I will see them made hot."

Chapter 20:

Distant Drums

Harper awoke warm and happy with her arms and legs fully wrapped around Calista. Gently, in the hope of not awaking her partner, she touched a few of the parts of Calista's body that she found coldest the night before. Her endeavor not to be caught failed almost immediately.

"If I were a deeper sleeper, would you molest me to your heart's content?" Calista asked.

"I was seeing if you were still chilly," Harper said.

"I am warmed to perfection, but don't let that stop you from touching what you wish to touch." Calista lifted her head to kiss Harper in a long, sweet embrace.

Harper could already feel her desire for Calista rising. It was an insatiable craving that didn't seem remotely diminished by intimacy. If anything, the more Calista pleased her, the more she craved. Already, before the kiss even broke, her thinking was far too chaotic to focus on anything but the woman in her bed.

"I have something to ask you," Calista whispered.

"Anything," Harper cooed, willing Calista to know how pliable she was.

"I want to travel south for the winter," Calista said, "and I want you and Aerial to come with me."

This shocked Harper from the entirely erotic place her mind had gone. "What do you mean? What about the Dagger Falls Company?"

"We're not a good fit for them," Calista said. "We are destined for greater things than drinking and hunting easy treasure."

"Then you think me a capable warrior?" Harper asked, her heart already on the verge of cracking should Calista say anything remotely negative.

"I think you are amazing." Calista pulled away far enough as if to see if Harper was joking. "You fought Jevvon to a standstill—the same veteran warrior who bested both brothers at once. You're so magnificent and inspiring that I think you capable of leading the Sea Queen's Exalted Armies someday."

Harper could feel the sting of happy tears at the corners of her eyes. "But what of the company? They need us both."

"They need us to leave," Calista said with a light shake of her head. "They rely too heavily upon you to ever grow and excel. With me there, that will only get worse. Besides, I'm certain Brandinne would return to the company if we were gone, and she seemed to get along far better with the brothers after a little drinking contest."

It all made so much sense when Calista laid it out in such a way. Harper could see precisely what she meant about the brothers' skills stagnating as they relied more and more on her and Aerial. The loss of a Jack the season prior hadn't even stopped them seeking work, but Aerial being partially blinded did. Harper's long held belief that Athol was the greatest warrior among them and Ezra the most important piece to the company's tactics was apparently completely erroneous.

"What of us?" Harper asked. "Is this simply professional courtesy and desire for warmer weather?"

"It is adoration, infatuation, and lust as well," Calista said with a bright smile. "To say I am growing increasingly fond of you would hardly do my feelings justice. In time I would share more than just a bed with you."

Harper could hardly believe her ears and her heart would not heed any advice to venture cautiously into such lovely words. She could think of no impediment to leaving with Calista—it felt fated and wonderful. "Yes, yes of course I will travel south with you," Harper said.

"Then we must go to the marketplace today and book passage for the last merchant caravan leaving tomorrow," Calista said.

"So soon?"

"It is best not to linger with such a thing." Calista moved to slip from the bed, but Harper grasped her by the hip and drew her back.

"Perhaps we could tarry a moment longer," Harper whispered to her.

Calista's hand slid down the rigid muscles of Harper's stomach and between her powerful thighs. She pressed her fingers down the length of Harper's slit and found her not only wet, but her clit eager for attention. "It would seem you have need of me," Calista purred.

Harper pondered something clever or lovely to say in reply, but Calista was already on her way down Harper's body, beneath the covers. Before she could even murmur a reply, Calista's mouth covered the part of her that always promised pleasure and Harper's focus was lost to the much craved sensation. Inside her, the flicker of the Goddess's power that Harper always knew to be blue, grew with her building ecstasy and began turning a shade of purple. It wasn't something she could see with her eyes, but felt with her heart. When she opened her mouth to try to articulate the exceedingly strange magical transformation taking place within her mystical spark, the only thing that could escape her lips were gasps and moans of pleasure.

Calista licked at her hardened nub with increased vigor at such verbal encouragement until all Harper could see within her mind's eye was the glowing purple fire of her divine touched power and all she could feel was the explosive gratification coursing through her body. The building wave of pleasure crested as it had before and brought with it a wave of unimaginable bliss. In the afterglow of such joy, the divine spark within her subsided some, but remained larger, more intense, and still purple rather than blue. The transformation should have vexed Harper, but her thundering heart could only focus on Calista.

She pulled her lover up from between her legs and kissed her fiercely, tasting herself on Calista's mouth. The taste and feel of Calista's tongue only drove Harper's desire to grow. She was not in control of her emotions, yet she could not bring herself to care as her mind was already sparked to wonder what Calista tasted like.

"I want you to guide me to know how best to please you with my mouth," Harper murmured, wishing the request hadn't sounded so stilted.

"I suppose our efforts last night were more palliative than strictly pleasurable," Calista said. "Very well, I will show you my preferred position."

Harper allowed herself to be guided to having her upper body propped up partially on the pillows. She watched in great comfort and eager anticipation as Calista's alluring body rose above her to kneel on the bed with her knees to either side of the pillows cradling Harper's head. From her vantage point of having Calista spread fully around her, Harper could see up Calista's body as her lover leaned forward to grasp the headboard. Harper believed Calista was lovely from most any angle, but the entirely different view offered only the most erotic aspects of Calista in new and exciting ways.

Harper thought to crane her neck up to taste of the lovely woman's line above her, but Calista instead spread her legs, slowly lowering herself to Harper's mouth. Harper reached her hands up the backs of Calista's incredibly limber legs to grasp at her thighs as she buried her face into what she'd wished to taste ever since the notion of licking to provide pleasure was introduced to her.

For her part in the guidance, Calista wordlessly moved her body to place Harper's tongue and lips where they would feel the best. She rolled her hips as though in the middle of an alluring belly dance, never losing contact between Harper's mouth and the soft folds between her own legs.

Harper held onto Calista's silken thighs more out of the need to touch as much of her lover as possible than any need to guide her. She could taste and smell Calista in entirely new ways and she thrilled in the differences between the taste of herself on Calista's kiss and the pure, unadulterated taste of Calista directly pressed onto her mouth. Harper was eager to give pleasure, and she was gratified to hear Calista's blissful moans, but equally she derived her own enjoyment from the act. She liked the taste of the wetness from between Calista's fold, she liked the feel of her lover parting over her mouth, and she delighted in noticing the change in Calista's nub as it sought out attention in much the same way her own did. Harper found she also favored the position Calista was showing her and looked forward to trying it from the other end as well although she doubted she could ever match Calista's graceful, full-body undulations.

To Harper's surprise, Calista reached down from the headboard with one of her hands, and guided Harper's gripped fingers away from her thigh. "You are meant to use only your mouth in this position so you might pleasure yourself with your hands," Calista said in between gasping breaths.

Harper complied with the instruction, removing her hands from Calista's thighs to run them down her own body where her right hand stopped at her breasts and her left continued on to the slit between her legs. Rather than return her hand to the headboard, Calista instead gripped at Harper's hair in an intense, yet loving way as she continued her writhing dance upon Harper's mouth.

The sensations were nearly overwhelming. The tangy taste of Calista on her tongue, the almost spicy scent of her wetness, and the beautiful view up her body where Calista's arm that crossed to hold Harper's hair pressed her already heavenly breasts somewhat together to give Harper an all too beautiful view up at the bottom of Calista's artistic bust. Harper had never known such a loss of control even as the desire for Calista gripped her fully; she rubbed at her own pleasure nub furiously driving herself toward another wave of ecstasy—she kneaded her own breast finding it too provided pleasure when touched in such a way at such a time. A small, frivolous part of Harper wished for her and Calista to experience at the same time the satisfaction she did not even have a word for yet. She felt she might be behind as Calista appeared to be on the verge of explosion, yet when her lover's writhing became more irregular, and her moans more intense, Calista didn't stop or slow. Harper, under the pressure of her own rubbing, experienced something of a distracted wave, while Calista seemed to be finishing her third as the pleasure rose and fell quickly in her once the waves began.

Calista slipped from Harper's mouth, sliding down her body rather than un-straddling herself. She kissed Harper as if in a daze, taking a few moments to lick the ample slick of herself from Harper's mouth and lower face. There was something infinitely gratifying for Harper in seeing Calista's body dappled with sweat and still glowing from arousal well-tended.

"You experienced pleasure?" Harper asked.

"Thrice over," Calista said, "and the word for it is orgasm."

"You can orgasm thrice?"

Divine Touched

"With such a giving lover as yourself, I could have as many as I could stand," Calista said, drawing Harper's lips to hers for another kiss. "As could you most likely if you should so desire. It's just a matter of finding what brings it out in you."

"There are so many things I must know, so many names for things I have no words for," Harper said, a little in awe of the entire experience.

"I would gladly instruct you," Calista purred. Her hand made its way down between Harper's legs. She seemed pleased at the work Harper had done on herself during the exceptionally intense lovemaking. Her fingers caressed across Harper's folds in delicate touches. "Although it has many names, this, as a whole, shares a word with a cat and a plant. By my preference, it is known as a pussy."

Harper had heard reference to it as such long ago, although the favored terminology for it among the brothers and most adventurers was a short, clipped, vulgar sounding word that Harper didn't care for at all. She was glad Calista seemed to prefer the name pussy as it sounded velvety to match the way it felt.

"And this, does it have a name?" Harper guided Calista's fingers up to her hardened nub, half out of direction of the question and half because she desperately wanted Calista to touch her there.

"It is a cute, short word for a cute, short appendage." Calista leaned in closer to Harper's mouth until their lips danced across each other with the speaking of every word. Breathlessly she whispered, "clit."

It was good to have preferred words for such things. The vague terms she'd learned from animal husbandry, the drunken talk of other mercenaries, and the awkward explanations of her mother long ago never seemed to fit things in quite the way Calista's words did. It all felt wonderfully beautiful when Calista said such things, especially in her sultry tone and southland accent.

"Will you show me other ways to give you pleasure?" Harper asked.

"Should you like, I would show you every way in which your body can give and receive carnal delights," Calista whispered. "The ways in which we are meant to fit with one another are too numerous to count, and, in time, you will come to learn what you like best as well. I have shown you but a few of the places on your

176

body where touching and licking provides pleasing sensations, but these are not the only ones and they can often be combined—touching here, licking there—to create entirely new enjoyments."

It all sounded like such a grand adventure to Harper and one she was infinitely pleased to be taking with Calista. She felt vulnerable and safe at once, such was the trust Harper felt was growing between them. Wherever Calista wished to go, Harper felt eager to follow not only as it pertained to what they might do in the comfort of a bed, but also in whatever direction Calista might wish to go after they headed south for the winter.

Getting passage booked with the merchant caravan wasn't an easy matter. With the port closed by ice, the people looking to travel or ship goods south were all pushed to the final wagon train. The bag of coins stolen from Brandinne was indeed mostly gold, but even at that, Harper had to make up the rest of the money required for Calista's passage. It wounded Calista's pride a little to have someone, especially Harper, pay her way. She only consoled herself with the fact that when they reached Ovid, Calista would have money enough to pay Harper back and much, much more.

The rest of the preparations ate up most of the day. Harper's money was tied up in the temple rather than the inn like the other members of the Dagger Falls Company, which made it far easier to collect without drawing suspicion. They would tell Sven, Athol, and Ezra of their intentions to leave over dinner, sleep well one last night in the inn, sign papers of severance from the company with the guild in the morning, and be on their way south after breakfast.

Calista didn't like mentally spending money for a job done, but not yet collected on. She felt it distracted her from tasks at hand and payment wasn't always guaranteed upon completion in her line of work. There was also the matter of Jacks owing their livelihood to luck and never wanting to jinx a job by counting on the outcome. Lesser thieves and rogues talked fancifully or dejectedly about a final grand job of epic difficulty and even greater reward that would finally allow them to retire—most dreamed of such an unattainable goal while the rest quashed such dreams by stating they never knew anyone to have done it. But that was just the point, and Calista knew it. Anyone good enough to acquire such an opportunity and succeed at it would know enough to vanish in their retirement, which was precisely what Calista planned to do. Once they reached Ovid, she would set herself up as a shadow benefactor, purchase a mercenary company for Harper, and travel with her under an alias. When they grew tired of adventure they would retire into opulence in the warm south, perhaps both taking on new names for anonymity.

Calista cuddled closer to Harper's side as they walked up the hill toward the Thundering Dawn. The late afternoon brought with it a reprieve from the weather. The autumn sky broke through the clouds with a pale blue dome and a biting cold. Calista took it as a good omen, although Harper said it portended of lousy sailing weather to come. That was fine with Calista since they were traveling by land.

Within the Thunder Dawn's main hall, the drinking and reverie was already picking up where it left off the night before. Harper and Calista parted ways briefly so that Harper might see to packing the rest of her items. Calista made her way to the bar to partake in a celebratory brandy. The wait for service from the harried bar staff was lengthy, but Calista didn't mind. She didn't plan on drinking to excess anyway so as long as the barkeep noticed her before dinner, there wasn't any hurry.

"You ruined a perfectly good pair of boots," Brandinne said, practically materializing on the barstool next to where Calista stood.

"Technically *you* ruined the boots since the trap was your own," Calista said.

"I don't suppose it would do me any good to search your room for my money," Brandinne said.

"Since you probably already did, I suppose you know the answer to that," Calista replied. "Let me save you time in further searching though—the money is spent."

Brandinne shrugged and turned her attention to the bar. "No doubt spent on leaving town on that last merchant caravan. It's not how I would have liked to get rid of you, but it was a way I considered regardless: paying to have you gone. I am surprised it was enough though, unless you've made money elsewhere to add to what you stole from me."

"Some, but not enough," Calista said, finally getting the barkeep's attention to order her drink. "Harper made up the rest. She's coming with me." Calista took up the brandy poured for her, turned to Brandinne, and polished off the tumbler of cheery liquid in a single gulp. "The game is at an end, and you lost."

"We'll just see about that," Brandinne hissed.

"Whatever you're planning on doing, you'd better do it soon." Calista directed Brandinne's attention to a shady group of Dwarves entering through one of the smaller side doors meant for busboy children. "Because I think those bearded gentlemen are here to see you." Calista distanced herself enough from Brandinne to make sure the Havvish woman could see who the Dwarves were actually interested in. Calista didn't need to watch the Dwarves to know their triangulations through the inn were focused on Brandinne; the look on Brandinne's face said it all. "I didn't have a burning ship or angry mob at my disposal, so I decided to use something that would actually work. I feel like we should say our goodbyes now since you might not be around tomorrow morning."

Calista left Brandinne to her fate. Even amid the crowded room, Calista knew of a dozen ways a person might kill another without drawing too much undue attention. If Brandinne ran, that would make it all the easier. Calista practically floated to the Dagger Falls Company booth where Athol, Sven, and Ezra were deep in a philosophical discussion about burial rites.

"I'm just saying, doesn't it strike you as odd that the way we dispose of our dead is often the same way we dispose of our garbage," Sven said.

"Yes, yes, you've made your case for burning and burying, but what of the north men who send their dead out into the sea on funeral ships?" Ezra asked.

"Some larger cities that are unafraid of the Sea Queen's wrath use unmanned garbage barges," Sven countered.

"Confound you, brother, you're forgetting the most important part of a funeral in your comparison," Athol said.

"Which is?"

"Taking drunken advantage of the mourning, lonely widow!" Athol smacked his brother on the shoulder, nearly knocking him from the booth. "Make no mistake, once I have burned and buried your body like garbage, I will find mutual consolation in the arms and bed of your wife. No one participates in such blatant debauchery after disposing of garbage."

"Conceding, of course, that some people are indeed garbage to be disposed of," Ezra added.

"Agreed," Athol so conceded.

"Then consider me departed of this world and see to my wife," Sven said. "She awaits me at home even now to shout me silly, belittle my manhood, and demand coin. You're likelier to find a frying pan to the side of the head than the marital bed though."

"You lack husbandly charm." Athol let out a long, multi-toned belch to punctuate his point.

"Perhaps our lovely Jack here could give you pointers in seduction," Ezra said, indicating Calista who had long stood at the edge of the table, watching with a bemused grin. "She appears a proper tramp, able to bed those formerly believed unbedable."

"I wouldn't have thought you the type to mistake meanings of words," Calista chided. "Tramp implies I am easily lured to sex while the rest of your statement praises my ability to seduce those not easily lured."

"Harlot then?" Ezra sneered.

Calista laughed at this. If Ezra knew how close that was to true in light of Harper's paying half of Calista's ticket aboard the merchant caravan, the comment would've held teeth. As it stood, Ezra was blindly reaching for a word that might nick Calista's impervious veneer.

"I come from a land where that term is hardly an insult," Calista said. "Harlot is accurate enough in this case, although you are unwitting to the reasons why, so call me a harlot and let us move on from there."

"Challenge," Brandinne said from behind Calista. A mandolin clattered onto the table before anyone could even take notice of the Havvish woman who threw it.

Calista smirked down to the stringed instrument. Brandinne's plan was painfully obvious. She needed to make herself the center of attention so a hidden dagger or poisoned dart wouldn't find its way into her without being noticed by all.

"Stakes?" Calista asked.

"A secret kept weighed against a chest delivered," Brandinne said.

Calista turned to finally face her. Brandinne actually looked a little nervous. The chest delivered would no doubt contain Brandinne and the delivery method would involve Calista and Harper taking the chest south with them when they departed. Calista could also guess the secret kept would be in regards to her own divine touched status rather than the more obvious news of departure to be delivered later that night. Calista could play a mandolin, although only passably well. In truth, she played only slightly better than she sang, which certainly didn't leave her with much hope of winning any challenges in either. Still, she did have one trick up her sleeve…

"Terms being to the audience's favor?" Calista asked.

"Certainly," Brandinne said, chancing a few furtive glances over her shoulders to see if the Dwarves were closing in.

"Accepted." Calista scooped up the mandolin, slung the strap over her shoulder, and tested the tune of the instrument with a strum.

"Challenge!" Athol shouted to collect the attention of the inn.

After the heated and wholly entertaining riddle competition, the gathered adventurers populating the inn were all too eager to see a rematch between the two talented Jacks. Calista directed Athol to construct easily traversed pathways between the multiple bars around the edge of the main hall using tables. The mercenaries, excited for a show, willingly gave up tables and chairs. Calista and her mandolin were carried to stand on one of the countertops while Brandinne and her lute were ferried to another.

"I defer to the challenger in this," Calista said loud enough to silence the excited throng of half-drunk adventurers. "Age before beauty being the reason before—this time I will defer on the grounds that the poor thing is always the last to know when it rains."

The gathered mercenaries let out a collective chuckle, turning their attention to Brandinne, expecting a witty retort. Sadly, the Havvish Jack seemed more interested in getting the competition underway and began strumming out a tune on her lute. Calista took the opportunity to untie the top strings on her tunic to create an astounding amount of cleavage, tussled her hair, and gathered all the trinket jewels from the bag she'd originally taken from the mugger she'd rolled, adorning her hands with it until her fingers positively gleamed and slung on both necklaces, letting the pendants dangle between her breasts. Judging from the soft, sweet music flowing from Brandinne's lute, Calista was over matched in talent. She only knew a couple songs, but they were fast, catchy, and easy to whip a crowd up with.

When Brandinne finished her soft, dulcet ballad, leaving the gathered mercenaries a little stunned and touched, they turned to Calista, some seemingly surprised by her slight transformation. Calista started off in a flurry of simple, yet pleasing chords strummed out on the mandolin. She took long-legged strides down the bar top, leaning down occasionally as she walked and played to show off her cleavage above the instrument. The firelight and candles in the inn caught the rings on her fingers to sparkle as she strummed quickly, and she whipped her hair with every flourish to add visual appeal to the entirely basic tune she played.

The gathered men and woman, addicts of adventure and excitement already, were wet clay in her hands. She swung her hips this way through the music, and they followed, she brought it back around, tossing a glance and a wink with a flurry of strumming, and they were falling over each other to get into her line of sight. The song she was playing was little more than a collection of basic chords alternating with an occasional changeup, but Calista rightly guessed her audience knew little of music, yet adored a good spectacle—adventurers were an immature, unrefined lot.

Calista threw the attention back to Brandinne knowing full well her little display of shiny rings, exposed cleavage, and a fast-paced catchy song, were winning the audience away from a far more talented musician. Brandinne smiled though with her entirely too-toothy grin and started off on her own musical tear. She didn't have the raw sex appeal Calista did, but she tried her best to make up for it with a brilliant show of musical prowess. Her fingers flew across the strings plucking out an incredibly complex tune.

She cut off at one point in the music, throwing it back to Calista as if she were meant to continue the same piece. Calista tried her best, although she was forced to strum out only the

Cassandra Duffy

simpler rhythm rather than the incredibly dexterous plucking portions. She made her way across the bar tops, hips swaying, hair swishing back and forth, and a twirl added in here and there whenever she royally screwed up a portion as if to give visual apology to her faulty playing. Brandinne figured out what she was doing entirely too late. By the time Calista shot the music back to her, they were standing next to each other, well within the audience's field of vision. Brandinne was going to out play her, but Calista would hold people's attention, even when she wasn't playing, simply by being eye candy beside the superior musician.

Brandinne picked out an increasingly simple tune, drawing herself closer to Calista in the playing of it. Calista glanced down in surprise at the Havvish woman who was standing directly next to her, putting on something of her own show, although not nearly with the style Calista could muster. One of Brandinne's turns didn't fully bring her all the way around to face the audience again, which Calista initially thought was a mistake.

"I'm sorry, okay?" Brandinne said, using the partial pirouette to shield her speech from the audience. "You can have Harper, I swear to keep your secret about being divine touched, and you don't even have to smuggle me out of here if you don't want to. You're better than me and you win. You don't need to have me killed to prove that anymore since I readily admit it"

Calista thought she was going soft in the heart or the head for even considering what she was considering. She strolled away from Brandinne in something of a show, letting the Havvish woman think she was rejecting the proposal. As Brandinne's playing began to fade, Calista picked up the music, adding her own strummed mandolin to the song, carrying a rhythm over Brandinne's melody until they matched. The song was simple enough that Calista could keep up, but still displayed both their talents.

The audience seemed to like the sudden shift of competition into an impromptu concert, cheering and pounding their fists upon tables to match the beat. Calista made her way back down the bar under the adulations to shoot a single comment in Brandinne's direction.

"Call it a momentary reprieve, but you owe me now," Calista whispered as she walked past.

Divine Touched

At the end of the bar, Calista hopped down to a table amid the crowd, which whipped the audience into a frenzy. Surrounded on three sides by cheering mercenaries, she opened her mouth to sing, knowing her voice didn't need to be perfect to be adored at that point.

Her song was cut off before it could begin by the thunder of hurled rocks striking stone walls. The music tapered out and the entirety of the main hall went silent. Several more crashes were followed by the warning bell ringing in the bay and the rumble of distant drums of war.

Chapter 21.

Chaos Behind a Slamming Door

Calista vanished from the tumult that followed. She didn't see where Brandinne went, and she didn't care. She was well on her way back up the stairs toward Harper's room when she ran into the Sword Maiden.

"What's going on?" Harper asked.

"Go upstairs," Calista said, ushering her back the way she came. "We need to get armed and armored."

"Why? Where are we going?"

Harper's questions didn't stop her from being herded, which was a small favor in Calista's mind. Explaining everything wouldn't be possible or all that helpful in the moment, and so she was glad they could at least keep moving forward while they discussed things. Back in the room, Calista began donning her own armor, knowing she could easily help Harper with the more complex plate when she was done.

"We're going to try to get to the caravan and see if they'd be willing to leave early based on new developments," Calista said.

"What new developments?" Harper already had her under padding and chain suit on by the time Calista finished with her own gear.

Calista immediately turned her attention to fortifying Harper with the metal plates. There was something excitingly united to helping Harper with her armor. It couldn't accurately be considered domestic, but it certainly spoke of an intimacy that Calista enjoyed.

"The city is under attack," Calista said, knowing full well Harper might demand they stay to help, such was her altruistic temperament. "The window to escape what might end up being a brutal siege is closing quickly. If we can make it south, we can rally others to the cause of liberating the city." She hoped the last bit would convince Harper they could do more good outside the walls than inside.

"Who would attack Griffon's Rock?" Surprisingly, Harper's questions weren't slowing her down at all in donning her armor. She was fully encased in magically imbued steel, wrapped in the tabard of her faith, and shrugging on the cloak Calista was offering her before she'd even gotten through most of her inquiries.

Calista weighed her answers knowing if she revealed too much, she would implicate herself if she hadn't already. "Armies out of the north, I would imagine," Calista said. "No other band would begin a war as the snow is starting to fall—Fir'bolgs probably or maybe Cyclops."

Harper took up her sword and slung it across her back. "There hasn't been a March of the Giants in a thousand years," she said, although it was clear from her tone she wasn't hoping too much in history to save them. "Very well, we must see what is going on first, and then see if we might make an escape to find help."

Calista breathed a sigh of relief. Pragmatism was winning out, even if she had no intention of ever returning to Griffon's Rock. She could deal with Harper's wishes to return with a liberation army once they were safe. It wouldn't matter, and Calista knew why—if the invasion army was what she thought they were, they wouldn't lay siege to Griffon's Rock for very long after she left.

They ran to the stables first, saddling Aerial and the tan gelding they'd taken from Jevvon's group. Harper stated that barding and lances would have been nice, but from the sounds of combat in the city, their time was up. Calista and Harper rode fast for the marketplace. They passed people in the street seeking shelter from the boulders flying over the walls and the city guards rallying to the defense. Calista took the lead to give Aerial an easy target to follow with her remaining good eye, although it was clear she could have easily outpaced Calista's horse in an open field.

They rounded the corner to cut across the gate opening up on the Last Road, and found the drawbridge gate not only open, but the portcullis only about halfway down. Harper pulled up to stop in the courtyard on the immediate interior of the gate. Calista slowed and turned her horse back to see what held Harper's attention.

"If this gate isn't closed, the city will be sacked," Harper said.

Calista strained in her saddle, searching the snowy night for someone, anyone capable of closing the gate. The attack striking the eastern wall and gate drew every last guard and mercenary to the defense, leaving the largest gate in the city open and waiting for a secondary force to walk right in. It made sense, Calista mused, why run drills on how best to defend a city no one had a reason to attack. If they closed the gate though, leaving would become nearly impossible since it clearly wasn't manned. But she could see from the stern set of Harper's jaw that arguing wasn't going to do her any good. If she abandoned the gate, she would be leaving by herself.

"Fine," Calista grumbled. "I'll get the gate. You keep an eye out for trouble."

"Hurry, my love." Harper grasped Calista by the front of her cloak, and nearly pulled her from the saddle in drawing her over for a kiss.

It was frivolous and courtly, but exhilarating all the same for Calista. It was also expected considering whom she was romantically involved with—knights will be knights regardless of gender, Calista decided. Only after the fact did she realize what Harper called her. She shrugged off the possible declaration of love, believing she didn't have the time to process it until the gate was closed.

Harper galloped Aerial toward the yawning gate while Calista rode hard for the gatehouse set in the thick stone wall. Harper dismounted and ushered her loyal mount away while she stood as a lone defender of the gap with her cloak billowing in the snowy wind and her faintly glowing sword drawn. Calista caught one last fleeting glance of her chivalrous lover before she ran into the gate house. There was something to be said for the allure of knights.

Within the darkened gatehouse Calista expected everything to be fairly self-explanatory. Sadly, she overestimated her ability to sort a gate's mechanisms or she underestimated the complexity of such mechanisms. Something clearly had gone wrong with the portcullis machinery, although she was at a total loss to figure out what. There were chains gone slack and dangling in odd ways and ropes strapped around gears in strained webs that she couldn't imagine were intentional.

Divine Touched

She ran up the stairs winding around the outside of the great room filled with all sorts of wheels and gears for which she had no understanding. Height didn't seem to help her much in deducing how best to raise a drawbridge and lower a portcullis, but it did offer her a slightly obscured view down into the gap of the wall where the gate would close and lock. Harper was standing her ground amid the snow while thumping footsteps were coming for her. Calista debated whether or not she should continue her futile attempts at figuring out the gate gears or if she should drop what she was doing and join an equally futile attempt to hold the open gate against an army.

While she was trying to decide, the first heavy figures reached Harper. They were massive, although not large enough to be Fir'bolgs. Cyclops scouts by the look of their long, burly arms, gargantuan hairless heads, and back humps. They stood easily a couple feet taller than Harper and outweighed her by likely triple. Even with their size advantage, they were no match for her weapon, armor, and speed. She met their rush with one of her own, easily cutting through the first two Cyclops while their clubs were still raised. Harper was going to best them one or two at a time, but a quick glance out one of the arrow slits facing the outer edge of the wall told Calista they were going to arrive in numbers shortly. She didn't have time to figure out the mechanisms without losing Harper to the coming onslaught.

Calista glanced around to find the weighted ballasts and other counterbalances to the defense's raising and lowering. It was easy for the portcullis, as the ropes clearly held up the heavy grate's descent. She drew her dagger and cut them away. The massive wooden wheel spun freely, chains clattered, and the huge metal fence fell into place with a resounding crash.

"That's it!" Harper shouted. "Now the drawbridge!"

Calista sighed. She was sealing them in by closing the barriers the way she was. They might be able to wedge open the portcullis even if they couldn't raise it with the wheel and winch, but if she cut free the gate to let it slam shut, only a team of oxen pulling from the outside would lower it again. She glanced again to the coming rush of a dozen Cyclops scouts and made up her mind. She raced through the gatehouse, cutting away the ropes holding the massive iron weights counterbalancing the gate. A few spooled

188

out easily and the gate came rushing up to the stone wall, smashing into place with a thump so loud it shook dust from the rafters down onto her.

Calista tried to console herself with the thought that the caravan likely couldn't have escaped with the Cyclops outside anyway. This rang false though; she and Harper could have killed the scouting party easily to clear the way, but Harper wouldn't have left with the gate still open. When it came right down to it, Calista chose staying behind with Harper above her last chance to escape. If the stupid Fir'bolgs and Cyclops just waited one more day to invade...

Calista sullenly trod out of the gatehouse to find Harper happy in their apparent success. She'd killed a third Cyclops at some point before the defenses smashed into place. The hulking, brutish trio of Cyclops she'd felled lay bleeding into the white snow of the courtyard with Harper in their center. Calista glanced to the fallen enemies as she and Harper came together. The invaders wore the mammoth hides of the Stone Club Clan, which was about the only clan of Cyclops Calista knew anything about.

"Everything slammed shut so quickly," Harper said breathlessly. "I thought it would take you longer." Harper embraced her and Calista nestled into the hug.

Hugging Harper with her plate armor on wasn't particularly satisfying, but Calista did enjoy breathing in the scent of Harper's long, blond hair. "They're shut permanently," Calista said. "I didn't know how to work the gears, so I cut the ropes holding them open."

Harper pulled back to look Calista in the eyes. Her hand gently caressed away a few snowflakes that clung to Calista's eyebrows. "We did what we had to," Harper said. "We'll have to hope we can hold out until spring or that someone else makes it out to rally help."

"Cold comfort for those likely to die in the coming months," Calista said. She couldn't bring herself to tell Harper the truth of any of it, nor could she bring herself to watch Harper die or leave her behind. She was getting soft.

Calista pulled Harper in for another hug, forgetting how unsatisfying it was while they both wore armor. Even still, the embrace reminded her of the one good thing to come from the loss of her last escape route. Eventually, a patrol of city guards came to the gate and secured the bars and locks required to truly close the entrance. Calista and Harper watched them in their work even as the night got colder and the snow fell thicker. When archers from the guard and militia showed up to man the posts on the walls, Harper and Calista collected their horses to return to the inn.

They walked their steeds slowly. The streets were deathly calm around them. As they neared the Thundering Dawn, armed mercenaries began populating the narrow lanes. The rumors were difficult to sort from truth, but the word among the fighting men and women who aided in defending the eastern gate was that an army of Fir'bolgs was on the east and an army of Cyclops was swinging around from the south. With the mountains to the north and the sea to the west, there was little doubt they were trapped.

Before Calista and Harper could reach the stables to return their horses to stalls, Sven retrieved them for a meeting with the benefactor of their company, his father, and the Duke's personal advisor in matters of war. Calista was curious to meet such a man and even more curious to know what he intended to do in defense of a walled city with no standing army inside and two armies outside.

They were ushered into the upper floors at the top of the oldest part of the Thundering Dawn Inn. Calista guessed the original purposes for the rooms and hallways off the back of the main armory turned into an inn were barracks for the guards meant to protect the arms. In the domicile no doubt meant for the commander of the Dwarven detachment that once guarded the building in its original incarnation as a weapon depot, they found Athol and Sven's father.

The old warrior looked far more like his older son than the younger. Even in his advanced years, he was a bear of a man, furthering the ursine appearance by bedecking himself in bear pelts. He walked with a pronounced limp, favoring his right side heavily. He moved amid the dimly lit room like a wounded animal, making great noises of strain with every jolting step he took. The room's low ceiling didn't seem to bother him as he'd been hunched by age and whatever wound destroyed his left side. Athol, however, had to duck to get through the doorway.

"About time my sons finished the simple task before them," the old man growled as if speaking out only one side of his mouth. He settled into a massive stone chair, again, leaning heavily to the left.

Calista finally caught her first real look at his face, heavily scarred, ruddy, and mostly covered by a thick gray beard. The left side of his face drooped, indicating he'd had a brain bleed at one point that paralyzed, at least in part, most of one side of his body. It finally made sense why the company's benefactor would hide away from the world. For a former adventurer to be so afflicted would be a great source of embarrassment even though it was fairly remarkable he lived through such a condition at all.

"The Sword Maiden and our new Jack were securing the gate to the Last Road," Sven explained.

"That bodes well if it can be guarded." The old man leaned forward in his chair to press the majority of his weight down on his one good arm propped on his one good leg. "For the new Jack girl, my name is Bjorn of the Stone Hammer. I have other titles, among them Defender of the City, but none of that matters as you'll only address me as Father."

"Yes, Father," Calista said, not really liking the sound of it at all.

"Now that we're all acquainted, let me get to the point," Bjorn said. "You're all idiot children without experience in real war, but in the coming months, you'll get all you can stand and then some." The words, strangely formed by his partially paralyzed mouth rang true in the solemn little room. He waited a moment to catch his breath before continuing. "The soldiers charged with defense of Griffon's Rock depart in the late summer to make room for the returning mercenaries. Invading this far north would normally be impossible, unless you had an army of ice giants or Cyclops."

"Or both in this case," Ezra said.

"Just so." Bjorn nodded.

"What do they want, Father?" Sven asked.

"To pillage, most likely," Bjorn answered. "This is the richest time of year for the city in terms of gold and goods. You don't march for weeks out of the Crown of the World Mountains without a prize in mind. We have too many warm months here for them to want the land and they couldn't hold the ground anyway since the orchards are too vital for too many to give up." The old man readjusted himself awkwardly in his chair, breathing heavily both from the effort to move and the long explanations he was forced to speak. "If their vanguard hadn't rushed in too soon, we'd be overrun by morning. As it stands, their advanced scouts were pushed out and we managed to close off the city. We are besieged, but the news is not so bleak as it might seem."

"If it is a fight they wish, then it is a fight we will give them!" Athol said, rearing up to bonk his head against the low ceiling, taking much of the bluster out of his posturing.

"And so we will, my vertically blessed son," Bjorn said with a laugh that dissolved into a hacking cough. "The city does not re-supply through the winter regardless, so they cannot simply starve us out as we already planned to last on what we have until the spring thaw that will open our bay. Time and supplies are on our side, although that is where the good news ends. We have five hundred guards and perhaps that number again in untrained militia. These men cannot hold the walls alone since I assume the enemies numbers will be in the thousands. This paltry force will not be our army though."

"The mercenary guild…" Sven murmured.

"Indeed," Bjorn said. "We have a little more than two-thousand hardened adventurers and sell-swords within the city. The wealth the invaders seek to steal is wealth owned by these mercenaries, and we already know they're motivated to fight when gold is on the line. They're fragmented though. Each mercenary band has its own commander, fights with its own tactics, and many of them have fought against each other on opposite sides of various conflicts over the years creating long held grudges. The Duke wishes me to unite them and lead them in the city's defense, but for obvious reasons, I cannot do this. I might have the mind for war still, but my body has long since ceased to inspire confidence."

And here it was, Calista thought. The old man would name his eldest son his proxy in the field. Out of the corner of her eye, she could already see Athol swelling with the pride necessary to accept such a responsibility. The only real leadership quality she'd seen Athol display to that point was the ability to easily be spotted in a crowd. He was more of an effortlessly located rallying point than a general of the field.

"This falls to you, Sword Maiden Harper," Bjorn said, practically sucking the air from the room with the announcement. "You will be my proxy on the field, the general to rally the men to our cause, and the beacon of hope for the civilians to look to. I will plan our strategies from here, but you must be the one to carry them out."

Instinctively, Harper took Calista's hand. Calista responded by giving it a reassuring squeeze. In spite of herself, Calista felt a little swell of pride at Harper's elevation to field commander. She rather liked the idea of taking orders from the Sword Maiden, and believed it would be far easier to keep her safe if she had an entire army helping her. She could see on Sven and Athol's faces that they did not share in her joy.

"Seek out the commanders of the largest mercenary forces taking their rest here," Bjorn instructed. "Take the Sorceress as your steward—she will know how to use the mercenary guild records to find the leaders of each band and how best to placate them. If I may make a suggestion, find the Ash twins—they lead the Dead Watch Pikes, which is still four-hundred men strong." Bjorn stood with great effort and gestured toward the door with his good hand. "If you'll excuse me, ladies, I must speak with my sons alone."

They quit the room, leaving Athol and Sven where they stood. Harper held fast to Calista's hand even after they were well on their way down to the main hall. Ezra followed a few steps behind, possibly stunned from the news or unhappy with her own posting as steward.

Calista, sensing Harper's reticence, leaned in and kissed the Sword Maiden on the neck, whispering hotly against her ear. "You were meant for this. The Sea Queen and I are not the only ones who see greatness in you. Seize upon it and shine, my love." The last part almost came out as a reflex in wanting to balance some scale between them after Harper had said something similar to her at the gate. In truth, she didn't know if love was quite what she meant yet.

Divine Touched

Harper visibly calmed under the influence of Calista's words though, which was the entire purpose. Calista already missed every opportunity to remain ahead of the storm and now she would need to find her way through it. She decided she could have no better captain to guide her through such a maelstrom than a Sword Maiden of the Sea Queen.

Chapter 22:

Rallied

Harper thought she could handle things if the tasks kept coming to her one at a time. Closing the gate, meeting with Bjorn, and now finding the Ash twins all came easily to her as they came to her single file. She took comfort from Calista at her side and Ezra at her back. She trusted them and knew they were invested in her success in more than just the general continued survival sort of way that everyone in the city was.

The Ash twins would be easy to find and likely easy to sway toward unity. They were tall, muscular, handsome, and incredibly dark of skin. The logic of seeking them out first made sense as they were also well-liked and widely respected. Harper certainly thought she was on friendly terms with the Dead Watch Pike leaders as they were devout believers in Maraline and came to the temple often during resting seasons.

She spotted the twins among a small contingent of their men within the great hall. They were already in full banded black armor and adorned in the telltale purple cloaks of their mercenary band. Harper assumed at the beginning of their adventuring careers the identical twins were impossible to tell apart, but over the years they'd taken scars in different places making it clear which was which. Their heads were shaved to the scalp, displaying a three clawed slash scar from a wyvern along the right side of Romulus's head while a crescent scar cut around the outside of Remus's left eye from where a helmet had been smashed into his flesh. They smiled wide with their gleaming white teeth upon Harper's approach.

"Greetings, Sword Maiden," Romulus said. His smile never faded, showing off a few gold teeth mixed into the bunch.

"The rumors around the hall say you and one other companion secured the Last Road gate before the Cyclops could charge in," Remus said.

"We did," Harper replied, indicating Calista at her side.

"A necessary task, although we would've been glad to have your sword at the eastern gate," Romulus said. "A dozen Fir'bolgs made a rush, hurling rocks and insults in their hacking and spitting language."

"We met their charge with one of our own, Athol and Sven of your company joining our numbers, and we put pikes to good use in felling half the giants and sending the other half fleeing," Remus finished the story for his brother.

"That is part of what I meant to speak with you about," Harper said. "Bjorn is collecting mercenaries under a unified banner to defend the city as the guard and militia might not suffice."

"He thinks this is an invasion force…?" Remus started to ask.

"Who is he expecting to lead this patchwork army?" Romulus interrupted his brother. Whereas such a move might have caused trouble between Sven and Athol, the twins immediately seemed to understand one another's motivations, and Remus suddenly was more interested in an answer to his brother's question than his own.

"Me, it would seem," Harper said.

Romulus and Remus exchanged a look and a smirk before turning their attention back in unison. "How can we be of service, Sword Maiden?" they said together.

Enlisting Romulus and Remus appeared to start something of a chain reaction. Moreover, Sven and Athol returned from their private meeting with their father and began enlisting the help of other mercenary groups around town. The rallying cry of the Sword Maiden carried easily among the mercenaries spread throughout, and though a few grumbled about needing space from other specific groups, there was largely enough solitary postings for everyone to have the elbow room they demanded. Before the sky was to gray with the coming dawn, there was a plan in place to ensure the walls would be manned and the tenuous alliances struck to hold the city, for the moment.

Harper was exhausted in the dead on her feet sort of way, and increasingly sorry she didn't change from her armor as the night wore on. Her armor, sword, and tabard were iconic though and did seem to aid some in commanding loyalty from various mercenary bands even if she didn't need any of it for combat in her current duties.

At long last, Harper and Calista mounted the stairs to their room with their task mostly completed. Ezra promised to continue in some of the work, using the brothers as runners for errands. The orders flooding out of Bjorn's command post were extensive and ever changing. They made good use of every report Harper could send back regarding another mercenary group's agreement to join the cause and adjustment orders were issued whenever the Duke voiced a new concern. The tumult of it was almost more than Harper could stand and she increasingly leaned on Calista and Ezra to help her keep it all straight. By the time she and Calista stumbled through the door in the dwindling hours of the night, she was also literally leaning on her lover.

"You know that sensation when you will have to don your armor again in a few hours, but you know you won't be able to stand the sight of it even after rest?" Harper asked as Calista helped her remove the metal plates.

"All too well, I'm afraid," Calista said.

"I think I passed that point a few hours ago and now I'm in an entirely new realm of hating all things heavy." To Harper's delight, Calista smiled and chuckled weakly at her joke.

After Harper's plates were removed, Calista began seeing to her own armor, leaving Harper's chain suit and padding to be removed by Harper alone. In only a few hours, Harper had already begun adoring being the center of attention and focus of so many. Even the tiny, momentary loss of Calista's consideration in armor removal made Harper a bit needy.

"You do believe I can do this," Harper said, "lead an army, that is?"

"Of course I do. I've said as much a few times now."

"And you do still think me beautiful, tired and harried as I might be at the moment?"

Calista turned her attention from removing her own armor at this and smiled to Harper with something of a knowing grin that sent Harper's stomach aflutter. "Fishing for compliments, are we?"

"Perhaps a little," Harper said sheepishly.

"Very well, I'll humor you since you've been wearing metal armor and I've been wearing leather." Calista put her hands on her hips and looked Harper over. "What kind of compliment would you like? Clean enough for polite company or dirty even behind closed doors?"

"One of each, please."

"Look at how much I care for you," Calista said with an overly dramatic sigh, which was tempered by the infectious smile she couldn't keep from spoiling the put-upon act. "You are a beautiful, courtly knight fit for ballads and poetry even as you fall into a state of hating all things heavy." Calista didn't wait long for the polite company compliment to completely settle before she took a step to press her body flush against Harper's whispering the second compliment in a low, husky tone. "And you have the thickest, tastiest clit I've ever wrapped my lips around."

Harper was entirely certain she'd never experienced such a duet of compliments. She could feel the heat of a flattered blush rising in her cheeks and further felt a kindling of her desire for Calista. It would all have to wait though. She was exhausted and she could see that as flirtatious as Calista's words were, she wasn't anymore up for fun than Harper was.

"Thank you," Harper said, adding as almost an afterthought, "my love."

They'd both said it a couple times during the course of the night, and there was no doubt a conversation was needing to take place regarding whether it was simply an affectionate way to refer to one another or if they both truly meant it. Their exhaustion prevented such a conversation from taking place though. Harper wasn't sure she meant it the first time the words slipped from her mouth at the gate, but she knew she meant it every subsequent time. She could only hope Calista wasn't simply calling her 'my love' out of a sense of reciprocity or decorum.

They finished removing their armor, preferring to sleep naked even though the room was chilly as neither of them could stand the idea of putting on any new clothes after removing so much. Harper and Calista slid into the comfortable bed together, intertwining their limbs into one of the many conformations they'd learned fit them both for sleeping. There were things Harper wanted to say to unburden herself of countless doubts and fears, but with her arms wrapped around Calista protectively and Calista's talented fingertips caressing up and down her back, Harper lost all motivation to do anything but sleep.

Calista awoke rested, far too rested for what was going on within the city. More surprising still, she awoke before Harper who was resting comfortably beside her in the snug bed. Calista was certain someone would come collect them shortly after dawn or possibly earlier, but, judging from the position of the faint autumn sun outside the window, they'd slept well into midmorning.

Calista slipped from the bed and began dressing. No sooner had she started the task of clothing herself to see what was going on in the world than a knock came at the door. Harper remained asleep through the gentle tapping and Calista scampered silently over to the door to open it before another knock came. She'd managed to pull on a tunic that barely covered her, though she thought she could use the door to shield her lower half. Calista half expected to find Brandinne on the other side of the door, although a little consideration dispelled that fear—if the Havvish Jack was smart, she'd already be gone from the city or looking for a spectacular place to hide.

Ezra peered into the crack when Calista opened the door. From the smell of the parcel she carried, it appeared the Sorceress came bearing gifts. Calista was glad to see Ezra, or, at the very least, glad she brought bacon. Without a word spent between them, Calista let Ezra into the room.

"I don't suppose the Fir'bolgs and Cyclops decided to go home," Calista said as Ezra walked past her into the room.

"No such luck, I'm afraid." Ezra walked directly to the table in the room and began setting out her bundle of breakfast.

"What other reason could there be for the late hour we were allowed to sleep to?" Calista asked.

Harper chose this moment to awaken to the smell of cooked meat, a pot of coffee, and freshly baked rock berry nut biscuits. She came to the world a little bewildered at the smell and then a little horrified that Ezra was in the room, laying out the breakfast spread.

"I'm naked under here," Harper said, bundling the blankets up to her chin.

"We've both seen it all," Ezra said, never losing focus on her unpacking of the basket she carried.

"Oh, right." Harper slipped from the bed on the other side, careful to keep her back to Calista and Ezra while she pulled on the nearest tunic and trousers available.

"You're due to meet with a few of the company leaders on the eastern wall after breakfast," Ezra said. "Then we're set to meet with the Duke before the combined rally this afternoon meant to bolster militia recruitment. He'll play up the patriotic angle and you'll focus on the spiritual. You'll finish your day in a tactical meeting with Bjorn and those who will be your officers in this makeshift army."

"This sounds dreadfully like an itinerary." Calista took a seat in front of one of the plates Ezra set out and began loading it up with food.

"I've written it down if you wish to see it," Ezra said, "although, if you don't like organized activities, you're welcome to skip all of it, since none of it entails answering riddles or flouncing around to music."

"How much of it might involve saving your life?" Calista asked, winking to Ezra. "Since that's the third thing you've seen me do."

Dressed in her hastily assembled and dreadfully mismatched clothes, Harper took the seat opposite Calista at the table. "I need her with me," Harper said. "And she's right about saving your life. If the need to fight does arise, she's exactly who we want along. In fact, if this itinerary is going to be a formal thing, I'd like her added as my bodyguard wherever we go."

"Splendid," Ezra moaned. "It'll make an enormous amount of sense to list a buxom harlot in leather as the bodyguard to the Sea Queen's own Sword Maiden bedecked in mystical plate armor."

Calista tucked an entire strip of bacon into her mouth and moved it to her cheek to reply. "It makes far more sense to list a cantankerous old spell-flinger as a steward to the same amazing Sword Maiden." Calista leaned forward to trace her fingertip down the curve of Harper's powerful bicep. "You also forgot to mention how much stronger than me she is."

Ezra set the mostly unpacked basket beside the table and stormed toward the door. "When you're done canoodling and eating, I will return to help you into your armor, Harper."

Calista and Harper smiled to one another. They were increasingly familiar and comfortable in communicating without speaking. They ate easily, polished off the coffee, and spoke sparingly, although they made every effort to canoodle as much as possible so they might get it out of their systems before starting on their itinerary where Ezra likely wouldn't allow for such flirtations.

Calista didn't much care for the itinerary as it stood. There was something off about it all. If Harper was indeed meant to be the general of the defense army, she should be doing far more than simply admiring fortifications and chatting with nobles. She had to console herself with the fact that she knew bugger-all about building an army or waging war; what Harper was doing might be right down the line for a general for all Calista knew. It was a new army and so it did make some sense that Harper should help build it. The oddness of the schedule didn't rate as the largest looming problem either, and she was an expert on the other, more pressing issue.

The thieves guild would likely be gearing up for a grand time of pillaging the city from within. Sieges were marvelous opportunities for profit among the unscrupulous. They'd be stealing whatever necessities they could get their hands on over the next few days. In a month, bread would be worth more than gold, but at the moment, it wouldn't be nearly as well-guarded. After the rationing became unbearable, the thieves would sell the bread, possibly even to the people they'd stolen the flour from, at extortive prices. If they were a truly wicked organization, and Calista suspected they were since they appeared to be lead by Dwarves and Dwarves were all greedy, evil bastards, they would likely also sell people an escape from the city through the old Dwarven tunnels. Of course, the escape would actually just be a dead end where the escapee would be killed and all their possessions taken.

Calista couldn't decide if she would do anything about it though. She didn't have a particular ethical objection to any of it. She was a thief and a killer in her own right, although she typically only stole from those who could most afford to be stolen from or those who already stole. She was a little less discerning in whom she killed, but that came with other rewards far more valuable than gold, which was always part of the deal in one way or another. There were things in the world worth killing for, and she had a built in motivation that almost no one else did.

"What are you thinking about?" Harper asked, snapping Calista out of her musing.

"I guess I'm wondering if you see issues arising from what we are," Calista said. "A Dark Stalker and a Sword Maiden make for an odd couple to say the least."

"I hadn't considered it," Harper said. "I suppose I assumed you were more of a Jack than an actual assassin. Aside from the conflict with Jevvon's company, you haven't killed anyone, have you?"

"Not since we met, no," Calista said. It was odd to tell the truth in such a thing, although her answer would have been the same regardless. In addition to being a thief and killer, she was also a superb liar.

"I don't see a problem then." Harper smiled in such a way that made Calista's heart ache a little.

Calista probably wouldn't have to lie to Harper too often since she seemed determined to lie to herself. Harper easily could have pointed out that Calista modified her answer to list only activities since they'd met, or she could have asked a follow up question regarding Calista's future murderous plans, or she could have asked about Calista's thievery, which was getting pretty excessive. But she'd let the matter drop entirely instead—Harper left the topic alone because she didn't *want* to know what Calista really was.

Without a real point of reference for what a normal, healthy relationship between two people might look like, Calista shrugged it off as being good enough. All her partners in the past were like her, which hadn't worked out too well. Maybe having Harper curb some of her more illegal proclivities would be a good thing since her girlfriends in the past always seemed to amplify them in ways that were ultimately self-destructive.

"We should braid your hair with lace and ribbon today," Calista said, feeling the matter of their vastly divergent codes of conduct was settled. "You'll look comported as you did on our date." Even as she was saying the words and refilling Harper's coffee cup, Calista was thinking of ways she might take advantage of the thieves guild's future illegal activities. Stopping them or ignoring them were only the black and white options available to her. She could also find some grayer area between to make her own stay within Griffon's Rock a little more comfortable until spring.

"I was thinking we also might find you something to wear that looks more official and is a little warmer to spend so much time outside in, at least when we're away from the wall," Harper said.

"Good idea." Calista couldn't tell if Harper meant it solely as a concern for her comfort or if she also didn't want to be seen with someone dressed in such sinister armor. A warmer poncho over the entire thing with ample room to move her arms and legs wouldn't hurt, although the request brought up another twinge of concern about the propriety of Harper's itinerary.

"Do we have enough time to...?" Harper began, but shortly after a knock came at the door.

"Ask me again tonight," Calista whispered even as Ezra walked through the door unbidden.

Chapter 23:

Not All the News is Bad—Some of it is Downright Wicked

The eastern gate was in a state of partial combat when Harper, Ezra, and Calista arrived. Harper made to support the warriors atop the wall, but Ezra held her back and instead directed her to the Ash twins who were awaiting her arrival with a couple other company commanders.

"The fight isn't going anywhere and it's not the sort of a thing a woman with a sword could help with," Ezra said.

A rotund old Sorcerer stood with the Ash twins. He wore a heavy red coat and a floppy, fur-lined hat with a drooping point on the top. He twirled the most impressive moustache Harper had ever seen that fluttered down to touch the top of his chest when one of the ends wasn't wrapped around a pudgy finger. Harper knew him as Wizardly Willard, the commander of the Mystical Multitude, a company comprised of seven Sorcerers, not to be confused with the Sorcerous Seven who were stationed near the Last Road gate. Ezra told Harper the two Sorcerer groups couldn't be anywhere near each other as the naming rights issue wasn't settled to either's satisfaction.

Wizardly Willard bowed to Harper as much as his puffy coat and bulbous belly would allow, and directed her to the staircase up toward the defensive positions atop the wall where men in black banded armor with crossbows were fighting alongside a handful of Sorcerers in red coats.

"I would have wondered what a wall of fifty feet could do to keep out giants of thirty feet, but it would seem the greater threat is their spiders," Wizardly Willard explained as they walked up the stairs.

This caused Harper to falter, enough so that Ezra bonked into the back of her. "Spiders?" Harper asked.

"Oh yes! Ice spiders that would look like your average Black Widow excepting they are a whitish-gray and weigh roughly as much as a healthy milking bovine," Wizardly Willard said, not remotely catching on to Harper's reticence. "The Fir'bolgs raise them as pets in much the same way people breed hunting hounds."

Harper reluctantly followed when the collective weight of Ezra, Calista, and the Ash twins pushed at her back. She finally crested the wall to stand among the men and women defending the position. The Dead Watch Pikes with their heavy crossbows and long spears looked to have little to do most of the time as the six sorcerers in their ranks were hurling healthy amounts of magic into the slow trickle of ice giants and their pet spiders. The halo of destruction within the groves ringing the wall appeared partially due to the battle and partially planned as though the giants might have harvested trees to construct siege items.

"Are there settlements outside the walls we should worry about?" Harper asked, noting the halo of destruction appeared to be growing larger by the minute. Magical fireballs, lightning bolts, energy blasts, and conjured rocks were not only felling the attackers, but were tearing up the territory outside the wall as well. Harper was concerned farmers might not only be caught by the ice giant army, but also might get struck by an errant spell.

"We asked about that and we were informed farmsteads were pushed out long ago to make more room for groves," Remus offered. "There might be some holdout hermits a few miles out, but we doubt the Fir'bolgs care to stomp on far flung shacks."

"Besides, they're well beyond reaching now," Romulus added.

Harper stepped closer to the edge of the wall to get a better look. The spiders may have weighed a couple thousand pounds like most cows, but they spread such weight over a much larger area. Even the burned and curled husks of the dead arachnids were enormous. She shuddered, hoping her armor covered the revulsion.

Fir'bolgs weren't quite what Harper expected. They were tall, thirty feet as Wizardly Willard explained, but they weren't brawny. Most were lanky and some were downright thin. They wore their silvery white hair, beards, and eyebrows long with giant hooked noses drooping down in front of their mouths. Their armor appeared to be made of wooden plates and animal pelts and their weapons were stone clubs and axes or hurled boulders.

A few rocks pelted the wall and occasionally clipped one of the armored pike men. Typically the large rocks seemed to wound, rather than kill, and the soldiers covered their own with shields until they could be revived or moved off the wall. All in all, it looked like something of an awkward stalemate to Harper. The giants generally stayed out of range of spells and crossbow bolts, hurling inaccurate rocks toward the wall while sending their spiders racing across the war torn field to try to reach the wall before they were felled by magic.

"Why are they waiting to assault us in numbers?" Harper asked.

"They fear the might of the Magical Seven…er…the Mystical Multitude," Wizardly Willard explained. "That's the name we settled on, isn't it?"

"Yes, Willard," one of the nearby Sorcerers confirmed.

"More likely they're testing our defenses while waiting for their full force to arrive," Remus said.

"We've estimated their current strength at about a thousand with ten times that number in spiders, but we expect that'll change," Romulus continued.

"There are around six thousand Cyclops at the Last Road gate, with half that number in riding bears," Remus said.

"We don't know how many more might join that army," Romulus said with a sigh. "They're not building fortifications the way the Fir'bolgs are."

"Riding bears?" Harper turned to Calista as if for confirmation, but also partially at the marvel of seeing Cyclops riding on giant bears.

Calista simply shrugged. "There are a lot of weird things in the frozen north," she said.

"What are we doing to fortify the wall?" Harper asked, assuming she shouldn't simply be sightseeing to watch Sorcerers vaporizing giant spiders, as interesting as all that was.

"Little needs to be done for the wall other than to repair the ballista on the towers, which have all seen better days," Remus said. "We have what passes for engineers working on that now, although we have our doubts about them being fixed anytime soon, if at all."

"We're piling snow behind the gate to freeze into ice when night falls. This will turn the weakest part of our defense into the strongest with time," Romulus continued.

"Although it also blocks us from making retaliatory charges," Remus finished glumly.

"What ill-conceived charge will we need to make on them so long as the magical practitioners of the Sorcerous Seven..." Wizardly Willard began.

"That's the other group," Ezra corrected him.

"...the Mystical Menagerie..." Wizardly Willard tried again.

"I think that's a traveling circus and freak show," Calista said.

"...the Magical..." Wizardly Willard mumbled the rest, turned hastily, and stormed down the wall as if there were some great breach in the defenses only he could plug, which of course there wasn't. "Onward, brave men!" he shouted as he trundled along.

"Is there anything else you might need?" Harper asked of Romulus and Remus, shaking off the sneaking suspicion many of the mercenary company commanders might be ghastly eccentrics or raging alcoholics or probably both in Wizardly Willard's case.

"Axe men for the low parts of the walls and bowmen for the towers," Romulus said, to which his brother simply nodded his agreement. "When they attack in numbers, and they will eventually, a handful of spells won't stop the charge."

"I'll start searching and see who I can come up with." Harper looked to Ezra to ask her to write down the request, but found the Sorceress was already scratching away on a bit of parchment regarding axe men and archers.

"It would also do us a bit of good if you would walk the wall once to offer solace and blessing to the men," Remus said.

"We'll provide shields for you, of course," Romulus added quickly. "We wouldn't want an errant rock striking our field commander."

Harper couldn't see the harm in it. She looked to Ezra to see if her itinerary would allow for such a walk and Ezra nodded. She then looked to Calista who simply shrugged. It was strange. As excited and afraid as Harper was by the whole war and the prospect of commanding soldiers, it all seemed fairly easy so far. It wasn't remotely surprising that Calista seemed bored and Ezra appeared more interested in paperwork than fearful for her life. She might have asked Romulus and Remus if they knew how a siege war was meant to feel, but she didn't want to appear inexperienced in their eyes.

"Very well, we'll walk the wall," Harper announced.

≈♥≈

The stroll down the defensive line did indeed seem to help with morale. The giants targeted the shield turtle around Harper a few times, but they seldom landed hits and the few they did were easily deflected. Harper stopped on occasion to heal one of the mercenaries with a broken arm or bloodied head, further increasing the will of the men to fight.

By the time they were due to meet with the Duke, Harper was practically beaming from the good she'd done and Calista was almost falling asleep on her feet from the boredom. Ezra made it all too clear to Calista that they would not allow her kind anywhere near the Duke and so she might watch from the crowd with everyone else at the appointed time.

Calista wasn't remotely offended by the implications, nor did she protest although Harper voiced concerns. Calista said she was fine with running a few important errands while Harper met with nobility—something to clear her mind and keep her from slipping into a coma. They parted ways at the Duke's keep with a brief kiss.

Calista turned to walk down into town, specifically the marketplace where she hoped to find the merchant caravan still within the bazaar. If they weren't leaving, and she couldn't see anyway they could now, she thought a refund was in order.

Tension wound through the city, clearly written on the faces of the people she passed. Everyone was going about their business, albeit in hushed tones with furtive glances over their shoulders and occasionally skyward. The threat of Fir'bolg hurled rocks, ice spider swarms, and Cyclops charging on the backs of mighty bears consumed so much focus of the citizenry that Calista suspected she could walk the streets naked, proclaiming herself the assassin queen of the world and nobody would even remember what color her hair was five seconds later. The tension of the strangely non-violent siege would certainly work in the favor of the thieves guild as they plucked the city clean of all goods.

The merchant caravan hadn't made it out, and Calista was able to procure a refund for their passage with only a few minor threats of the grumpy merchant leader. The hiccup causing trouble in acquiring such a refund was the sudden disappearance of the passenger manifest. The merchant leader's oldest son remembered Calista and Harper, and recalled exactly how much they'd paid, smoothing the process along even without the written log.

As Calista was walking away from the bazaar, heavy laden with gold coins, she was struck by the oddness of a manifest going missing before a caravan's departure. She knew a merchant might lie about such things to avoid giving a refund, but she didn't think the particular merchant in question was a good enough actor for the performance given. Besides, she'd gotten the full refund without real altercation, which didn't support a ruse on the merchant's part. Losing a manifest of any kind, especially before departing a city, simply wasn't done by any caravan leader. Most merchant caravans carried several logs of their dealings, some legitimate, others not so much, and the merchant leader knew where all of them were at all times so the right one might be presented at the right time to the right authority for the right effect.

Certainly a manifest from a merchant caravan held resale value if someone knew a rival interested in buying it, but a smart thief wouldn't steal the book itself. A few pages here and there could be removed without drawing too much immediate attention, allowing the thief ample time to sell the information and escape to a safe distance. Stealing the entire book was brazen, especially when the thief had no hope of leaving the city. Calista's paranoia got the better of her, and she wondered if maybe whoever stole the book couldn't have simply stolen the page containing her and Harper's information, because if that page was discovered missing amid an otherwise complete manifest, Calista would know as soon as she went for her refund. There were two people Calista could think of in the city who might like that information and might know to cover their tracks by stealing the entire book.

Calista arrived back at the square before the temple of the Sea Queen in time for the gathering of the frightened masses. The

Duke, who looked like an amiable enough fellow with his curly black hair and delicate features, stood next to Harper and a few of the affirmed sisters. The Duke was all smiles and pageantry while Harper looked positively miserable at his side.

The call to arms rally did little that Calista didn't expect and the longer the Duke spoke of civic duty, the foreign horde at the gates, and the strange religions they represented, the more Calista felt like gagging. She could see the similar disgust on Harper's face, and so, it wasn't all that surprising that Harper was never given leave to speak. "That's my girl," Calista muttered under her breath. The goal, and no doubt one thought up by Bjorn since the Duke didn't seem a tremendously cunning sort, was to turn the entire conflict into a holy war between the faithful of Maraline and whatever heathen Gods the Fir'bolgs and Cyclops worshipped. Gallingly, it also seemed to work with or without Harper's direct participation. By the end of his tirade, the Duke had the gathered masses believing they need only prove their devotion to the Sea Queen for divine intervention on their behalf.

It did hold a hint of irony that wasn't lost on Calista. It was a holy war, although the only person on the human side of the wall who should have known that was her. They'd gotten some of the details of the spiritual conflict incorrect, but Calista didn't see anything wrong with the people of Griffon's Rock being mislead into something that was generally true by those who were unwittingly telling the truth. In fact, she actually kind of liked the serendipity of it all. Gazing up at Harper, who had clearly figured out what her actual role was in it all, put and end to how pleased Calista felt.

Calista vanished from the crowd before the speech came to the call to action portion where men and women would begin volunteering for posts and signing up for the militia. Since her suspicions were all but confirmed regarding what they were actually doing with Harper, she decided it was well within her flexible moral code to begin her own acts of war profiteering. She had gold enough on her to make some moves before any but the most opportunistic people in the city. The thing about mercenaries was most would take paying work over patriotic work even if it meant decreasing their own chances of survival in the long run.

She was well on her way back to the Thundering Dawn Inn when the familiar shape of a tall guard and his stocky companion stepped from an alleyway to block her path. They were smart enough to approach her during daylight hours, even though the sun was on its way to setting. If they tried the same shakedown routine after dark, she fully planned on killing them both.

"Our informant friend here has been suspiciously silent lately, Turbald," Ulrich said when he seemed sure Calista was close enough to hear his feigned offhand comment.

"Makes a person wonder why nobody is havin' any accidents," Turbald agreed.

Calista decided she might get some information from them before turning them away all the same. "With the bay frozen, I don't need the coin so much anymore," Calista said, hoping the dopier, shorter of the two might let slip if they stole the merchant's passenger manifest. "Besides, with the whole city in peril, it seems like a person could just wait awhile and see who gets squished by a thrown rock. What would be the point in looking for accidents?"

"Then I suppose we're reduced to threats," Ulrich said.

"Then threaten me." Calista folded her arms over her chest and cocked her hip to one side in a posture that positively screamed 'I dare you.'

"We got evidence, solid evidence, of what you are," Turbald said. "Maybe we take that evidence to our guard captain."

Calista faked an overly dramatic yawn. "With two armies outside his gates, I would imagine your guard captain cares far more about why you two aren't at your posts. Besides, so many people have figured out what I am that it'd hardly matter if you added a few more to the list. What else do you have?"

"We've got some unfriendly business associates who might be interested in learning who was behind the deaths of a couple of their friends," Ulrich said, apparently a little shaken by the sudden shift in Calista's attitude toward them.

"Short guys with shaved heads and unshaven beards?" Calista asked. "I'd be curious to see how they would fare against the army surrounding the Sword Maiden. You may have noticed I'm often found at her side in the middle of a host of mercenaries charged with her safekeeping. I would imagine any attempt on my life could easily be mistaken as an attempt on her life, and then what do you suppose would happen to your business associates and their organization?" Here was the point where Calista found out if they were the ones who stole the manifest. They were out of cards save that one and she knew they would have to play it if there was any hope of keeping her in their employ. "Is that all you've got?"

"We won't forget this," Ulrich said.

Calista snorted. "You'll likely be eaten by ice spiders before the end of the week. If you come back to pester me, you'll wish you had."

Calista brushed past the two guards who parted before her. That settled the question of who stole the manifest, she thought. Now she just had to figure out what Brandinne was going to do with it.

By the time Calista managed her little mischief with a particularly surly group of Rangers, who had something of a reputation as being highwaymen during lean years, she made her way up to the room she shared with Harper. She was rather proud of herself in the problems she was planning on causing and the discount price she'd managed. The benefit of following Harper and Ezra around to recruit groups for combat was that she knew precisely who weren't being sought out and who had said no. The group she'd hired for her little plan was of the former type, although they'd made it clear they planned on being the latter if anyone bothered to ask them. "We don't fucking fight for free!" they'd exclaimed. And so Calista paid them. The Red Dale Riders, a band of a dozen ruffians, was on the case for a discount price, scouring the city for shady Dwarves up to no good with full permission to kill and rob any they found with Calista's personal assurance the guards were far too busy to concern themselves.

If the competition was afraid of catching an arrow in the back whenever they ventured out, Calista could take to the city at night and begin her own war profiteering business. She suspected she would make back the entirety of her investment a dozen times over before the winter was out. The money would be nice, but her real motivation was staving off boredom. If she was right about what was going on with Harper's posting, nothing interesting would happen anywhere near her.

Calista gently knocked at their door before stepping inside. Harper was in the midst of the room, frustrated by taking off her armor alone and something else less immediate. Calista offered her a wan smile and crossed the room to help her with her armor. Harper's irritation didn't diminish at all with Calista's help, which gave credence to Calista's belief the armor was only a small part of what was wrong.

"You heard the speech?" Harper asked.

"I heard the Duke speak," Calista replied.

"I'm not in charge of anyone or anything, am I?" Harper asked, stopping Calista's hands between her own.

"No," Calista said.

"Did you know?" Harper released Calista's hands and took a step back.

"I think I figured it out about the same time you did."

"So I'm meant to be a symbol, paraded around while others fight, made to look like I am in charge so the people might see me and believe the Goddess is on our side," Harper said. It was phrased as a question, but spoken as a statement. "Who is really in charge?"

"My guess would be the Ash twins," Calista said.

"I'll quit, or tell people the truth, or…"

Calista cut off Harper's tirade by gathering up Harper's face in her hands. "You won't. You won't even let on that you know. The only thing more valuable than you as a living symbol is you as a martyr. They can parade your memory far more easily than they can parade you."

Harper calmed a little under the gesture, placing her hands on the outside of Calista's. "You're the only one I can trust," she whispered. "I can trust you, can't I?"

"Of course you can," Calista said. "I swear I will keep you safe."

The thought hadn't even occurred to her until Harper threatened to shatter the entire plan put in motion by Bjorn, the Duke, and likely the Ash twins. Keeping Harper safe could be a boring task supported by an army, or it might turn out to be Calista against a widespread conspiracy to create a powerful martyr. She needed to enlist an army of her own. Setting up a black market would be the first step and then she could fund her own force out of the malcontents who wouldn't willingly join Bjorn's patchwork army. If they thought to harm Harper to fuel their false holy war, they would find another war waiting for them inside the walls.

Chapter 24.

Brittle From the Cold

More than a week passed without any major incursion. The Fir'bolgs even quit sending their spiders to attack the walls. The numbers of ice giants and Cyclops outside the city steadily grew and so too did the pressure within. Calista could only liken it to the strange change in the weight of the air before a tornado tore across the open plains of the south. It made animals go nuts and caused a general ill-ease among people. After seven days of it, the city seemed ready to collectively pull its hair out and go screaming onto the frozen bay. Uncertainty and fear were good for one kind of business though, and Calista was in that business.

Harper's depression at the realization she wasn't actually a field commander weighed heavily on her. She went to bed early and slept late. Rather than let Harper feel entirely useless, which was something Bjorn and the Ash twins seemed perfectly fine with, Calista opted to seek out honest work for her in training the new recruits to the militia. Harper's mood elevated some, her sword skills remained sharp, and her body responded well to the resumption of physical work. Even still, a dark cloud followed the Sword Maiden, which Calista could neither mend with work, nor chase away with love making.

Calista seized upon the extra time alone to sneak out at night to burgle here and there. With the Red Dale Riders giving the thieves guild fits, she found the city was generally open for the taking. Still, she wasn't in the business of making a name for herself and so she only took what might not be noticed from a plethora of victims; a little here and there from several places added up to a lot over several nights. Stealing only what she could carry was slow but satisfying work. She found in the cousins who ran the Ghaf'nashi tea house a viable option for the legal front of her black market; the secretive nature and predilection toward illicit activities of her countrywomen made them the perfect entrepreneurs to sell what she'd stolen. Money started trickling in and Calista began eyeing other malcontent mercenary groups who might be interested in joining her clandestine business ventures.

Calista awoke early, slipped from Harper's arms, and dressed quietly in the early hours of the morning. She had a meeting with Caleb the Callous, the lead Ranger of the Red Dale Riders. She ventured down into the main hall to find half the Riders gathered around a long table, some standing, a couple sitting, admiring a pile of something or other. As Calista got closer, she spotted through the burly, dirty limbs of the Rangers a heap of what looked like furs on the table.

Upon spotting Calista, Caleb stood from the table and took a few steps away from the rest of the group to greet her. He towered a good foot taller than Calista, as did most of his men, and had the dirty, utilitarian look common to most Rangers. The uniform of the Red Dale Riders was little more than a burgundy sash and a brown cloak, although they all had leathery skin, haphazard beards, and hair hacked short by shears—coincidence, Calista guessed. The only item setting Caleb apart from his men was the tarnished iron girdle he wore around his waist.

"You're our kind of employer, Calista," Caleb said before any sort of salutation. "You leave us to our work without comment or question of our methods."

"You know your trade," Calista said. "It'd be foolish for me to tell a Ranger how to hunt."

She'd encountered highwaymen and Rangers before. They all lacked social graces less out of overt rudeness and more out of the need for frugality in all things, including words. Pleasantries like hello, goodbye, please, and thank you were all wastes of time and breath that might be better spent on other things.

"Well spoken, Patroness." Caleb put his arm around Calista's shoulder and guided her toward the table. From the dirty appearance of the Rangers, she expected them to smell terrible, but even when held to their leader's side she couldn't smell any of them. It made sense only after the fact—what good was a hunter if their scent gave them away? Upon closer inspection of what they were counting out on the table, Calista found several of the Dwarven long knives like the ones she'd taken off the two she'd killed while seeking out the Ogre's treasure, along with several face pelts.

"You've been hacking off their beards?" Calista asked, trying to keep her voice even despite being unreasonably angry.

"We have, although we've found little interest in them," Caleb said. "There are no rival thieves willing to pay bounties, which was our original plan. We hoped you or the guards might buy them."

Calista didn't like hirelings for a lot of reasons. Even if hirelings could be made to understand the grander scheme, it typically wouldn't make them any better in aiding it and often resulted in them asking for a bigger slice. Getting hirelings to do the right thing always involved a perfect mixture of truth and lie, but even then they were unreliable and prone to erratic, detrimental behavior like cutting beards off dead Dwarves in hopes someone would buy them.

"The entire point of hiring mercenaries to do the work is to not have it easily traced back to me, so buying beard scalps would provide an overly obvious link I don't want," Calista said, which was true. "I also wouldn't recommend turning them in to the guards since many of them are in league with the very Dwarves you're killing." The second part was only possibly true. It was true enough in terms of Ulrich and Turbald, or so they said, but for all Calista knew they were the only ones double-dealing.

Caleb didn't seem too pleased by the news that the beards they'd taken weren't worth anything to anyone. He sucked his rotting teeth violently and sighed. "The take off them wasn't very much," he finally said.

"Then I guess it's good you're getting paid for simply doing the job," Calista hissed. Caleb took a step back from her. "You're no good to me if you can't keep this quiet and you know too much to leave the contract now." She always tried to go the gold route with hirelings and it almost always ended up having to go another way. She wanted to leave the choice in Caleb's hands, but she suspected he was going to be as thickheaded as all the other mercenaries she'd hired in the past.

"That sounded a lot like a…"

Calista assumed Caleb was going to say 'threat' before the breath was literally stopped in his lungs. Tendrils of black magic escaped from around the edges of her fingertips suddenly wrapped around his ropey throat. His eyes faded from brown to solid white and his heart began thumping at irregular intervals. Before his body succumbed to the darkness flooding into it through his neck, Calista let go of Caleb's throat. The Ranger dropped to his hands and knees at her feet, weeping openly in such a pitiful and genuine way that the other half-dozen men took a frightened step back from her.

"Yes, that was a threat." Calista knelt by Caleb, whispering calmly to him, but still loud enough to be heard by the gathered men. "Do you feel sufficiently threatened?" Caleb nodded weakly. "Good. I'd hate to have to do that again, and I *know* you don't want me to."

Calista stood, wiped her hand with a napkin from the table, and turned to address the rest of the Red Dale Riders. "Get rid of the scalps and don't take any more," Calista said. "In fact, begin varying how you leave the bodies to make it seem as though several different groups with several distinct calling cards are killing the Dwarves." She dropped the napkin on the back of Caleb's head and walked away. "I'll see you lovely gentlemen next week."

The snaking, dark magic she'd left inside Caleb would spread to his men with every word he spoke to them until she wouldn't even have to pay them anymore for their service. Before their next meeting, the whole of the Red Dale Riders would sacrifice themselves to protect her without a moment's hesitation, believing with every fiber of their beings that they did so in the name of her Goddess. Hirelings had their uses, but thralls were far more reliable. Sadly, the magic she left within them would eventually return to her, leaving them hollow in some places and completely cut off from the divine. No great loss in most cases, Calista decided. She couldn't think of a reason any deity would care what happened to the Red Dale Riders.

A light snow fell on the training arena where the new militia recruits had gathered to take on the Sword Maiden with their new found skills. Calista stood just outside the ring, watching with a faintly amused grin on her face. Harper was dressed only in her armor padding vest and trousers, armed with a large, wooden training sword. The sword had a lead core, and thus was far heavier than her normal blade, meant to build her muscles up so they might swing her magically imbued sword with greater ease in real combat. Harper liked the strain and burn wielding the training sword put through her arms and shoulders, but she loved the way Calista leered at her muscles while she practiced.

Her trainees came at her three at a time on the first charge, lowering blunted, wood-tipped spears at her flank. They let out unsure battle cries at the outset of the charge, tipping Harper off to their attack. She pivoted and swung her sword down across the front of her body to sweep aside all three spears as they came for her. She stepped through the deflection, put her shoulder into the first man, taking him off his feet, swung her sword down to knock the middle attacker's knees out from behind, and followed through, stepping over the top of the two men she'd dropped, to knock the third and final attacker senseless with a strike from her elbow.

The gathered trainees laughed at their fallen compatriots and cheered for their commander. Harper turned to catch Calista's gaze and her ever widening smile. Harper returned the smile before focusing on the ring of men around her.

Four new recruits came at her from all four sides, wielding wooden swords and practice shields. They'd seen their fellows dropped easily after a mad dash and so chose a more measured approach. They circled her, inching their way closer.

Before any of them could make their attack, Harper leapt from the center, striking out at the first man to pass before her. She feinted with a swing on his shield side, which he raised his defenses to block. He braced for the impact of the massive wooden sword that never came. She turned the blade back around and smacked the pommel into his stomach, following through with the blade to drag it across his upper thighs. Before any of his companions could get into position to attack her, she was already charging the next man to her left, carrying with her the momentum from the slash across the first man's legs.

The second trainee gave ground, but not nearly enough or fast enough. Harper swatted the practice sword from his hand using her own blade and then knocked him out of the ring with a thrust kick to the shield he held out as his last resort. Her powerful kick lifted the man from his feet and hurled him into the waiting arms of the men gathered to watch.

She turned to the last two trainees who huddled beside one another to draw strength from each other. Harper smiled to this. "What did the first two do wrong?" Harper asked of the gathered trainees.

"They hesitated," a man shouted from somewhere in the ring.

"Yes, and in doing so, they let me dictate the speed and nature of the combat," Harper said. "And these two, why aren't they defeated so easily?" Harper swung her practice sword in a wide arc at the remaining two, sending them leaping backward.

"They clustered together to guard each other," another voice called.

"Precisely," Harper said. "They are stronger as two. Remember this: none of you can defeat a Cyclops or Fir'bolg alone. You will need to coordinate your attacks and defend one another to survive."

Harper slid her practice sword back into its resting place across her back in the rope loops meant to represent her scabbard. She bowed to the remaining two trainees who bowed in return.

"Practice in squads the rest of the afternoon," Harper said.

She walked from the ring as the men broke apart to carry out her orders. They were fishermen, shopkeepers, stable hands, and laborers, but Harper saw promise in many of them to be soldiers someday. She hoped she would have more than just a few weeks to teach them the new trade.

Calista came to her before she was fully from the training grounds that were already echoing with the clacking of practice swords against shields and wooden targets. Harper collected Calista into her arms and kissed her. Calista took on the demure role and melted into the muscular arms around her.

"You're building quite the following here," Calista murmured when their lips parted.

"Let's hope the city's survival doesn't hinge on a couple hundred tradesmen turned soldier and trained in haste," Harper said.

"Battles have hinged on less," Calista replied, "and they're fortunate to find a leader so worthy to believe in. The mercenaries gathered by Bjorn might be more skilled, but these are your men because they chose to follow you. Take heart in that knowledge. It's not so easy a thing to gain."

Ezra practically materialized in front of Harper and Calista, snapping both of them from their conversation with almost an audible pop. "There's something happening at the Last Road gate that you need to see," Ezra said breathlessly.

The trio mounted horses provided by a Dead Watch Pike mercenary. They rode hard for the gate, scattering people from the slushy, muddy streets. Harper took the lead, her hair trailing behind her like winter sunshine, drawing the attention of people who began gathering at the edges of the road to watch the riders pass. As they neared the massive gate, the bellowing of a great horn found their ears. The sound was earthshaking, slow, and repetitive as though someone with massive lungs was blowing every bit of their breath through the horn and pausing only long enough to refill his lungs before blowing again.

"What is that?" Harper asked as they dismounted, handing their horses off to another mercenary.

"It's easier to see than explain," Ezra said.

They were met at the stairs to the top of the gatehouse by Michael the Magician, the leader of the Sorcerous Seven. Unlike Wizardly Willard, Michael dressed in more traditional blue, satin robes adorned with bejeweled moons and stars. He was tall, slender, and likely older than eighty. With his wide brimmed hat on, he looked a bit like an open blue umbrella with a long white beard.

"He's still blowing away on that infernal horn," Michael the Magician said.

"Who is?" Calista asked.

"The blind Cyclops," Ezra explained.

"How do you know he's blind?" Harper asked.

"You know how most Cyclops have one eye?" Michael asked.

Harper and Calista nodded.

"Well, this Cyclops has none," Michael explained.

"Then you can't really call him a Cyclops anymore, now can you?" Calista said, apparently a little sad that nobody thought her joke was funny enough to laugh.

They crested the top floor of the gatehouse and emerged on the snowy roof where several other Sorcerers of Michael's company were collected, casting a protective globe of magic over the top of the building. Ezra directed Harper to the edge of the roof where a stone wall guarded her from the chest down.

Below them, standing on the stone and mortar landing platform for the draw bridge, blowing on a great curled horn set in the back of a specially designed wagon, was an old Cyclops who did indeed seem to have lost his lone eye at some point; for good measure, someone apparently had sewn the upper and lower lids of the empty eye socket together. It was immediately obvious why nobody had bothered killing the hapless horn blower. The Cyclops was clearly crippled as well as blind. Judging from the winding, irregular tracks through the snow left by the wagon with the heavy horn on it, it must have taken hours for him to get into position.

"He's an oddity," Michael the Magician said in his increasingly nasal voice. "Certainly, we could kill him, but we didn't think it wise or indeed worth the effort. Aside from being a little irritating, he hasn't done anything."

"Unlike the Fir'bolgs, the Cyclops haven't attacked us even by proxy since that first night when they rushed the open gate," Ezra said. "The orders from Bjorn are very clear: don't antagonize them."

"Could it be a magical horn meant to bring down the walls?" Harper asked. The horn was peculiar. It looked like it came off a big horned sheep, but the sheep would likely be as large as most cargo ships to grow such a horn. There was something ancient and important about the horn, and by extension the Cyclops blowing it, which Harper assumed could mean magic.

"We've cast a dozen divinations out of just that concern, but nothing is detectable," Michael said. "If it is magic, it is of a kind unknown to humanity."

"He's an oracle," Calista said, drawing everyone's attention to her.

"How do you know that?" Ezra demanded.

"It's not important," Calista said. "He's here to deliver a message from the Gods."

"To whom?" Michael asked.

"To Harper."

"Any message for the commander should…" Ezra began, but stopped short of finishing her sentence.

It felt like a spear in the stomach, which Harper had actually felt twice in her many years of fighting. Ezra was in on the whole thing. She knew Harper wasn't really a commander, yet played along the entire time. A very tangible thread of friendship Harper believed existed between her and the Sorceress suffered a violent severing. The betrayal by Ezra hurt a good deal more than when Harper learned Sven and Athol were in on the charade.

"It is for Harper," Calista said. "She is the spiritual leader of the city regardless of who is actually in charge of the army. Oracles aren't military leaders so he wouldn't be interested in talking with Bjorn or the Ash twins."

"How am I supposed to talk to him?" Harper asked.

"I imagine you can just shout," Calista replied. "They wouldn't have sent him if he wasn't going to understand our speech, and I can translate what he says for you since I don't think you speak Cyclops."

Harper nodded with more certainty than she felt. She stepped to the edge of the roof, trusting in the magic barriers shimmering around the top of the gatehouse parapet to protect her from a hale of arrows or other such ambush. She wetted her lips, took a deep breath, waited for the horn blower to pause to fill his lungs, and shouted down to the oracle.

"I am the Sword Maiden Harper, divine touched servant of the Sea Queen Maraline," Harper shouted. "I would hear your message!"

The old, hunched Cyclops stopped with his lips mere inches from the mouthpiece of the horn. He limped forward away from the wagon, walking dangerously close to the edge of the ravine serving as a moat around part of the southern wall of the city. He shouted up at the wall in the general direction of Harper in the strange, guttural language of the Cyclops, which involved an odd combination of hacking, spitting, popping of lips, and even a little belching.

"He says the armies outside the walls are not an invasion force," Calista translated. "He says they were directed by their Gods to seek something within this city."

"If we can deliver what you seek, will you leave peacefully?" Harper yelled in response.

The Cyclops shook his head and shouted a shorter reply.

"He says he cannot trust us in this. They need to find the thing themselves," Calista said.

"What is it you seek?" Harper shouted. "I give you my word as a fellow servant of the pantheon that I will find it for you!"

The Cyclops seemed to consider this for a moment. After several tense moments, he shouted up a softer reply.

Calista paused as if she were having a hard time understanding the answer. Harper looked to her, as well as Ezra and Michael. "What did he say?" Harper asked.

"He's not sure what it is, but he'll know it when he sees it," Calista said. "He wants us to open the gates to…"

"Liar!" Ezra shrieked. From beneath her robe, she produced a glowing sphere of magic swirling around her hand. "I've been using a tongues spell to understand him the entire time. You lie!"

Harper glanced from Ezra to Calista, unsure of whom to side with. She trusted Calista more than anyone, and Ezra was increasingly untrustworthy, although she'd never known the Sorceress to lie. Ezra was a bit of a crank and hated most everyone, but she wasn't deceitful…except when it came to lying to Harper about being the field commander.

Calista seemed to read the doubt on Harper's face, the moment of hesitation in her action, and took it as a betrayal. She lunged for Ezra, well before any of them could do anything, moving far faster than Harper even thought a human could. Magic, divine magic from another realm of the pantheon shot across the roof of the parapet, striking the translation spell wrapped around Ezra's hand. The magic exploded in a shock of energy, hurling Ezra back down the stairs with mystical power crackling around her as she fell through the bottom edge of the protective barriers.

Harper glanced to where she thought Calista would have come to a stop, but found the top of the parapet contained two fewer people than it had a moment ago. Harper looked to Michael the Magician for explanation. The old man looked to be on the verge of a heart attack.

"What did the oracle say?" Harper demanded.

Michael just shrugged and shook his head, sending his long white beard in a dopey sway below his agape mouth. Harper sighed and shoved her way past the useless Wizard to chase after the fallen body of Ezra. The Sorceress lived, although her clothing was still smoldering in a few places. Harper reached out to pour healing energies into her stricken friend, but found a strange barrier holding her out with powerful divine magic feeding on the Sorceress herself to keep the spell in place. Harper had heard of such a stasis, although she'd never seen one personally. If Calista cast the spell, and it certainly seemed as though she had, she would have to be the one to remove it.

Harper sighed and sat back on the step above Ezra. She couldn't even venture a guess at what Calista truly was other than an amazing liar. Still, if Calista could cast such a remarkable stasis spell, she could have just as easily killed Ezra, which could only mean…Harper still wanted to believe the best of Calista.

"You couldn't have said something more useful than 'liar' before you got knocked into a coma?" Harper muttered at Ezra's snoozing form.

As if in response, Ezra let out a snorting snore and continued her magically induced nap.

Chapter 25:

Shattered

Harper was well on her way to deliver the news to Bjorn about the complete catastrophe that took place on the Last Road gate parapet. A few of her men, actually her men from the militia, carried Ezra on a stretcher back to the Thundering Dawn Inn, following closely behind Harper. Try as she might, Harper couldn't feel bad for Ezra. In truth, if Calista had given Harper the chance, she would have sided with her against Ezra. Even if Calista was lying about what the Cyclops said, and Harper was fairly certain she was, she believed Calista must have had a good reason. At least, a far better reason than Ezra had to lie to Harper about the field commander posting.

Harper didn't believe Bjorn would do much with the information from the Cyclops oracle or the sudden disappearance of Calista. The old bear was a rigid thinker and already decided on the plan of bunkering down until spring. Appeasement of the Cyclops and Fir'bolgs by giving them what they wanted simply wasn't in Bjorn's nature. Nor did Harper think he would turn the city upside down to try to find Calista to learn what the invaders wanted that he wasn't going to give to them anyway. From the meetings she'd had with Bjorn over the past week, it actually seemed like he was a little perturbed the war wasn't starting in earnest yet. He might thumb his nose at the enemies outside the gates just to get the fighting going.

Harper's entourage followed her into the main hall of the Thundering Dawn Inn. Sven, Athol, and Brandinne were at the Dagger Falls booth. In the middle of the big stone table sat a book and a handful of strange looking pelts. Harper directed her men to take Ezra to the makeshift infirmary set up in one of the other, lesser halls of the inn, before she made her way over to the table to see what was going on.

"What happened to her?" Athol asked, his eyes following Ezra's form on the stretcher.

"That's kind of a complex and lengthy story," Harper said. "Are the book and pelts easier to explain?"

"That depends," Sven said. "It would seem you made plans to leave our company shortly before the siege began."

Brandinne opened the large book on the table and turned it toward Harper. In the manifest, as the last entry on the page, was Harper's signature, the amount paid, and planned date of departure. Harper shrugged at the news. She'd intended to tell them anyway and it wasn't like she was planning on staying part of the group anymore regardless. Sven, Athol, and Ezra all made it clear they thought she was little more than a puppet to use. Still, Calista's words echoed in her head—she couldn't let on that she knew what they were doing as much as she wanted to hurl their betrayal back in their faces. She suspected entirely justifiable self-righteous indignation often preceded martyrdom.

"We were planning on telling you that night," Harper said.

"You don't think you owe us more of an explanation than that?" Sven sputtered.

Harper really didn't, and she felt like saying so, but she swallowed the harsh words and tried to calm herself to reply. "Calista pointed out that the group was stagnating with me in it. I agreed we would all be better off if the two of us left and the company found people more suited to your skill level," Harper said. She felt a little better after slipping the passive-aggressive insult in.

Brandinne and Sven looked stunned by Harper's explanation, but Athol was enraged. His eyes were stretched wide, his nostrils flared, and there was a slight shake to his head as though he were saying 'no' to every word as it exited Harper's mouth.

"You think you're better than us?" Athol growled.

"I think there's a reason you never wanted me to use my magic when we sparred," Harper said. "And I'm not the only one." Harper glanced meaningfully to Brandinne.

"I may have said something to that effect, although it was meant to be taken in confidence," Brandinne said quickly. "Pleasant conversations held over stink weed are not meant to be spread to others after the fact. If everyone blabblered about

Divine Touched

everything they overheard while passing around a pipe the entire Havvish people would…"

"Shut it, you little viper," Athol bellowed. He worked himself out of the booth to tower over Harper. "We should settle this to your satisfaction then, Sword Maiden. If you think I am afraid of your full prowess, let me prove you wrong."

Harper thought that was a fine idea and an excellent opportunity to hurt someone who had wronged her. "Find your hammer then." Harper calmly removed the wooden training sword from the ropes across her back.

"Wait," Brandinne said, "shouldn't you put your armor on or demand he use a practice hammer or something? It's hardly fair to…"

"No need," Harper said. "It'd take longer to put my armor on than it will to best him." She could see in Athol's eyes her words were having the desired effect. Harper smirked inwardly—she used to be such a nice, deferential girl.

Athol hefted his hammer from its resting place beside the booth, let forth a mighty bellow, and charged the space between them. Harper dashed forward to place herself inside Athol's defenses. It was the same mistake the Cyclops made against her, and after seeing how well it worked on larger, slower foes, Harper was all too glad to show Athol what she'd learned. She drove the pommel of her great sword into his stomach left fully exposed from hefting his hammer. He attempted to drop his elbows onto her back, a move she'd seen him use before when something got inside his guard. She flung her hand up to meet the massive arms about to crash down upon her, calling the power of the Goddess to shield her with the will of the storm. Athol's elbows collided with Harper's extended hand, but found it as immovable as rock or ice. Harper swung her sword up into Athol's exposed underarms, knocking his hammer from his grasp.

"You convinced me for so long that you were stronger," Harper said, backing away to allow Athol the chance to pick up his hammer. "But I finally figured out why. You're afraid of me."

Athol hefted his massive hammer for another attack. The rage within him fueled his wild assault. Rather than dodge his stampede-like rush, which would have been a simple matter, Harper decided to meet it, to break his strength with her own. The

228

power of the Sea Queen filled her, surrounded her, drawn from the divine spark within her that was amplified and changed by her relationship with Calista. Harper could feel the difference in the mystical spark. The divine fire, which formerly glowed blue, was far stronger in the purple shade it transformed into with continued contact with Calista. The trickle of power became a rushing torrent, and Harper bent the flood of magic to her will. She could see the rage fade from Athol's face when it was replaced by shock and fear. Her wooden sword, imbued with the power of the Sea Queen, crashed through the metal shaft of Athol's maul, shattering his weapon like brittle glass.

Athol dropped to his knees in the midst of the tiny metal fragments that his mighty hammer was reduced to. His beard and hair swirled around his head, blown by the ocean winds still flowing from Harper. He'd yielded less out of being bested in combat and more out of being awed into submission.

"Whoa," Brandinned peeped.

"You've made your point, Harper," Sven yelled. Everyone looked to him, including the crestfallen Athol. "We all knew you were stronger…"

"I didn't," Athol muttered.

"Fine, we all knew except my idiot brother, and now he knows too," Sven sighed. "Blast it all, you're touched by one of the most powerful Goddesses in the pantheon. Only a drunken barbarian like the one you just bested would think you were weak. Felix, Ezra, and I pretended for your sake because you didn't seem to want to be treated differently. When Felix died, we told Mettler and then Brandinne after him, which was obviously a mistake."

Harper shot Brandinne a harsh glare.

"People tell me stuff all the time," Brandinne protested. "I'm too much of a talker to be much of a listener."

"After the fight with Jevvon's company, Ezra and I started figuring out that you didn't actually know how powerful you really are," Sven said. "When my father asked us if you could be controlled, we told him you could. Obviously we were wrong. For what it's worth, I'm sorry."

"I normally have to pay good money to get beaten like that by a woman," Athol grunted. "If I'd known you had it in you, I would have let you thrash me on a weekly basis to save myself the coin."

He offered his hand to Harper. She took his hand and helped him to his feet. He reached out with his massive arms and embraced her. Athol parted the hug reluctantly. "Enough of that. I'm already turned on from the whipping and I don't want the Sea Queen striking me down for rubbing my arousal against her favored servant."

Harper's nerves broke and she burst into tears despite her best efforts to hold them back. She'd thought she'd lost every friend she had in the world to betrayal and suddenly they all came rushing back with heartfelt apologies. She wanted to trust the brothers again as they'd always trusted in her. Try as they might, Athol and Sven were not like their father. Neither was ruthless. How could they be when neither of them bothered to fully grow up?

"That's all well and good that you're friends again," Brandinne said, "but you're still ignoring the scalped Dwarf beard collection we have here and the unconscious Sorceress that Harper brought in with her."

Sven sighed. "Every time you talk, I fantasize about strangling you," he said. "Does it bother you at all knowing that, Brandinne?"

"Not in the slightest," Brandinne said. "Which thing should we talk about first?"

"I think they're probably both related to the same person, so why don't we cut to the chase," Harper said. "Calista is really, really, really not what she seemed."

"We think she hired mercenaries to kill thieves," Sven said. "Clearing out the competition according to Brandinne, but we already know Brandinne is a liar."

"Granted," Brandinne said, "but that doesn't necessarily mean I'm lying now."

"Did Ezra tangle with Calista?" Athol asked. "Was hair pulling and clothes tearing involved? Let me sit down and get a drink before you recount the details."

"Yes to the first—no to the rest," Harper said. "She's divine touched."

"By the Thief Lord?" Sven asked.

Harper shook her head. "I don't think so."

Brandinne seemed genuinely shocked by the news, and a little surprised in the vehemence of her own reaction. "It has to be him!"

Harper gave her a puzzled look. "Why does it have to be him?"

"Because…well, I said to her…and then she…she lied to me when I was trying to blackmail her!" Brandinne said. Sven, Athol, and Harper all stared at Brandinne with unabashed apathy. "Are you insinuating it was okay for her to lie just because I was blackmailing her?"

"Anyway," Sven said. "Brandinne's foolishness aside, why do you think it isn't the Thief Lord granting her power?"

"There was something else in there," Harper said. "She didn't use enough power or use it long enough for me to tell what was going on, but it wasn't like when I've encountered other divine touched. She hides it better than anyone I've ever met and I might never have known if she hadn't used the stasis spell on Ezra. She's no doubt trained to fight as a Dark Stalker, but that doesn't necessarily mean she owes the Thief Lord her allegiance." Only after the words were out of her mouth did Harper understand the change of her own divine spark caused by Calista. She didn't know what it meant, but it clearly had to do with the similar fire within Calista unintentionally touching something inside her. Part of Harper wondered if Calista sensed her own divine spark as red— she desperately wanted to ask her to see if the colors combined to make purple. Harper had to shake off the silliness of that being the question in the forefront of her mind regarding Calista.

"Did Ezra finally say something truly unforgivable to Calista?" Athol asked. "Not that we all haven't felt like rendering the Sorceress unconscious, but most of us just call her a name and drink until we forget what she said."

"That's actually a good question…" Sven said.

"It was? I mean, damn right it was!" Athol interrupted.

"…of all of us, Calista seemed the least perturbed by Ezra's barbs," Sven finished. "It doesn't make sense that she would render her speechless from an insult."

"Ezra called her a liar, but I don't think that was it," Harper said.

"We know she is a liar," Brandinne protested. "She lied to me and probably was lying when Ezra called her a liar. Do we even know if Calista is her real name? I bet it's actually something like Ethel, Bertha, or Mildred."

Of course she hadn't taken offense at being called a liar, Harper mused. Ezra had called Calista far worse without so much as a flicker of anger. Calista was shutting up Ezra to prevent her from saying what the Cyclops and Fir'bolgs were really after because Calista must have it. Harper felt thunderously stupid for not seeing that immediately and only managed to console herself some with the thought that she must truly love Calista to be that blinded about her motives. The truth was Harper still likely would side with Calista in not giving over whatever it was to the invaders.

"The Cyclops and Fir'bolgs want something Calista has," Harper said.

"Is it valuable?" Brandinne perked up.

"It must be," Harper said. "The northern tribes sent two armies to retrieve it."

"Walk us through the whole thing," Sven said.

"Wait until we order food and drink and then walk us through the whole thing," Athol amended his brother's statement.

Calista came to the conclusion vanishing was a whole lot easier when the city wasn't under siege. Everywhere she could think to go was already a known haunt for her and when the sun went down, the streets would be running red with the blood of a war she'd started within the city. If no other options presented themselves, she decided she might as well join in on the thief hunting.

The damnable Sorceress could just spend the rest of the winter asleep, dreaming of whatever mundane things spell-flingers dreamed of. Calista determined once again that she must be going soft—time was she would have slit Ezra's throat to keep her quiet in a far more permanent way. That would have hurt Harper though, and Calista still found herself wanting to make the Sword Maiden happy. If things kept on the way they were going with Harper, Calista imagined she might end up feeding orphans and bathing lepers with a dopy grin on her face.

The sun set as Calista continued her search of the city for a safe place to hold up until she could think of her next move. She realized she was being followed long before the lamplighters began their stilted walks to illuminate the streets. The darkness was as much cover for her as it was for those on her tail and so she made good use of it to lead her pursuers toward the eastern gate where she suspected the Red Dale Riders would begin their nightly purge of Dwarven thieves within the city.

Short, shadowy figures flashed across the ends of alleyways as she ran, cutting off any chance she had at turning a corner. All too soon, she realized she was being herded toward an ambush. The barricades around the exits of a small courtyard below the Thundering Dawn Inn came as no surprise. She slowed to a walk, and casually made her way to the open snowy ground at the center of the clearing.

"I don't know what you did to that Havvish woman, but she is determined to end you," Ulrich's familiar voice echoed out of the shadows. "If we were still friends, I might have opted to kill her for you and asked for a taste of the valuables she mentioned as a reward, but you made it pretty clear I could take my friendship and shove it in whatever orifice pleased me most."

"Valuables?" Calista asked. "I hate to say it, but I think you've been played by her."

"The valuables the Cyclops and Fir'bolg marched an army to retrieve," Ulrich said. "The Havvish woman said you knew where they were."

Calista rolled her eyes and let out a little laugh. Normally it would have been a show to make the accusation seem preposterous, but in this case, she was being absolutely genuine in her incredulity. "You don't even know what it is," Calista said.

"I know you must still have it since you didn't want to stick around after the shipwreck."

"Did she also tell you I was the one who hired the mercenaries hunting down thieves in the city?" Calista asked.

"She did not," Ulrich replied.

"You can tell Randolph I'll work my way up to him eventually."

"You can tell him yourself soon enough."

"Can we just skip to the part of this where you fail at trying to kill me?" Calista slid her curved dagger from its sheath along her lower back, well hidden beneath the poncho she'd started wearing for Harper's sake.

"We're not going to kill you," Ulrich said, "at least, not until we torture the location of the valuables out of you."

Dwarves armed with truncheons flooded from the shadows. She sidestepped a few clumsy attacks and took off running for the edge of the clearing, hoping to use the walls of the two story buildings as cover for one of her flanks. She jumped over a swung stick, slashing her dagger across the face of the Dwarf who attacked her as she sailed by. The Dwarf shrieked, dropped his bat, and gripped his face.

As much as Calista wanted to use her powers to cleave the life from everyone in the area, she knew she couldn't. Drawing any more attention to her true nature than she already did in binding Ezra and creating thralls of the Red Dale Riders would be completely foolish. Her Dark Stalker weapons delivered magical poison with every strike without linking the power back to her and she could still drink in their deaths regardless of how they died. She could already feel the Dwarf she'd slashed fading quickly toward death, transferring his life force to her.

A Dwarf armed with a net flashed into view at the top of the building ahead of her. Before he could even lift the net to shoulder height, Calista flung her handheld harpoon at him. The little barbed head buried itself in his stomach. She yanked hard on the chain bringing the howling Dwarf down from the roof, snarled in his own net. When she tried to pull her harpoon free, the chain tangled in the net, stopping her in her tracks.

She released her grip on the chain to draw her straight blade dagger from her boot. The reel attaching the chain to her belt wasn't easily removed, tethering her to the fallen Dwarf until she could clear enough space to cut the net.

Her attackers appeared to figure this out as two of the Dwarves dropped their clubs to grasp the chain buried in their screaming fellow. They yanked back hard, thinking to pull Calista off her feet. Calista skipped once backward, pulled by the chain, before she turned into the attack, jumping past the two Dwarves, slashing them with the daggers in her hands as she passed by. She tucked into a roll on the other side and popped up to defend herself again. The two wounded Dwarves fell over their screaming compatriot, adding their own agonizing yelps and writhing forms to the mix.

Calista had no idea how many Dwarves it was going to take to bring her down, but a quick headcount of those charging her let her know how many they were going to use. She stopped counting after twenty, which was far more than she could reasonably kill. Nets and lassos flew from the attacking gang. Even as she was dodging them, she could see several of the Dwarves breaking away to once again grasp at the chain on her entangled harpoon.

Before she could move to clear the four Dwarves fumbling among their dying companions for the farthest end of the chain, a lasso landed on Calista's right arm. She managed to slash it away with the dagger in her left hand a second after it was tugged tight. The momentary distraction was all the Dwarves needed to bum rush her.

She slashed and stabbed at the beards and batons flying at her. She felt her knives catching again and again on flesh and weapons. A net fell over her head even as she lashed out wildly to clear some space. She tried to get the serrated back of her curved dagger up to clear away the binding, but a hard club strike on her hip knocked a good deal of the fight from her. More blows rained in, dropping her first to her knees, and then over onto her side in a fetal position to protect her head.

A familiar bellow echoed through the night followed by a flash of light. The Dwarves attempted to gather her up in the netting to flee with her. The harpoon chain prevented them from getting very far though as the dying Dwarf on the other end was buried under two other bodies of now fully dead Dwarves.

Calista seized upon their struggles to free the other end of the chain from the tangle of bodies and netting to cut away some of the ropes and nets binding her. She caught a glimpse of a great barbarian swinging a giant hammer through a field of Dwarves. Dark, bloody bodies of the diminutive men sailed into the night off the edge of every backswing.

Calista had expected the Red Dale Riders, or perhaps a contingent of guards, but instead found her rescuers were far more familiar faces. Harper, Sven, and Athol crashed through the Dwarven horde with great glee. Judging from the lethality of the Dagger Falls Company against the Dwarves, Calista guessed the thieves were not permitted to bring deadly weapons for the ambush out of fear of killing someone with valuable information. When

Divine Touched

people they might have liked to kill showed up, they were ill-equipped to retaliate.

Calista managed to wriggle her left arm free enough to drag the blade of her curved dagger along one of her abductor's bare arms. The poison immediately seized him and her entire upper body fell to the ground. She sat up quickly and slashed at the two trying to hold her legs. From the howls, she assumed she'd cut both of them deeply enough to inflict the poison.

Harper was at her side moments after, pulling away the netting and ropes as best she could while Sven and Athol cleared a halo of safety around them. The brothers fought far better together when they were on the offensive against largely unarmed Dwarves and soon they had a vast territory around Calista cleared of any attackers. Clearly having lost their prize, the thieves vanished into the night, leaving nearly a score of their numbers behind as dead or wounded.

Calista dropped her daggers and Harper dropped her sword. Kneeling in the bloody snow, Harper collected Calista into her arms. "You're safe, my love," Harper whispered. "I won't let anyone take you from me now."

Part of Calista wanted to believe her even though the rest of her knew it was a promise born out of not knowing what Calista truly was.

Chapter 26:

The Hard Edge Restored

Harper took Calista back to the Thundering Dawn under the watchful guard of Sven and Athol. The brothers were in fine spirits about their victory over the army of small bearded men wielding clubs, speaking animatedly about how they sent the sawed-off brigands running. Harper wondered if they were getting a little antsy about not seeing any action at the walls.

It was difficult to tell how hurt Calista was. She felt weak, leaned heavily on Harper as they walked, and seemed to flinch often. Harper wondered what fresh hell she would find beneath the armor and poncho once she set to work healing her.

Once in the main hall of the Thundering Dawn, the brothers took their leave, bidding Harper come speak with their father once she was done patching Calista up. Harper wasn't sure what their plan might be, and she didn't care. Until she knew Calista was going to be okay, nothing else mattered.

Within her room, Harper summoned servants to fill the large, stone tub in hopes of warming Calista once her wounds were tended. Servant girls hauled great cauldrons of hot water to the room in groups of two on the ends of poles used to suspend the vast pots. Harper focused on undressing Calista who had unceremoniously collapsed on the bed.

"You must have questions," Calista murmured.

"Nothing beyond 'where does it hurt?' at the moment," Harper replied as she gingerly stripped away Calista's black armor.

"Oh, that's easily answered: everywhere," Calista replied.

As Calista's skin finally came into view with the removal of the leather plates, Harper could see she wasn't lying. Calista was more bruise than anything else and there were no doubt countless fractured bones as well. Harper set to healing the wounds as she found them, which she knew wasn't the most efficient tactic; try as she might, she couldn't stand to look at the ugly injuries knowing what pain they were causing while she finished removing Calista's armor.

"Ask other, more important questions as well," Calista said. "It would do me good to think of something else besides how often I was hit and kicked."

"Your divine spark, it's red, isn't it?" Harper asked.

"It was," Calista replied.

"But now it's purple?"

Calista smiled faintly. "Yes."

"It's hard to explain the divine spark to people—where it is, how I can see it, but not with my eyes," Harper said.

"I've honestly never tried," Calista replied.

"Which God gave you your divine spark?"

Calista waited a moment before answering as though she were considering her words carefully. "You wouldn't have heard of her," she finally said.

"Try me."

"Her name is Solancacae," Calista said.

"You're right, I've never heard of her. What sphere does she claim?"

"Secrets, among other things," Calista said with a smirk.

"Solancacae Mistress of Secrets," Harper said.

"Precisely," Calista said.

Harper healed what she guessed was a fracture or torn ligaments in Calista's left knee, straightening it out slowly until she felt the bones and tissues knitting back together beneath her magic touch. The purple divine spark within her, glowing brighter the longer she spent around Calista, was more powerful in healing just as it was with combat magic. Typically mending so many wounds would have exhausted her, but Harper found she was energized by it when it came to Calista. She had Calista nearly naked and nearly healed by the time the servant girls finished filling the tub with steaming water.

"Are you truly a Dark Stalker then since you don't worship the Thief Lord?" Harper asked.

"There is no word for what I am," Calista said, "although that is how I was trained in combat, so it will suffice."

Harper finished stripping away the last of Calista's armor, pressed her hands over Calista's swollen right ankle, and eased the wound back to a normal state. She closed the door behind the last servant girl and turned back to gaze upon Calista lying completely still on the bed, nude and gloriously whole once again.

"What did the Cyclops say that made you silence Ezra?" Harper asked.

"That they're looking for a divine assassin and thief." Calista sat up, testing the flexibility of her freshly healed joints a little before pulling herself to the edge of the bed.

"He didn't call you by name?"

"How could he? They don't know my name," Calista said, "but I could see on Ezra's face she'd pieced it together."

"Do I know your real name?"

"I inherited a surname from my father, a moon name from my mother, and they gave me two other names as their gifts to me as is the tradition of my culture," Calista said. "Of my four names, yes, Calista is one of them."

Harper felt reasonably satisfied with this. She'd heard of the southern practice of every child receiving two names from each parent—an inherited one and a given one. Judging from some of the names her childhood friends had, she guessed many northerners might have liked a few name options to choose from.

She helped Calista to her feet, even though she knew she was likely as spry as she'd always been, and walked with her over to the tub. Calista settled into the steaming water slowly, letting out a satisfied hiss when she was fully submerged.

"Did you steal or assassinate to upset the Cyclops and Fir'bolgs so much?" Harper finally asked.

"Both," Calista replied.

"What did you steal?"

Calista smiled an enigmatic smile Harper had never seen before on her. It was self-satisfied, wily, and a little sinister. "The most valuable thing that ever was and ever will be."

"I don't suppose you would be willing to give it back."

Calista shook her head. "They would have to kill me to take it back, and even then, I don't think they'd be satisfied."

"That isn't an option then."

Calista opened her eyes to tiny slit of sparkling blue and looked up to Harper. "Have I told you that I love you?"

Harper's heart threatened to break free of the moorings in her chest at the question and the wickedly feline look within Calista's eyes. "Not yet."

"I will soon," Calista replied, letting her eyes slide shut again.

Before Calista's bathwater could even cool to uncomfortable, Athol and Sven came to collect them. Calista dressed while Harper remained in her armor for some reason. Calista assumed it was a readiness born of practicality. Harper probably believed, and reasonably so, that the Cyclops would attack at any minute or the Dwarven thieves would spring from the shadows. There were a lot of enemies both inside and outside the walls—Calista was used to the idea, but apparently Harper wasn't yet.

Calista dressed in more typical clothes, but still armed herself with her daggers. The four of them walked up through the darkened hallways and corridors toward the old Dwarven section of the inn where Bjorn held his meetings. It struck Calista as passing odd that no one asked her to remove the spell from Ezra. She assumed Harper would have told the brothers, and there was little doubt she'd already figured it out, yet the topic hadn't even come up.

"I appreciate the timely rescue," Calista said, "but how did you know where to find me?"

"Brandinne," Athol replied as they walked.

"I wouldn't have thought she'd want to help," Calista said.

"She didn't," Sven said. "We figured out pretty quickly she was looking for information about you to sell to the thieves guild, so we gave her a little, and then followed her to the rendezvous. She passed the information to a couple guards and then we followed them to the ambush."

"We're not sure where Brandinne is now," Harper said. "We suspect she'll surface again since we don't think she knows that we know she betrayed us."

"Betrayed me, you mean," Calista said.

"You're part of the Dagger Falls Company still," Athol said. "If she betrays one of us, she betrays us all."

"Technically, you didn't leave our employ or steal our Sword Maiden, yet," Sven said with a wry smile. "Which means my brother is right, after a fashion."

"Plus, we eventually need you to release the spell on Ezra," Athol said. "Not too soon, mind you, but in due course."

Calista smiled and glanced to Harper.

"I have my own reasons that I will make clear to you later," Harper said.

When they reached the door to Bjorn's office and domicile, Athol and Sven held Harper back from entering with Calista.

"He'll have a conversation with all of us after," Sven explained.

"For now he wants to meet with just the instigator of this grand fun," Athol added.

Calista shrugged and walked in on her own. There might have been a time when Bjorn would have been a physical threat to her, but she likely hadn't even had her woman's blood yet the last time that was true. The room was faintly lit from just the fireplace. Bjorn sat before it in a large, metal chair, blocking much of the light and a good deal of the heat. He was bundled in bear hides, and he looked even older than the last time Calista saw him a couple weeks prior.

"My sons tell me I have you to thank for all of this," Bjorn said, waving his hand weakly for emphasis.

Calista couldn't rightly say if he was being sarcastic. The brain injury causing paralysis on half his body made him fairly difficult to understand at the best of times and made subtler inflections like sarcasm essentially impossible to discern.

"You're welcome?" Calista replied.

"I wanted to die in a great battle." Bjorn seemed to think things over for a minute, coughed, and then shook his head. "No, that's not right. I wanted to be mortally wounded, carried from the field as the triumph was assured, and died that night listening to the drums of victory." He turned to look at her finally. The flickering firelight lit up half his face, the good half as it turned out, but even still he looked very old and very tired. "This will have to do for my final battle, and I must spend it here, in a low ceiling room that I won't leave alive regardless of the outcome."

"You wouldn't have me given over to the Cyclops and Fir'bolgs for the sake of peace?" Calista asked.

Bjorn practically roared with laughter. "By the fires of the afterworld, I would have you spit in their eyes and demand they come for us with all they've brought," Bjorn declared. "If what my sons say is true, you could do precisely that if you so chose. You could force their hand and set this battle to burn at long last."

"The tall Sorcerer, Magical Michael or whatever his name is, said you didn't want the Cyclops antagonized."

"I don't want them antagonized; I want them bloody well infuriated, which that buffoon and his prancing, spell-flinging lot could never accomplish. But you...you've done them some great wrong, stolen something by the sound of it. It must be valuable for them to send so much after you. Do you think they want it badly enough to truly go to war with us?"

Calista nodded. "I *know* it's valuable enough that they would bleed their armies dry in its retrieval."

Bjorn slapped his good hand against the arm of his chair and grunted. "That is what I wanted to hear. I never desired anything more than this epic fight of impossible odds, on a snowy field, against a monstrous army. It's finally here and I'm too feeble to wade in with axe and hammer in hand."

"I could give you that chance," Calista said, taking a step closer. "You could be what you were, if only briefly."

"I could fight again?"

Calista nodded.

"I could leave this room, feel the cold of winter upon my skin, and face down the enemy once more?"

Calista nodded and took another step forward. "For a time, but you will die before it is over." There were questions a sane man would have asked her, but she could see in Bjorn's eyes his full senses had long since fled him. Hope sprung in him at the mere mention of attaining what he knew to be impossible only moments ago. She knew he would sacrifice everything for the chance and wouldn't question how or why for fear she might retract the offer.

"I would give anything for this, anything at all." Bjorn pulled himself from his chair, struggling greatly in the effort to fall on his knees before Calista. He crawled to her in an awkward shuffle to take her hand between his.

"Name Harper as your true successor, commander of the forces and guardian of the city," Calista said, "and I will restore your strength to fight and provide the epic battle you've always craved."

"Tonight, it will be done tonight before you or I or anyone else is allowed to sleep, but please, let me know what it is to hold my axe again," Bjorn pleaded.

It was all so easy that for a moment Calista considered asking for more. He would give more just as readily, but she couldn't honestly think of anything else she could want from him. Calista leaned down, taking both of Bjorn's hands in her own. The withered husk that was his dead side lay only slightly weaker than his supposed good side. Black tendrils of magic snaked down her arms and into his. The life forces stolen from her slaying of half a dozen Dwarves earlier that night poured into the old bear of a man, restoring his strength, pumping strong blood through revived tissue, and sweeping away the necrotic wounds of his mind that left half his body paralyzed. It was a temporary gift, and one that would eventually return to Calista regardless of what either of them did. Unlike Harper's healing magic, the power Calista used to restore was not truly hers to give. When Bjorn fell on the field, it would return to her; if he survived the battle, it would return to her in a few days anyway. Regardless, it would bring with it what little life he still had in him.

Bjorn might not survive the winter at any rate. Calista needed to look to her own future. If the mantle of commander of the defense forces fell to anyone but Harper, she would be in danger of being turned over to the Cyclops and Fir'bolgs in hopes of bartering a peace treaty. Certainly Bjorn said he wouldn't, which she believed, but Calista didn't believe he had three months of life left even under the best of conditions. If Harper supplanted Bjorn, Calista would be safe until the spring thaw as she knew the Sword Maiden would never let her be taken, knowing it would mean Calista's death.

Bjorn slowly rose, stretched to his full height, and nearly knocked his head against the ceiling. He flexed his fingers before him, surprised when both hands functioned. Before Calista could make comment, he stormed from her, back across the room, rooting about in some dark corner with the clank of metal against stone. Finally he came away with two massive weapons, one for each hand. In his right fist, which seemed to be growing larger and stronger by the moment, he held a massive, double-bladed battle axe. In his left that was every inch the match of its fellow, he held a gnarled war hammer with a spike on the top and a hook upon the back.

"I threw them there months ago, believing I would never again possess the strength to lift them," Bjorn whispered in awed tones. "They feel lighter than when I swung them as part of myself." He finally looked to her and she could have sworn, even by the low firelight, that he had tears in his eyes. "Thank you for this."

"Listen closely," Calista said, not particularly interested in the old warrior's reunion with his draconian weapons. "The Cyclops will come if I reveal myself to their oracle, but they won't come for the wall. They never intended to assault the gate of the Last Road."

Bjorn nodded his understanding. "They'll ride their bears for the frozen bay and try to get in over the ice."

Calista smiled at this. "Yes, that is what they will do."

"I've seen it before," Bjorn said. "They attacked the outpost of Archangel in the early spring before the ice broke. When I was a young man, I used to take my resting seasons up there. The stone and ice walls could keep out the whole of the north if it marched over land, but the bay…"

Archangel, above the Crown of the World Mountains, was where Calista took ship from on the *Enola* months ago. It seemed like a lifetime away that she'd boarded that ship only to have it dashed upon the rocks outside Griffon's Rock. She'd seen the Cyclops use that same tactic before as well, although much farther north in a land few humans had seen. The Cyclops were attacking a Fir'bolg occupied human village in the midst of a holy war that threatened to consume the entire tundra regions. The ice giants couldn't walk on the bay, even when it was frozen to its thickest. Before the Fir'bolgs could mount a proper defense, the Cyclops razed the city. It was under the cover of this destruction that she took her prize and escaped into the night. Apparently, a tense truce was struck after the fact to chase a common enemy down to retrieve what they were fighting a bloody war over in the first place.

"If you take the fight to them far enough out, fall back in good order, and bleed them along the way, you can collapse the bay when their reinforcements make a charge," Calista explained.

"The hot blood spilled will weaken the ice..." Bjorn mused.

"...and the glorious victory in death you've always wished for can finally be yours," Calista finished for him.

Chapter 27:

War on the Ice

The combat engineers gleaned from every mercenary group that boasted one worked tirelessly throughout the night to create anti-cavalry fortifications on the ice of the bay's bottleneck. As the sun crested the mountains in the east, shining cold winter light over the shimmering frozen bay, the walls, parapets, and spike embankments almost entirely constructed of ice and snow stood like a deadly extension from the city wall in the south to the lighthouse in the north.

Calista still couldn't bring herself to walk on the frozen bay. If the Sea Queen was angry with her, and she had several reasons to believe she was, standing on frozen salt water would be foolish beyond reason. From her vantage point at the top of the Last Road gatehouse, she could see all the way down to the bay where the white and blue banners of Harper's brigades stood out among the men and women fortifying the bay's defenses. Calista resolved to join the fight in something of a support role. There were archers in and around the lighthouse she could aid without actually stepping on Maraline's domain.

Bjorn was good to his word regarding Harper's ascension upon his death. He actually strode that very night up to the Duke's palace with his astounded sons in his wake, banged his restored fists upon the door until the Duke awoke, and then declared Harper his successor with all rights and titles pertaining to the position. It was difficult to tell whether the Duke was more flummoxed by the sudden change in Bjorn's plan or the fact that the old bear was restored to a semblance of his former glory. Regardless, the Duke, standing about in his night clothes, was in no position to argue. He agreed, stating it was at Bjorn's discretion.

The Red Dale Riders were at Calista's hip most of the time. This was the only drawback to Harper's sudden true ascendancy to the future commander of the defense forces. She seemed to think

Calista was in mortal danger after the Dwarf ambush. Apparently a dozen zealot Rangers following her around was the only thing that would satisfy Harper that her lover was safe. Calista didn't care for the entourage, but she supposed, if she had to have a personal guard, she was glad they were Rangers capable of keeping up with her sneaky ways. Glancing around to the stoic men atop the gatehouse tower with her, she could see the thrall spell was fully spread among them already. They looked to her as though she was the Goddess incarnate, and, for all they knew, she was.

Calista liberated the same bow she'd used on the Ogre excursion from the Thundering Dawn armory early that morning. Aside from not being able to use her daggers for much of the coming fighting, she was also a little skittish about going back into the fray after taking such a tremendous beating the last time. She still carried her daggers, but she truly hoped she wouldn't have to use them again anytime soon.

The blind Cyclops oracle still stood at his horn, blowing the low, rumbling note for the umpteenth hour without rest. One sure way existed to rile the Cyclops without actually enraging the Fir'bolgs as well, and Calista knew precisely what it was.

"Oracle, I spit on your ineffectual Gods and mock your pathetic attempts to appease them," Calista shouted down in Cyclops to the oracle. She spoke in their hideous tongue not for the benefit of the oracle, but so the other Cyclops within hearing range who likely didn't speak the human tongue would hear her words. She spoke only a strange, stilted form of Cyclops that she knew sounded eccentric, but was as close as a human could come to being understood in the harsh tongue. The oracle likely wouldn't care what she said, but the average soldier could be inflamed by her words.

The oracle briefly ceased his horn blowing to look up to where he thought the shout came from. He opened his mouth to respond, but before he could put breath to words, Calista put an arrow through his head. Inflamed by words might have done the job, but Calista decided adding deed to words would seal the decision to attack.

"Tell your next oracle to wear a helmet," Calista shouted in the Cyclops tongue so they might know it wasn't an accident.

All she could do was done at the wall, and so she directed her company of Rangers to follow her down to the waiting horses. They filed after her in good order. In the courtyard on the interior of the wall, thirteen horses awaited them, including Aerial on loan from Harper. The warhorse chomped at her bit and urged Calista aboard. Calista led the charge at the head of the Red Dale Riders. The drums and horns of war outside the wall echoed long before they could even see the lighthouse amid the snowy buildings. The warning bell above the bay rang out in response.

Calista thundered down the terraces on a galloping Aerial. The defenses on the bay were readying for the charge that Calista hoped would be sloppy and rage-driven. Bjorn guessed correctly when he guessed Calista knew precisely how to infuriate the Cyclops in ways the rank and file defenders couldn't. Calista and her riders were nearly to the jetty road leading to the lighthouse when the first bear cavalry emerged on the frozen sea.

She urged Aerial on faster. The warhorse jumped to, and galloped down the frozen rocky outcropping at a full charge, outdistancing the lesser horses ridden by the Red Dale Riders. Calista clattered to a stop among the already manned lighthouse base. Her riders finally caught up to her as she was dismounting. She directed them to the top of the lighthouse where they might do the most good with their deadly longbows. For a second after their departure, she considered riding Aerial out onto the ice to join Harper's line. More than simple concern for her own wellbeing overrode the desire though. If Maraline chose to shatter the bay to get at Calista, it would far more than deadly just for her as the collateral damage might consume Harper and anyone else near her in the Sea Queen's wrath. Gods and Goddesses weren't above sacrificing their servants to get what they wanted, and Calista couldn't abide the thought of Harper dying at the hands of her own deity simply to get at what Calista carried.

Calista gave over the string of horses with Aerial at the lead to one of the militia members and instructed the lad to take the horses back to the Thundering Dawn. The boy of only fourteen seasons did as he was told, struggling to get the horses to move until Calista told Aerial to go. Calista watched the horses finally leave before she strode up the winding spiral staircase within the lighthouse to join the Red Dale Raiders at the pinnacle.

From the top of the lighthouse she could see the entire bay to the south and the frozen ocean to the west. The Cyclops cavalry stood in gathering formation atop their colossal bears; they didn't manage proper formations the way heavy mounted human warriors did. Instead, they clustered in clan groups based on speed, which created long, disorganized rivulets of riders rather than a wall of charging lances. Calista believed this was based on their mounts. Bears weren't good distance runners, were far slower than horses, and typically fought rather than simply carrying their rider to the fray. The northern bears ridden by the Cyclops were also huge, five thousand pounds usually, which was to play an integral part in the plan to collapse the bay.

No archers on the defensive side fired. They needed to bring them in close before the killing began. The tense moments mounted as the Cyclops gathered for their charge. They numbered in the thousands, Calista was sure of that. In truth, it was the first large scale battle Calista openly participated in. She'd snuck through war zones in the past, but never actually fought as part of an army. At the northern most edge of the line, she was in a well defended position with unassailable rock cliffs guarding one side of the lighthouse's position and twenty feet of icy, jagged rocks leading up to the landing the lighthouse sat upon. Any Cyclops intending to take their position would have to ride through the multiple lines of defense on the bay, across the full bay itself, mount the end of the jetty at the city's edge, and ride down the length of the lighthouse road. Even knowing this, Calista felt nervous.

The horns signaling the charge blew out of the enemy's formation. The bears with their heavy barding and even heavier riders began rumbling across the frozen ocean toward the bay. As Calista had seen before, they stretched out to long, strangely shaped formations like water running down a window pane. She and her men knocked arrows, but didn't draw bowstrings yet. There wouldn't be any need to even aim when the Cyclops entered the killing zone. Once the Cyclops were close enough, her archers could fire into the mass without fear any of their arrows would strike ice.

Before the first bear riders could reach the front line of the bay's defenses, the magical blast that would be the signal to fire erupted down the line. Fireballs, lightning bolts, and all other manner of mystical attack exploded from amidst the human line, tearing great swaths of destruction in the Cyclops cavalry charge.

Calista and her men drew their bows back and fired at will. Arrows rained down into the Cyclops following their magically devastated brethren. All the arrows they'd brought to the lighthouse held wickedly serrated heads. They flew awkwardly because of it, but caused uncontrollable bleeding upon impact. They needed blood, lots of hot blood both bear and Cyclops to melt the ice. With the rear ranks of the cavalry charge stumbling into the fallen front ranks, accuracy wasn't a concern even though the arrows fluttered and snapped like angry snakes off their firing bows.

Calista fell into the repetitive pattern of knocking an arrow, drawing the string back to aim toward the sky, and letting fly. It was unlikely such volley-fired arrows would slay anything amid the chaotic crush of the rear ranks they were falling into, but they would cause bleeding, and that was more valuable than an occasional kill.

Harper's brigade stood watch over the northern edge of the line, which was irritating yet understandable. Her trained militia certainly wasn't meant for center of the line conflict. Bjorn and the Ash twins held the center with the Dead Watch Pikes while Athol and Sven were entrusted with the southern edge, leading an organized contingent of a dozen or so mercenary groups.

In seeing the bear cavalry for the first time across the frozen ocean, Harper didn't think the walls they'd built were nearly tall enough. The Cyclops formation looked taller by double that of any human mounted warrior and likely weighed five times as much. Her men were equipped with long spears behind the shoulder height ice walls, but even still, she wondered if the bears might not simply break through the hastily constructed fortifications. She had to remind herself again and again that the plan was not to stop the charge—they were to bleed it out, draw the fight across the bay, and let the frigid water beneath do the rest of the work once they'd pulled the majority of the enemy force onto the thin ice.

Awaiting the charge, she decided, was worse than the charge itself. She had nothing to compare it to, of course, but the hour of waiting for the enemy to form up to charge felt like an eternity. When the Cyclops horns sounded and the bears began barreling down on them like a thundering storm of death, Harper quickly revised her opinion about waiting being the worst part. The ice beneath her feet trembled with the coming charge. She could see on the faces of her men around her that she wasn't the only one unsettled by this.

"It's all part of the plan," Harper said, hoping she was right.

Her men seemed to glean some courage from this, holding fast to their extended spears. Even still, Harper wondered about their resolve to fight. They were hastily trained militia. Certainly they were well armed and armored from the supplies within the Thunder Dawn's armory, but they weren't hardened troops by any stretch of the definition. They would run when it came down to it, and Harper knew this, but that actually was part of the plan so long as they didn't run all the way back to the town when they did. Calista's words echoed in her head—they believed in her and she thought she would do well to believe in them.

Harper's fears about the defenses being inadequate to slow a charge of two-thousand Cyclops riding giant bears were only supported the closer the cavalry got. She drew her sword all the same and readied for the imminent collision of thousands of mounted warriors crashing into their ice walls. The bears, bigger than any bear Harper had ever seen, puffed great billows of steam from their mouths upon the charge, hurling ice chips from their massive paws in their gallop. She could see from the shaking in the tips of the spears of her defensive line that she wasn't the only one unnerved by the ferocity of the mounts barreling down upon them. Charging horses were unsettling enough, but Harper couldn't think of a single situation where a bear wasn't dangerous while she could think of plenty where horses weren't frightening.

The wait for the magical assault felt interminable, coming far too late for Harper's tastes. Wizardly Willard was the Sorcerer assigned to her specific section of the line. The paunchy, mustachioed mystical practitioner carried himself with such pomp and confidence that Harper found herself a little reassured by his presence. She glanced back to him standing in the back of the wagon that was pointed toward the city, ready to move their magical artillery piece as soon as the line fell back. His great mustache blew in the wind while the ends of his red coat whipped and snapped around his thick legs. For a moment, Harper wished they had Ezra, although she was still deep in a mystical slumber since the company voted unanimously to leave her there for a few days. Still, she knew Wizardly Willard, despite his foppish appearance, was a far more powerful practitioner of mystical arts than Ezra.

The red bedecked Sorcerer conjured a powerful spell from the air, waving it into shape with his pudgy hands and giving it direction with quickly chanted words. He extended his arms to full length in front of him, flinging his hands wide open, palms toward the enemy. An enormous fireball erupted from the space before him, shooting toward the charging cavalry like an angry comet.

Harper's gaze followed the magical projectile as it sailed over her formation, striking the front ranks of the bears. The fireball exploded in a shower of mystical flame, consuming several of the neighboring bears in the process. The cavalry behind the fallen bears stumbled through the charred corpses, slowing their attack and even pitching a few riders over the fronts of their mounts. Harper could hear Wizardly Willard already conjuring up another spell when the first of the charging bears broke through the fallen tangle of bodies.

A colossal gray bear reared up at the frozen wall defended with spears. Her men made good efforts to thrust at the bear's underbelly, but found thick scale barding guarding the bear's stomach. Their spear points bounced off the armor harmlessly. A moment after, the bear brought its full weight down on the ice wall, shattering a great hole in it and scattering the four men defending the section.

Harper led the reserves in a counterattack to plug the gap. She swung her blade down in a mighty arc, cleaving the bear's head from its body at an awkward, diagonal angle. The bear collapsed forward and her men leapt upon the Cyclops rider who tumbled out of the saddle upon the death of his mount. They plunged their spears into the armored brute again and again, finally pulling back when they were certain they'd secured the kill.

Harper glanced to the center of the line in the brief moment of calm. She spotted the Ash twins and Bjorn amid an immense rush of the Cyclops. The great general Bjorn was battling his way through the charge, axe in one hand and hammer in the other, shouting for the enemy to send him more victims. It seemed all the Ash twins could do to keep up with their commander.

Harper's focus shot back to her own battle when a handful of riders managed to veer across the top of her line along the face of the jetty. She rushed to cut them off from their goal of crushing Wizardly Willard and his wagon. Several of her men already made the same attempt, falling beneath a great swiping paw and the follow up stabbing of the rider's spear.

She altered her angle of attack to place herself in the path of the charge in hopes of turning the bears back toward the center where her men might have a better chance of felling a slowed rider. The lead bear reared again, towering over her, larger than anything she'd ever faced. She called upon the power of the Goddess to aid in her strike, drawing the same spell she'd used to shatter Athol's hammer. She swung hard for the center of the bear's armored breastplate with her sword. Her strike carried the full force of the Goddess through the attack, shattering the armor and burying her blade deep within the bear's stomach. The stricken bear and surprised rider pitched to the side, carried back by the force of the blow. The next rider in line made the turn as Harper hoped, stumbling directly into the waiting spears of her men. Harper didn't know if it was the ice hampering the bear cavalry's lateral movements or if they simply weren't as nimble in turns as traditional horse cavalry. Regardless, Harper planned on forcing them to turn as often as possible from then on.

Harper pulled her sword from the bear's chest. A gush of steaming hot blood followed the blade out, melting a river through the thick ice before it could cool. She shook off the momentary surprise at how superficially well the plan seemed to be working. Scrambling up the bear's corpse, she found the Cyclops rider working to dislodge his leg from where it was pinned between the corpse of his mount and the rock face of the jetty. Harper swung her sword in a horizontal slash, snapping the shaft of the spear he threw up to defend himself, and then the Cyclops's head immediately after.

Divine Touched

The warning bell within the tower at the edge of the docks rang once, signaling the retreat to the second tier of defenses. Harper glanced back to find Wizardly Willard and his wagon were already rolling back toward the second row of walls, pulled by two mules and driven by the Sorcerer's apprentice. Her men didn't seem to hear or understand the bell as they continued to stab at the onslaught of bears and riders with their spears.

Harper shouted to them and waved her bloody sword above her head to get their attention. A few heeded her orders, but many did not. She slid down the body of the bear she'd climbed, grabbed at the backs of the men she passed, and again tried to rally them to the second level. She turned back to retrieve the handful of men who hadn't heard her or were too deep in the frenzy of battle to understand. Before she could make it two steps toward the frontline, the full Cyclops charge crashed through the weakened position. The men were lifted in powerful bear jaws, crushed beneath pounding paws, or run through by the spearmen riders.

Harper cursed her slow reaction, but turned away her rising desire to charge in to save those beyond saving. She punctured the oil barrel on her way back toward the next line of the defense, sending a slick of rock berry nut oil pouring across the ice behind her. As bloody and horrible as the fight felt from the ground level, she had to assume by the single ring of the warning bell that it must be going well. If the line suffered any meaningful break, the signal to retreat of constant ringing of the bell would already have sounded and they would be fleeing blindly while their Sorcerers attempted to collapse the bay in a panicked rush.

Harper rallied her men to the walls of the second tier of defenses. There were already fresh reinforcements waiting to support them, taking up the primary act of fighting with unbroken spears and confidence in their goal. Wizardly Willard appeared exhilarated by the action, still standing atop his wagon. All in all, Harper was pleased with her militia's progress.

She glanced to her right, spotting Calista and her Red Dale Riders atop the lighthouse. They seemed perfectly safe, raining arrows down into the rear ranks of the enemy without any real return fire. Cyclops spears bounced off the walls of the lighthouse, but none appeared able to throw high enough to reach even three-quarters up the face of the structure.

Harper's confidence in their imminent success faded when she looked to her left and the center of the line. Bjorn was well out in front of his men, creating something of a bulge in the line that looked to be cleaved from the whole at any moment. The Ash twins and their black armored pike men seemed torn between falling back and staying with the general. An instant after, the oil barrels ignited prematurely on the southern edge of the line where Athol and Sven's forces were fighting.

Chapter 28:

And the Sea Shall Come Up to Meet Them

Calista saw the catastrophic failure in the line from a perfect vantage point. Harper's militia portion was the only section to fall back in good order, leaving two very chaotic regions of the bay to the south. If Harper continued on with the plan, which she appeared to be doing, she would open Bjorn's flank for an attack. But if she moved forward again to support the general, who had advanced himself completely out of position, the entire army would have to march forward onto the ice they'd just thinned.

The fire that exploded on the southern edge of the line only added to the already compounding problems. Athol and Sven's forces were cut in twain by the fiery swath. Even before the fire separated them, half had fallen back in good order while the rest seemed to be torn between following through with the plan and helping Bjorn's forces. A wall of fire separated them, putting that entire end of the line in danger of being dumped into the frigid bay. With their backs to the wall, they looked to be fighting for their very existence, pushing in the only direction left to them—west onto the ocean.

"Down," Calista shouted to her men.

The Red Dale Riders responded without question or comment. They gathered their arrows and descended the lighthouse. Calista followed closely behind them, making her way to the front when they emerged before the road again. She pointed at the open flank on Bjorn's forces created when Harper fell back.

"Clear them out," Calista directed her archers' fire. The handful of other archers around the base, who hadn't been knocked out by spears hurled by Cyclops, followed the lead of the Red Dale Riders in fanning out along the edge of the jetty to pour a close-range salvo into the disorganized Cyclops charge.

Calista joined them on the farthest east edge of the line, firing into the openings as she walked. She needed to direct Harper, to get her moving in some direction since she couldn't very well sit there and hope the rest of the line figured out what they were meant to do. In truth, Calista had no idea what was tactically smart for the situation. Harper couldn't stay where she was though, she couldn't scale the jetty, and she couldn't return to her original position without risking her own men. The only option Calista saw available was to turn south and try to snap the Cyclops line at the center.

The Red Dale Riders, aided by another dozen or so militia archers, were making good progress in sweeping out the Cyclops. Firing from an elevated position at such short range turned their six-foot longbows into powerful killing machines as so many of their targets were completely defenseless on their flank.

Calista shouted down to Harper when she got into range to be heard. "You need to join up with Bjorn's forces and make a charge! I'll cover your side!"

Harper looked up to Calista atop the jetty and nodded her understanding. It was all Calista could do not to slide down the rocks to join her lover's side. Harper rallied to her men to push up toward the middle and Calista followed suit.

The Red Dale Riders again responded to her commands without question, adding legitimacy to Calista's orders that she didn't really deserve. The militia archers deferred to her orders as well, maybe because they lost their own officer or perhaps simply because she seemed to know what she was doing and the mercenaries present appeared to believe in her—as far as Calista was concerned, they didn't need to know it was because the Red Dale Riders were enthralled.

The Cyclops rallied and began to return fire on the archers with hurled spears. Calista directed her men back up the jetty to continue sweeping out the area to the north of where Harper's charge would land. The spears hurled by the Cyclops were inaccurate, which made sense—having only one eye, they likely lacked any real depth perception. A few militia archers fell under the hurled spears regardless; however, the Red Dale Riders side stepped and fired while walking as though the entire battle was old hat to them.

Harper's charge began with a mighty shout from the Sword Maiden. Calista glanced back to find Harper running full speed across the oily, bloody ice, glowing sword raised over her head, and blond hair trailing behind her. The ferocity of the charge took not only Calista by surprise, but the Cyclops as well. The bear riders, who had long since lost the momentum of their charge, seemed to believe they were on a slow advancing march until suddenly the force they'd just believed routed came hurtling back at them.

Calista pushed her men up the line toward the lighthouse, killing everything below them along the jetty's base. She fired, edged forward, sidestepped incoming attacks, and repeated the process again as soon as the next Cyclops in line fell from his bear under a hail of arrows.

Back at the base of the lighthouse, with the northern edge of the Cyclops line struggling to fall back through the second and third wave assaults. The Cyclops rallied, realizing they were only dealing with a couple dozen archers against a couple hundred riders. They beat the drums to direct a new charge. Calista realized all too late this new attack wasn't intended to counter Harper's advance, but instead looked to be heading toward the pile of bodies at the base of the jetty. With every kill Calista and her arches piled on the ice, the larger the ramp they built for the bear cavalry. Unlike traditional human and horse riders, the Cyclops and their bears could climb anything the bear's claws could find purchase in, and the mountain of dead created by their arrows certainly qualified.

"Back!" Calista shouted. She didn't have a plan beyond beating the bear riders to the likeliest ramp up point to avoid being cut off from the city.

The fifty or so bear riders in the charge were moving far faster than Calista and her men could on foot. Their arrows fired on the run weren't remotely sufficient to even slow the charge. The bears were scrambling up the pile of dead twenty yards ahead of Calista's group.

Calista halted her men to fire at the bears that would soon be rumbling down the jetty at them. The only other option was the lighthouse, and she didn't think they could make it back before they were ridden down. Before any of them could even draw a bowstring, the entire ramp of dead bodies with the bear cavalry scrambling up it exploded in a massive pillar of fire. Wizardly

Willard followed in the wake of Harper's charge. He was sweating profusely and clearly a little unnerved by the new developments in the battle, but he was still safely standing atop the back of his wagon driven by his apprentice. He saluted Calista, catching the ends of his mustache on his coat sleeve as he did. The fire spell spread, igniting the oil spilled across the ice by Harper's men in their initial retreat. The northern edge of the bay exploded in a conflagration that Wizardly Willard and his wagon only narrowly escaped.

Their path of retreat was gone in a firestorm, which left little else for Calista and her men to do than to return to the lighthouse and the duty of thinning the rear ranks. Calista directed her men to the end of the jetty. She could get a better look at the field from the top of the lighthouse regardless, and it was once again the safest place to be even though their influence over the rest of the battle would be altogether negligible. Calista hated the feel of retreat it all had even though she was technically heading toward the enemy.

Harper well knew the disorienting effects a bull rush could have on an enemy. She routinely charged the doors on mercenary jobs since she liked the overwhelming panic a sudden rush produced. In many cases, she found animals often responded with retreat to such tactics as well. This was the case with the Cyclops and their bear mounts that seemed to uniformly believe they were suddenly on the defensive.

Bears and their riders scrambled to escape the rush, stumbling over one another, pitching Cyclops to the ice in some cases, and colliding with rear ranks who weren't aware yet of the hundred or so men led on a retaliatory charge by a shouting Sword Maiden. Harper slashed through the chaotic ranks without losing momentum in her assault. Her massive sword wounded, adding an edge of mystical ice through the divinely charged blade. Her men, following her lead, continued her attacks, often felling the bears and Cyclops she wounded on her way through.

The Cyclops line hardened when she struck the rear ranks trying to push their way through. Even still, her sudden emergence through the bloody line caught many off guard. She hacked off the front paw from a bear. The mount pitched over sideways, depositing its brawny rider in her path. Harper lowered her shoulder, collided with the stumbled rider, and ran him over with the resounding clank of her steel shoulder plate knocking against the Cyclops's skull. A handful of men still following her finished off the wounded bear and the concussed Cyclops with their swords and spears.

Harper found herself on the other side of the Cyclops force. She'd broken the line with her charge, but she'd done so too far from Bjorn to do either of them much good. The ocean side of the battle was a bloody mess as well. Calista and her archers were back in the lighthouse raining razor arrows down onto those still on the open ice. Several bleeding bears were limping about, peppered with arrow shafts, devoid of riders, and aimlessly wandering as though they only wished a place to hide from being shot again. Strangely, Harper's heart went out to the animals despite the fact that she'd slain several already.

The rest of her men pushed through the gap she'd created, joining her on the other side. The battle was still raging to the south of them. To the north, the ice between them and the lighthouse was covered in dead bears and a handful of riders seeking to flee the fireballs being flung at them by Wizardly Willard and the arrows fired down on them by Calista's men.

Harper turned her back on the smashed end of the Cyclops line. No sooner had her focus shifted to Bjorn's rescue than she heard the groan and crack she'd dreaded. It was a sound unlike any other, unmistakable as anything else, and louder than a shouting God. She wheeled back around in time to watch the fiery bay shattering beneath the fleeing bears and Cyclops beside the jetty. Water rushed up to put out the fires on them before they fell into the growing cracks. Many splashed about still before the shifting plates of ice crushed them or knocked them below the frigid water. Bjorn's situation was forgotten. If Harper didn't do something, her own soldiers would soon join the enemy in their doom.

"Forward!" Harper shouted. There wasn't anywhere else to go. The enemy was on their left, broken ice was to their right, fire and ice was behind them, which only left running out onto the frozen sea.

Her men followed her insane order without question, rushing toward the horizon as if they intended on attacking the sun when it tried to set. A handful of wounded Cyclops, injured mounts, and what Harper guessed to be cowards fled the incredibly strange forward retreat of a hundred men still bearing the battle standards of the Sword Maiden.

When Harper was certain they were far enough out that the ice was stable again, she brought her formation to a halt and directed them into porcupine formations to guard one another's backs. It took a bit to calm them enough to get into the proper positions with shields and spears facing out around four gathered rings of twenty-five men a piece. The fifty or so Cyclops and bears still out on the ocean didn't appear to have any interest in attacking the spiked clusters of Harper's militia. Instead, the wounded enemy appeared to flee toward the south, apparently hoping to get out of range of the arrows should they start raining down again.

Harper glanced up to the lighthouse. She could see dark figures around the top even with the gathering of dark storm clouds behind them. They weren't firing any longer, apparently didn't have anything else in range to fire at now that Harper scattered the last of the Cyclops stragglers.

To that point, the cold winter sun shone down on their conflict. This was only a momentary break in the harsh weather of the season, and one that was quickly coming to an end. Unforgiving winds blew in violent storm clouds out of the north, no doubt carrying snow and freezing rain with them. It would complicate an already immeasurably complex situation.

Harper found her horn blowers and directed them to pipe out the signal for a general rally. The colossal melee still taking place on the cracking bay was so chaotic she couldn't tell if Bjorn, Athol, Sven, or the Ash twins were winning, losing, or holding even. What she could see from her vantage point of a quarter mile out to sea was the two fires on the north and south ends of the battle heading toward the middle and bringing with them the creeping doom of broken ice. She didn't know what to do beyond directing her men to continue trumpeting out the rally call. If she marched them back in, the added weight might well send the entire battle into the briny deep. If she remained on the ocean, well beyond the protection of the wall, they might be wiped out by

Cyclops infantry should they choose to march onto the ice in support of their cavalry. To that point, she'd taken orders from Bjorn and Calista without making any serious decisions on her own. She needed to make a choice, direct her men to do something other than fruitlessly blow on horns while standing about in the open field.

Her thoughts were cut short when the unthinkable, yet planned event finally took place. The entire bay shattered beneath the battle with a sound that could only be likened to a thousand thunderstorms attempting to break free of the ice. Fighting became a secondary concern for all involved as fleeing in all directions took over both armies. That was it then, Harper surmised. They succeeded in the plan even if her and her men were on the wrong side of the broken ice when it happened.

"Create a defensive perimeter around this spot," Harper ordered her men. "Haul in any bear bodies you can find to start creating fortifications. Keep on those rally horns to draw in whatever we can. If it's a soldier, add them to our line, if it's a Cyclops or bear, kill them and add their corpse to our defenses." This was the first order Harper could see her men struggling with and she could completely understand their reticence. A storm was blowing in, they were standing in the middle of a frozen ocean completely alone, and death was all around them. "Get on it! The ice will freeze again after dark and we can return to the city in the morning, but only if we bunker down and survive the night."

Her men finally jumped to in a somewhat awkward jumble. Harper didn't mind their slow progress in their tasks. It wasn't like she'd covered what they were doing in any of the training sessions of the past couple of weeks. They'd performed admirably to that point and were operating above and beyond already.

Harper about laughed herself silly with a nervous burst of giggles when she spotted a band of fur-laden barbarians chasing a fleeing contingent of bear-less Cyclops across the ice to the south. At the head of the formation, hurling every insult and name after the fleeing enemy, was Athol. Apparently the Cyclops could flee faster than Athol or his barbarian cohort could chase and soon it was clear they were going to escape into the south without being caught.

"Athol!" Harper shouted, which snapped his head around.

"Harper!" he bellowed back.

The barbarian contingent of thirty or so with their beaming leader marched over to Harper's increasingly impressive fortifications. Harper and Athol embraced while the axe and hammer wielding north men jumped into the work of showing Harper's men how to construct a proper wall out of bear corpses.

"How did you end up out here?" Athol asked. "And why are you building a bear fort on the ocean?"

"Everything kind of went wrong," Harper said, believing it properly answered both questions in just five words.

Athol laughed so hard he nearly fell over from the effort of it. Harper joined in on the cathartic guffawing. They were stressed, tired, and completely out of their element. The nervous laughter was a fine release and gave off a cavalier aura their men likely appreciated.

"That it did," Athol said, "and this is a fine response to such failure."

"This was hardly a failure," Harper corrected him. "We intended on sinking the enemy in the bay and we did precisely that. Certainly our plan stated we were meant to be on the other side when it happened, but the plan's success was not contingent upon that."

"There is truth enough in that, although I'd like to live through this to receive a reward for completing such a plan."

"Where are Sven and your father?" Harper asked.

"Sven was on the city side of the bay when our idiot Sorcerer accidentally lit our oil barrels with what looked a bit like a fireworks spell. I don't mean to speak ill of the dead, since he was one of the handful who burned up in that catastrophe, but the spell-flinger's bungle nearly ended us all. As for my father, I lost sight of him more than an hour ago."

Athol nudged Harper away from her thoughts and pointed toward a strange sight creaking and clacking its way across the ice to the north. Harper wound her way through the bustle within her quickly forming bear fort to see what Athol was pointing to as she didn't have nearly the height he did to see over her men.

Wizardly Willard, the tails of his mustache trailing behind him, was riding across the ice on the back of his wagon driven by his apprentice. He was firing fairly minor spells at a group of fleeing bears. It appeared the foppish Sorcerer was out of primary combat spell energy and was resorting to some truly bizarre combinations in an effort to harm the four ursine he was slowly chasing. Cooking pots, chickens, and other useful flotsam appeared via conjuring magic, falling onto the heads of the confused bears, but doing no real damage in the effort.

"Stop your nonsense, you daft old codger!" Athol shouted to Willard, who nearly lost his balance in the wagon in the process. Indeed, he did lose his footing, but didn't fall out as he apparently had the foresight to tie a rope around his rotund belly, affixing the other end to a beam in the wagon. He swayed around on the rope a bit though before he regained his composure.

The bears escaped by scattering in the window provided by the distraction. Wizardly Willard allowed his prey to flee at that point, directing his apprentice to drive him over toward the growing fortress on the ice. He looked flushed and exhausted, but also exhilarated by the fun. He attempted a bow to Harper, nearly pitching sideways out of the wagon again in the process. The rope saved him for a second time in a few minutes.

"When it became a choice of retreating or following the only officer on the field that appeared to have the faintest clue what they were doing, I chose to follow," Wizardly Willard said. "Looking over the fine proverbial circling of the wagons you've accomplished out here, it would seem I chose wisely."

"I'm afraid we can't claim victory quite yet," Harper said. "We've still a night to survive."

"Nonsense." Willard struggled with trembling, fat fingers to untie the rope around his waist. When it proved a task too difficult, he simply cleared his throat, pointed to the rope, and directed his apprentice to cut it off him. The boy produced a knife from his belt and scrambled back to cut the rope off in an eager sawing motion. Freed from his lifesaving rigging, Wizardly Willard climbed awkwardly out of the back of the wagon. "We'll claim victory in the morning, marching over the frozen bodies of the dead enemy forever held captive in the ice of the bay. Well, not forever, until the spring anyway. Safety tonight is practically assured. The Sword Maiden stands upon the realm of her deity, surrounded by stout warriors loyal to the cause. What more could any soldier ask?"

Harper rather liked the sound of that and when she looked to Athol for reassurance, he simply smiled to her. Their conversation was cut short by shouting for aid by familiar voices. Harper, Willard, and Athol scrambled to attention.

The Ash twins and a squadron of their Dead Watch Pikes were struggling to guard something they carried. Upon coming closer, it became apparent they were fleeing toward the fortification with a massive body in tow. A contingent of Cyclops barreled down on them.

"To their defense!" Harper commanded.

The sun was setting behind raging storm clouds in the west. A cold wind whipped across the frozen ocean. And the sounds of battle resumed in the gathering dark.

Chapter 29.

The North Wind Valkyries

Calista rushed out of the lighthouse when the bay shattered in a tumult so great she suspected it could be heard a thousand miles away. The fires were put out, but that felt like a small blessing as the frigid water roiled with chunks of ice and bodies struggling to find anything to hold onto. The few hopeful escapees that managed to swim to the jetty were dashed against the jagged line of ice and rocks by floating chunks knocked about in the chaotic bay. It ended in a slow whimper with only a handful of bears still struggling long after most of the armored men and Cyclops sank into the freezing water. Eventually, even the bears succumbed to the cold with only a handful actually escaping the watery grave.

It looked as though a few hundred soldiers on the furthest western edge of the battle managed to escape when the bay collapsed, but the majority of the seven hundred defenders and two-thousand attackers were dumped into the water. On the open ocean, barely visible from the end of the jetty, Calista could see Harper's battle standards still flying above a large contingent of men. She'd been well ahead of the rush to escape the crumbling bay and thus seemed to still hold the largest force. Water strewn with floating bits of ice encapsulated the entire end of the jetty though, leaving Calista without an option to help. Beyond Harper's men, who appeared to be constructing fortifications from fallen bodies, the rest of the combatants still on the field appeared to be too disorganized to continue the fight at the moment.

Calista was torn between seeking out help from the handful of men on the city side of the bay and trying to figure out a way onto the ice. The more she looked over her options, the more she came to the conclusion the only way to bridge the enormous gap between frozen edges would be a boat that she didn't have.

She turned her men back to walk down the empty jetty even as the sounds of combat resumed out on the frozen ocean. Harper appeared to have the upper hand for the moment, and so, as much as Calista detested abandoning the battle, she had to find help.

Wizardly Willard's protective flames died out shortly before the bay collapsed. Calista didn't know if that meant the old Sorcerer was dead as well or if the spell simply ran its course. Regardless, the way was clear for her and her men to walk back to the city.

Amid the frozen docks and the still iced over eastern edge of the bay, she spotted a solid contingent of soldiers that successfully escaped to the city side at some point. She followed them with her eyes even as she directed the Red Dale Riders and handful of militia archers to step lively into a jog. As they rounded the bay back toward the docks, she saw among them a familiar banner of a white bear on a red field. Beneath the banner was Sven with a group of mercenaries.

Calista immediately turned her forces to intercept his as they scrambled up the stair embankments beside the larger docks. They met on the frozen promenade meant for fishmonger stands, which was left vacant during the snowy months. Sven seemed as happy to see Calista as she was to see him.

"On the ocean side, there are still survivors, hundreds even," Calista said.

"Is my father or brother among them?" Sven asked.

"I don't know," Calista replied. "I only saw Harper's banners."

"We need to rally a force to row across the bay before it starts to ice over again," Sven said. "If we can deliver some supplies before it is fully dark, it'll help their chances of survival immeasurably."

"What about getting enough boats together to bring them all back?" Calista asked.

"There isn't enough time," Sven said. "If what you say is true about there being hundreds on the other side, it'd take all night to find enough boats and even longer to row them all across. We have two or three hours at most."

"You start rounding up the boats and supplies; I'll go awake Ezra and gather some fresh men," Calista said.

Sven nodded and they parted ways. They'd lost so many magic users when the bay collapsed. It really was humanity's greatest advantage in the conflict since Fir'bolgs and Cyclops had far fewer practitioners of mystical arts and the ones they did have barely rose to the level of an apprentice Sorcerer. They still had Ezra and the Sorcerous Seven in reserve, which was an incredible benefit to draw upon after such a costly battle.

Calista and the Red Dale Riders pushed their way through the crowds gathered to watch the bay's collapse. The general tone of the populace was mixed. Many thought it was a crushing defeat while others stated it was a grand victory destroying one of the two armies allied against them. The truth was somewhere in the middle, but Calista didn't have the time or inclination to make any proclamations since the battle was technically still ongoing and she was well out of it at the moment.

The Thundering Dawn's main hall was abuzz with a fresh mustering of mercenary groups not assigned to a particular wall. Calista pushed through these without concern. On the other side of the hall, she turned to direct her soldiers to a more important task than simply following her about.

"Find me twenty stout warriors," Calista said. "Look for groups who do most of their work in the north. I need people that are familiar with cold nights and surviving on ice."

The Red Dale Riders, who appeared to be acting in unison rather than upon direction from Caleb, nodded their understanding, saluted Calista, and then dispersed to find what they were instructed to seek out. The handful of militia archers who had followed them wandered off, apparently realizing they weren't meant for the work ahead.

Calista ran down the hall toward the infirmary where she was certain to find Ezra. A score of mercenaries capable of rowing across an ice-strewn bay would be helpful, but a fresh Sorceress who hadn't burned through all her spells was immeasurably valuable—Ezra's extreme dislike of Calista notwithstanding.

The Sorceress was snoring away, mouth wide open, one of her arms dangling off the side of the cot she was left to rest upon. Calista touched her hand to Ezra's forehead and pulled away the spell holding her in stasis. There were other, gentler ways to bring a dreamer back to the waking world, but they were time consuming. Certainly they were in too much of a hurry for the kinder ways, but Calista also didn't like Ezra enough to bother being gentle even if time wasn't a factor. Having the spell torn away was a little like someone sneaking up on another person snoozing in a hammock, and then swinging the entire contraption until it dumped its occupant on the ground after a couple revolutions. Ezra's bewildered and angry scowl spoke of precisely this sort of awakening.

"You're a liar!" Ezra shouted.

"Yes, you've said as much twice now," Calista said.

"Where am I? And don't you dare lie to me."

"You're at a grand ball for the Duke's third daughter's wedding, you twit," Calista said. "Where do you think you are?"

"Fine, why am I in the infirmary?" Ezra said through clenched teeth.

"Because someone thought you were sick. Look, these are really trivial questions in the grander scheme of things. You're needed for an important and dangerous mission, and it's the sort of thing that can't wait for me to answer the rest of your asinine queries if you want half of the Dagger Falls Company to survive."

This galvanized Ezra to pull herself from the cot. She practically snapped her teeth at Calista when she attempted to help her up. "Lead the way, but you will not be coming," Ezra said. "I know full well what you are now."

"I seriously doubt that, but I had no intention of going regardless." Calista directed Ezra to the door and followed along a half-step behind.

The Sorceress glared at her, but said no more. It was a bluff and an obvious one that Ezra actually knew what Calista was. In the southlands, everyone boasted an impossible to read stoic expression when bluffing. It made gambling incredibly difficult in Calista's homeland. Most people outside of the southlands wore their bluffs far too obviously in their facial expressions and body language, and Ezra was no different.

Unknowingly, Ezra gave Calista the excuse she needed for not accompanying the expedition onto the ice. Ezra would be far more useful than her and if Ezra didn't want her going, Calista would stay behind for the sake of peace.

The Red Dale Riders had found a group of northern adventurers counting seventeen members. The Riders were happily awaiting Calista with their find when she walked back into the main hall behind Ezra. The mercenaries in question were all women, all well over six feet tall, and all dressed in hide armor and furs. There was little doubt they were northern women from above the Crown of the World Mountains. How they'd found their way into each other's company and south of the mountains was what really interested Calista.

"I am Ingrid Ironshield," the lead woman said, stepping away from her cohort to greet Calista. "Your men here say you are looking for mercenaries fit to row across icy waters and then do battle with bears upon the frozen ocean. I assure you, you'll find no one better for such a mission than the North Wind Valkyries."

Ingrid stood a good head and a bit taller than Calista and even a little taller than the other giant women she called companions. She had a solid jaw, a powerful frame, steely blue eyes, and a braid of the thickest blond hair Calista had ever seen. There was little doubt from the look of the Valkyries and their brawny shoulders that they'd rowed longboats before.

"I am Calista of the Southlands," Calista replied.

"And a liar," Ezra added.

"Why hasn't your group been commissioned yet?" Calista asked, ignoring Ezra's barb.

"We wear only light armor and never fight at range," Ingrid explained. "This makes us unfit defenders of walls, but ideal for beach incursions in the night."

Calista nodded her understanding. She believed some good old fashioned sexism was involved as well since Bjorn and the Ash twins didn't seem to value female warriors as equal to male warriors, even if the female warriors in question were practically oak trees.

"And how did so many of you find one another to form this band?" Calista asked.

"We're sisters and cousins of the North Wind Tribe," Ingrid said. "A few of us were displeased with our martial matches and so left the village. More joined out of familial solidarity and…other reasons."

Calista chuckled and raised a curious eyebrow. "Do you mean a preference to couple with other women?"

Ingrid nodded. "Yes, that provided reasons for three of our members."

"You'll find yourself in good company in my employment then," Calista said.

"We would not be contracted with the city defenders?" Ingrid asked.

"No, you would join the Red Dale Riders in my personal guard," Calista said. "I would prefer to put your specialized skills to better use than simply walking about on a wall."

"And how exactly did you come by the money to hire so many on your own?" Ezra asked.

"Prestidigitation, my dear spell-flinger," Calista replied.

"Liar," Ezra said.

"So you've said before." Calista turned her attention away from the sniping Sorceress and back to the north women. "Your typical rate for combat until the siege is broken?"

Ingrid nodded. "Our axes and shields are yours until such a time, Mistress Calista."

"Excellent, let's put oars to water then before the bay becomes impassable."

Calista led her new army of a dozen rangers, nearly a score of northland women, and one surly Sorceress out of the Thundering Dawn on a quick march to the bay. Ingrid explained along the way what Sven only glossed over: there was a tiny window when a couple of shallow draft boats might make it across the water. In a couple hours more, the water would be too slushy to row through, yet still hours away from thick enough to stand on, especially by so many. Even if the Red Dale Riders hadn't found anyone nearly so suited for the task, Calista would have had to accept whatever help they could find.

The North Wind Valkyries were a superb choice as Calista saw it and would be a fine addition to the group she was already building. That the Red Dale Riders chose them and the North Wind Valkyries didn't object meant there was no pre-existing animosity between the two groups that might be a problem in the future.

Once they were at the bay, they found Sven had three longboats meant for hauling crab pots. The provisions were loaded, and the Valkyries added their shields to the sides in traditional defensive positions for the rowers. Sven and Ezra embraced before climbing into the boats to be crewed by colossal northland women.

For a moment, Sven seemed perplexed that neither Calista, nor her Rangers, were joining them in the already crowded fishing boats.

"You're not coming?" Sven asked as the boats pushed into the dark waters of the bay.

The night was upon them and the storm blowing in was threatening the entire endeavor if they didn't move immediately. Calista didn't think they had the time to discuss or debate her voluntary exclusion.

"You're better off taking Ezra and she doesn't wish me along," Calista explained. "I'll take my men to the lighthouse to give you a beacon to navigate by." Everything in Calista wanted to join them, to run out to Harper's aid, to fight at the side of her lover in the coming tribulations, but she still couldn't shake the feeling she would only be a liability should the Sea Queen choose to make another attempt on her life.

The long boats, expertly rowed and navigated by the north women were well on their way out through the iceberg strewn bay, slipping between the huge pieces of floating ice and frozen dead bodies as if they were little more than lily pads and reeds. Sven reluctantly took his seat and turned his attention to the other side of the bay.

Calista marched her men back up to the dock landing. There, upon the promenade, stood Aerial, looking expectantly as though Harper might be coming back on the boats.

"She'll be home in the morning." Calista ran her hand down Aerial's muzzle. The horse seemed to calm some under her touch. "Want to stay with me until then?" By way of answer, Aerial began following at Calista's side on the long walk down the snowy jetty toward the darkened lighthouse.

The storm and the blackness of night enveloped the city shortly after they reached the lighthouse tower. The Red Dale Riders battened down the structure as well as they were able. The Rangers apparently didn't know much about lighthouses, although they were experts in fortifying unusual structures, which came in handy.

Calista left Aerial's company in the lowest and largest room of the tower. She climbed the stairs to light the beacon that marked the entrance to the bay. Frigid wind blew in sleet from the north. Calista could barely see in the darkness and violence of the howling storm to light the mirror-amplified pyre at the top of the lighthouse. By and by, it sprung to life with plenty of priming from oil and repeated sparking from a flint and steel. The pyre bathed the entire top of the tower in a powerful light while large, bronze mirrors magnified the beacon out to sea.

Through the darkness of the night, made all the darker by the thick storm clouds blocking out the moons and stars, Calista could see a few flickering lights out on the ocean. She didn't know if they were part of Harper's fortifications or if the Cyclops were reinforced and setting up another charge.

She could only sit by and hope.

Chapter 30:

Battle of the Frozen Bear Fort

Harper's men were already hunkered down, exhausted from building the fort of corpses, and less than immediate in their response to her cry to resume the battle. Athol's barbarians, however, were not so reticent. The thirty men swinging massive axes and mauls rushed to the fray with renewed glee. Harper was barely able to keep pace.

The Ash twins and their men struggled along, hampered by what looked to be Bjorn's body and a dozen or so wounded of their own to carry. The rallied Cyclops and bears turned their attention away from the limping column to the more immediate threat of the charging barbarians, allowing the Dead Watch Pikes a slim chance to escape to the relative safety of the bear fort.

The majority of the Cyclops force arrayed against them appeared to be on foot, having lost their mounts somewhere along the way. The dismounted Cyclops cavalry wasn't nearly as effective on the open ice as proper infantry. Harper, Athol, and the barbarians, despite being outnumbered nearly three to one, found their foes unused to and ill-equipped for such combat without a plan to organize them.

Harper lost focus on the larger scheme of things in the bloodlust that followed. Cold winds blew her hair around her face until the ends were blood-soaked and sticky. The freezing rains and snow began falling, but she ignored this as well. The only task in her mind was the task before her: killing whoever came within range of her sword. She certainly didn't lack for attackers to dispatch. No sooner had she slashed through a Cyclops at her front than a spear point bounced off the armor plates on her back or flank. She turned to fight, sustained a handful of actual wounds along the weakened joints of her armor, but nothing serious enough to slow her. In the midst of what she thought would be an endless task of slaying the Cyclops, she found a sudden ebb in the tide of battle. Only after the enemy began their retreat did she hear the low bellow of a horn calling the Cyclops away.

She was exhausted when the field cleared of foes, leaving her to take a knee amidst the blood and bodies of her personal fight against so many. She rested her elbow across her knee, head bowed, and breathed heavily to try to force her lungs into accepting the frigid air blowing across the frozen ocean. It was a small blessing from the Sea Queen that the wind blew away much of the scent of the gory mess around her, and she thanked her Goddess for the favor.

"They caught hell on this side, it would seem," Athol said from above her.

She glanced up to find he'd suffered far more serious injuries than herself. His lighter armor and slower responses against larger foes was apparently beginning to wear on him after a long day of fighting that wasn't nearly over. Harper accepted his help to rise to her feet, but believed she would likely be helping to heal his wounds in short order. This thought carried with it a streak of panic; Athol certainly wouldn't be the only wounded in need of healing.

"For a time, I forgot I wasn't born fighting Cyclops," Harper said.

"One day can feel like an eternity if it's the wrong kind of day," Athol agreed.

"Or a fleeting moment if it's the right kind," Harper countered.

"With luck, we'll both see more of those to come."

Athol and Harper limped back to the bear fort with significantly fewer barbarians at their sides. There were plenty of fresh dead to add to the walls created by the piled bears, Harper thought grimly. Her plan for survival was functional, but increasingly distasteful even with such inhuman enemies.

Within the confines of the makeshift fort, Athol left Harper's side to seek out his father. Harper followed at something of a respectful distance. The Ash twins and Wizardly Willard were in attendance, although Harper could see on their faces that hope wasn't appropriate anymore.

"He was alive when we pulled him from the fray," Romulus said.

"He must have died along the way," Remus added.

Athol stood above his father's body. His head was unbent, his shoulders weren't slumped, and he looked more heartened by the news than stricken by it. Athol nodded his understanding after a brief moment of consideration. "It's better than he could have asked for," Athol said. "I only wish he'd lived long enough to see the grand frozen bear fort on the sea. A warrior could die happy after witnessing this marvel." Athol turned and smiled to Harper. "It would seem you are meant to lead the men now."

"We are aware of the notifications naming the Sword Maiden his successor," Romulus said.

"But that doesn't mean we agree with the judgment of it," Remus finished.

"You'd better get yourselves used to the idea," Wizardly Willard said. "Between the two of you, I'm sure one is good enough with math to notice she commands the lion's share of the men in this fort she ordered the building of. Your troops number at forty-five with more than a dozen others wounded to weigh them down. She still has a contingent of close to a hundred with two Sorcerers and an apprentice in the mix. The Magical Men-at-arms, or whatever the blazes we're calling ourselves these days, stand by the Sword Maiden—all three of us in attendance."

Harper looked around to check the validity of Wizardly Willard's statement. The remaining Sorcerers, which only included one other of the red coats and the apprentice who drove Willard's wagon, did indeed appear to be standing with her. The other mercenaries who trickled in clearly pieced together from the battle standards and tunics worn by the majority of the men within the bear fort that Harper's force was the largest by more than double anything else. Certainly they were militia, but they'd comported themselves admirably in the battle and then built a marvelous defensive position in the unlikeliest of places. Apparently the Ash twins made their own survey of the situation at the same time Harper did and came to much the same conclusion.

"Very well," Romulus said.

"We'll acquiesce for the good of all," Remus said.

Harper accepted the position as being tenuous from the Ash twin's acquiescence, but believed she could strengthen their fealty through success. Her thoughts on what to do next toward that goal were interrupted by a peculiar signal. The lighthouse, which typically remained dark through the winter after the bay froze, suddenly sprung to life, shining like a beacon of hope amid the rocky cliffs.

Their brief conversation about Bjorn's desires faded under a strange, warm awe. They walked to one of the two, ten-foot wide entrances on opposite sides of the ring to get a better look. At such a distance, the light was enough to see, but not enough to see much by. Still, it illuminated something on the bay at the edge of the ice. Three long boats were coming across.

"It would seem we aren't meant to spend the night alone," Wizardly Willard said grandly, pointing everyone's attention to the barely lit figures along the edge of the ice.

The boats rushed at the far shore of the bay, running up onto the ice with enough force to beach their respective boats. Figures leapt from the front, hauling hard to drag the vessels even farther onto the ice. As they did, more figures leapt from the sides, taking up shields to set off at a jog toward the bear fort. The entire enterprise had a look of polished grace to it, disembarking a small contingent quietly in the dark in a matter of a few moments.

The camp of Cyclops, which was equally difficult to see to the south, also apparently took note of the added reinforcements on their way to the bear fort. They rallied a party to try to intercept the score or so warriors on their way across the ice, mustering what looked to be a dozen bear riders to chase them down.

"Are they going to make it to us before the riders get them?" Athol asked.

"Not likely, but neither would we," Romulus said.

"Since anyone we sent to help would be on foot," Remus finished.

Harper looked on with knots turning over and over in her stomach. Calista might be among the two dozen warriors on their way across the ice. The Ash twins were right though. She was too tired to run very far or very fast and she wasn't particularly swift in her armor anyway. Still, sitting idly by wasn't in her nature.

"I don't care," Harper said. "I'm going and anyone with the spine to follow me is welcome to try to keep up."

Harper leapt through the gap and began her own run toward the reinforcements. It didn't take long before she heard the pounding of footsteps beside her, accompanied by the clinking of metal armor. Shortly after that, she regretted adding the last part about people keeping up with her since it looked as though she might be among the last to arrive at the battle. The Ash twins and a dozen of their uninjured men were on a quick double step, catching Harper and then quickly passing her.

"We'll try to save some for you," Romulus said as he jogged past.

"To lead from the front, you'll have to run faster," Remus added a second after.

Their point was well made and their gesture to join her appreciated, but it was all apparently for naught. Even from the lousy vantage point at the back of the formation, Harper could see the imminent collide of the two forces ahead of them. The reinforcements from the bay stopped, changed direction on a dime, and began veering to the north of a span of nondescript ice. The bear riders sped on, heedless of what the shift in direction might mean. Suddenly, the entire charge of two dozen cavalry came to a sudden stop, pitching the riders forward out of the saddle. When the riders struck the ice, they slid for a second and then stopped just as suddenly as their mounts had.

"Ezra!" Harper shouted, recognizing her slip-and-stick spell. It was a remarkable bit of magic they'd used to good effect in the past that created an area of immeasurably slippery ground-covering that instantly turned to equally immeasurably stickiness once impacted with enough force.

Even with the sudden stop in the cavalry charge, it didn't appear Harper's contingent would get there in time for the full battle. The reinforcements turned back to the completely disabled bear riders. Harper could only describe the warriors as having mastered synchronized sprinting as they were moving far more like flowing water than a squadron of foot soldiers. The score of warriors from the bay struck the fallen bear riders with remarkable force and a surprisingly feminine chorus of battle cries.

As Harper got closer to what quickly dissolved into a one-sided slaughter, she got her first look at the mercenary band coming to their rescue. There were maybe twenty of the incredibly tall women, but the way they moved on the battlefield made it seem like there were far more. They all wore an animal pelt of some kind over their armor and all donned gleaming winged helmets over trailing braids. The stumbled Cyclops and bears put up only token resistance as the charging longboat raider women washed over them.

A second wave of bear riders appeared to be mounting in the south. Before their rush could even begin, the warrior women had dispatched the entirety of the first charge and were out on the ice on the opposite side, banging the flats of their swords and axes against the fronts of their shields. Their shouting and smacking of weapons was an astonishingly intimidating gesture and soon the second wave of bear riders was turning back toward their own camp, wanting no part of what had happened to the first wave.

Even the Ash twins and their seasoned men appeared a little confused by the sudden shift in battle. Certainly the Cyclops were as tired from the day of fighting as the Dead Watch Pikes were, and certainly the new warriors were fresh, but even at that, the quickly dealt rout spoke of a confidence and skill on the winning side.

The reinforcements appeared to be a mixture of a handful of people carrying supplies and a band of warriors, which was made all the clearer when one group remained behind while the other ran off to fight. The two groups rejoined and resumed their jog toward the bear fort and the contingent of the Ash twins' warriors who had come out to greet them.

Indeed, as the two bands neared one another, Harper recognized Ezra and Sven among their numbers. She was nearly as glad to see the Sorceress as she was to see Sven whom she believed may well have perished earlier in the day. Their reunion was short lived as the commander of the warrior women was eager to have their company off the open ice and into the safety of the makeshift fortifications. The Ash twins agreed and the lot of them marched at the quick back to the frozen bear fort without further harassment from the Cyclops camp.

Athol, who was too battered to run, and Wizardly Willard, who was too old and fat by his own estimation to join a charge, made good use of their time stewarding the fort. Men were working quickly to carve away pelts from the bear bodies encircling them before they froze, using the scavenged furs to create something of a carpet to keep them from having to stand or sit directly on the frozen salt water all night.

It was clear to Harper that the storm barreling down on them would prove far deadlier than the Cyclops that night if some fortifications against the cold couldn't be erected as well. The true battle might well be keeping her men alive through the harsh weather. She glanced back over her shoulder to the lighthouse to derive hope from the light.

"Calista didn't come with you?" Harper asked of Sven when he and Athol had finished their brotherly reunion.

"She sent the North Wind Valkyries here in her stead," Sven explained, "something about our boats not being large enough to keep her and Ezra from killing one another."

Harper tried to tamp down her disappointment. The thought that they might not survive the night, and even if they did it was going to be a miserable experience, helped in this—she certainly didn't want Calista suffering or dying of exposure. Besides, from the tactical standpoint, Ezra wasn't just hypothetically more valuable; she'd already shown precisely why, if a hard choice was to be made between the two, she was the one to send.

"I am Ingrid of the North Wind Valkyries," the largest of the warriors women snapped Harper from her thoughts. "We are here to fortify your position with our countless generations of knowledge about surviving the harshness of winter."

"We would certainly welcome the expertise," Harper said.

The imposing warrior woman smiled. "You've done well so far and what you've accomplished might well make the difference."

Harper replied with a wan smile of her own. "Whatever you might need, my men will see to helping with."

Even with the aid, they would be in for a long night, which was going to require healthy soldiers to man the fortifications. Harper beckoned Ezra to her side to begin the rounds of healing the wounded within their camp.

"Care to be my assistant again?" Harper asked.

Ezra smiled sheepishly and nodded. "Sven filled me in on much of what transpired while I was *sleeping*."

"Whatever you might think of Calista or her motives, she's been honest with me in things I wouldn't have expected her to be,"

Harper said. "Moreover, you should know I love her deeply. If your next words are to disparage her, I wouldn't expect them to be received well, were I you."

"I wonder if we compared her story to what I know if you would still believe her so honest."

"We have other, more pressing concerns at the moment," Harper explained as they reached the first cluster of wounded resting fitfully on a pulled off hunk of bear pelt. "Were you able to estimate how many are out there from your vantage point on the way across the ice?"

"Four-hundred once they've gathered up the all the stragglers, maybe a little more," Ezra said. "I only saw around a hundred usable bears though."

"Then we need to get as many of our own back to fighting form as possible." Harper began the slow, cumbersome process of trying to heal through armor and clothing. Her magic worked best with skin against skin contact, laying her hands directly upon the wound, but in the increasingly cold, wet night, she would likely kill with hypothermia while healing a cut or broken bone.

Four-hundred was a problem. It meant they were outnumbered by close to four to one. If the infantry arrived in the morning, that number would rise to a hundred to one. Harper couldn't decide if it was better for the Cyclops to remain in a holding pattern awaiting reinforcements from the infantry in the morning or if both sides might be better served to fight it out on the ice in the night to settle things for good and all. Regardless of what might be preferable, Harper chose to leave things up to the Cyclops while still making ready for either eventuality.

Strangely, the more she healed, the more she felt the power of the Sea Queen flowing through her. Harper and Ezra worked their way through the two or three dozen wounded, including Athol, and by the end of it, when Harper knew she should have been exhausted, she instead felt reinvigorated. She glanced to Wizardly Willard who smiled knowingly to her. Somehow the old Sorcerer knew something she didn't about her own powers.

Morale soared even in the face of the winter gale pounding the little fortress. They were whole again and the North Wind Valkyries were good to their word about improving the dead bear ring into a proper fort. Things were looking up and everyone appeared to believe the worst of it was past them. A few men were even comfortable enough to find some sleep.

The sound of bears rumbling across the ice broke the endurable night with the resumption of battle. Harper scaled the mound of bodies that constituted their six foot high walls to stand atop the completely frozen stockade. The last of the Cyclops cavalry was charging on the hundred bears they had left with the forced infantry of three-hundred more following on foot.

"We came here to finish off their cavalry and that's precisely what we will do!" Harper shouted to rouse her men. "To arms and let's end this before the dawn."

Her men took to the order in reasonably good cheer. Their reticence was only noticeable in comparison to the North Wind Valkyries who appeared positively giddy to finally be let in on the war.

"The Dead Watch Pikes will hold the entrances," Romulus announced to Harper.

"That's the benefit of having two of us," Remus said. "We're the only captains who can be in two places at once."

The Ash twins ran off with their scimitars gleaming, leading their pike men to the two gaps on opposite ends of the ring. Their momentary insubordination from earlier aside, Harper was glad they both survived to join her. When they said they would hold the entrances, the only true weaknesses in the fort, she believed they would.

The original members of the Dagger Falls Company stood on the outermost curve of the fortress, awaiting the bear charge, flanked by the North Wind Valkyries and Athol's remaining barbarians. Harper felt strong and at peace with the chosen location for their final stand in the midst of her friends. If she were to die on the ice during one of the Sea Queen's storms, surrounded by her compatriots, it would be a good death.

The first wave of bears quite literally crested upon the fortress walls. Apparently the cavalry believed the piled bodies of haphazard construction would tumble when pushed. Frozen together, the stacked corpses were every bit as strong as a stone rampart, and the first thirty or so riders found this out the hard way.

The North Wind Valkyries took full advantage of the stunned, initial assault. They pulled the riders from their mounts, stabbing and hacking at them before hurling the barely breathing bodies back into the ring for the rest of Harper's men to finish off. When this left them with little else to do in the moment, they leapt upon the stunned bear mounts, felling them with deeply thrust broadswords through the empty saddles. Harper managed a single kill in the earliest stages of the battle, stabbing at a Cyclops hurled face-first at her feet. Such was the ferocity of the Valkyries.

Seeing the catastrophic end of their vanguard, the rest of the cavalry split their charge, and made slow turns to begin riding circles around the bear fort ring in hopes of finding a more approachable entrance. This opened them up to the long spears of Harper's men as the Cyclops tried their first slow revolution. Her militia men, who were clearly revitalized by their commander's mood and having their wounds healed, made a good show of knocking a few riders from their bears. The real damage done to the confused cavalry was done on the ends by the Ash twins.

The Dead Watch Pikes swung out in perfect lines like wings unfurling from a bird. They brought a full line of their long pikes to assault on the disorganized cavalry as it tried to circle the equator of the bear fort. Some tried to turn rather than strike the sudden roadblock, but as Harper had already seen, such sharp turns were difficult for the bear cavalry to execute, especially when in large clusters in the middle of a storm in the dark. The split cavalry impaled themselves upon the pikes, stumbled, faltered, and were struck down by thrusting spears from rear ranks of the Dead Watch Pikes' tightly packed phalanx that stood three men deep.

Harper's triumphant glee at seeing how well her fortress worked with such remarkable defenders was short lived. The infantry that was comprised of cavalry members who couldn't find bears to ride anymore made a proper charge, clearly learning from their last disastrous attempt. It occurred to Harper only after the fact that the three to one advantage possessed by the Cyclops might not mean much against the North Wind Valkyries when fighting from an elevated position, but if their initial line broke and the Cyclops flooded into the confines of the fort, the militia men who made up the majority of their force would be slaughtered.

Their victory relied entirely upon the ring holding. Without stating as much, the soldiers around her seemed to implicitly know.

They fanned out along the wall, awaiting the charging Cyclops as the burly warriors scrambled up over the fallen ranks of the first wave of cavalry. In a maneuver Harper could only describe as a perfect mirror of the bum rush she'd used earlier in the day, the North Wind Valkyries let loose with another knee-weakening chorus of battle cries and leapt off the wall into the fray. Harper's men, seeing the wall vacated, rushed up to take their places with swords and spears at the ready. With little other options left to them, Harper, Sven, and Athol followed the Valkyries into the growing melee.

Ingrid and her women warriors gleefully hacked into the struggling Cyclops with axe and broadsword. The poor footing of standing on dead bodies didn't seem to bother the Valkyries in the slightest while it appeared to hamper the enemy in the extreme. Harper struggled to keep up with them as they created a second wall of dead, pushing out into the coming attackers. Soon, the three members of the Dagger Falls Company were relegated to finishing off the Cyclops only mortally wounded by the charging raider women.

A strange surge on their left flank crushed a small contingent of Harper's men, giving up a portion of the wall to open attack. The rest of the Cyclops seemed to flow to the spot as though it were the only hope to truly take the fort. Harper, Sven, and Athol, hampered by the bodies they were attempting to walk on, reacted too slowly and suddenly the Cyclops were pouring into the breach, threatening to swing in behind their forward position.

A redheaded Valkyrie on the end of the line attempted to lead a countercharge against the incursion's flank while Romulus moved to cut the attack off from the other side. The duo appeared to do a reasonable job of stemming the tide, but the damage was done. Fifty or so of the Cyclops warriors were already within the fortress with a small trickle still pushing through.

Harper, Sven, and Athol were nearly back to the wall when a blast of magical energy hurled back a good portion of the Cyclops within. Harper's joy at seeing Ezra enter the fight in such a remarkable fashion was short-lived. The blast of energy reminded the Cyclops of the devastating losses they suffered earlier in the day at the hands of Sorcerers. The counterattack was swift and fierce, overtaking the personal guard of Harper's spearmen encircling Ezra's position. The entire group of ten men and one woman went spilling over the back side of the wall into the fortress with a dozen Cyclops following them down.

Harper screamed. She struggled to haul herself up the wall as her armor seemed to catch on everything around her in her panicked rush. In the darkness and stormy weather, she couldn't be sure of what she'd seen and her mind refused to accept it as true. Even still, the rage that took over told her that her eyes hadn't betrayed her. Ezra was cut down in the charge.

Chapter 31:

The Break

Harper scrambled up over the edge of the parapet to find the fort beneath her in chaos. Her men were disorganized, fighting in fragmented clusters against better organized Cyclops troops who already held the advantage of being physically larger and stronger. In the snow storm and darkness, she couldn't find Ezra among the bedlam. It suddenly dawned on her why the Cyclops were fairing so much better in the darkness and the cold—they were used to both. Harper remembered Bjorn talking long ago about the northern most reaches of the world having nights that contained months of darkness and winters so cold spit would freeze in a mans mouth if he dared open it. The Cyclops came from a region that couldn't wage war if they couldn't wage it in such inhospitable conditions.

Calling upon the magic of the Goddess, Harper raised her sword above her head. The beacon spell she'd used to light the harbor on her first night back in Griffon's Rock flooded through her with far more force than she'd ever used before. She could feel the power surging up through the ocean all around them, fueling the spell in an astounding way. Daylight broke out in the middle of the night, radiating out of the great sword held above her head.

The flash of light served to disorient all combatants, but the Cyclops far more than the humans. Her own army, that was struggling to see by the radiant light held in beneath the cloud cover, suddenly saw the world as if it were noon on a clear day. The Cyclops were struck senseless by the brightness of the light, temporarily blinded by their superior night vision reacting poorly with the powerful and unexpected radiance.

"Find each other and fight together or find yourselves lost!" Harper ordered her soldiers. Her men apparently remembered well the lesson she'd taught them in relying upon each other in small groups to increase their survival chances. The battle swung to their advantage as they turned the odds against the Cyclops, forming larger groups to take down the bewildered enemy.

Sven and Athol rejoined her atop the wall, holding back the Cyclops horde that sought to extinguish the source of light so damaging to their chances. The brothers fought well together from the fortified position, striking down foes with hammer and sword or simply knocking them from the wall to either side where Harper's men or the Valkyries finished the task. Harper stood tall, her sword above her head, lighting the fort and snow swirling around her in an ever-growing blizzard.

The Valkyries split the incoming line and were working their way back around to close the breach. The Ash twins broke the last of the cavalry charge, giving them a clear advantage in holding the entrances of the stockade ring despite fighting enemies both inside and outside the fort. Seeing all this around her, Harper's main focus remained on seeking out Ezra among the fallen. Whenever the crowd parted on an open area, her eyes would immediately light on it only to find it devoid of the Sorceress.

Magic was still being cast amidst the battle, although it wasn't cast by Ezra and it wasn't of the particularly harmful variety. Wizardly Willard, his remaining Sorcerer companion, and his apprentice were standing in the back of his wagon, defended well by a double line of Harper's spearmen. The trio was casting spells at whatever Cyclops happened by, but their combat magic appeared to be long spent. An attacking Cyclops might suddenly find himself bright purple in color or covered in chicken feathers, which did serve to disorient some of them without causing any real damage. Wizardly Willard's apprentice brought only two spells to the combat, which he alternated to no appreciable effect by lighting candle sized flames on some Cyclops and then almost immediately smothering the tiny flame he'd just conjured under a dollop of strawberry jam. He was trying though, and Harper admired his stoicism in the face of such combat when he was armed only with magic enough to light a lantern or jelly his toast.

The Cyclops still on the outside of the fortress lost their will to fight when it became clear they couldn't make it over the wall while blinded by Harper's light and beset by the Valkyrie or push through the phalanx of black armor pike men standing strong at the entrances. The general retreat was called for by rumbling horns, and the remaining tatters of forces fell back, leaving their compatriots who had managed to surge into the fort to their fate.

Ingrid and her Valkyries didn't seem to care for the sudden loss of their dance partners. They turned their attention from the backs of the fleeing enemy to sprint up and over the parapet to either side of Harper, determined to find the trapped quarry before someone else could slay them all. The abandoned Cyclops within the fort fell quickly. The Valkyries ran through the melee with their winged helmets gleaming in the light of Harper's sword, stabbing and hacking at the Cyclops warriors who were already engaged in other combat.

A great cry of victory arose out of the fortress even as the storm beating down on them intensified. The enemy's ranks were broken. Their bear cavalry destroyed. And though they paid a heavy price for such a rousing defeat of a great threat, the patchwork army within the fort seemed to feel they'd brought about a noteworthy shift in the war.

Despite her almost overwhelming urge to drop her sword and seek out Ezra among the wounded or dead, Harper held fast, letting the power of the ocean flow through her via a slow trickle until it came out her blade as light. The Valkyries and barbarians collected burnable items off the dead and built small fires, sheltered by strange tenting, along the top of the walls. Harper had never seen such adept survival skills at keeping a fire alive during a raging snowstorm, although it seemed all the northerners among the army knew the trick of protecting a fire with a small tent of cloth or hide.

Harper let the spell within her peter out. The firelight of the two or three dozen little pyres wasn't nearly as impressive, although served the purpose of being able to see by without melting the ice beneath their feet. She sheathed her blade and slid down the interior edge of the wall to begin her search for Ezra.

Other soldiers were already digging into the piles of bodies, seeking out moaning, wounded companions when Harper began her search. Try as she might to keep moving, whenever she founded a wounded man among the bodies, she couldn't leave him in his broken state to continue her search for her friend. She healed as she went, rationalizing the merciful act as also being practical— the more hands at the work of clearing the fortress of bodies, the sooner someone might find the Sorceress.

Athol was the one to find Ezra among several Cyclops bodies that she'd apparently electrocuted with her dying breath. Harper helped the brothers clear away the charred Cyclops to reveal Ezra's body. The Sorceress had suffered spear impalement and nearly a dozen knife stabs before succumbing. The remaining members of the Dagger Falls Company collected around their fallen fourth.

The loss stung every bit as much as when Felix had died, but appeared to be tempered slightly for Athol and Sven in knowing she'd perished in the service of a far grander duty than simply protecting a caravan. Harper was not so lucky. Her last words with Ezra were spoken in a heated moment and carried more of a tone of chiding than friendship. A small part of Harper, that she hated as soon as it reared its ugly little head, was glad it was Ezra and not Calista dead within the bear fort. Try as she might, Harper couldn't entirely clear away the scrap of relief that was coloring her mourning for her deceased friend. She finally had to accept the despicable gladness that would rather see Ezra dead than Calista if one of them had to fall.

Harper's time to reflect on Ezra's death was cut short though as Wizardly Willard galvanized her on to help in the healing of the remaining wounded. At some point in the battle, Wizardly Willard's moustache suffered an amputation. The right side, which formerly stretched down nearly to his belly, was cut short enough to barely tickle the bottom of his jaw line. In the grander scheme of things, it was a minor wound, but he appeared to be taking the loss of half his facial hair as though it were a depressing defeat.

The snow storm slowed some during the long hours of healing that Harper slogged her way through. She felt emotionally numb and in a bit of a daze from it all, which stretched well beyond simply being cold. In truth, she didn't feel the chill of the storm. Her armor offered some insulation from the weather, but not nearly enough for how comfortable she felt. Many of the men she healed were suffering from the early stages of frostbite on their extremities. A quick glance at those around her revealed that only the Valkyries weren't huddled together against the cold. With the last of the wounded healed, Harper walked past the laid out dead. The Cyclops bodies were removed, hurled from the fortress after being looted of anything burnable, leaving only the solemn bodies of her fallen men. They'd started the day with so many, a grand army of more than seven hundred. What remained, shivering in the bottom of a bloody, frozen rampart numbered less than a hundred including the Dead Watch Pikes and the North Wind Valkyries. Harper walked past Sven and Athol who were still standing vigil over Ezra's body at the end of the line of the fallen. They didn't appear to see her and she didn't draw their attention away from their quiet conversation.

Ingrid approached Harper, bowing low and removing her winged helmet as she did. "Well fought, Sword Maiden," the Valkyrie commander said.

"It's difficult to see the victory when still standing in the midst of dead friends." Harper hated the sour note her words sang over what was a triumphant moment, and she immediately wished she hadn't spoken them. "We likely would not have survived the battle had you not come to our aid. Thank you."

"Think nothing of it," Ingrid said. "It has been many years since I've slaughtered Cyclops and I was glad to see my skill hasn't waned much."

"There was one of your numbers, a red haired woman with two braids who helped to close the breach that nearly cost us the fort," Harper said. "I should like to offer her a commendation from the field commander of the defense forces."

"You speak of Sofea," Ingrid said. "She's my cousin's daughter and the youngest member of our band. I wouldn't imagine a commendation could do anything more to further her already overflowing confidence, but we are not part of the city's defense force."

"Oh," Harper said, stunned a little by the revelation. "What brought you to the ice then?"

"Your lover hired us on with her personal coin," Ingrid replied. "The blue eyed assassin from the southlands is your lover, yes?"

"Yes," Harper said, glad to say so without reservation.

"I thought as much, but I didn't want to presume," Ingrid said. "I do regret that it will likely be unhappy news for Sofea—I believe the girl is a bit infatuated with you, and likely only more so after seeing you in all your glory. The power of the Sea Queen's divine touched is legendary, even in the north, but none of us had witnessed it first hand to this point." Ingrid replaced the winged helmet atop her head. "I will fetch Sofea to receive your thanks."

Harper stood a little stunned at the entire conversation. Calista was apparently hiring mercenaries and exceptional ones at that. Harper couldn't imagine where Calista was coming by so much coin or why she would be spending it thusly. It also lingered with Harper that she had admirers of that specific nature. Certainly she'd known people to respect and revere her within the temple and her position as a messenger of the Goddess, but none of the admiration could be mistaken for infatuation. Her thoughts on both matters were cut short by the return of Ingrid with Sofea at her side.

Sofea removed her winged helmet and bowed to Harper. Her twin red braids fell over her shoulders as she did. When she arose to look Harper boldly in the eyes, an excited smile lit her face. Upon closer inspection, Harper was surprised to find the ferocious warrior who contributed so valiantly to saving the fort was young, perhaps seventeen seasons only. Next to one another, Harper could also see the familial resemblance between the much larger and more imposing Ingrid and the slighter, younger Sofea.

"I would like to offer thanks and a commendation for your bravery in closing the breach," Harper said.

"Thank you, Sword Maiden. I acted on instinct only." Sofea bowed awkwardly again and her smile brightened, setting a twinkle to her sky blue eyes. The girl was a bit taller than Harper, but of slighter build than either the Sword Maiden or the other Valkyries.

"Then you have fine instincts," Harper said. "I'm sure the Ash twins would offer their thanks as well."

"Your words are all the recognition I need." Sofea beamed.

"Then tend to the fires on your section, girl," Ingrid said. "I would have a final word with the Sword Maiden before we must make ready to depart."

Sofea reluctantly walked away, glancing back over her shoulder to Harper several times.

Ingrid turned back to Harper, dropping her voice a little lower to conceal it from others in the area of the formerly crowded fortress. "The Cyclops will return with infantry in the morning,"

Ingrid said. "Single minded determination is their way. We must be ready to march before the dawn if we are to slip past them."

"I appreciate your counsel in this," Harper said. "Would they charge the harbor again with their infantry once it is frozen enough again to hold such large numbers?"

"Undoubtedly," Ingrid replied. "It will take several more crushing defeats like this before they will turn away from such an old and reliable tactic."

The words sent a shiver through Harper at the thought of having to do the entire thing several more times if the city's defenders could even muster the forces for that many more battles like the one they'd just finished. Something on Harper's face must have translated this worry to Ingrid. The Valkyrie captain put her gloved hand on Harper's shoulder plate.

"Take heart, Sword Maiden," Ingrid said. "We have done well enough to give them pause."

Ingrid departed to see to her own force's preparations for abandoning the bear fort while Harper turned to see to the rest. The Ash twins were already well ahead of her on the task, having anticipated her orders from the assembling of the Valkyrie forces. Their own men were already up from their all too brief rest and were drawing others to the task of departure. It was just as well, thought Harper. She'd spent all her inspirational calls and orders for the day and she didn't know when she might have more.

Dawn was nearly upon them when they reached the edge of where the bay collapsed the prior evening. The new ice looked lumpy, strange, and not nearly as thick. Harper didn't want the entire host of them trying to walk over it in formation, especially not since many were dragging the bodies of the dead. The night was cold, but not nearly as cold as Harper hoped it would be as was evident by the inclusion of rain among the snow for several hours. The storm held some warmer air from somewhere or other and thus didn't hit the region with quite the freezing force it might have.

Ingrid's prediction about the Cyclops bore itself out. To the south, gathered on the tattered remains of what was the Cyclops camp the night before, a force of a thousand or more in infantry were marching into position. By daybreak, Harper imagined their number would double, and by midday, all four-thousand of the Cyclops that remained would be in position to march on the bay.

A vanguard looked to be breaking away from the main force. The Cyclops had seen what Harper and her men were doing and intended on finishing what their cavalry started. Something spoke within Harper in a way she'd never felt before. It was a voice without words, but still it beckoned her to a patch of ice illuminated by the rising sun through a break in the clouds.

"Take the men across as soon as you are able," Harper directed the Ash twins as she began walking toward the patch of ice a hundred yards to the south.

She could hear people talking to her, but not what they said. Her focus was entirely on the illuminated patch of ice and the wordless voice within her speaking in a language of emotions. Her divine spark seemed to understand the voice even if Harper could not and responded by flickering in a way Harper had never seen or felt. All she knew was that she must stand on that section of ice to know what might come next.

The Cyclops vanguard saw her walking toward them and began their charge. Several hundred of the fastest runners were lumbering across the ice at her even as she strolled slowly toward the illuminated spot on the bay.

When she reached the patch, the flickering of her divine spark told her to draw her sword against the charging enemy barreling down upon her. She did as she was instructed. Every movement felt effortless. She was in perfect harmony with something powerful and unseen. The only comparison she could think of was when a strong wind caught the sails of a small boat and pushed it across glassy, calm waters. She was that boat and she believed the wind was her Goddess finally speaking to her.

Harper plunged her sword into the ice with all the force she could muster. The mighty blade sank easily into the frozen salt water that might well have been harder than the stoutest granite. Her divine spark flashed white and became almost blinding to her mind's eye. The ice shattered away from her sword. The break continued out into a colossal crescent of instantly thawed water. The charging vanguard's assault ended abruptly when the ice beneath their feet ceased to be ice. Their splashing ended as quickly as it began when the ocean itself pulled them under far faster than simply sinking could have accomplished.

Harper slid her blade from the ice and stood to her full height. Several hundred square yards of the ocean that formerly was frozen solid had miraculously returned to liquid in a matter of seconds. The turbulent gray water warmed to almost blue as the morning sun broke free of the clouds to shine upon it.

The Cyclops army on the other side of the gap looked on in awe. Then, slowly at first, they began falling to their knees. Harper looked on in utter amazement at the army humbled before the miracle that completely cut off any chance of crossing the bay short of using boats.

"They're a superstitious lot," Wizardly Willard said from beside her. Despite his enormous girth, the old Sorcerer did seem quite adept at sneaking about. He twirled the remaining half of his grand moustache around a pudgy finger and nodded at his own words. "That may be the last we see of them."

"What do you mean?" Harper said, still in awe of the power of the Goddess that flowed through her not moments ago.

"The pantheon ruling above the Crown of the World Mountains is far more tumultuous than our own," Wizardly Willard explained. "Gods and Goddesses war with one another constantly, drawing their mortal pawns into their conflicts often. We are accustomed to being ignored by our deities while the denizens of the north know the wrath of their pantheon all too intimately." Wizardly Willard stopped twirling the remaining half of his moustache and stepped gingerly toward the edge of the ice and water. "If they believe your Goddess does not want them crossing this bay, they will not cross it. Your display of power here should sufficiently convince them of this."

"It was the Sea Queen working through me," Harper whispered.

Wizardly Willard looked back over his shoulder to her and smiled. "If it is a true miracle of the divine, we can expect the remaining Cyclops army to depart in the coming days then." He turned to face the groveling army and waved grandly to them. "The favor you've gained with your Goddess might well win this war for us yet."

Harper sheathed her sword and turned to leave. Wizardly Willard's voice stopped her after a few paces though.

"She's going to ask for something in return for this—mark my words," he said.

Chapter 32.

Precious

Getting everyone back across the ice was a long, arduous process that Calista couldn't have over with soon enough even though her role in the entire thing was simply as an observer. She stood on the docks with Aerial and the Red Dale Riders, passively watching the hundred or so survivors struggle across the weakened part of the bay. Even spread out, moving slowly, and entirely diminished in numbers, the soldiers caused the ice to creak and groan loud enough to be heard all the way on shore. Several times the people crossing stopped entirely and waited to see what the new ice was going to do before resuming their trek at an even slower pace. There was little doubt in Calista's mind—had Harper not blocked off the Cyclops infantry, the returning forces would have been easily slain during the slow, spread out walk. They were entirely vulnerable and something as simple as fleeing might well cause the newly formed ice to fail.

Calista didn't need to be told that Harper performed a miracle. She could feel the overwhelming rush of divine power even from shore. The Sea Queen could have simply smashed the bay on her own, but she wanted Harper to do it for her. Calista suspected she knew why as well, which only confirmed her earlier concerns that the Sea Queen had a vested interest in what Calista stole. Obviously the Sea Queen didn't want the Cyclops getting back what she planned to take for herself. Taken altogether with the rest of the evidence, Calista had to assume the Sea Queen was in opposition to her and would likely set Harper to the task since Calista hadn't ventured into the Goddess's domain again.

Harper and Wizardly Willard were among the last to cross. The soldiers began filing past Calista up into the city before the duo took their first steps onto the fresh ice. Sven and Athol were nearly across, dragging the body of their father behind them. Calista didn't need to be told the body belonged to Bjorn—she felt the power she'd infused him with trickling back to her the moment he died. Then came the North Wind Valkyries, all seventeen of them still intact although their armor and wooden shields had seen better days. Finally Harper and Willard finished the crossing. They too were hauling a body, and Calista needed venture only one guess to know who it was as she hadn't seen Ezra to that point.

Part of her was glad Ezra was dead, which wasn't a particularly attractive emotion and certainly one she planned to keep to herself. The Sorceress didn't like her, had valid suspicions about her, and had overheard what the Cyclops seer actually said. Her death solved all those problems. And that's about where Calista's feelings on the matter ended. She certainly didn't hate Ezra, nor did she like her. Perhaps Calista didn't kill wantonly, but that hardly made her a soft touch on the topic of death. Still, Harper would take it hard and Calista needed to at least appear human in her reaction even if her true response was that of an indifferent assassin that recently had an inconvenience removed.

Calista nodded to Sven and Athol as they passed; they nodded in return. They weren't in a chatty mood and neither was she. They'd survived, which was more than she expected them to do.

The North Wind Valkyries came next up onto the promenade. Calista bade them go to the inn to rest and see her in the evening about their next task. The northern ladies were eager for more after getting their first taste of combat in weeks, but accepted the day of rest regardless.

Harper crested the slope that was slush and mud by that point. Her armor was dented, scratched, and stained. Her hair was disheveled and also held darkened tips from dried blood. But her eyes were alive with the spark Calista knew. The essential part of Harper made it through even if the superficial parts suffered greatly.

Calista practically threw herself onto the Sword Maiden who managed to catch her despite the surprise of it. Aerial even joined in on the embrace, nudging Harper's side several times with the top of her head to try to express her own excitement. For several moments Harper and Calista simply held one another with Aerial in close attendance. Calista could smell the lovely combined scents of Harper's skin, the steel plates of her armor in the cold, and the blood of slaughter clinging to her sword. It was a remarkable amalgamation that she could only describe as a knight's perfume.

"If you two would prefer to ride back for your well-deserved rest, I'm sure my apprentice and I can find a wagon to convey your friend's body," Wizardly Willard offered.

"I would not burden you with such a task when..." Harper began.

"I would not consider it a burden," Wizardly Willard interjected. "Ezra was one of our kind and we are honored to see to her."

Harper looked to be on the verge of dropping, but still reticent to take the offer. Calista chose to push the decision over the edge for both Harper's sake and her own.

"You've not slept or eaten in a day," Calista said. "Ezra would understand and insist you take better care of yourself. Or, barring that, allow me to take better care of you."

This settled the matter. Harper nodded, took Aerial's reins, and hauled herself into the saddle in an almost painfully slow mounting. Calista took Harper's offered hand and leapt up to ride behind her. Whatever adrenaline or divine energy left over from the miracle was draining fast from Harper, and Calista wondered if she might end up dragging the Sword Maiden's sleeping form up the stairs to the room if they didn't hurry. Harper took one last glance at the wrapped body lying on the ground between Wizardly Willard and his apprentice. She turned Aerial away from the scene and gently nudged her toward the inn. Aerial, eager to be back in the stable after a long night in a lighthouse, took off like a shot, forcing Calista to hold tightly to Harper.

Calista took Harper away from her mercenary band, stole her away from Brandinne's advances, and she would steal her away from the Sea Queen next if that's what was required. Harper was *hers* and she'd made up her mind to keep it that way no matter what.

Calista ordered food on their way through the main hall, although Harper protested that she was too tired to eat. Back in the room, Harper's weariness took on a morose edge while Calista helped her remove her armor. Even as Calista was carefully stacking the increasingly worn plates of Harper's once magnificent shell, the Sword Maiden began weeping softly. Calista collected up the partially unarmored Harper and gently caressed her hair.

"My last words to her were harsh," Harper said.

"I'm sure that's not true," Calista replied. Without hearing what Harper said, Calista couldn't believe it was anything remotely mean enough to make it through Ezra's thick emotional shielding. The Sorceress was far too prickly and Harper was far too sweet. "Friendships can be complex and war is brutal. Sometimes these truths collide in unfortunate ways."

"Have you lost friends in war?"

It was an expected question that Calista knew she should have an answer for. "I've had few friends and never fought on a defined side in a war."

"I don't know how much more of a war we'll have here. Wizardly Willard said the Cyclops would leave after witnessing the miracle for fear of angering the Sea Queen."

"Did he?" Calista asked. Already her mind was working over things. The old Sorcerer's assessment of the situation matched what she knew perfectly. The Fir'bolgs wouldn't be as easily dissuaded from their path, especially not with their competition voluntarily departing, but Calista could think of one thing that could be done to even the odds still further. The ice giants never took to the sea, even to walk upon the ice, and thus had no fear of the Sea Queen, but there were other weaknesses she might exploit if she could find her way outside the walls and behind their lines. She would need to find the leader of the thieves guild, Randolph, and convince him to give her access to a genuine Dwarven tunnel out of the city, preferably on the eastern side, for her plan to even stand a chance.

"It was a remarkable victory with a steep price," Harper said.

Calista couldn't agree more. They'd lost nearly a third of the city's total defenders in the battle, Harper lost a friend in Ezra, and there was the looming threat of what the Sea Queen might want in exchange for her miracle. Calista knew all too well that no God or Goddess did something so grand without asking for something even grander in return. Calista suspected she already knew what would be asked.

Divine Touched

Despite Harper's insistence that she was too tired to eat, when the food arrived, her tune changed. A serving girl brought in two crusty loafs of sourdough bread that were hollowed out and filled with lamb stew. The edible food containers delighted Harper and the scent of cooked lamb, rosemary, potatoes, and carrots momentarily pushed back her need for sleep. Calista ate as well, although not nearly as voraciously as Harper.

"It's nice to be able to come home to you after an ordeal like that." Harper glanced up from her eating. She looked ineffably tired, but ultimately relieved.

"It's nice to be here to come home to," Calista replied.

She waited for awhile after, letting Harper eat her fill, which included much of the bread bowl the consumed stew once sat in. Calista knew Harper would be more pliable if she was fed, relaxed, and ultimately ready for bed, which was precisely the point she'd reached.

"The miracle the Sea Queen offered you will need to be repaid," Calista said.

"Wizardly Willard mentioned as much. I've never performed one so I don't really know the etiquette of such a thing, although I should hate to appear rude or ungrateful." Harper yawned, plucked a strand of her hair up for inspection, sniffed it, and made a sour face. "My hair smells awful."

"Cyclops blood putrefies quickly," Calista said. "We'll need to wash it out before you go to bed." During her time in the far north, Calista saw precisely how quickly Cyclops blood became vile and odorous after being spilled. The Cyclops relied a lot on their noses to sense the world around them as they had half the vision of most, and so it was a way for them to detect danger to their kind by knowing when something wounded or killed one of them—or so the stories went, anyway.

Calista led Harper to the great stone tub and helped her to settle on the steps with her head resting on the lip and her hair dangling into the basin. She used some of the offered water sitting next to the roaring fire and began washing out Harper's long, silken blond hair. The act of stroking her hair, massaging her scalp, and cleaning away the awful smell worked to further relax Harper until Calista was certain she was amenable to just about anything in the vulnerable moment.

"The Sea Queen wants what I've stolen," Calista said. "That's what she'll ask for in exchange for the miracle."

"You're sure of this?" Harper's eyes fluttered open. They were bloodshot around the edges, but still bright blue in the middle and kind, so very kind.

"As sure as a person can be when speculating on the motivations of the divine," Calista said.

"The shipwreck of the *Enolla...*"

"Was meant to kill me and take what I carry." When added to the second attempt on her life during the disastrous assassination job, there was little doubt in Calista's mind the Sea Queen took the two chances to kill her and then tried something else when Calista didn't give her a third.

"What is it you've stolen exactly?" Harper asked.

The question was fair and beyond due, if Calista was being honest with herself. Harper's need to protect their relationship from what was no doubt going to be an issue served them both well to that point, but Calista knew it was a fool's desire to think they might never have a conversation about it. She could get ahead of the Sea Queen by bringing honesty first though, and the timing of it couldn't have been better.

"The essence of a new God," Calista said.

This drew Harper from the tub, hair wet, eyes suddenly sharp and aware. It wasn't quite the panicked reaction Calista expected; the stew, exhaustion, and candor likely tempered the response a bit.

"Explain, please," Harper said softly.

"The type of assassin I am, my divine spark, allows me to take the life force of my victims," Calista said. "The power isn't mine to keep, but I can use it some and then trade it to my Goddess for favors. After years of my being highly successful in this, she approached me with a favor of her own to ask." Calista could see on Harper's face the disdain for such a craft, and the worst part wasn't even spoken yet. "The immortal life force of a new deity comes along rarely, tens of thousands of years in the lands below the Crown of the World Mountains. The pantheon here has become relatively stable. But in the far north, Gods and Goddesses slay one another all the time and so a new deity can be born every few hundred years. In the weakened state of emerging, an immortal can be slain by a mortal such as myself. If that mortal also happens to be imbued with the power to take life forces from victims, a power only granted by a specific Goddess, you can see how an immortal essence might be stolen."

"You slew a God and stole their immortality?" Harper asked in astonishment.

"It was nothing so grand as it sounds," Calista explained. "To watch what I physically did, it would literally look like I simply broke an egg before it hatched. The future God was within, unborn or unhatched or whatever, and the life force passed to me along the same channels as any other life force I've stolen. It isn't mine, holding onto it doesn't make me immortal, and I can't do anything with it but transport it from one place to another."

"Why would the Sea Queen want it?"

"To create a daughter, revive a long deceased ally, elevate a servant to immortality so they might better serve her...I really don't know," Calista said. "In the right hands, what I carry is the creation of an immortal of colossal power—the reasons to try to take such a thing are as numerous as the stars. The Cyclops and Fir'bolgs who were fighting over this burgeoning God set aside their differences to march two armies south of the Crown of the World Mountains to try to retrieve it, which speaks to the value of the thing, but not the specific motives the Sea Queen might have."

"Why does your Goddess want it? Or do you even know?"

"She didn't tell me, but I believe I've figured it out," Calista replied. "I can't tell you though. Questioning the motives of my own Goddess would be blasphemy and whatever information I give you might well pass to your Goddess through your divine spark. For both our sakes, I can only say that I believe in her reasons and think them worthy of what I've undergone."

"What about everyone else involved in this?" Harper asked. "Do you believe such a thing is worthy of all those who have died?"

"I cannot say, nor is their blood truly on my hands. I tried my best to stay ahead of those who would pursue me to reduce any collateral damage. The Sea Queen and I believe maybe even the Thief Lord actively sought to keep me from completing my task. The blood spilled since is on their hands as I would have been in

Ovid months ago and long since done with my task had they not interfered."

"The Cyclops and Fir'bolg armies though…"

"…are siege forces," Calista finished for Harper. "They knew I would be stranded here because the God or Goddess or both preventing me from leaving told them so."

"You couldn't simply surrender the essence back to the Fir'bolgs?"

"The only person, immortal or mortal, that I can willingly give the essence to is my Goddess. Anyone else seeking to take it will have to tear it from me in brutal fashion. I don't have to consciously defend it any more than your rib cage has to consciously defend your heart." Calista shook her head. These were the questions she was prepared for although she didn't feel her answers were doing much good. "It's not *their* essence anyway. The Fir'bolgs, the Cyclops, the Sea Queen, the Thief Lord…none of them has any stronger claim to it than my Goddess. The God I prevented from existing was to be a dragon deity summoned by a cult intent on restoring dragons to prominence in the far north. The Cyclops and Fir'bolgs destroyed much of the cult in fighting over the essence and slaughtered an entire city of believers while they warred with each other over which group could claim the prize. I slipped in during the chaos, took what both armies were fighting for, and ended the massacre by removing the purpose for it. Either the Fir'bolgs would have taken the egg and likely smashed it to prevent the Cyclops from having it or the Cyclops would have offered it to one of their barbaric Gods as a sacrifice. There wasn't going to be any dragon God regardless of what I did."

"What am I supposed to say to the Sea Queen when she finally calls upon me to repay the miracle?"

"I don't know," Calista said. "I've told you everything I can. You'll have to decide the rest for yourself."

The moment, a seminal moment in their relationship when Harper knew everything Calista could say, came and went with little in the way of fireworks. Harper's exhaustion likely played a role. She shook her head and shrugged. "That's more than I care to think about at the moment and certainly nothing I'll decide until the Sea Queen forces me to," Harper said. "Come to bed with me.

It's only the dinner hour, but I'm tired and wish to find comfort in my lover's arms."

Calista accepted Harper's invitation, stripped off her own armor with a little help, and they both fell quickly into bed. They wrapped themselves around each other beneath the blankets without another word. Calista fell asleep easily, listening to Harper's slow, rhythmic heartbeat and feeling the strength in the powerful arms around her. In time, if things succeeded, she would be able to tell Harper the reason why. If Harper was the person Calista hoped she was, it would justify everything Calista had done and still might have to do.

It felt good to unburden herself to someone she trusted even if she didn't know yet what would come of it all. Calista fell asleep shortly after Harper.

Chapter 33:

Love, Loyalty, and Lies

Calista had planned on seducing Harper whenever they both woke up. The act of making love, she believed, would help solidify the goodwill she'd accumulated the night before. Her plans were dashed, however, when she awoke to find Harper well into the act of seducing her. It wasn't the first time Calista came to the waking world at the exploring hands of a lover, although the last occasion was some time ago and not nearly as enjoyable. Her body was already well on its way to a deep, abiding satisfaction before she was even aware of the world around her. Indeed, she had no idea what time it was or even what day. She did know Harper was caressing and stroking her with eager fingers between her legs, which was all that mattered.

Calista nuzzled into her partner's caresses and kissed Harper's neck. The Sword Maiden increased her efforts as Calista spread her legs to allow her easier access. Calista's hand found its way to Harper's strapping arm to stroke her fingertips along the rounded lines of her muscles that shifted beneath her smooth, soft skin with every motion. Calista moaned softly to which Harper responded by covering her mouth with a dominant kiss.

Not to be outdone by her lover, Calista shifted to her side and sought out Harper's body with her own hand. She found the Sword Maiden's strong thighs already eager to part for her hand and the thick nub of her clit anticipating her touch. There was little doubt in her course, although she found herself well behind Harper in dealing pleasure as Calista awoke on the cusp of an orgasm and was heading over the edge quickly. When she climaxed, peeling her lips from Harper's to breathe and let loose a series of sleepy moans, she became acutely focused on the woman beside her and the unquenchable desire for more of Harper.

Calista pushed Harper onto her back and nestled her way down beneath the thick blankets. Harper made a single attempt to pull her upper body from the bed to do something or other, but Calista quickly pushed her back down with an insistent hand, leaving it upon Harper's chest to caress the large, enticing breast it happened to land upon. Calista plunged her mouth over Harper's clit and tongued at it with great relish. More than simply wishing to give pleasure to her lover, Calista enjoyed the act as a way to explore Harper's body. Her lover's form was a wonder and Calista found herself lusting after it in every way. The lines of her muscles were marvelous, the smell of her skin was intoxicating, the map of scars across her physique was intriguing, and the impressive love button between her legs occupied Calista's thoughts until she was able to explore the object of her desire, which only served to feed her yearning.

Harper's body responded both of her free-will and of its own volition. Calista could taste Harper, feel the slipperiness dripping onto her chin, the heat from Harper's skin, and the nipple beneath her fingers going rigid. To add to her body's reflexive response to pleasure, Harper added an eager hand to the back of Calista's head, grasping wantonly at her hair while she writhed and moaned in pleasure.

One climax came quickly, then another as Calista pressed on, and one more frantic explosion of pleasure before Harper's hand on the back of her head pulled her away from her work at the overwhelming sensations. The Sword Maiden was breathless, glowing, and suddenly eager to once again hold Calista in her arms. Calista found herself plucked up into a strong embrace and kissed upon the forehead, cheeks, and mouth.

"That was a wonderful way to be awoken," Calista murmured, nuzzling her head beneath Harper's chin.

"Your body called to me," Harper replied breathlessly. "I began to wonder if you would awaken at all."

"I must have been more tired than I thought."

"I am glad my advances were appreciated," Harper said. "I sat awake for quite some time before I could work up the courage."

"Consider it always a welcome way to revive me, my love."

Silence hung between them for a moment. Harper's breathing calmed and Calista began to wonder if she'd fallen asleep.

"I would not give you up in exchange for anything," Harper finally said. "Do you believe me?"

"Yes," Calista replied. It was true enough in the moment and she believed that Harper believed her words, although she wondered if the promise could stand in the face of all a spurned Goddess could do. Harper was certainly physically strong, brave, and honest, but she was emotionally unpracticed in love and fragile in the tender newness of her feelings. Calista believed it would still remain to be seen if Harper could guard one with the other in a meaningful way when the time came.

"Loyalty is important to me," Harper said after a time.

Calista didn't know what to make of the statement. It was important to her as well, although she didn't know if Harper meant loyalty to her Goddess or loyalty to her lover—both seemed likely and in short order she might well have to decide which was more important. Calista couldn't imagine how she might make the decision were their positions reversed. Her relationship with her own Goddess wasn't typical; they were nearly friends in many habits and that made Calista partial in ways most divine touched weren't.

"It's important to me too," Calista replied.

"It's the middle of the night, but I'm hungry and restless," Harper said. "Let's go get something to eat."

Calista felt better by the time she and Harper parted company in the small hours of the night. Neither of them was interested in returning to sleep just yet, which was understandable. They both had full heads and even after they added full stomachs on top of it, they still weren't sleepy. Harper returned to their room to work on her armor while Calista dressed and took to the night to check on the progress of the Red Dale Riders on the streets.

The cold night air was invigorating and Calista made good time walking through the deserted lanes of the snowy city, confident her men were doing an excellent job of driving the thieves guild underground one way or the other. She briefly considered a few burglary jobs of her own to pad out the black market she was supplying. There was a cider house she thought she might be able to nick a small barrel or two from before sunrise, especially if she could locate a wheelbarrow on the premises.

The cider house sat on the edge of the marketplace, close enough that she could simply walk the stolen barrels over to the teahouse used as a front for her black market. She was certain one of her countrywomen would be awake at that hour to receive the stolen goods. She kept mostly to the shadows on the walk across town, and eventually found herself incidentally tailing a familiar duo plus one.

Guard Ulrich and Turbald were walking as brazen as you please with Brandinne between them, heading in the same general direction as Calista, but a dozen or so yards ahead. Calista focused on intentionally following them at that point to see where the unlikely trio might be headed. She couldn't hear what they were talking about from as far back as she was following and she dared not get closer since Brandinne no doubt had ears to rival most bats.

In an unhappy coincidence, they appeared to be walking straight for the marketplace and their destination, while not necessarily the cider house, was close enough to spoil Calista's brazen plan to steal a couple casks of cider using a wheelbarrow. Her musings on what she might do next came to an abrupt halt when her minions, likely starved for prey by that point, sprung upon the three.

Brandinne focused entirely on avoiding conflict in the first few seconds of the fight and managed to escape the quickly closing ring of Rangers somehow. Several of the Red Dale Riders gave chase. Calista hadn't instructed them to capture the Havvish woman, although she had little doubt that was precisely what they were about to do since she wasn't of the thieves guild and thus not on their list of people to kill.

Ulrich and Turbald stood their ground for the moment, seemingly relying upon their status and dress as guards to protect them from brigands. Of course, Calista long ago gave her men their names and descriptions, stating they were thieves no matter what cloak they were wearing at the time. Ulrich took an arrow in the shoulder, failed in getting his shield into position to block anything further, and ended up making a mad dash to escape. Turbald ducked behind his taller compatriot in this retreat, but broke away quickly, showing remarkable speed for a man of his size and encumbrance. Even injured, Ulrich appeared to be set to put up a fight and the Red Dale Riders had already split their numbers once. The Rangers seemed satisfied with their wounded prey of Ulrich and the hunt for Brandinne, and so let Turbald go, possibly with plans to track him later if the night allowed.

Calista chose to follow the fat guard who apparently was quite the runner. She tailed him mostly in the shadows, struggling to keep up at times with how quickly his choppy little gait carried him through the snow. He also didn't seem to tire. She was breathing heavily and on the verge of falling behind while he was only getting started.

He ran straight up the hill toward the high end of town at the foot of the mountains and the statue garden Calista suspected contained an entrance to the thieves guild lair. He was fumbling with something in his cloak; she guessed it was a key. His attempts at finding the key slowed him enough to allow her to close the gap. He found the key and nearly reached the threshold for the walled enclosure of Dwarven statues when she decided to take him.

Calista hurled her harpoon, catching Turbald in the back of the left leg. The pronged end caught in his armor, clothing, and flesh. He let out a little yelp of surprise and pain, which was quickly cut short when she yanked the chain, pulling him off his feet, to deposit him face first in the snow. He popped his head up, sputtering out the snow that went straight into his open mouth when he fell. She leapt upon his back, pinned his arms beneath her knees, and gave him a meaningful tap on the side of his neck with her straight blade dagger.

"Care to give me a tour of the old Dwarven tunnels on the way to Randolph?" Calista asked. "I doubt simply having your key will be enough to get in."

"I'll do you one better," Turbald said. "I'll introduce you to Randolph this second." His dockside accent was gone and his voice sounded far less gruff than she remembered.

"Wait a second…"

"I'm Randolph T. Minetrotter, the illustrious leader of the Bull Rush Boys," Turbald said.

"You're too slick by half," Calista grumbled and meant it. Hiding in plain sight the entire time, he was the least likely person in the world for the guards to suspect was in charge of the thieves guild. "I expected a Dwarf."

"So does everyone, most of all your hunters," Randolph said, completely dropping his Guard Turbald act. "No point in keeping up the charade with you since I'm certain you're willing to torture me to get an introduction to me. Let's skip the whole messy affair and cut to the quick."

"Very well." Calista slid her dagger back into the sheath in the top of her boot and plucked the harpoon from the back of Randolph's leg. He grunted at the pain, but seemed reasonably fine, all things considered.

He leapt to his feet in another surprising display of athleticism, dusted the snow off his guard uniform, and stood with suddenly perfect posture before Calista. "No point in pretending like you don't have me over a barrel," Randolph said. "I'm not much of a fighter, my boys aren't any match for yours, and that blasted Havvish woman has done a fine job of bleeding us dry by selling us information that doesn't go anywhere. To put it bluntly, I'm willing to barter away a great deal to be left alone. I'd like to get back to business as usual and I can't very well do that while your men slaughter my people. So, what is it you want?"

"I want guided passage through the old Dwarven tunnels to an exit in the east behind the Fir'bolg line," Calista said.

"And I would love to help you, but the only such passage I know of exits directly into an Ogre mound. A particularly odd old Ogre occupies the mound. He seems harmless enough, but has an unbearable stench regardless."

"I've got ways around the stench," Calista said.

"Then you've got yourself a guide, a map, and a tunnel whenever you like."

"Why are you being so helpful?"

"Why wouldn't I be?" Randolph shrugged and smiled. "We woefully underestimated what you are capable of. We entirely overestimated how well we'd do against your mercenaries, and I hear there are seventeen more joining the ranks. Now we're completely interested in being left alone. Like I said, I'm not a fighter; I'm a businessman. This sort of conflict is bad for my bottom line. Thieves ending up hunted and dead costs me money. Give me an escape as cheap and easy as showing you a tunnel out of the city and I'll be glad to provide it in exchange for letting us get back to our work."

"Your continued existence in exchange for passage through the tunnel?"

Randolph nodded. "We'll call it doing our bit for the war effort."

"Done," Calista said. The whole thing was entirely too easy. She believed most of what was said by Randolph was probably only half true. He would get something more out of their deal and likely look for a way to have her end up dead if she didn't keep her wits about her. "Stay in the open. I'll let you know when we're leaving."

"We?" Randolph asked.

"You'll be my guide to prevent any sort of double cross," Calista said.

"If I didn't have bad luck lately..."

"...you wouldn't have any luck at all," Calista said. "I'll throw in keeping Brandinne out of your hair as a bonus."

"I'd pay to have her thrown in a sack and buried," Randolph said, "but out of my hair would be a blessing worth turning religious over."

Even as tired as Harper was, she knew sleep wasn't a possibility. She'd hoped making love with Calista would calm her mind, but apparently the opposite was true. Sven and Athol always said a good romp put them into a napping mood—she would have to tell them that wasn't a universal truth when next she saw them. She ate with Calista and they parted ways after a lingering kiss.

Harper briefly went back to her room to tend her armor, which required little work to bring back to a gleaming state. The enchantments running through the metal worked out dents in time and shed tarnish like ice off a roof in the spring. Still, she took a few moments to wipe away the grime and reorganize the plates for easiest equipping.

Little else remained to do in the room and so she took a walk in the snow as the sky began to warm to gray with the coming dawn. Her head was too full for much of anything else, and the chilly walk did little to clear it. Perhaps it was a matter of habit or a matter of faith that she ended up standing outside the temple of the Sea Queen.

There was a certain impatience behind Harper's hasty entrance to the temple. The threat of what the Sea Queen might ask of her hung over her head and she didn't care for the feeling. She decided she would ask, expecting no answer, to see if Maraline truly intended what Calista said she did.

Harper was dressed for the cold of a long walk on the streets, but found herself overly warm in her bundled up state within the temple. There was a pleasant warmth in the air and the typical scent of salt water, seaweed, and sandstone. An alluring glow arose from the clamshell carving at the head of the temple, drawing Harper closer. A distant form of familiarity hung over the morning, harkening back to the day the Sea Queen imbued her with the divine spark.

There was little doubt in her mind that the orb was another miracle, floating above the shell like a golden pearl. The warmth it gave off drew her in with reverent steps, forcing her to shed a few of the warmer layers of her clothing until she was down to just her tunic, britches, and boots. She knelt before the altar bathed in lustrous light. The glowing pearl no longer looked like a sphere. The light source remained centralized, but a body of a woman grew out from it. It was as though the shimmering orb found itself within a glass sculpture of a beautiful mermaid only it wasn't glass. The surface was rippling like water. It was quite possibly the most beautiful sight Harper ever beheld.

"You have found your way home, Sword Maiden, after an interminable night upon the ocean," the radiant, watery mermaid said in a voice that echoed with the sound of surf crashing upon the shore. Her words struck upon Harper's divine spark, causing it to flicker, and she knew the watery apparition was a mouthpiece for her Goddess.

"I give you my thanks, Sea Queen." Harper hushed her tone and remained kneeling before the Goddess's avatar, glancing occasionally at it out of the corner of her eye.

"I ask not for your thanks, only your servitude," the Sea Queen's avatar said. "I can feel in you already that you know what you must do. What I ask is simple and well within the realm of your duty to me. Bring me your lover and lay her upon my altar so that I might take what she has stolen."

Obedience was required in all things to her Goddess. A deity rarely, if ever, spoke to a believer, and when they did, they were not to be questioned. Harper knew this, knew she was taking her life in her own hands by not immediately carrying out the command. Despite knowing she shouldn't question her Goddess, the words flowed from her.

"Calista said she would have to die to give up what she carries," Harper said.

"Many have already died in the service of this," the avatar replied.

Already, Harper was pushing her luck, but she pressed on nevertheless. "What would you do with the immortal essence?" she asked, knowing full well her question bordered on heresy. There was no justification for any mortal to ever ask anything about an immortal's plan. Her Goddess owed her no explanation. Even still, Harper could not turn away from the question. The Sea Queen made it clear she would kill Calista in taking the essence, and Harper had to know if there was a reason worthy of taking so much from one so loyal to her. Harper couldn't fathom an answer that would make her understand, but she also wasn't a Goddess and believed there might be some unknowable explanation that only her Goddess could give.

"That is not for you to know," the avatar's voice rumbled, sending ripples across the surface of her watery body. "I command and you obey."

"I cannot!" Harper replied, turning her gaze from the increasingly angry avatar. Blind obedience to her duty ruled her life to that point, but she couldn't imagine sacrificing her lover without so much as a justification of why. The reason to do such a thing would need to be astounding, making the Goddess's refusal to answer easy to reject.

The Sea Queen calmed even in the face of Harper's disobedience. The pleasant glow and serene surface returned to the avatar. A soothing wave passed through Harper's divine spark, bringing her breathing and heartbeat to an almost slumbering level.

"So many innocent lives are at risk. So many have already died in the name of keeping this cherished thing from deserving

Divine Touched

hands," the avatar said in an increasingly hypnotic voice. "I can grant you the power to end this without anyone within the city dying. You could be the holy chalice of my essence, slaughter the ice giants outside the walls, and save the city from further bloodshed. One, noble sacrifice is all I require and you will become the instrument of salvation for so many."

Harper hadn't expected the offer. She hadn't necessarily believed her questions would be answered. Indeed, she thought the Sea Queen might smite her where she knelt, but she never expected such a proposal. There was no reason to believe she was lying. The Sea Queen's avatar spoke to her through her divine spark in addition to vocalizations. The sacrifice would be noble and so many lives would be saved. It was an appealing end to a conflict that already brought about the death of so many. The euphoria flowing from her Goddess into Harper through her divine spark made the offer sound all the more alluring. Except it wasn't her sacrifice to make. Certainly she would lose Calista, but the altruism in it wouldn't be her own, nor did Calista seem willing to betray her own Goddess to end a conflict she wasn't truly responsible for.

"Were the sacrifice mine to make, I would," Harper said.

"You reject my offer?" the avatar stammered through a growing storm of rage.

"I cannot do as you ask in this…"

"I save your life and the lives of your men by performing a holy miracle through you, mend your body and the bodies of your compatriots countless times, offer you the means to end the war without further death or destruction, and even still you will not obey me?"

"I will serve as you ask in any other way you ask. I will give up my own life as recompense to spare Calista's. But I cannot give you what you desire."

"Your life is worthless to me and you are an unfit servant for the gifts I have given you!" The avatar grew in size and ferocity, taking on the form of a great sea serpent.

The air grew cold within the temple, as though an arctic storm blew away the warmth. Ice coated Harper quickly and she awaited the killing blow that she thought could only follow such blasphemy. She was resigned to her fate. She wished only to tell

314

Calista why she'd done what she'd done, although she suspected her lover would understand even without the explanation. Harper had prepared for just such an eventuality, enjoying everything she could with Calista with what little time she believed remained to her. Loyalty was important to her and she'd remained loyal to the person she loved. Slain by her Goddess in the name of saving the woman she loved was also a good death and she would go willingly to it. Harper defiantly looked upon her deity's monstrous avatar and smiled.

"Know a life of emptiness no doubt shortened by a brutal death in the coming months of war," the avatar roared at her. "I will have the essence and you will feel the loss of what I have given you before it is your end. You are not strong enough to be victorious without me—a lesson that will cost you more than you can imagine."

The storm building around the glowing, watery serpent snapped, the avatar vanished, and with it went the divine spark in Harper. She fell forward onto the steps of the altar. The tiny fire of the Goddess inside her was gone, replaced by a great emptiness that threatened to swallow her. She felt weak, not just physically, but emotionally and spiritually as well. Old wounds, healed by the Goddess's magic ached, her muscles felt suddenly insufficient to wield her sword or wear her armor, and a crushing sensation of utter aloneness overwhelmed her.

She knew the sun of a Goddess's love and attention for years. To have the eyes of the Sea Queen turn away from her tore purpose and love out of her life in a way that even rejection from her own parents couldn't accomplish. She didn't know loss and rejection could hurt so much.

Harper wept upon the sandstone believing death would have been a mercy.

Chapter 34:

Spiders Abound

Harper remained as she lay until the affirmed sisters of the temple found her. They whispered concerned words to one another, keeping just out of Harper's hearing. Eventually they left, returning after awhile with Sven and Athol. The brothers were of a sullen mood, no doubt still grieving their father. From what Harper knew of their family, he'd been a good father to them and despite the readiness of Bjorn to die, it seemed his sons weren't quite ready for him to go. They helped her to her feet and guided her to the door. Even walking seemed more difficult without the Goddess's light within her.

The cold outside bit through Harper's clothes and for a moment she forgot she'd shed most of them. Still, it'd been the first time in ages that she'd actually felt the full weight of weather, such was the power of the Goddess's protection over her. Athol wrapped her in his own bear cloak, which dragged upon the snow behind her, but kept out the winter's worst.

They returned to the Thundering Dawn Inn in time for midday meal. The brothers guided her to the usual circular booth and Harper sat, still wrapped in the bearskin cloak, staring blankly ahead. They gathered food and drink from serving girls before returning to her. They deposited great slabs of cold cured pork, brined okra, and flat loaves made from rock berry flour. In addition to the entirely unappealing food, they brought for themselves heaping tankards of ale with foamy heads. Harper watched one of the tankards curiously while Athol and Sven set about carving food from the central platters to put on their individual plates. Harper reached out, snatched up Athol's tankard of ale, and drank greedily of it until her throat burned too much to continue. She set down the still heavy tankard with a slosh and let out a mighty burp. Immediately her stomach churned and shortly after her head began to swim.

"Finish it as you will," Athol said. "I'll happily find another if you plan to join us from now on in our drinking."

"Not to overlook such a grand belch for the more mundane topic of vows, but doesn't your oath prevent you from imbibing spirits?" Sven asked. "Returning to the belch, it was a worthy first effort but you need to open your mouth wider and push out your jaw to truly let it ring."

"The Sea Queen has forsaken me, hurled me from her sight, I am a Sword Maiden no longer." Harper took up the tankard, which was now her tankard, and drank greedily again of the ale, which was bitter and thick and growing on her quickly. "I owe no vows to anyone now. My maidenhood I renounce as I've done plenty with the woman I love that I would constitute losing my virginity. Thus I am no longer a Sword Maiden." Harper wiped away the foam from her upper lip with the back of her arm and took another long drink. The beverage was making her feel fuzzy all over and a little warm. She could see why the brothers and Ezra enjoyed alcohol so much. "I am going to drink ale, do naked sweaty things with Calista, and spend all my money on pretty things without tithing a single copper to the temple. I will become a hedonistic wretch."

"You can't simply become a hedonistic wretch!" Athol beckoned a nearby serving girl to deliver him a new tankard of ale to replace the one Harper had nearly finished. "It takes years of practice, a lifetime of dedication, and a lack of any other realistic ambitions to become a hedonistic wretch."

"Begging your pardon, but why would the Sea Queen do such a thing?" Sven asked.

"She asked me to sacrifice Calista on her altar and I said I wouldn't," Harper replied.

"Bugger that briny wench and all her fishy followers," Athol said.

Harper looked at him curiously and then to Sven for confirmation of the blasphemous reaction. Sven nodded his approval and drank of his own tankard to put a final seal on the matter of buggering the Sea Queen.

"But she was my Goddess..." Harper stammered.

"And she mucked it all up by asking for something stupid," Sven said. "If I worshiped any of the pantheon, put in the dedication you have, and then they asked me to turn my wife into a

317

ritual sacrifice, I would have told them the same thing. And my wife hates me! Calista seems to genuinely love you—I couldn't tell you what I would do for a woman like that, but I certainly wouldn't hurl her upon an altar to please some soggy old apparition of the immortals."

"Those Gods and Goddesses with their unknowable gobbledygook," Athol slurred, having somehow found possession of a fresh tankard while Harper was listening to Sven. He drained most of it and waved for another. "Meddling about in their nonsense, demanding mortals beg and scrape for a tiny crumb of recognition, and then they ask you to give up a raucous piece of tail like Calista? I hope you told her to take her trident and whatever other maritime bric-a-brac she could find and shove it right up her undying ass."

"But my powers," Harper argued. "What am I to do without the divine spark?"

"You've got arms like oak branches, shoulders like the mountains, and the heart of the world in you," Sven said. "The Goddess didn't give you any of that."

"And a right pert set of tits!" Athol agreed. He hoisted his tankard, smacked it into Sven's when it was offered, and then looked to Harper expectantly. She reluctantly lifted her own drink, and he smacked his tankard against hers as well. They all drank deeply and set down their empty mugs in succession. "You know what I think?" Athol asked.

"I never do," Sven said, "so you should tell us."

"I think all the really amazing stuff you did, you did without her," Athol slurred. "You built a bear fort on the ocean. It was a fort large enough to hold more than a hundred men, constructed of the fallen corpses of bears, and you built it on the bloody ocean. A bear fort, built on the ocean…forget having seen it before, have you ever even heard of anyone doing something like that?"

"Not once in all my years," Sven said. "Bards will sing songs about that for decades. The miracle of the bay cracking and the Cyclops fleeing—the Cyclops are gone by the way, left this morning in a hurry they did—but like them, all that will fade. Gods and Goddesses do twaddle like that every couple of years just to prove they still exist. But the bear fort and the great battle at night…people just don't do things like that unless they're really, really…"

"Creative!" Athol finished for his brother.

"Close enough!" Sven hefted his new tankard, which he'd acquired at some point while Harper was feeling a little dizzy and clanked it against Athol's fresh one that he already had waiting in the wings.

Harper really was feeling better about the pep talk and even the food looked a good deal more appetizing after she finished her ale. The warm ease surrounding her faded quickly when the Ash twins stormed into the hall in full battle regalia.

"The Fir'bolgs sent a swarm to our battlements," Romulus said.

"Ice spiders threaten to overrun the city," Remus added.

Harper felt like throwing up the contents of the stomach she'd just filled with ale. Thought turned to deed, and she hurled the foamy mess onto the bench beside her.

By the Gods she hated spiders.

Dawn had broken by the time Calista started her way back down the hill to find out what became of Ulrich and Brandinne. She was, quite frankly, so sick of the both of them that if the Red Dale Riders ended up riddling them with arrows and leaving them for the crows that would have suited Calista just fine.

She found Ulrich first. He was dead, as she suspected he might be, and stripped of valuables. It really saved her a lot of time to have her men be so proactive. She hadn't liked that Ulrich blackmailed her and she had briefly suspected he was an agent of the Thief Lord, although his current state would argue he might not be. He certainly wasn't divine touched and if he acted unwittingly at the behest of a God it would just be another puppeteer pulling his strings as apparently Randolph had him completely fooled. Calista left the stripped and battered corpse to whatever might have him and continued following the tracks in the snow down toward the bay.

She found the Red Dale Riders, all twelve of them, lounging quite happily about on a pile of heavy lobster traps. Among them, under the boot of Caleb, was a writhing, angry sack. People occasionally passed by, giving the turbulent bag a sideways look, to which Caleb simply said, "Angry cat tiring itself out." This seemed to satisfy most pedestrians. In truth, many of the sounds Brandinne was making could have been mistaken for a cat of some kind. As unhappy as Brandinne was about being stuffed in a sack, the other option apparently was slain by arrows, looted for valuables, and left in an undignified heap to freeze in the street. Calista considered telling Brandinne to be grateful she didn't share Ulrich's fate.

"Let the angry little thing out of her bag," Calista said upon approach.

The Red Dale Riders stood with cavalier grace, gathered around the bag in a semi-circle to prevent Brandinne from escaping, and then Caleb upended the bag, depositing the ruffled Havvish woman onto the snow.

"I know it is against your nature, but for now, you need to listen only. Don't talk. Just nod or shake your head to answer," Calista instructed Brandinne. "Do you understand me?"

Brandinne glanced around the stoic faces of the hardened Rangers with the distant look of thrall in their eyes. Several had clubs in their hands, which weren't being used to menace, but simply dangled at their sides as though the Rangers had forgotten they were there—somehow this seemed even more threatening. Brandinne looked back to Calista and nodded.

"Good," Calista said. "You've been a proper pain in the ass. Normally, that would earn you a quick, if messy, death, but I find myself only half sorry my men didn't kill you. The other half thinks you might still be useful." Calista offered her hand to Brandinne, who initially flinched. Then, realizing Calista didn't intend to strike her, Brandinne took the offered hand and the help to her feet. "I want to offer you a job. It's dangerous, you'll likely die, I may very well pay you with some of your own coin, but the benefits of accepting can't be beat. Don't ask. I'll just tell you. The benefits are: you get paid to continue living. Sound good?"

Brandinne rolled her strange, violet eyes and nodded.

"That wasn't so bad, now was it? Go back up to the inn, stay in the main hall the rest of the day, and I'll come find you tonight before we are to leave," Calista said. "If you aren't there when I arrive, I'll have my men hunt you down and drown you in one of these lobster crates. Is that clear?"

Brandinne glanced back to the lobster crates as if to confirm she would fit in one. The glance satisfied everyone she would, which gave her all the motivation she needed to agree. Their conversation was about to be sealed with a handshake when the warning bells on the eastern wall began ringing with wild abandon.

"On second thought, we may well be needed at the wall," Calista said.

The lot of them raced through the city toward the sound of the clanging bells. As they neared the eastern wall, the fleeing citizenry began to choke the streets, slowing them immensely. Heading in the same direction as them, and having no less trouble pushing their way past the escaping people, were other adventurers, militia, and a few city guards.

The wall itself was in chaos, easily seen before they even arrived. Spiders were flooding up toward the wall from both directions somehow. Calista wondered after some sort of tunnel or a breach farther down the wall that circled back. Her wonderings were answered in short order though after the distant cracking of ropes and creaking of a catapult arm ended with a snap and suddenly a whole host of bunched spider bodies flew over the top of the wall. A few of the Sorcerers still assigned to its defense, Wizardly Willard among them, hurled spells up at the fresh salvo of incoming giant ice spiders. The magic struck all but one of the half dozen spiders, setting them aflame as they fell into the city.

"You don't see that every day," Brandinne mused.

Calista shot her an angry glance.

"What? You don't," Brandinne said in her own defense.

The magical fireballs, which were effective in killing the spiders mid-flight, were equally effective in setting parts of the city ablaze. Many of the guards diverted from defending the walls to fight the fires, hurling snow and ice upon them to quash the flames before they could spread.

"We need to get onto that wall," Calista said.

As if reading her intentions, the Red Dale Riders set bow and arrow to the undertaking. They fired up at the spiders wreaking such havoc on the wall ahead of them as they walked ever forward toward the stairs. Their arrows wounded rather than killed, but did enough damage to hamper the spiders, which in turn allowed the defenders of the wall a chance to rally. There were axe men among the mercenaries atop the stone parapet, freshly stationed as part of Harper's request, and their axes appeared to be just the tools for taking down the white widow spiders. With the spiders hampered by well-placed arrows from the Red Dale Riders, the axe men hacked their way through the lot of them, and secured the section of the wall that was seemingly lost only moments ago.

Calista and her men rushed through the gap with Brandinne following reluctantly. Before they could even reach the first landing of the stairs, the crack of another catapult firing drew their attention to the overcast sky. An additional bombardment of balled up spiders flew above them. This time, the Red Dale Riders added a flurry of arrows to the mix of spells thrown by the Sorcerers. Again, they managed to cut down many of the spiders before they could land, but more fires within the city were started in the process.

They finally crested the wall to stand among the embattlements. Her men fanned out easily into the open gaps and made good use of the fire arrows apparently abandoned by the original defenders of the walls. Soon the spiders attempting to cross the field were peppered with burning arrows fired expertly from Ranger longbows, and these arrows did more than wound, apparently serving to cook many of the spiders from within.

Brandinne followed Calista down the wall as she stalked among the chaos, eyes toward the horizon, looking for the catapults. She finally spotted a wooden bulwark or two among the Fir'bolgs which seemed to house the half-dozen catapults. They were well out of range of spells and guarded heavily by the ice giants and fortifications built from felled stone berry trees. Calista also suspected the six she saw were only a fraction of the total. Even if they did manage to destroy one of the catapults, the Fir'bolgs would simply bring up another to take its place. That was their way: wear down the enemy with large quantities of spiders and hurled items before risking their soldiers. They'd probably built fifty catapults they might never use on the off chance one broke or was destroyed. Her original plan remained the best plan, and from the look of the battlefield, she would need to enact it as soon as possible.

"What exactly do you want me to do?" Brandinne asked. "We haven't discussed payment yet, but I can tell you right now, anything you paid me to stand on this wall would be wasted coin. There's precious little I can do up here and you don't have enough money to convince me to go down there."

"You're going to come with me through the mountain and out of the city," Calista explained. She was still looking about the wall for a Sorcerer who might work for her purposes. Wizardly Willard was certainly one of the most powerful spell-flingers left, but he was integral to the wall's defense and Calista wondered how the portly old fellow might fair walking through miles of Dwarven tunnels. Calista needed a Sorcerer who was small enough to travel easily, but powerful enough to destroy upon arrival. Calista abandoned her inspection of the wall's defenders. She already knew the Sorceress she needed, although it was going to require her to do something fairly distasteful even by her own permissive standards.

A familiar battle roar drew Calista's attention from her wonderings. She glanced down the southern edge of the wall. Near the gate, fighting grandly against some of the largest ice spiders Calista had ever seen, were Athol, Sven, and Harper. Killing spiders appeared to be something the trio excelled at. Judging from the ruddy complexion on Sven's face, the spittle dotting Athol's beard, and the slight sway in Harper's posture even when simply standing, Calista had to guess the lot of them were at least half in the bag.

"Oh for the love of long-legged women...they're drunk!" Brandinne exclaimed, giving voice to Calista's concerns.

There was something else to Harper's fighting that seemed off. She was slower, more focused on technique than power, and a good deal more cautious than normal. It took a moment for Calista to piece things together—the drunkenness, the trepidation, the weakness—Harper had lost her divine spark!

Calista rushed down the wall toward Harper. Brandinne followed along with little else to do. A gangly set of spider legs sought to find purchase atop the wall, blocking their progress momentarily. Calista slashed out with her curved dagger, cleaving one of the legs off at the mid joint, spun through the attack, and buried the straight edge blade of her other dagger in one of the large eyes on the spider's head when it crested the wall. The spider had seven more eyes left, although seeing became less of a concern when Calista dragged the blade up, splitting the top of the spider's head in the process. The entire corpse tumbled back off the wall the same way it came, clearing the path once again.

By the time Calista and Brandinne reached Harper, Athol, and Sven, the Dagger Falls Company had mopped up the last of the spiders in their section and were taking a bit of a breather before moving on to another. Calista sheathed her daggers and fell to her knees to embrace the already kneeling Harper. She could empathize, better than anyone else in the city, with what Harper was going through. Calista couldn't imagine the shocking depression and pain that would accompany the removal of her own divine spark, and so she didn't begrudge Harper the desire to drink.

"She took it away," Harper said.

"I know," Calista murmured, kissing Harper's eyelids.

"Everything seems so difficult and cold without her," Harper said.

"I'm sorry." Calista drew Harper's face up in her hands. They rested their foreheads against one another, drawing comfort from the closeness. "I'm going to take a group beyond the wall tonight. There's an exit for a Dwarven tunnel at the Ogre mound. We'll kill the spider queen they brought and destroy her rookery. Then, in the morning, we'll end this."

Harper stood slowly, drawing Calista up with her. Some of the old steel and determination returned to the Sword Maiden in her furrowed brow and the stern set to her jaw. "I'll ready a cavalry charge and lead it myself."

"There will be disorder when the spider queen dies. Look for the fire to rival the rising sun in the east and seize upon the moment."

Harper collected Calista in her arms and kissed her fiercely. The memory of their night together flooded back through Calista, sweeping away any doubt in her course. Escape through the tunnel was possible, and may end the war when the reason for the siege was removed, but she wouldn't leave Harper no matter what. Victory was the only option left to end things, and she would see her Sword Maiden triumphant.

Chapter 35.

Beneath the Crown of the World

Finding Randolph still in the guise of Turbald was an easy matter. Calista backtracked from where she'd left Ulrich's body, which had been removed by his fellow guards at some point, and made her way up, toward the highborn estates around the base of the mountain. When she heard an angry, puffed up guard shouting obscenities in a dockside accent, she knew she was on the right track.

Guard Turbald stood in the middle of a snowy crossroads, shouting feebly at several noble children who had beset him like a pack of well-bundled dogs. They hurled snowballs at him along with insults, bonked at his armor and helmet with sticks, and mocked him viciously. All the while, he sputtered and cursed them, but dared not lay a finger on any of the hell spawn of wealthy nobles as a lowborn guard would know not to.

Calista stood for a time in the shadow of a building watching the ribald scene, made all the coarser by Turbald's colorful use of terms such as "cut-short dilly-whackers" and the like. To look at the man, nobody would ever guess the hapless guard in the ill-fitting armor was the thief king who had united under his control every gang in the largest northern city. To look at the man, most might guess he couldn't visit the chamber pot in the night without it ending up on his foot.

Calista held a certain soft spot for talented practitioners of shadowy arts. There were so many incompetent rogues, thieves, rakes, pick-pockets, burglars, muggers, assassins, and Jacks-of-all-Trades that she never felt comfortable killing one that showed talent. It seemed like it would cheapen the entire scoundrel trade if the best and brightest bumped each other off while leaving the dregs to inherit the craft. Randolph, his current predicament not withstanding, was even more impressive than Brandinne in his own way. No guard would ever suspect him of being the head of the thieves guild and likely no thief within could think of him as anything but Ulrich's lackey. Most thief kings fell to their own hubris and greed, but the display before her told Calista that Randolph didn't put pride before anything and likely preferred sustained profit to rampant avarice.

This thought vexed her as well. He'd told her his grandest secret to avoid torture—a smart tradeoff to be sure—but it left her with the sneaking suspicion he would prefer she died very soon. Obviously he didn't have the muscle at his disposal to kill her anymore. The thieves opted for capture with their best attempt and were thwarted. She doubted they could still muster the numbers to even try again. Regardless, Randolph would have *something* waiting for her within the Dwarven tunnel, of that she had no doubt.

She pulled the cowl from her armor over her face, tightened the cinch around her neck to obscure her voice, and set to the work of rescuing the powerful thief king from the fat little lordlings assaulting him. She kicked the legs out from one as he ran in front of her. The bundled up, sadistic little noble born fell face first onto the ice, slid a few feet, and began bawling in a whiny falsetto. She plucked the snowball out of the next child's hand an instant before he could hurl it and then gave him a swift kick to the rear when his awkward throw resulted in hurling only his empty hand forward. The last noble boy of about twelve years, and likely the ring leader from the way he ordered the others about, was dressed in fur-lined finery with golden buttons and chains holding it around his plump little body. He spotted what she was doing and made to storm over in order to tell her off. When he opened his noble little pie hole, Calista stuffed the snowball into it and shoved him into the nearest snow drift.

They were sadistic children who might never know rough treatment. Judging from their clothes, they were from families that would count on their gold to make up for their lack of honor. Calista was all too happy to teach the little lordlings that there were still people in the world bigger and stronger than them who didn't give a rip what their family name or title was.

The ringleader of the troupe managed to pluck the snowball from his mouth. Calista snatched the boy's own jewel-encrusted dagger from his belt and tapped at his jowls with the finely honed blade.

"Do you know who my father is?" the boy stammered.

"I imagine he'll be a very sad man when his fat son turns up in an alleyway stabbed, robbed, and possibly buggered," Calista growled in the low, hissing voice created by the cinch around her windpipe. "Perhaps to ease his sorrow, I should send him your roly-poly head to bury in the family crypt."

She could see on the young man's face he'd never had his threat fail to impress. His next tactic, which she knew he would attempt before even he did, was to bribe her. "I can give you money."

"You can't give me what I was already planning on taking," Calista replied in her raspy voice.

"Guard, help me!" the boy finally begged of the guard he'd just been tormenting.

"Why should he lift a finger to save you?" Calista stopped the boy's pleas for help by tapping under his chin with the flat of his dagger. "All he needs to do to take revenge on you is simply turn a blind eye."

"I'm sorry," the fat little lordling stammered through tears. "I'm so sorry, guard. Please help me!" The undignified crying reached a proper crescendo of honest wretchedness when he started blowing freezing snot bubbles between gasping cries. The blubbering was genuine as she didn't imagine any highborn would willingly debase themselves in such a way for a ruse.

In truth, it surprised Calista that he reached the desired state of sobbing remorse so quickly. "Get out of here before I slit your throat from ear to ear and pluck your tongue out through your new smile," Calista hissed at the boy. She pulled the knife away from beneath his neck and let him roll to safety.

The boy stumbled a few times in his escape while the other two children who had acted as his minions were already gone from the scene. Calista turned to Randolph and tossed the jeweled dagger to him. He snatched it out of the air and shook his head.

"I wouldn't have fancied you to be the parenting type," Randolph said.

"I wouldn't have fancied that parenting," Calista replied. She loosened the choker on her windpipe to restore her natural voice and pulled back the cowl to release her burnished locks. "After seeing what you're willing to endure to keep your guard persona, I do wonder what manner of trickery you employ to conceal yourself as thief king."

"All manner if you must know." Randolph sat stiffly on the edge of a fountain in front of one of the manors to begin clearing the snow from his helmet. "I have a hollowed throne and fake beard that I use to look like a Dwarven king, I dressed as a mummer's clown for awhile with face paint and stilts, shoulder pads and masks of course, and for a time a few years ago, a fresh crop of ne'er-do-wells only ever saw me while I wore a jack-o-lantern upon my head. If a guard should catch any two of my boys in the course of their duty, they would likely give two entirely conflicting descriptions of me, and neither would approach the truth."

"I am most impressed by your subterfuge, and so I should hate to have to kill you for some nonsense beneath the mountain," Calista said, a little pleased to find the unlikely thief king also had an interesting sense of humor. "Meet me and mine at the statue garden where you nearly lost your life, and we'll get this entire unpleasant business behind us as soon as possible."

"How many do you plan on tromping through my tunnels?" Randolph asked shrewdly.

"A grand army if you must know," Calista said. "I'll have a lich to protect, and before you can ask if I'm being facetious, know that I'm not."

"Then tonight it is." Randolph slipped back into his Turbald persona. "Get on yer way there, trollop! This neighborhood is for better than the likes of you."

Calista raised her hands in deference and backed away. "As you say, guardsman."

Before nightfall, the Valkyries, Randolph, and Brandinne were likely already awaiting the last member and their shady liege. Calista didn't fancy herself a leader of men or women, but she'd managed the position with as much aplomb as she could muster. She rather liked working with mercenaries and blackmail victims.

Grumbling or not, they generally did as they were told. This wouldn't be the case with the final member of their group.

Calista walked into the frigid storage room in the bowels of the Thundering Dawn Inn. Only a few bodies remained of the dead important enough to await spring's thaw for burial. Bjorn's body was burned on a pyre the night before, as was the custom of his people. Beside the massive empty space on the frost encrusted table left by the old bear's removal was a much smaller body wrapped in the burlap sacks and rough cord common to all the corpses in the room. Calista cut away the ropes and sacks around the face to reveal Ezra's blood splattered face. Even gray and frozen solid in the pallor of death, she looked unhappy.

"By the pantheon, spell-flinger, can you not even find peace in death?" Calista whispered.

It was going to take all the power she'd collected to that point, and she would likely still need to kill again soon to collect more to maintain the spell. Even with all that effort, all she had to offer Ezra by way of payment was a few moments longer in the world and an opportunity to go out with a proper bang rather than the whimper she initially exited with.

To restore Ezra to life, even for a few hours, she would have to recall all the energies she'd already spent. The Red Dale Rider's enthrallment would fade, although their usefulness was becoming rather limited at that point anyway. Regardless, they were on the wall fighting and still under contract to continue fighting even if they were no longer mystically compelled to do her bidding. Calista needed the tiny fraction of power she'd spent to maintain their state of compliance, and so she would have to trust them to continue their work for coin alone, or rather the promise of coin since she'd stopped paying them once they were enthralled.

Calista gathered all her strength, felt the power of life she'd stolen flow through her divine spark, and poured the entire content into Ezra's deceased form. The act of revival was nearly immediate. Color returned to Ezra's flesh and her eyes shot open. She began shivering straight away. Calista hurled the heavy bear cloak she'd brought with her over the resurrected Sorceress.

"I died!" Ezra exclaimed. Her eyes weren't focusing on anything in particular yet, but her hands seemed to recognize the comfort and warmth of the cloak draped over her and clung to it fiercely.

"You did," Calista said softly, "but I brought you back."

"How?" Ezra asked.

"Divine magic, although I'm sure you know it is not permanent," Calista said. "We don't really have time for a lengthy explanation. What I have done is akin to a mystical hourglass already set to pour and there is work to be done before the proverbial sand runs out."

Ezra sat up, further wrapping herself in the bearskin cloak. "What do you want?"

"I have an expedition force and a path outside the walls. I need a Sorceress to join us in destroying the brood mother providing the Fir'bolg spider army. I bet a lot on your willingness to be that Sorceress."

"I'm a lich…" Ezra said vacantly.

"An undead practitioner of magical arts, yes, in a sense, you are, but you are not cursed to an eternity as one," Calista explained. "As I said, you will return to death when the divine energy I've imbued your corpse with is spent. I don't know how long that will be, so we must hurry. In truth, I've never been to war and thus never held so much life energy taken by slaying, nor have I used so much life force to resurrect someone. Typically, I would use just what was needed to awaken a corpse long enough to answer a question or two: where is the gold, who hired you, or whatever. You may have hours or a day—I cannot say, but I do know we would do well not to waste time talking in a makeshift crypt."

"Then we should go." Ezra hopped from the table with a spryness Calista didn't expect the old, and still mostly dead, Sorceress to possess.

There was something fairly liberating about death, Calista supposed. Ezra came with her willingly, collected a staff from beside the door, as hers was likely left on the ice within the abandoned bear fort, and they were off. It made a morbid sort of sense to Calista only after the fact. Whatever dislike Ezra held for her mattered very little in the grander scheme of things; dead once with an imminent return to the afterlife likely put minor grudges into a certain diminutive perspective. They were well outside the

Thundering Dawn and on their way up the hill before Ezra spoke again.

"Do you want to know what lies beyond?" Ezra asked.

Calista noted that the Sorceress's breath no longer steamed in the cold air when she spoke, which reminded Calista of how little she knew of her own powers. "If you would like to tell me," Calista replied.

"Nothing," Ezra said flatly. "Blackness and nothing. I was gone, not as though I slept, but truly gone into nothingness, and then I awoke when you brought me back." They walked on for a time. Only the sounds of their shoes crunching dry snow followed them before Ezra spoke again. "I had thought there would be something there."

The words sent a chill through Calista. She had thought and hoped there would be more as well. She'd never bothered to ask the metaphysical questions surrounding death in the handful of prior instances of bringing a corpse back to life, and now she wished Ezra hadn't told her. Life seemed a good deal more precious knowing nothing existed beyond.

"It might be different for divine touched like you and Harper," Ezra said, "but for me, there is only the abyss."

These words replaced the chill with a stabbing pain. Harper wasn't divine touched anymore. Perhaps the Sorceress was right about divine touched receiving special treatment of a sort in death, but that wouldn't apply to Harper regardless. "Perhaps," Calista said quietly.

As Calista hoped, the Valkyries, Randolph, and even tiny Brandinne were waiting outside the garden statue in the gloom of the fading day when Calista and Ezra arrived. The Valkyries, being from the northlands, didn't bat an eyelash at the undead spell-flinger joining their company. Above the Crown of the World Mountains, a lich was as common as a Sorcerer. Randolph appeared to be resigned to whatever, and so Calista showing up with a Sorceress who had clearly been stabbed to death in the very robes she was still wearing, only carried a momentary wondering.

"Abomination!" Brandinne shouted, showing she was not nearly as comfortable with the idea of an undead Ezra. "Oh, sorry, I sometimes forget there are people in the world who can do stuff like bring bodies back to life. Was this a plan or...never mind. It doesn't matter. I'm probably going to be spider food anyway, so you'll forgive me if I don't feel like discussing how other people are cheating death since it's not like it's going to help me."

"A good deal more pragmatic than I've come to expect from you, Brandinne," Ezra said.

"I'm an ever-evolving enigma," Brandinne replied.

"Evolve quietly, if you can manage it, little sneak-thief," Randolph said to Brandinne. He turned his attention to Calista next. "Best that we set off sooner rather than later if we want to reach the surface on the other side by daybreak—the tunnel meanders and we might get lost once or twice."

Calista couldn't agree more. They filed into the statue garden behind Randolph with no further discussion of Ezra's undead condition or Brandinne's concerns. As Calista suspected, the entrance to the passage used by the thieves guild was of Dwarven make. Randolph produced an iron key from a chain squirreled away in his heavy coat. He inserted it into the left nostril of a statue of a Dwarf man holding a hammer in one hand and a loaf of bread in the other. The key turned and suddenly the statue was sinking into the ground as smooth as an old man settling into a hot bath. Randolph stepped through first and held his palm on a metal pressure plate within the tunnel to keep the entrance open. Ingrid and the Valkyries entered next, followed by Brandinne, Ezra, and finally Calista.

Torches burned in sconces along the wall, illuminating the subterranean tunnel in flickering lights. It took a moment for everyone's eyes to adjust to the gloom even with the way lit. Randolph strolled down the narrow corridor, which initially allowed only two people to walk side by side. He plucked a torch from the wall and a handful of the Valkyries did so as well until the light was following them into the interior of the mountain.

"I inherited this under-mountain stronghold from a Dwarven thieves guild a decade ago," Randolph explained as they walked. His voice echoed front and back, covering the distant sounds of dripping water and the soft scuffling of their feet as they walked. "It's difficult to say exactly how deep the original Dwarven builders burrowed into the mountain. The dragons that slew the Dwarves of Griffon's Rock burned most of the tunnels they couldn't fit into."

"I've read that dragon fire can melt stone," Brandinne explained to no one in particular.

"So we've discovered," Randolph said. "There are large portions of the old city below that are closed to us. Being thieves and not miners or stonemasons, we've left those passages as we found them: melted and impassable."

Despite Randolph's claim they might get lost once or twice, he didn't actually seem to struggle to find his way. Tunnels branched and turned, but he always walked directly to the one he wanted without hesitation. Calista initially tried to remain focused on following the path so she might find her way back if needs be, but she soon had to abandon any hopes of directing herself out after an hour or so of walking. The stonework was nondescript, the tunnel uniform, and the path winding—if one hadn't spent a decade learning the trail, one couldn't hope to do anything but get lost. In some places the ceiling was low enough to force many of the taller Valkyries to duck and in other places so high the darkness consumed the torch light before the ceiling could be illuminated. The whole thing made Calista drastically uncomfortable. She glanced to Ezra, who didn't appear to want to be more than a few feet from her at any time, and found the Sorceress as placid and calm as if she were strolling a sunny lane to afternoon tea.

"I don't suppose you've been keeping track of the way," Calista whispered to her.

"I don't suppose I'll live long enough for it to matter," Ezra replied placidly.

She had Calista there.

Just when Calista was planning on marking the wall to ensure they weren't simply walking in circles, the passage suddenly emptied into a massive hall. The room was so vast that Calista suspected the entire sprawling floor plan of the Thundering Dawn Inn could fit comfortably within. The relative warmth of the tunnels gave way to a deep and likely permanent cold within the cavernous hall. Remarkably, no pillars stood within to buttress the ceiling. They all wandered a bit out into the grand hall to marvel at the craftsmanship required to construct such an enormous subterranean hall.

"Douse your torches," Randolph instructed, pointing to a handful of buckets along the wall beside the tunnel entrance.

The Valkyries looked to Ingrid first, who in turn looked to Calista. "Do as he says," Calista said, although she wasn't entirely certain of the course.

The Valkyries dunked their torches into the water. For a moment, utter blackness surrounded them. Then, slowly, as their eyes adjusted, a faint blue light began illuminating the hall. Threads of something glowed with a strange, blue light, like rivers on a map through a fertile land, laced along the walls, growing brighter at the apex of the dome and trickling down the walls all around them.

"Frost fire," Ezra said.

"Is that what it's called?" Randolph asked.

"Tiny bioluminescent, aquatic insects that turn minerals in stone and cold water into light," Ezra explained.

"If you say so," Randolph replied. "All I know is we haven't been able to move them to other tunnels from here."

"The stonework probably isn't right or they might not have the water they need." Ezra pointed to the top of the dome hundreds of feet above them. "That's likely where the thawed ice comes in that gives them the water and minerals they need."

Indeed, the longer they spent in the strange blue glow of the frost fire the better they all saw. Little shiny, impurities in the stones around them reflected the light, giving outlines to the stone benches and pathways within the great hall. They followed Randolph through the open floor toward the center and a glowing gateway on the other side of the room, which appeared to be several hundred yards away.

The vastness of the room, which swallowed the sound of their footsteps to that point, suddenly filled with a strange, scraping noise, barely on the edge of hearing. Ingrid held up her hand and the Valkyries all came to a stop, drew their swords, axes, and shields, and set themselves in a defensive ring.

"Above us!" Brandinne shrieked.

Somehow the little Havvish woman had snuck up right beside her. Calista looked up in time to spot the black, vague outlines of massive descending spiders, blotting out the blue glow of the ceiling.

"This is where I take my leave," Randolph said. "I wish you the best of luck in whatever spider belly you find yourself..." The rest of his words, even as he faded into the darkness between two statues and likely a hidden pathway, came to an abrupt stop when a crossbow bolt sprouted from his left eye.

"Double-crossed!" Brandinne said from behind her crossbow. "Damn it, I should have said that before I shot him. Could whoever brought Ezra back to life resurrect Randolph a moment so he knows I double-crossed him?"

"Explain it later," Ingrid shouted. "Fight now!"

"Run for the portal over there," Brandinne said, nodding in the direction of the glowing gateway while she reloaded her crossbow. "Randolph's blood should briefly distract the spiders."

The Valkyries didn't need any more encouragement than that. The warrior women set off into a synchronized run, securing Calista, Ezra, and Brandinne in the protective shell of their formation. Calista could only focus on the act of running to keep up. They were moving so swiftly and the terrain was so surprisingly complex that it was all she could do to keep her feet and keep Ezra upright at her side. She resolved to get the whole story out of Brandinne later if they managed to survive.

The sound of hissing spiders came outside the formation from time to time, always followed by thudding against wooden shields and occasionally an axe or sword hacking at a chitin limb. Part of Calista wished she was on the exterior of the moving mass of northland women and part of her was glad she was firmly encased within a wall of running mercenaries.

The glowing portal before them, which appeared to be an archway designed to pool a considerable amount of the frost fire above its cornerstone, finally opened before them. The formation of Valkyries broke and for a moment they were running even faster than the breakneck speed they'd formerly held.

"Sofea, rearguard!" Ingrid bellowed as they crossed the threshold of the portal.

Several women at the back of the formation broke ranks, stopped, and turned to block the passage with their swords, axes, and shields. A tall, slender Valkyrie girl, who couldn't have been more than seventeen seasons old, leapt forward to command the rearguard.

"Whatever tries to cross my line will meet a quick but gruesome end," the girl shouted in response to Ingrid's command.

Calista turned to join the half dozen women stopping up the passage, but Ingrid ushered her forward. "Sofea has this well in hand, mistress," Ingrid explained. "We've other matters to attend to on the surface."

Calista chanced one final glance over her shoulder to the outlines of the women of the rearguard as they hacked at the fearful bodies of giant spiders hurling themselves against the Valkyries' wooden shields and steel weapons. They turned a corner, and then another, and finally the passage opened onto a colossal staircase. The Valkyries pushed the flagging Calista, Ezra, and Brandinne up the stairs even as the steps began to narrow. Soon Calista found herself running alongside Ingrid at the front of the strung out formation. Calista's legs burned from the exertion of climbing so many stairs until her feet felt like they were made of lead. Her lungs ached from breathing so heavily of cold air until she puffed in a huge waft of Ogre stench. She about retched from the massive influx of the odor, but in the next instant it was gone.

She glanced back over her shoulder to find the end of Ezra's staff glowing with a faint red light. "Harper wasn't the only one capable of creating a zone free of Ogre stench," Ezra explained.

Calista smiled to her, although the gesture was tainted with concern. Already the Sorceress was beginning to fade and Calista hadn't slain a single spider along the way to replenish her supply of life force. Her thoughts were interrupted by her footing going out from under her. Were it not for the quick intervention of Ingrid's stabilizing hand, Calista knew she would have fallen face first onto the stone steps.

Mud, which had long since frozen, began coating the stairs into an icy ramp. Even the sure-footed Valkyries were having trouble trudging up the mess. All of them sheathed their weapons and slung their shields on their backs to free their hands for the climb. At the top of the tunnel the sky opened up in a tiny portal, black, clear, and dotted with familiar stars. For a moment, a dark figure blocked out the top of the hole. A massive hand reached in, and plucked Calista from the slippery shaft before Ingrid could respond.

Calista found herself deposited gently on open and recognizable ground. She was in the middle of the field behind the Ogre mound, although the last time she'd seen it there wasn't such a thick covering of snow. The massive divine touched Ogre who had told her fortune in stew smiled down at her as he plucked Ingrid from the hole next.

"Move the boulder, so says the stew, visitors coming," the Ogre said. "And so did I find visitors of two known to me."

Calista fell to her knees in the trampled snow to catch her breath. A moment later, a wary Ingrid and a relieved Ezra were placed beside her by the steady-handed Ogre. After the last of the Valkyries was plucked from the tunnel and set gently on the snowy field, the Ogre remained hunched over the hole for a time, waiting for more.

"Six remain within the hole," Ingrid informed the Ogre.

"One more, the stew said," the Ogre replied.

After nearly a half hour, the Ogre reached down into the depths and plucked one last Valkyrie from the Dwarven tunnel. He deposited a wounded and bedraggled Sofea in the midst of her sister Valkyries. Her winged helmet was missing, one of her braids was pulled free, hanging hair in red cascades on her left side, and her shield was gone. She dropped the broadsword in her right hand and the double-bladed axe in her left before pitching forward onto the snow field to retch.

Ingrid immediately flipped the slender girl over and pushed a strange leaf-wrapped poultice into Sofea's mouth. The redheaded Valkyrie struggled to swallow it, but eventually managed to tamp it down. Her violent shuddering subsided a few moments after.

"Spider bitten," Ingrid explained. "The northern ice widows are well known to us and so is the remedy to their poison."

The Ogre rolled the boulder back into place over the tunnel's entrance with his massive, gangly arms, putting to rest any further notion of the remaining five Valkyries rejoining them.

"There was no end to them," Sofea murmured weakly.

"There will be soon," Ezra said as she walked past Calista toward the frozen river.

Calista let Ezra go and left the Valkyries to tend to their wounded. She sought out Brandinne who had faded to the edge of the formation and looked to be considering running or hiding as her next option.

"What did you mean: double-crossed?" Calista asked, although she already suspected the answer.

"Randolph hired me to help him get rid of you and your mercenaries. I think he thought you were going to bring the Rangers that gave him such fits, but instead you brought a bunch of crazy women in winged helmets. He spent all day unblocking the passages that fed into the main hall until he was sure it would fill with spiders. Then I was supposed to hamstring you, and we were both going to sneak away in a passage he opened up," Brandinne explained.

"And why didn't you carry out the plan?" Calista asked.

"A couple reasons, actually. For one, you paid me more, so the Jack code required me to side with the better deal. For two, I'd kind of like this stupid siege to end and Randolph made it clear he wanted it to continue so long as it continued without you. He was desperate and banking heavily on my dislike of you to see his plan through to success," Brandinne said. "Except, I don't really dislike you. Plus, you had Ezra with you, and I couldn't let spiders eat her, even though she's an abomination now. So, I think you owe me one."

"You can't have Harper."

"Fine, you can owe me a different one."

Chapter 36:

The War Beyond the Wall—Fire in a Field of Webs

The Ogre accepted their thanks and sent the party on its way. He directed them to where he saw the spider queen last. She was big, he'd said, bigger than most houses. He'd seen her coming in the stew, but even that didn't prepare him for the size of the beast when she arrived. Before they could leave, he imparted one final piece of wisdom to Calista, whispering it to her almost as an afterthought. It was actually a repeated piece of wisdom he'd given her on their first meeting.

"When she see the you that is real, burn the world around you," the Ogre told her again.

The dire warning in the disordered Ogre speech didn't mean anything new to Calista. She'd told Harper a good deal more truth since and a good deal more truth than she'd told anyone in a long time. Of course, hearing truth wasn't seeing the real her, but she didn't even know what that meant. It also wasn't clear from what the Ogre said who was to do the burning of the world around her. If it was a true prophecy and not just the ramblings of a stew brewing Ogre, Calista assumed she would know what it meant when it happened, and so let the matter drop from her mind.

They walked along the frozen river as it was easier and less obvious than trudging their full force through the virgin snow that was over two feet deep. The Valkyries were a somber lot, having lost nearly all six from their rearguard. Ezra was quiet as well, contemplating no doubt her imminent return to the abyss. Brandinne, however, was in fine spirits and chose Calista as her walking partner.

"It occurs to me that we have an opportunity here," Brandinne said.

"I doubt it *just* occurred to you," Calista replied.

"As if I'm the only one here with plots and schemes," Brandinne said dismissively. "Regardless of your judgmental attitude, I'll tell you about the opportunity. You and I are the only two people in all of Griffon's Rock, perhaps even the world, who are in possession of a certain pieces of valuable information."

The realization dawned on Calista before Brandinne could even give voice to the words. "You intend to take Randolph's place," Calista said. "You probably always did!"

"In short, yes," Brandinne said. "We're the only ones who know he is dead, we're the only ones who know what he looked like, and the spiders will almost certainly dispose of his body for us. The thief king crown in the city is open, but we're the only ones who know it is available."

"That's the real reason you killed him," Calista said.

"One of them, and the real reason he trusted me, disgusting as it is, was that he seemed to think we might one day be lovers," Brandinne said. "Can you even imagine me getting bug-squashed beneath that scruffy oaf?"

"And you no doubt let him believe that." Calista didn't always prefer to use her feminine charms to accomplish her ends, excepting when it came to Harper, but she didn't begrudge Brandinne the use of her own. The Havvish woman likely ran into precious few situations in which she could utilize her womanly graces. "Never mind that," Calista said. "The crown is yours and you're welcome to it."

"I didn't think you would mind since you appear to have your own agenda in the world with the zenith of your plans being in the distant south," Brandinne said. "Still, I wished to tell you of my intentions so you wouldn't believe Randolph somehow survived to resume his work and come looking for your revenge on him."

"He met a strange end for a thief king," Calista said. "It wouldn't have been strange to think it a ruse."

"Not so strange an end if you think about it," Brandinne replied. "He fell to betrayal by a woman he believed he loved, or at least lusted after, died quietly in a dark place, and had his mantel usurped by his murderer. As far as I know, those are the leading causes of death among thief kings."

"A fair point—see that you don't fall to the same."

"There's always danger of the first as I am a hopeless romantic. It comes with the Havvish blood," Brandinne replied.

They walked on in relative silence for some time before reaching a log bridge, as the Ogre said they would. This was their signal to turn west to come upon the Fir'bolg encampment from the rear. The sun was beginning to pink the sky in the east with the coming dawn when they scrambled up the banks of the river to either side of the bridge and set out through the snow, following the path of the cleared road into the stone berry orchards.

Soon the trail eased and their tracks vanished among the trampled snow of Fir'bolg patrols along the road. The company took the trodden path as a sign to heighten their guard. The Valkyries removed shields from their backs and placed weapons in their hands. Brandinne loaded her crossbow.

They saw the brood mother long before they could find a way to reach her. The great spider sat atop a wooden palisade in the midst of a cleared portion of the orchards. The rising sun struck the ice crystals clinging to the great widow's body, causing the colossal spider to glisten in the morning light. Calista directed her group to take cover in a tiny finger of trees the Fir'bolgs hadn't cleared yet. They'd snuck up on the unsuspecting army with such ease that she wondered if they weren't walking into a trap.

"How exactly do we plan to kill a spider the size of most sailing galleons?" Brandinne whispered to her.

"We have a Sorceress and the Fir'bolgs blessedly chained their grand spider queen to the top of a wooden structure," Calista explained. "Dare I say fire will be the best way?"

"And how do we get close enough to accomplish such an obvious task?" Brandinne asked.

This question held more weight and demanded a longer consideration than the first. It wasn't difficult to see the field before them contained countless spider nests, webs galore, and no doubt hundreds of spiders of various sizes hidden within. Then, once they crossed the field, it appeared a dozen or so of the ice giants were standing guard beneath the large, wooden structure the spider sat upon.

"I'm open to suggestions." Calista didn't fancy herself a tactician beyond her own activities. As silly as it would sound to say aloud, she'd rather thought the spider's nest would be in such a place that Ezra could easily rain fire upon it from above without any real risk.

"Take the Havvish woman and Sofea to sneak across the spider field with your Sorceress," Ingrid suggested. "I will lead the rest of my force around the other side, there, near that rocky outcropping where no spiders reside; we will draw the giants to us and slay them." She pointed out the locations she meant and then to the redheaded girl from the rearguard who had been spider bitten yet survived.

Calista normally would have objected to taking such a young woman into such a dangerous mission, but she'd watched the girl since her miraculous emerging from the tunnel. She moved as silently as Calista or Brandinne and was apparently favored by the Valkyries as a potential replacement for Ingrid in time. Calista happily accepted the extra blade in protecting Ezra despite Sofea's extreme youth.

"That plan will suffice," Calista said.

The Valkyries, save Sofea, retreated around the edge of the trees and vanished into the groves quietly to loop around to the opposite side. Calista turned to the remaining three women with her. Sofea's face alit with a proud smile as did Brandinne's, but Ezra looked bored.

"Killing giant spiders doesn't excite you, spell-flinger?" Calista asked of Ezra.

"Our company specializes in killing giant arachnids," Ezra replied. "We've cleared out large nests of spiders and scorpions countless times before. This is simply a larger example of what the Dagger Falls Company does best."

Calista wondered after why Harper, Athol, and Sven seemed so adept at slaying spiders and that was her answer. Still, she'd hoped the sheer size of the brood mother would elicit some sort of excitement from the increasingly weary Sorceress.

"Very well, let us set to the boring task then so we might have time later to do more exciting chores like copying ledgers," Calista said.

They snuck out low into the webs and nests of the spider field, careful to keep to the great widow's bulbous hind side. The tiny spiders crawling through the haystack sized web nests around them were easily the size of Calista's hand. The skittering little creatures crawled back into the web alcoves upon the quartet's approach. Calista hoped that was as large as the rookery spiders came, although she couldn't imagine she would be so lucky.

"Tell us when we are in range of your most devastating fire spells," Calista whispered to Ezra at her side to which the Sorceress simply nodded. The new, sullen Ezra was somehow even more irritating than the old, insulting Ezra.

The ground became increasingly sticky and fraught with web traps as they crept closer and closer to the grand palisade topped with the gargantuan spider queen. Calista well knew her blades would do no good in cutting away the trip lines set out among the growing mounds of spider nests surrounding them. Spider silk was stronger than steel and the trip webs were the thickest of the bunch. If any of them happened to fall into one of the chaotic webs, only fire would free them and would alert the entire spider field via the vibrations along the trap lines.

To Calista's dismay, three things continued past her comfort level. The nests were getting larger, growing to the size of houses as they neared the wooden palisade. The spiders within them were getting larger as well, some of them more than two feet in diameter. And Ezra still hadn't said a word about their range being close enough. A quick glance to Sofea and Brandinne told her she wasn't the only one concerned with the mounting peril of their situation.

They weaved around the massive columns of webs and eggs finding more and more of the pathways blocked with the strange, haphazard webs spun by the ice widows. Finally, at long last, Ezra tapped Calista on the back of her shoulder with her staff.

"This is close enough," Ezra whispered.

Only after the fact, when they were far too drawn into the plan, did Calista see a major flaw. Sneaking into the nests with a distraction of the Fir'bolg guards would keep the giants from pelting Ezra with boulders when she began casting, but it also left them with few options of flight once the fires began. Calista glanced around furtively for an escape route only to realize they were ages away from the edges of the spider field and none of the paths to freedom were direct. This wasn't a concern for Ezra as she was dead already, but Calista didn't plan on dying there.

Calista turned to voice her objections, but the entire field exploded in chaos before she could utter a single word. The willowy ice giants spotted the Valkyries at the edge of the orchards before they could even reach the rock outcropping. They shouted warnings in their hacking and spitting language, blew baleful alarm horns, and began hurling rocks at the trees. The brood mother atop the great palisade let loose a knee-weakening shriek and the spiders within the field heeded her cry.

It was all Calista, Brandinne, and Sofea could do to get their weapons into their hands to defend against the sudden rush of juvenile spiders with bulbous bodies as large as over-ripe pumpkins. Calista slashed out at the first spider to emerge from the nest nearest them. Her dagger cut through the hideous eight-eyed head, sending it back down the hole it emerged from.

"They don't see well despite all the eyes," Sofea shouted. Her broadsword and axe were in her hands. "Turn the morning light off your blades to trick them." She reflected a shaft of sunlight creeping between the nesting towers to create a glow on the ground that a swarm of spiders suddenly leapt upon. Before they could realize the spot of light was little more than a reflection, Sofea pounced, stomping with her heavy boots and hacking away with axe and sword.

Ezra plucked the spell component chain up from her belt, searched through it for an item, and began chanting. Calista stepped in close to her side, warily watching the field of webs around them for the glistening bodies of the spiders that might leap out at any moment.

Brandinne was far more proactive in her defense of the tiny patch of ground they'd been forced to make their stand on. She walked close in behind Sofea's back, letting the Valkyrie girl keep the immediate area clear of spiders, while she fired exceptionally accurate bolts from her crossbow. The heavy, metal-tipped projectiles struck targets near and far. The spiders Brandinne's shots didn't outright kill retreated, apparently wanting nothing more to do with the fight after taking a crossbow bolt to the thorax.

A spider leapt from the webbing, aimed directly at the back of Ezra's head. Calista spotted the shadow just in time to leap between the Sorceress and the airborne arachnid. The spider landed on her shoulder and grasped at her armor. An instant before the spider could sink its fangs into Calista's neck, a crossbow bolt pierced the spider's bulbous abdomen. The spider shrieked in pain rather than complete its attack, giving Calista enough of an opening to stab her straight-blade dagger into the spider's mouth.

The flood of energy flowing into Calista from the slaying of spiders she poured directly across the divine connection she'd created to keep Ezra alive. The increasingly vacant vessel of the undead Sorceress trickled to fill a tiny iota with every spider she killed. It was a little like trying to refill a barrel one spoonful at a time though and Calista began to wonder if Ezra would survive long enough to do the damage that needed to be done.

Her question was quickly answered when Ezra completed her spell. A dragon, whose body appeared to be constructed entirely of black smoke, billowed forth from Ezra's hands. The dragon apparition soared above the brood mother, drawing the attention of the Fir'bolg guards, many of which broke off their pursuit of the Valkyries to begin hurling rocks at the smoke dragon. Their projectiles passed harmlessly through the dragon's ethereal black body. Ezra opened her hands and the dragon's jaws stretched wide in mimic of her gesture. She spoke the old Sylvan word for fire and the smoke dragon spewed forth a stream of flame along the front of the palisade, blinding the great widow queen and setting to blaze the structure meant to protect her.

The chained brood mother screamed a response and attempted to flee, but the frost steel mounted chains upon the palisade held her in place. A second pass of the smoke dragon cut another fiery swath across the wooden structure, hemming the ice queen in on two sides. Calista spotted Ezra's intention a moment before the calamity of it all struck. The huge spider fled the flames at her front and to her right, stumbling backward off the wooden fortress. The chains caught on the far side, but broke free with great burning chunks of wood still attached. The spider pitched over the edge backward with its front legs flying free as the chains gave way. The rear chains, still mounted to unburned wood, held firm, anchoring the spider's rear limbs to the palisade. The brood mother fell partway down the side, snapping several of her hind legs with resounding cracks of the ancient chitin shells on her limbs. The Fir'bolgs coming to her aid were surprised to find most of the burning spider queen falling upon them. The massive spider body striking the ground set the earth to tremble. The smoke dragon took another pass, this time aimed at the field of webs the brood mother had fallen into, and lit a fiery swath through the highly flammable webbing.

Calista looked to Ezra. The Sorceress was no longer concerned with the dying brood mother, yet her casting continued. The smoke dragon soared over them and began pouring fire into the field of webs they'd crossed. The army of Fir'bolgs, clearly rushing in to defend the rear of their formation, leapt back from the burning rookery field as the mystical dragon set it to blaze. Calista felt a tightening in her chest as she realized Ezra had tapped into the direct connection between them, drawing more magic from the divine spark within Calista to fuel the spell in ways that might not otherwise be possible.

"She means to kill us all!" Sofea shouted above the inferno encroaching upon them.

One look in the undead Sorceress's eyes told Calista the Valkyrie girl was right. Ezra had nothing left to lose and apparently was finding great joy in raining fiery destruction upon the world with her dying moments. The power held within Calista's divine spark was a source of magic she could never have fathomed and the rush of such great power carried with it a sense of euphoria as Calista well knew. The answer of what to do about it came quickly and in an increasingly familiar manner. A crossbow bolt impaled Ezra's head, striking her directly in the eye as it had with Randolph.

"I liked Ezra well enough, but I like myself more," Brandinne explained.

The soaring smoke dragon above them dissipated into nothingness before Ezra's body could even strike the ground. The fires the dragon set though were not so tied to the continued existence of the Sorceress. The flames burning across the open field of nests shifted with the winds, cutting to the south and west. The dead brood mother lay to the north, leaving only the east for their escape. Calista hadn't thought shooting Ezra was strictly necessary until she saw the direness of their situation. If the dragon had finished its final pass on the east, escape wouldn't have been possible.

Calista shouted her intent and began running with Brandinne and Sofea quick at her heels. Thankfully, the spiders within the fields were long past their concern for the three women in their midst. Most of the juvenile spiders fled into their web nests to be burned, but a few tried their best to run.

Calista scanned the field ahead of her, spotted trip lines as they arose, and leapt over them to set the example for the two women following her. The size of the nests they fled through slowly diminished as they neared the edge of the field until they were able to run hard with little concern for falling into a web trap.

Ahead, to the northeast, the remaining Valkyries were fighting ice giants amid the stone berry trees. Their numbers were culled again with less than half a dozen of the warrior women remaining. The four Fir'bolgs pursuing them limped and favored limbs, but appeared to be on the winning side of the engagement.

As Calista, Sofea, and Brandinne emerged from the spider field, they veered north to render aid to the other half of their company. Brandinne stopped to fire her crossbow to little effect against the towering giants in their petrified wooden armor. Sofea charged along the ground to join her sisters in their proven tactics of turning the giants in circles to get at the tendons along the backs of their legs. While Calista leapt to the trees to gain some altitude on the vertically advantaged giants.

Calista jumped from limb to limb as best she could. The ice and snow clinging to the branches slowed her acrobatic attempts a great deal. In a stroke of luck though, the Valkyries drew the Fir'bolgs close enough for her to strike. One of the ice giants swung a tree-sized club down at a group of the warrior women, who scattered before the blow could land. Calista seized upon the opportunity to dive from her tree onto the ice giant's exposed back. She used her drawn daggers as climbing picks to hold onto the giant. The Fir'bolg reared and bucked beneath her, trying to shake the tiny attacker. When this failed, he reached a hand over his shoulder to pluck Calista from his spine, but one of Brandinne's crossbow bolts halted the grab by striking deep in the giant's wrist.

Climbing up would leave a longer fall when the giant was slain, and so Calista slid down the Fir'bolg's back, leaving two long, bloody trails in her wake. She lashed out with her mystically poisoned blades, sinking one in the Fir'bolgs' kidney and the other as close to his spine as she could manage. The sapping power of the poison was taking its toll on the giant by that point and it staggered out beneath her, jolting violently in a painful death seizure. Calista pushed her feet off the giant's leg as best she could and tucked to roll when she struck the snowy ground. Instead, her shoulder hit a stone berry tree branch, and she tumbled awkwardly down for a soft, if ungainly landing in the snow.

Calista popped out of the snow, knowing full well she'd done serious damage to her shoulder in the fall. It burned and ached in a way that told her she'd broken something she needed for it to function correctly. The pain shooting through her left arm whenever she tried to move it confirmed what she feared. Worse still, she'd dropped both of her daggers. Even if she'd wanted to search for them, and she didn't think she had time to, the enchantment on them would likely prevent them from being found.

She limped through the deep snow away from the fight and the dying giant beside her. Apparently she'd turned her ankle on her landing as well, although that injury paled in comparison to her wounded shoulder. The Valkyries, bolstered by Sofea and supported by Brandinne, were finishing off another one of the giants. Of the remaining two, the more wounded of the Fir'bolgs broke away from the attack on the north women to pursue Calista. The giant limped along behind her while Calista attempted to hobble away.

She gritted her teeth through the pain shooting through her shoulder and ankle brought about by every step through deep snow. She was unarmed, egregiously wounded, and fleeing far too slowly to ever hope to escape her Fir'bolg pursuer. The sound of the wounded giant crashing through the orchard limbs behind her told her it was only a matter of a few more steps before he would have her. In the north, she'd seen what giants did to people when they caught them. Their favored form of executing humans they managed to lay their hands on was to rip them in half. Since the giant had a wounded arm of his own, Calista guessed he would simply squeeze her in his good hand until she popped.

The giant's hand descended for her and she lunged to her right, offering only a momentary reprieve from the grasping fingers. Before the Fir'bolg could sweep his hand to her new position, the largest, crudest meat cleaver Calista had ever seen hacked down out of the trees, nearly severing the Fir'bolgs hand at the wrist. The stew seer Ogre stepped from between the trees, followed closely by his overwhelming stench. He pressed his awkward attack on the now helpless Fir'bolg.

The Ogre was about a third of the size of the giant, but from the look on the Fir'bolgs' face, Calista could tell the ice giant had no desire to tangle with the oily-hide Ogre armed with an iron frying pan in one hand and the meat cleaver in the other. Calista's eyes were watering from the Ogre stench and her stomach churned, but she forced herself to watch her unlikely savior's gallant defense of her.

The Ogre attacked with all the style and methodical nature of butchering meat. The lack of battle prowess wasn't a problem though as apparently she wasn't the only one struggling to see and breathe through the Ogre's scent; the ice giant focused more on coughing and gagging than seeing to his own defense, and thus left himself open to any manner of attack the Ogre felt like hurling at him. The Ogre went for the giant's knees. Then his bowels when the giant attempted to flee on cut legs. A stunning blow from the massive frying pan in the Ogre's left hand staggered the giant long enough for the cleaver to find its way beneath the Fir'bolgs' chin to open his throat.

The Ogre, satisfied with his limited participation in the conflict, hacked free one of the Fir'bolgs' arms, slung it over his shoulder, and marched back toward Calista with his cleaver in one hand and the frying pan tucked into the chain belt around his waist. Calista tried her best to smile to him through the overpowering stench.

"Words of mine you will remember," the Ogre said as he walked past. "Too important you are to fall so soon. Arm of ice giant feed will my stew now."

Calista fell back into the snow and awaited rescue by the victorious Valkyries who were already shouting and clapping their weapons against their wooden shields after their triumph over the last of the Fir'bolg pursuers. The air around her finally cleared enough to breathe easily. Staring up at the pale blue of the early morning sky, Calista inhaled deeply, which sent a shock of pain through her shoulder. She whispered a prayer of thanks to her Goddess. She felt Solancacae the Mistress of Secrets smile down upon her and knew the Ogre's intervention was not happenstance.

Chapter 37:

The War Beyond the Wall—A Charge of Heavy Horse

Building a cavalry charge in a city full of mercenaries was akin to being awash in an ocean, dying of thirst. Horses within the city were plentiful, but only a handful were trained as heavy warhorses. Volunteers to ride also numbered in the hundreds, but only a fraction had ever even held a lance. She could easily field a massive cavalry charge that failed to land even a handful of its lances or worse still, fell from their horses before arriving at the target. Training a horse to charge at full speed into a stationary enemy took years; teaching a rider to remain on such a horse while accurately delivering a lance two or three times as long as themselves could take even longer.

By the time the sun set, the war upon the wall petered out. The giants could no longer accurately strike the city with their catapults in the dark, but this didn't mean the fighting was over for the defenders within the walls. Many spiders remained inside the city, requiring hunting parties to brave the darkened lanes to look for the vicious, hiding widows. Additionally, the fires set by the spiders struck by magic still burned in many places. Both problems exacerbated each other as spiders harassed groups sent to extinguish the fires while burning buildings slowed the progress of the hunter groups charged with exterminating the spiders. Harper would have traded places with any member of either group.

She sat at a massive table in the main hall of the Thundering Dawn Inn, speaking with a long line of volunteers who wished to join in the cavalry charge. She could have used Ezra to help her keep better books, but, by her own rough estimates, only one in a dozen requesting a spot knew the first thing about riding with a lance. Mounted knights and heavy horsemen were commonplace in the south where open fields and tournaments reigned, but in the north among rocky hills and thick forests, the mounted charge was relegated to the Cyclops on their bear mounts. With the orchards cleared by giants, the fields to charge upon were finally available within arms reach of the walls if Harper could only find the men to manage the devastating military feat.

A hush rippled through the expansive line that reached nearly the front door on the opposite side of the great hall. Harper didn't notice the shift in the amassed volunteers that was a haphazard mix of guards, militia, and mercenaries until the source of the disquiet was nearly upon her.

The Duke of Griffon's Rock stepped grandly to her table with five members of his personal guard in attendance. The Duke's tabards and armor of royal blue hemmed in green and purple followed him as the only clean uniforms Harper had seen in weeks. She stood and curtsied to the ruling noble of the city who bowed tersely in return.

"Rumors say you are planning a cavalry charge. Might I see your accounting, Sword Maiden?" the Duke asked in his casual, nasal sort of way. He held out a soft hand hemmed in lace to accept the pieces of paper she'd been scribbling on.

Harper relinquished her chaotic notes. She'd failed in her duties at commander that required her to keep the Duke informed of her plans. She suspected this insult was the reason for his visit and the brusqueness of his demeanor. "I had intended to send a runner with a message to you when one became available...I'm afraid my clerical skills are lacking."

"When last I saw you, a Sorceress attended you to see to such things," the Duke said, immediately perusing Harper's paltry figures on heavy warhorses and capable riders. "A dower woman with a large nose and quickly graying hair, I believe."

"I'm afraid she died on the ice in the battle against the Cyclops," Harper said, trying to hold the emotion from her voice.

"My apologies." The Duke's eyes never left the pages as he spokes. "A talented steward of figures and message writing can be difficult to find, especially in the shadow of the Screeching Peak."

Harper only ever heard natives of Griffon's Rock and the surrounding hamlets use the phrase: 'in the shadow of the Screeching Peak.' She looked hard at the Duke, wondering how such a man came to be born and raised in the northern jewel. Up close, he looked older than from a distance. His curly black hair held an occasional gray strand and lines around his hawkish eyes told her that he wasn't as young as he pretended. She'd thought him a pampered fop, likely born in the north, but schooled and warded in the south. Upon closer inspection, she saw a lot more of the north in him than before.

"From what I can see here, you're managing a one in ten average," the Duke said. "I passed seventy five men on the way in, giving you eight more at most. This will leave you less than two-hundred heavy horse, yes?"

"I had thought to augment our numbers with Sorcerers in the backs of wagons. I saw such a tactic work well in the fight against the Cyclops," Harper explained.

"An interesting plan. And how many of these mystical charioteers do you have?" The Duke handed back Harper's papers unceremoniously.

"Nine," Harper said, "although the smallness of the number is misleading. The nine I have are among the most powerful practitioners of magic in the north."

"Then it would be a shame to see them die because your line of heavy horse was entirely too short and easily broken," the Duke said. "My personal jousting squadron is in the city for their winter's rest. In addition, my own household guard is comprised of southern soldiers trained in mounted tactics. I believe I can augment your numbers by another two-hundred, if that would help."

"It would change everything," Harper said, thunderstruck by the offer.

"I begrudgingly accepted Bjorn's plan to allow the siege to last until spring thaw as needed," the Duke said. "I am glad to see you will not deign to follow it now. Let me be clear: I should like very much for the siege to be broken as soon as possible. We've spiders and fires in the eastern quarters, the crafting industries of the winter months are failing for want of workers who have joined the militia, ice fishermen who should be plucking delicacies from the bay are afraid to even venture off land, a thieves war is raging in our streets nightly as we have too few guards to patrol, and we're quickly eating through a harvest I planned to sell in the spring. I am not a noble blind to the woes of those I rule over, nor am I one to ignore the complaints of merchants; my people are suffering under the siege and they will suffer more under the economic hardships it will press upon us in the years to come. I need those infernal giants and their vermin pets out of the orchards they've already ravaged. Dead or fled, I want them gone."

"I will see to it, my lord," Harper said.

"Excellent. I will have the captain of my private guard, Ser Pierce, report to you immediately with the full force he commands."

The Duke and his guard departed, leaving Harper feeling lighter than before in finishing her task of sorting the last of the volunteers. Strengthening an already strong force seemed far less daunting than building a cavalry from scratch.

It took another two hours, well into the darkest part of the night, to sort the remaining seventy men in the line. As the Duke had estimated, only eight were worthy and two of those were a stretch. Harper figured she could bury the weakest of the lot in the rear ranks as needed and so if they fell behind or dropped their lances, it would hardly be noticed.

Knowing Calista was beneath the mountain at that very moment, trying to skirt the Fir'bolg line and accomplish an impossible task made Harper feel a little sheepish about her own grumblings. She would sleep, or more likely lay awake worrying, in a warm bed that night. She would have food, drink, and the comfort provided by stone walls and armed guards.

To alleviate some of her guilt over her creature comforts, Harper decided to walk the eastern wall in hopes of rousing morale. The last time she'd done so it worked well for both sides: the soldiers guarding the eastern gate were heartened by her attendance and she in turn felt bolstered by their confidence.

Sven and Athol greeted her at the wall, a surprising turn of events considering she thought they would still be out hunting spiders. The brothers were bundled and weary, sitting upon the steps leading up to one of the mid-towers. They were passing a wineskin back and forth, taking special care to hold it under a cloak between drinks so it wouldn't freeze.

"If I never see another spider again, it'll be too soon," Athol grumbled at Harper's approach.

"Or a house fire," Sven agreed.

"I'm afraid you'll probably see more of both in six or seven hours," Harper said.

"Explain again why we might not join you in riding with pointed sticks at giants?" Athol asked.

"Because you're afraid of horses and the one time I titled against Sven he actually leapt from his mount rather than take the strike," Harper said.

"I still maintain I took fewer bruises in the fall than I would have if I'd let you hit me," Sven said. "You were pointing that giant stick directly at my chest."

"Yes, that is generally where a lance gets pointed," Harper said.

"Unless your opponent is a giant," Athol said.

"And then you point the lance at their groin," Sven announced.

Harper had considered going for a knee or hip, but Sven made a good point—a heavy lance to the testicles might well level the playing field, so to speak. "I might do just that," Harper said. Both brothers winced. "If it makes you feel any better, imagine you are remaining behind on the wall to guard against spiders as you are both experts in slaying them."

"Meaning we are glorified bug squashers," Athol said, "and you're a castrator of giants."

"Then it's settled." Harper passed by the brothers on her way up the icy steps and gave each of them a pat on the shoulder. Before she could even turn south to walk down the wall, Sven's voice stopped her.

"Do we have a contingency plan if Calista fails?"

Harper turned back to look at him. "We won't need one."

Doubt couldn't creep in. Not then. Not when she was feeling so weak. She left the brothers to their wine and scaled the stairs up to the windy, cold walkway on the wall. The guards sat huddled against the protective stone bulwarks along the top. The watch commander refused to allow pyres to warm themselves as the light might provide ranging indicators for the Fir'bolg catapults. The lack of fire weighed heavily on the men. When the guards barely glanced to her as she walked, she began bidding them good evening, asking after their condition, and stopped to listen to what they might say. The black armor and purple cloaks of the Ash twins' men were almost entirely gone. In their place, bedraggled volunteer militia and city guards took their place.

She regretted her attempt at engaging the men almost immediately. The soldiers wanted fire, which she could not give them. They had wounds that needed healing, but she could no longer heal. She tried to explain both situations when they arose, but it was to no avail. They pleaded to have just a small fire and begged that she just try to heal without her magic even after she explained why they could have neither.

By the time she stepped off the stairs near the Thundering Dawn Inn, tears burned at the corners of her eyes. She'd promised the Duke she would break the siege for him, but now she knew she had to end the war for the men who froze on the wall with wounds she could no longer heal.

Harper slept little that night and the dawn, that at once seemed interminably far away, came all too quickly once she finally did manage to find sleep. She took her breakfast in her room and struggled to eat. After she'd finished picking over toasted bread covered in fried eggs and onions, she heard a knock at the door. She expected one of the serving girls to check on her progress, or perhaps the Ash twins wishing to speak with her about the city's defense. Instead, when she opened the door, she found a young man, perhaps sixteen years old, dressed in functional chain mail and adorned with the blue, purple, and green tabard of the Duke's noble house.

"Lady Harper, I am meant to squire for you this day," the young man said. He made an awkward attempt at a courtly bow, and then stood stiffly at attention.

"And your name, lad?" Harper asked. Being the daughter of a fisherman, she wasn't deserving of the title lady, but in the north such things were common to high ranking religious officials, although she wasn't that anymore either. She was glad the young man had not called her 'ser' though, as she had never taken a knight's vows. Addressing her as one might address any random townsperson would have been more accurate.

"Timon of the family Wulfe," the young man said. "I am nephew to the Duke's wife."

Divine Touched

That explains it, thought Harper. The Duke was setting up a grand battle of knights and lords on horseback, charging out to valiantly save the city, in an honorable battle that would be sung about for ages. A rag tag group of mercenaries and militia battling Cyclops on the bay probably didn't appeal to the Duke in the same way an early morning charge against ice giants did. Victory on her own terms wasn't a requirement for the day, as far as Harper was concerned. If the Duke wished to have his name at the forefront of the city's deliverance, Harper was fine with that, so long as the city was delivered.

"Very well, Timon Wulfe, let us set to our work," Harper said.

Regardless of Harper's original feelings about the matter, the assistance of a trained squire made every detail of preparing for battle infinitely easier. He knew how to equip plate upon a warrior expertly and even commented on how much easier it was to armor someone similar to his own height. He helped her change out her cloak and tabard from the temple of the Sea Queen to the noble house of the Duke as she was no longer divine touched and would soon be a sworn knight of the realm.

When she was armored properly and bedecked in blue, purple, and green, he carried her helmet and sword for her while they descended the stairs into an orderly assembly of knights. The Duke, wearing his own resplendent plate armor was walking down the line of her makeshift cavalry, who knelt before him with their heads bowed to receive their knighthood. Without land or a retainership, the knighthoods were largely ceremonial, but Harper thought it an interesting gesture on the Duke's part. When he reached the end of the line, and incidentally where she'd chosen to stand, he bowed grandly to her. She responded with a formal curtsey.

"Would you kneel to take your vows?" the Duke asked.

"By your leave." Harper knelt before the Duke, swore the truncated, honorable oath commonplace to hedge knights, and felt the tapping of the Duke's sword upon her shoulder plates. That was the rub of the thing, Harper supposed. They weren't to pledge themselves to the Duke's house, but for the fantasy to be complete, they must be sworn. For many of the mercenaries it was an honor that would open up other opportunities to serve noble lords, should they survive the battle. For Harper, it seemed a silly edge of pageantry to what would likely be a horrific battle.

The Duke departed immediately after, apparently looking to find a suitable location to watch from. Harper gave the marching orders for her men, and they walked in what might have been thought of as a loose formation, out of the inn to find their horses for the general mustering outside the gate of the Last Road.

Timon followed Harper dutifully to the stables where she planned to equip Aerial in her barding and ride her trusty, if half-blind mount, in the largest cavalry charge she'd ever taken part in. Timon offered to help her in equipping her horse's chain barding and specialized plates, but Harper refused. She wished to take the quiet moments before the battle alone with her old friend. Timon took his leave to see to his own horse.

"We need to trust one another today," Harper whispered to Aerial as she set about armoring her horse. Aerial raised her head to receive a hug when Harper entered the stall. Harper gripped fiercely to her horse's neck, feeling Aerial's heavy chin against her back, pulling her in closer. Harper laughed a little when she felt Aerial idly mouthing her hair. "Okay, you're right, enough of the sentimentality." Harper pulled away with nervous tears in her eyes. Warhorses died often and brutally in cavalry charges, but Harper couldn't imagine riding any other horse since she might well die too, and she would rather do so with a trusted friend.

Aerial, perhaps sensing what was to come, seemed more excited than timid. She stood with her head up, ears perked, and nostrils flared. The powerful muscles along her flanks twitched eagerly as Harper settled the padding and chain mail over the great mare. Retirement hadn't even lasted a month before Aerial was back to an armored charge. When Aerial was properly appointed for battle, Harper hoisted herself into the saddle, feeling comfortable atop her steady mount, with both of them protected by the finest armor. She turned Aerial slowly and walked her out through the run's gate to find her cavalry already mounted and awaiting her arrival.

She passed through their ranks, leading them out in good order to march through the city toward the gate of the Last Road. Already the sound of catapults filled the air and the battle at the eastern gate resumed. People stood at their windows watching the knights pass, cheering and hurling favors down to the mounted warriors. It was a strange combination of foreboding and jubilation in the city as spiders rained in from one gate while the saviors rode out the other.

The sky broke unevenly with a few tenacious banks of clouds clinging here and there while the golden morning sun poured through the ample gaps. The snow beneath their horses' hooves glistened and the steam of breath from riders and mounts caught white in the virgin light of dawn. In the east, Harper saw the pillar of smoke that could only be the signal Calista spoke of. The pillar grew quickly until it was a mountain of smoke half the size of the entire Fir'bolg line. Slowly, the smoke spread until it partially obscured the rising sun, setting the entire battlefield under a strange haze.

"Is this what was intended?" Timon asked from beside Harper. His horse, a tan gelding, was as lightly armored as he was. His task in the battle to come was to hand Harper fresh lances and to protect the supply line as well as the Sorcerers in their wagons, which counted not only Wizardly Willard among their number, but also Michael the Magician in his resplendent blue robes and his huge hat.

"I seldom know what Calista intends," Harper murmured. She pulled on her great helm with the t-slit visor and marine adornment along the crest of a shark fin. "It's a sign though and she said I would see it."

Trumpeters and banner holders ordered the mustered assembling to fan out into the proper line as they reached the edge of the cleared orchard. Behind them, the orderly second wave of the Duke's own men settled upon the leeward side of the low rise, led into position by Ser Pierce. Behind them still were the Sorcerers in wagons and the supply caravan bristling with fresh lances and readied with spare shields, guarded all by the squires and a contingent of foot soldiers armed with long spears.

The first target was the defensive line around the bulwarks protecting the catapults. One lance per charge was the order disseminated among the officers. Harper took her own offered lance from Timon. The heavy wooden spear with the barbed iron head felt good in her gauntleted hand. She could sense Aerial tensing beneath her, ready for the charge to come. The other knights and mounts strained under the apprehension before the charge as well.

Harper nudged Aerial out to the front of the formation, raised her lance high so the officers might find her and follow her lead. Her heart was thumping loudly in her chest and for the first time since she'd lost her divine spark, she felt fully alive again. The formation started following her at a walk, which she kicked into a trot as they descended the low rise into the cleared field. The thundering of several hundred armored horses echoed off the mountains themselves as the charge went from trot to canter. The hooves scattered mud and snow as the lances lowered from pointing up to the heavens toward the front and the enemy who stood unready. Men around Harper shouted battle cries although their exact nature was lost in the din of armor clanking and hoof beats. The charge settled into a full gallop before the Fir'bolgs could even scramble a hastily formed defensive line. Whatever Calista had done in the rear of their encampment left them disorganized and unprepared for an immediate counter attack.

As they roared across the open, snowy field, Harper spotted one of the giant's knees was unarmored. It was a large target, around the size of a barrel, which would be an easy hit considering she could put the lance through a ringlet no bigger than a goblet even at a full charge. She focused in on the area to strike through the narrow slit of her helmet. The world fell away around her, the noise of the charge became an afterthought, and then she hit. The head of the lance struck home, the handle bit and she held on until she felt the wood crack. Aerial leapt over the giant's foot and Harper released the lance. The giant howled in crippling pain. Harper settled in low behind Aerial's head, rose up in the saddle, and rode hard for the edge of the field where the formation could make its turn and begin the trip back across beneath the watchful arrows of the eastern wall.

Another giant went down, felled by two or three lances from rear riders. The stricken Fir'bolg pitched sideways, landing on the edge of a pen intended to hold spiders awaiting their turn to be launched at the wall. Several of the spiders wandered out into Harper's path. The chance to make a decision came up quick and Harper missed it. She spurred Aerial forward as her only option and led her charge directly over the top of the huge spiders. The first spider bounced off the metal plate protecting Aerial's chest. Heavy hooves crunched over the stunned spider's limbs behind her. Harper slid the sword from her back with the free second and continued the charge through the bewildered spiders. She cleaved two in half before she was finally free of the field and into the turn.

Harper held her sword high above her head, letting the blade catch in the early morning light to call the rally to her. Aerial galloped to the east, leading out the knights, most of which had successfully delivered their lances. They needed to clear the battle quickly for the second charge, which would be led by the Duke's jousting team and Ser Pierce. It would also comprise the majority of the professional knights in their force, and thus do the majority of the damage. Harper led her makeshift cavalry west toward the wall where the Ash twins, Athol, and Sven led the city's defenders against the spiders already launched. Harper dared not glance to the top of the wall, which was already teaming with arachnids, for fear she might see someone she recognized in a fight for their life, but she could hear the battle above raging with shouting men and hissing spiders. She also didn't look to the riders who had survived the charge for fear their numbers would be so low as to dishearten her. A dozen yards from the wall, she turned south, let Aerial drop into a canter, and returned her sword to its scabbard along her back. It was a moment to breathe and look to the battle in the east.

The professional jousting team leading a charge of two-hundred expert heavy cavalry hit the scattered Fir'bolg line with a crash of lance, angry shouts from giants, and the screams of frightened horses. Harper had been so focused on her own strike during the last charge that she must have blocked out all the same horrible sounds that she now heard perfectly from across the field.

The Sorcerers in their wagons were quick on the cavalry's heels, moving up with the supply line, guarded by squires and foot soldiers once they were in range. Among their numbers, Harper spotted the portly red blob of Wizardly Willard and the lanky blue line of Michael the Magician. The two old rivals were parked directly next to one another, hurling spectacular spells at the wooden fortifications surrounding the catapults. The Fir'bolg line erupted under half a dozen devastating magical attacks that sent burning timbers and spider bodies sailing into the smoky sky.

Harper led her force around the back of the Sorcerers' line where their squires awaited with fresh lances and horses should they need them. Timon waved her banner when she came near to call her in. She rode over to where he stood and accepted a new lance. Only then did she glance back to the number of riders in her charge. They'd lost a couple dozen, maybe more.

"Five or six were unhorsed and ran for the middle of the field as they were instructed," Timon informed her. "We'll get them fresh horses and lances when they get back to us and throw them into the rotation at your command." Timon looked flushed with excitement and eager to join her on the next charge if she so allowed. "It was a splendid strike on their line, slaying or wounding no less than fifty of them."

Harper could remember the momentary glee of success she felt in the battle against the Cyclops. It came right before everything went horribly wrong. She couldn't even let herself enjoy Timon's optimism through the memory of it. Faith in a plan felt like a perfect way to ensure it would fail. In response, she only nodded her understanding, and led Aerial back out to the other side of the supply line to begin general mustering of her cavalry again.

Ser Pierce, a mountain of an old man, well into his fifties, but still imposing, awaited Harper's arrival upon his great black charger. His helmet was crested with a golden dragon, wings spread and maw agape. He hailed her with a raised hand when she drew along side him. His mount dwarfed Aerial, indeed, might have outsized northland plow horses in a direct comparison. His visor was up to show off his steely eyes and little else.

"I sent my squires to scout the edge of their formation," Ser Pierce began. "One of the boys returned with news that the spider fields are aflame and the brood mother dead. Another said the Fir'bolgs are moving to flank us. And the third stated a small group of armed women are trying to cross the line to the southeast."

"If they flank us, they'll use the trees to prevent another charge until they're upon us," Harper said.

"That was my fear as well," Ser Pierce replied gruffly. "If we can break their troop movement, we might take advantage of the burning spider fields to force them into the flames before they can get into position for a counter attack." He lowered his visor as if the subject were already settled.

Harper didn't like the sound of the plan. It would mean a solid strike against a hardened line without any hope of turning back out to make another charge. Once they were engaged, they would have to force the giants into the fire or die in close-quarter combat in the attempt. She looked to Ser Pierce who was the picture of immovability on the matter. Men who never knew the divine spark made their stand and fought their battles without the added strength or healing powers of the pantheon—it was a strange realization for Harper to come to in such a moment.

"Ready the charge then," Harper said, "but first send a small group to retrieve the women responsible for the death of the brood mother." She mentally chided Timon for jinxing their plan by pointing out how well it was going.

"If I place your contingent on the southern edge of the line, you could see to this retrieval on your own," Ser Pierce said.

Harper initially grimaced at the implication. Her men were inferior, she knew that. The southern edge of the line would see the fewest giants with the most opportunities to break off the attack should things go wrong. A moment after, knowing full well it was not Ser Pierce's intention, she realized it also would put her in a position to rescue Calista. Her honor demanded she request a position in the center of the line while her love for Calista begged her to accept the lesser duty on the southern edge.

"Let my men take the southern flank," Harper said, "but I will ride in the center." Even as the words left her mouth, she could hear Calista's voice screaming in her head not to be foolish. She shook off the nagging doubt. The urge to spit in the Sea Queen's eye, to show her former Goddess what she'd lost, was overwhelming. She vowed that her greatest victory would come without the help of Maraline and she didn't doubt for an instant that her former deity would be watching as she rode victorious against an army of giants.

Ser Pierce nodded and led her out with the returning heavy cavalry. In juxtaposition to the chaotic jumble of her own charge, the next mustering was orderly and precise. The professional knights also had far more success in their first charge, returning nearly their full number and slaying more than twice as many giants as Harper's men had. Harper tucked Aerial in beside the Captain's black charger in the center of the line. A ripple ran down the formation of knights tapping the next lance in line with the previous. The clatter of wood ran the length of nearly four-hundred riders. It was a brilliantly exciting moment before another charge that sent Harper's heart soaring.

As they mobilized, wheeling the great line to the south, the exhilaration ebbed. The smoke and fire within the Fir'bolg line crept through the remaining orchards like an insidious, prowling hell beast. The giants were forming up, still in something of a disorganized jumble, but far more were armed and ready than met the first charge. The cavalry set into a trot, pressing in toward the fire and smoke accompanied by the clank of armor.

"For Griffon's Rock!" Ser Pierce shouted above the rumble of running horses. The cry echoed down the line, rebounding from the furthest reaches of both before they set into a canter.

Lances lowered along the line a moment before they reached a gallop. The charge was engaged. Three solid lines of men on heavy horses raced across the torn and muddy field, directly at a line of ice giants armed with clubs made from tree trunks. The smoke reached the cavalry long before their charge landed, stinging eyes and burning lungs.

Harper struggled to find a target amid the line of Fir'bolgs. She would need to make her lance strike count as it would be the only one she would get before she would have to battle with her sword alone. She spotted an immense giant, a head taller than the rest, standing in the center of their line with his legs wide and a club in each hand. She raised the point of her lance, and spurred Aerial toward the gap between the giant's legs. The giant raised one club to swing, but she'd covered the distance too quickly for him to bring it down. The lance struck directly in the soft spot between his legs and snapped off in the middle almost immediately. Aerial and Harper shot between the giant's legs as they buckled to either side.

Harper immediately grabbed for her sword, unable to take even a moment of satisfaction from such a perfect lance hit. Aerial threatened to slow, feeling Harper shift for the great sword across her back, but Harper spurred her back to a gallop. She gripped her horse with her thighs and held her blade with both hands. There would be time enough to trot when they won.

She slashed at the first gargantuan leg she saw. Her sword strike, made all the more powerful by the force of the gallop, cleaved the limb off below the knee. Harper twirled her bloody blade through the air above her head and brought it around to the other side to take another swing at the next leg she saw. This one was protected by a petrified wooden plate. Her sword bounced off it with a resounding clunk, sending a shock of pain up her shoulders and threatening to pluck the blade from her hand. She pushed on into the thickening smoke, regaining her balance as she rode.

A club smashed down to her right, but somehow Aerial saw it coming and dipped low to run around the edge of the impact zone. In the smoke and haze of the field, Harper saw as Aerial must out of her wounded eye. Shapes shot into view as she came close to them, but there was no clarity to any of it. Flames were ahead, giants walked among the smoke, and all around her other riders raced along as well, but beyond those things, it was difficult to tell where anything truly was. Another club smashed down to her left, well out of range of striking her. Harper veered toward it this time and slashed at the hand holding the weapon. Her blade bit higher than she'd intended, severing the muscles and tendons along the giant's elbow, but not taking off his hand.

She spotted another rider to her right, making his own rush through the smoke. She took heart in knowing she wasn't alone. In the moment immediately after, a giant's club swatted horse and rider from their path. The man and his mount sailed up into the smoke and were gone from sight. She glanced about to find another rider in her charge and saw the same occurrence take place a dozen more times. Her own success suddenly felt paltry in comparison to the overall thrashing they seemed to be taking.

A giant fell before her, dropped by something on its other side she couldn't see amid the haze. Aerial leapt over the Fir'bolg's outstretched arm putting Harper at the perfect level to slash her blade across the giant's face as they passed by. Her sword bit into the flesh, caught in the bone of its forehead, and for an instant they were bound in fate. Harper had to choose between keeping her blade and keeping her mount. The hard choice, which she was only given a split second to make, flashed before her mind and she made it, gripping fiercely to the handle of her sword with both hands. Try as she might to clench Aerial with her thighs, she felt herself pulled from the saddle. She nearly lost her grip on the blade when her body weight, amplified by her armor, tugged in the opposite direction of the sword's handle. Blessedly, the blade pulled free from the giant's skull at the exact right time, and Harper was sent rolling through the mud, still in possession of her sword.

She sprang to her feet and struggled to hurl her strangling cloak off her shoulders. The cloak's clasps came away easily as one was already damaged from the fall. She held her sword at the ready, scanning the haze around her for friend or foe. A rush of tree trunk sized limbs dashed past her from the direction she'd just came, fleeing into the flames ahead. She made a half-hearted slash at the giant's ankle, but came up well short, and then the retreating giant was gone from her limited sight.

The smoke threatened to choke the life from her, making her eyes water and sapping her strength as she walked cautiously through the muddy field. She found fallen horses, dead riders, wounded giants, and even a few burning spider corpses. The sounds of battle were fading out beyond hearing as though it were a storm passing in the distance. She opened her mouth to cry out for Aerial, but the smoke caught in her lungs and all she could do was cough. She fell to her knees to try to find cleaner air near the ground.

After a momentary rest, breathing what little un-fouled air there was to be had, she trudged on, turning right to skirt the fire in hopes of finding a way off the field. Men shouted in the distance, horses screeched, and wounded giants blubbered in their bizarre language, but it all seemed so far away. Through her burning, watery eyes, she spotted a darkened shape ahead. She lunged and swung for what she thought was a Fir'bolg leg, instead burying her blade into the side of a stone berry tree at what would have been calf-height on a giant.

A nervous fit of laughter overcame her, which dissolved into a lengthy bout of coughing. She tried to pull her blade from the tree, but she was too tired and weak from the smoke to yank the sword free. The adrenaline of fright apparently had drained from her, leaving her weaker than when she'd swung the blow. She settled at the foot of the tree beneath her sword and rested.

She didn't know how long she sat within the silence and calm. Eventually, the wind shifted and much of the smoke cleared, expanding her vision and allowing her to fill her lungs with relatively clean air. She stood wearily and made another attempt at working her sword free of the tree trunk. The wood finally relented and her sword was liberated. She turned a slow circle, inspecting the widening ring of smoke that still prevented her from finding any landmark or aid. The heavily trampled, muddy ground with the tenacious patches of snow around the base of the tree concealed her tracks leaving her with little clue as to which direction she might try walking first. Even as the smoke cleared, the sky above darkened with storm clouds. The day dimmed and fog crept in among the smoke.

The decision was made for her while she mulled over her options. A horse and rider materialized out of the haze as a light snow began to fall. Harper stood on her guard, blade ahead of her until the silhouette of the rider came into focus. The horse was her own and so too was the woman in the saddle. Harper let the point of her sword drop. Aerial whinnied a greeting and trotted a little faster toward her.

Harper took Aerial's reins in her hands and helped Calista out of the saddle. Calista's left arm was bound to her chest in a hasty sling and she favored her right ankle when Harper helped her from the horse. They embraced gingerly, and when the hug would not satisfy, they kissed. The smell of smoke and battle clung to them both, but Harper didn't care. Her craving for Calista had never been so strong and her relief in their reunion nearly knocked her from her feet.

"The Fir'bolg line broke and fled," Calista explained when their lips parted. "Aerial found me and brought me to you." Calista winced a little at a pain in her shoulder or ankle or both, which seemed to remind her of something. She took a step back and looked Harper over with an incredulous eye. "There isn't a scratch on you."

"I wish I could heal your wounds to say the same," Harper said.

Calista shook her head and smiled. "You're able bodied enough to dote on me while I recover. I rather like the idea of having the hero of Griffon's Rock waiting on me hand and foot."

They kissed again, lingering even longer this time. Harper helped Calista back into the saddle and then hauled herself up to ride in front. Aerial turned back to the city, walking like she knew the way to a warm stall and a bucket of oats.

When they broke free of the smoky haze, the remnants of the triumphant cavalry were waiting, apparently for them on the field of victory. Ser Pierce rode out to meet them with Timon in attendance. Harper spotted Wizardly Willard and Michael the Magician among the survivors; both Sorcerers looked infinitely pleased with themselves and each other—Michael's lost hat and Willard's half clipped moustache apparently being the only wounds either suffered during the entire war. As Harper and Calista rode into the midst of the knights, the cries of victory began, following them all the way into the city where the citizenry joined in.

Chapter 38:

Rewards

Breaking the siege came at a price, although not nearly as costly a one as Harper expected. The real damage to the north wouldn't be known until much later; this was how war went, the Duke explained to the people in his triumph speech. The mercenary guild's final accounting of what was lost would take months, perhaps years to fully understand how much labor perished in what was quickly being called the Winter War. The orchards in the east were devastated by the Fir'bolgs harvesting the trees and many of the more knowledgeable Rangers said the spiders that escaped from the ice giant camp would likely remain a problem for years to come.

Within the Dagger Falls Company, the damage was severe. The company's patron, Bjorn, was dead. The disappearance of Ezra's body remained a mystery that Calista guarded well. To add to the already mounting problems for the company in the week after the final battle, Sven lost his right leg when a poorly treated spider bite festered. He took the amputation with as much cheer as he could manage, healing from the debilitating wound at home with his wife and children. Athol relinquished his first born rights to Bjorn's place as the family's patriarch in favor of his younger brother, stating he had no head for business or figures and far too many years of adventuring still ahead. When this gift didn't serve to alleviate Athol's guilt about his brother's lost limb, he carved a wooden leg from a captured Fir'bolg giant's club. Sven said it was the ugliest, most unwieldy attempt at woodcarving he'd ever seen. Athol offered to make another attempt, but Sven refused, stating he would wear his brother's failure at leg carving as a beacon to his brother's incompetence at anything other than swinging a hammer and emptying a flagon. Athol agreed this was a fair trade. Only later did Harper learn it was Athol who had attempted to treat the spider bite; no amount of reassuring Athol it wasn't his fault could assuage his guilt. She struggled with her own regret in the matter as she felt she could have preserved Sven's leg if only she had retained her healing powers. Sven would hear none of it from either of them though. He hobbled about on his new wooden leg, wore his father's bearskin cloak, and swore that if the father could tend the books with only half his body working, then certainly the son could manage while only missing the better part of one leg.

Calista made good on her promise to put Harper to work in the weeks after the siege. Her dislocated shoulder and turned ankle healed quickly, but her demands of Harper never waned. Harper made the mistake of offering Calista quill, ink, and parchment for her to create a list of things that might help speed her convalescence. Among the more traditional demands of basic comforts, Calista added several whimsical needs Harper was to attend to, including copious amounts of bacon, burning incense, a hot bath for two every day, and that Harper never wear a stitch of clothing when they were alone in their room. In waiting upon her lover, Harper found she derived a good deal of her own pleasure within the list of Calista's demands.

The Ash twins collected the tattered remains of the best mercenary groups they could find to replenish their devastated numbers, including nine of the ten surviving members of the Red Dale Riders. Caleb, the group's former leader, said he chaffed under the rules of engagement the Ash twins required, although some of the Rangers stated he wasn't the same after coming out of Calista's thrall—he'd become a religious man, which didn't match well with being a brigand. The Dead Watch Pikes were well and truly gone, after boasting hundreds. What the Ash twins managed to piece together to replace their once glorious band involved a good deal more archery than before, but they were survivors and so made the change required by what remained to them.

The North Wind Valkyries, after suffering fifty percent losses including their leader Ingrid in the final battle, swore to return to the northlands with their riches, all excepting Sofea who began searching for new opportunities in the south, unwilling or unable to go back to the village so soon. Calista paid them with every coin she could scrape together from her illegal black market activities to add to whatever they'd scavenged from their victories, but even that felt paltry in comparison to what they'd lost. They'd wanted battle, glorious battle, and they had it. The Valkyries wanted none of Calista's apologies. They were returning to their village with Fir'bolg scalps and Cyclops ears—their positions among their people would forever be elevated by their bravery.

Michael the Magician, having lost none of his members within the siege, signed up his company with the mercenary guild under all the incarnations of names formerly desired by Wizardly Willard. The leader of the Sorcerous Seven stated the return to a frosty state of affairs with Willard was attributed to the matter of a missing hat. Wizardly Willard was soon after spotted on the street in Michael the Magician's fantastical hat, now dyed bright red, and announcing that it was a case of finders keepers.

Brandinne vanished for all intents and purposes as she'd promised. The thieves guild within the city resumed its activities without missing a beat, although the whispers among drinking guards in the Thundering Dawn's main hall was that the blasted thieves had taken to playing pranks along with their usual larceny. Calista was certain of Brandinne's ascension to thief queen when rumors spread that the thieves guild filled the guard captain's house with brightly dyed chickens after pilfering all his socks. It was a good distraction during the rebuilding to have the once feared gang of Dwarves become a source of wonderment and entertainment for the people of Griffon's Rock. Rumors spread with every prank, Calista assumed Brandinne helped in their spreading, until the thieves guild held a place of near folk heroes among the city's citizenry.

After a month, Calista felt healed enough to return to something of her usual duties, although she did so reluctantly, and somehow managed to talk Harper into continuing with many of her more fanciful requests, chiefly among them the required nudity and daily hot bath for two. She found the main hall of the Thundering Dawn alive as ever and the Dagger Falls Company booth well occupied in discussing a familiar problem. Athol was joined by Wizardly Willard, the Sorcerer's apprentice, the former Valkyrie Sofea, and Caleb the banished leader of the Red Dale Riders. The new members of the Dagger Falls Company were discussing how they might find and hire a Jack for the coming adventuring season. Old man Sven, their new patron, was cranky from spending so much time with his wife and children and wasn't in the mood for any of their excuses, Athol explained it to them.

Calista left them to their business, passing only a knowing smile to Athol as she sought out Harper amid the knights of her cavalry charge. Timon had earned a full knighthood under Ser Pierce's command after the battle, but still seemed to prefer to remain near Harper whenever she was out and about within the city. The former Sword Maiden, once sworn to never imbibe spirits, hadn't paid for a drink once since the end of the siege. Knights, of the hedge and sworn varieties, lined up to purchase whatever she liked so long as she would toast with them and regale them with the tale of how she'd castrated the Fir'bolg's field commander with a lance. Harper, ever humble, always explained she hadn't known it was the ice giant's general when she'd made the strike, and gave ample due to Athol and Sven for even having the idea in the first place. Her humility won her as many friends as her increasingly impressive storytelling prowess.

Calista wrapped her arms around Harper from behind and kissed her on the neck. The knights toasted the show of affection since they happily toasted most things those days. Harper had taken to referring to Calista as her betrothed, and that suited Calista just fine. The laws of the lands in the north didn't permit such pairings, but the citizens of Griffon's Rock petitioned the Duke for a change in such traditions to accommodate the betrothal of the heroes of the Winter War. The Duke seemed pleased to consider the petition, but slow to enact change—courtly love between a brave, yet manly, knight and a fair maiden was a hard dying ideal in his mind apparently.

"Have you packed to leave, my love?" Calista whispered hotly in Harper's ear.

"Yes, but I still don't see how…"

"I've read the signs," Calista replied cryptically.

They bid the knights goodbye and walked from the inn into an unseasonably warm day for the middle of the midwinter month. Snow melted until the cobblestones of the streets were uncovered and nearly dry. Blue skies and a warm sun made everyone swear spring had come two months too early. The marvels continued as Calista led Harper toward the gate of the Last Road where the watch blew a warning horn to notify the city of an approaching caravan. Calista led a stunned Harper up to the parapets to watch the arrival from an elevated vantage point. The couple held one another close, warmed by the sun, watching gypsy wagons upon their arrival.

The six wheeled wagons of southland gypsies were hauled by shaggy, two-humped camels. The tinkling of thousands of tiny bells was accompanied by the rolling pebbles of rain sticks upon the gypsies' approach. Strong men in leather vests walked along the sides of the wagons, showing off the tattoos that covered every inch of their skin and their great moustaches that glistened with dozens of golden rings a piece. Beautiful women, many of which resembled Calista with square jaws and burnished hair, danced or played instruments upon the platforms atop the covered wagons, their sumptuous bodies adorned in dyed silks and coins strung together into garments.

"These are the loyal servants of the Wandering Goddess Lyndria. They will feast, trade, swindle, and steal for four days," Calista explained, "and then they will carry us to Ovid where my Goddess awaits the prize I carry."

By the time the gypsies departed, the feelings of the people in Griffon's Rock were split. Many were happy for the goods and coin the gypsies brought in trade while many others felt cheated by the entire affair. Calista explained four days was the perfect amount of time for such a caravan to glean as much as they could without arousing enough ire for forcible removal from the city.

Calista, Harper, and Aerial departed with the gypsies, receiving a send off befitting their lofty accomplishments. Athol promised to lead the revived Dagger Falls Company south after the spring thaw to seek out work and pay Harper and Calista a visit.

As the wagons were pulling away down the Last Road, Harper looked back to the city she'd helped save. A fresh winter storm was already rolling in from the ocean and black clouds loomed heavy with snow above the Screeching Peak. The warm weather, as she'd suspected, was of divine origin, intended to bring Calista home once it was safe. She released the heavy cover across the back of their wagon and returned her attention to her betrothed.

Calista was relaxing happily amid the cushioned pillows and plush rugs, dressed as one of the gypsy women. She'd taken to wearing a gold chain that ran from her nose ring to another piercing in her ear in addition to flowing skirts and a revealing top constructed from gold coins.

"I could lose you amidst your people," Harper said. And it was true. Calista blended so seamlessly amongst the other gypsy women that in the past four days Harper had already accidentally touched several women on the back mistaking them for Calista from behind.

"Perhaps you should mark me as yours." Calista's voice dropped to a sultry purr and she beckoned Harper over with an inviting curl of her finger.

Harper took the invitation as entirely sexual, and in part it was, as Calista didn't waste any time in stripping the clothing from both of them to indulge in some much-needed oral pleasuring. Afterward, when they were lying amid the comfortably appointed wagon, entangled in one another's sweaty limbs, Calista invited Harper to find a location on her body for a tattoo of her choosing. Harper, having learned as much as she could of Calista's culture in the past four days, knew the seriousness of the invitation. The men of the southlands wore tattoos like camouflage; all the men had copious amounts of them, which helped male assassins blend in with one another. But the women of the southlands were unadorned for the very same reason. Coming from a society renowned for unidentifiable assassins, to offer creation of an identifiable mark upon her body as a sign of devotion was an extraordinary gesture on Calista's part.

Not wishing to spoil Calista's future career, even though Harper objected to the work of assassinating, Harper selected a spot on the top of Calista's left upper thigh. She placed her hand over the intimate spot, kissed her betrothed fiercely, giving the silken thigh a soft squeeze at the same time. "Here," Harper whispered against Calista's lips, "my name written in the Sylvan tongue."

And so it was agreed. Calista took Harper's mark upon her body that night when the wagon train stopped in the towering forests of the hinterlands. The gypsy tattoo artist, a voluptuous woman in her forties with plentiful piercings and tattoos of her own, smiled and complimented their union the entire way through the process of tattooing Calista. Harper accepted her compliments graciously, although she was uncomfortable by the amount and verve of them as most of the gypsies were fairly taciturn when speaking with one another. Later, when Calista's skin was washed over in soothing oil and left to air in the warmth beside the campfire, she pulled Harper close and explained.

"By their standards," Calista whispered to Harper, "that was as good as marrying me."

"And by your standards?" Harper asked.

"I am happy to be your betrothed until whatever ceremony you deem appropriate," Calista said.

The following day, Harper began referring to Calista as her wife, which immediately drew requests by the gypsies to see the tattoo. Calista started wearing a sash over a skirt with a daringly high slit so she might proudly and easily show off her marital ink whenever anyone should ask. In return, she gifted to Harper a beautiful platinum ring etched with a scene of a man fishing among the stars made of blue diamonds. When Harper asked where she came by the ring, Calista said she'd stolen it a few towns back with the intention of giving it to Harper when the time was right.

Harper wore the ring proudly and told anyone who asked, and many people who didn't, the symbolic meaning behind it. The weeks spent traveling with the gypsy caravan was easily the happiest time in Harper's life and she feared the day it would come to an end.

They reached the grand capital of Ovid shortly after dusk. The great, sprawling city was awash in the oppressive winter rains common to the rolling hills of the midlands. The season was known as the time of mud and flood in and around the capitol, and Harper could see why. She'd only ever been to Ovid during the summer when the hills were green with nubile wheat crops, verdant vineyards, and fluffy white sheep. In the late evening as they arrived amid another torrential rainstorm, the same fields were covered over in mud with several temporary levies gathering up the water into murky reservoirs. It was all so ugly and bleak that Harper could see why so many adventurers chose to spend their resting season in the warm halls and snowy orchards of Griffon's Peak.

The gypsies dropped off Harper and Calista at a familiar inn favored by southland visitors. Their farewell was terse, as Harper had come to expect of the gypsy travelers. It seemed the fewer words, and the more abruptness with which they were spoken, the more a gypsy showed familiarity with someone. Calista explained Harper could truly feel loved by a southlander if they should start snatching things out of her hands without asking.

They boarded Aerial at the inn's tiny stables, saw their belongings delivered to a room, and immediately set off into the darkened, rainy city streets. Harper followed Calista through narrow, shadowy lanes into the darkest, dankest sections of the city where the towering buildings threatened to block out what little light pushed through the stormy skies. The change from the narrow allies into a proper tunnel was so subtle that Harper didn't realize they'd even descended into the catacombs until she noticed rain was no longer striking the hood of her cloak.

Calista silently led on into utter blackness. Harper clung tenaciously to her wife's hand, trusting that she knew the way through the interminable darkness. A scant few moments before Harper was about to ask where they were going, the tunnel opened up into a faint purple glow of heart stone crystals. Harper didn't need to be told the subterranean building they were looking upon was a temple. She could feel the holiness of the strange place constructed entirely of the glowing purple rocks.

They walked lightly through the arched entryway that contained no door. The interior of the temple was a tiered circle with countless locked boxes set upon the multilayered floor. It was a small hall, less than a quarter the size of the Sea Queen's temple in Griffon's Rock, but it felt no less important. There was no central focus, no dais to administer sermons from, just boxes, many boxes of many types, all of apparently equal value and importance.

Calista led Harper to a specific box among the multitude. It was constructed of hand-carved rosewood panels held together with bronze ribbing, hinges, and latches. As soon as she saw it, Harper knew it belonged to Calista.

Calista knelt before her box, which was no bigger than a small chest, lifted the lid, and placed her hands within. She held something that remained hidden in the darkened interior of the chest. A faint, white glow illuminated her arms and face, but not the dark inside the box. When she was done with the simple ritual, she closed the box again, stood, and waited in silence.

Harper waited alongside her. The longer she remained within the purple, glowing temple, the more her eyes adjusted to the light. As more details came into focus, Harper noticed writing was etched into the faces of the crystal walls. Secrets in a thousand different languages were written throughout the interior of the temple. Some of the languages she recognized, and some of the secrets she believed she could even read if she got close enough. Most of the symbols were so foreign and ancient that she doubted anyone who lived could even guess at what language it was. Her marveling inspection of the walls came to a quick halt when her eyes passed over two cloaked women standing in front of the entryway.

The shadowy women walked first to Calista and then to her box. They were tall and slender, easily a head and a half taller than Athol even. When they came closer, Harper realized they were not wearing shadowy cloaks; the women themselves were made of shadow. One of the shadow women knelt before the box as Calista had and retrieved what was placed within. Her ethereal hands closed over the glowing white light, but tendrils of it snaked out between her ghostly fingers. She rose and handed the God's essence to the other shadow woman who accepted it with a bow. Harper looked to Calista who was smiling proudly—happy tears rimmed her sapphire eyes.

The second shadow woman who accepted the God's essence held it close as though it were a precious child. Slowly the light shifted, grew, and pulsed at a blinding level, becoming golden rather than white as it took the form of a woman made of light, held within the shadow woman's arms.

"Dahlia," Calista named the golden woman in a reverent whisper.

The shapes of the women solidified before Harper's eyes. No longer were they simply figures of shadow and light, but she saw in them features. The two shadow women had the same long, slender nose, arched eyebrows, and pert mouth. The glowing woman of light looked much like the other gypsy women Harper had grown accustomed to while traveling south, and in many ways, looked a lot like Calista.

"The Wandering Goddess Lyndria is sister to Solancacae the Mistress of Secrets," Calista explained to Harper. "The essence I stole was to restore Lyndria's long dead lover, Dahlia, and raise her to the pantheon so they might never be parted again."

"The Dahlia Feast's story…" Harper murmured.

"Not just a story, as it turns out," Calista said, the smile never leaving her face.

"I wondered if my clever servant might figure out our purpose," one of the shadow woman said, identifying herself as Solancacae.

"A plan a thousand years in the making," Lyndria, the other shadow woman said. "But what is such time to an immortal when waiting for one so capable to restore one so worthy?"

"I am nothing if not resourceful," Calista said.

The Goddess Solancacae smirked at Calista. Harper could see and feel in her very core the love of their relationship. It was unlike anything she'd ever had with Maraline—the Sea Queen was alien and unknowable to her, while Calista and the Mistress of Secrets clearly knew and understood one another very well.

The glowing Goddess Dahlia beckoned Harper to her with only her eyes. Harper stood before the towering Goddess of beauty and light. The new Goddess spoke to her through a growing pink divine spark in the place within Harper left vacant by the Sea Queen.

"I have no followers yet," Dahlia said to her, "but I see in you a pure heart. Would you serve me knowing I have little to offer right now but my love?"

Harper fell on her knees before the glowing Goddess, accepting the divine spark with tears in her eyes. The essence of Dahlia filled her completely, feeling pure and right in ways the Sea Queen's never had. They matched. Dahlia of the Faithful Heart had loving, benevolent goals, and they all aligned with Harper's. Every direction she already wished to go, every good and virtuous thing she wished to do, felt perfectly united with Dahlia's desires. The love and life Harper wished to share with the world was precisely the message Dahlia wished of her in displaying her faith. It was as though Harper had been crawling her entire life and suddenly learned to fly.

"My followers never weep so," Lyndria said.

"Nor do mine," agreed Solancacae.

Calista shrugged and smirked to her deity. "I show my fealty in other, more subtle ways."

Solancacae smiled back. "So you do."

Dahlia of the Faithful Heart and the Wandering Goddess Lyndria embraced again, shadow and light within the crystal temple, and faded from sight. Harper could see them go, but she still felt the presence of Dahlia glowing within. The divine spark was white swirled with pink like the most beautiful opal she'd ever seen. It felt right to be a Knight of the Faithful Heart in ways being a Sword Maiden of the Sea Queen never did. There were no vows spoken, no oaths taken, no rules to follow. Spread love and happiness, be a beacon of faithfulness, and bring light to those who know darkness, this was her edict. Harper wished to live in such a way regardless and she knew it was what Dahlia wished done in her name.

"Your reward, my lovely Calista, shall be the fulfillment of a prophecy centuries in the making. There are others who have attempted what you accomplished, but none were successful and thus none were worthy of the gift I offer," Solancacae said, turning to Calista. Whatever reward Calista expected to receive was clearly not what she was given, as was evident by the ineffably startled look that overtook her an instant after the Goddess touched both her and Harper ever so briefly upon the forehead. "You will carry a child born of two women, a daughter granted by three Goddesses, and the world will burn for her greatness. Stand strong, Harper and Calista—being the mothers of this fated child will be a trial unto itself."

As quickly as the words were spoken, the temple was once again only occupied by two. Calista sat back on the tier containing her chest. She glanced first to the wooden box that was meant for her offerings of secrets to her Goddess and then to her own stomach where she knew, beyond a shadow of a doubt, she carried a child that was part her and part Harper. The 'reward beyond believing' that Solancacae had promised her if she succeeded was not monetary as Calista assumed. This threw into new light her reluctance to count on a job's payment before she received it; rather than being rich beyond belief, she was penniless and pregnant.

Harper was instantly at her side, holding her close, not knowing what else to do. "What did she mean?" Harper asked.

"I'm pregnant, apparently with your child," Calista said, not understanding or believing the impossible words herself. The fear and uncertainty born of such a statement paled in comparison to the strangest joy she'd ever known. She was going to do the impossible—she was going to have a daughter with the woman she loved. It was nothing she'd ever wanted, yet more than she could have hoped for. Now that this treasure she'd never wanted was finally to be hers, she couldn't fathom her good fortune. "And the world will burn before her."

The End

The Adventure Continues in…

About the Author

Cassandra Duffy spent most of her childhood being precocious, which stopped being entertaining or impressive when she grew into an adult, at which point she had to start being precious. After being an outcast child prodigy it was no surprise when she graduated from one of the many fine University of California schools a year early to follow her girlfriend in a cross country move.

Two of her greatest prides are being a true California girl and author of some truly naughty things. She is a dutiful partially-Asian daughter who is beloved by her fairly traditional Korean father who thinks having a gay daughter is just fine as long as she keeps playing coed flag football. She is a stereotypical younger sister, and an adoring aunt of a hilarious little boy. Being a modern techno-freak, gamer-girl, she spent most of her childhood dreaming of being a video game designer, but changed her mind and brought her dreams of world building and story-weaving to writing unique romance novels.

Cassandra is a gleefully monogamous girlfriend to an earthbound goddess who was once her high school bully, but has done a magnificent job of making up for all the school girl nastiness ever since. When she isn't being an avid fang girl (vampire fan girl) or tormenting people in online gaming, she lives and writes in Winter Park, Florida with her partner and soul mate Nichole and their two cats: Dragon and Josephine.